Crystal's Story

Diane Brooks

Olympus Story House

CONTENTS

Preface

CRYSTALS STORY had to be told!!!

IT'S CRYSTAL CLEAR AND ALL ABOUT THE DAD was going to be a stand alone story, but as I tried to go on to other projects, some of the characters weren't done talking to me, a few of them had their own story to tell. Therefore we'll start at the beginning with Crystal and follow her and her antics though her life. We'll learn about highs and lows, loves, sorrows, accomplishments and illegal shenanigans. It's like learning about your favorite Aunt and not believing the life she lived!

Crystal's family and friends and husband, Dad, Maryland and Massachusetts neighborhoods have been living in my head long enough without paying rent. The Maryland neighborhood of 5 Lost Road is a picture in my head of the road I grew up on in Grafton, as is the orchard on Speer Street! They are beginning to drive me crazy. It's time to move on! So as not to torment my Dad, husband and friends, or EVERYONE I talk to, this is the end!

I hope you enjoy the "rest of the story." Crystal turned out to be quite the woman! It's been fun for me. But now I can go on to MY BROOKLYN and TABLE TALK... two more stories starting to keep me up at night!

Thanks for Reading
Diane Brooks

Chapter I

Once again Crystal sat in her room alone, sad, crying and hating everything about herself. These four walls have been her constant companion and her sounding board since she could remember. They went from pink ballerina to to green ivy and lace as soon as she had a say in the matter. They were her four walls and she learned young to speak up for herself. She was not an unattractive girl, quite to the contrary. With a few more years to fill-out and achieve a more mature posture to enhance her budding body, her height will no longer be a hindrance but rather make her the beauty with the striking silver, platinum hair stand out in any room. These in-between years in every growing girls life are the awkward, gangly, with self-hatred, sleepless night and tearful pillow ones. Crystal is no different, except for the feelings she has about her last name. She has first and second ribbons she has won from assorted piano recitals, proudly with her full name in gold fleck prominent across each one. Her full name in bold black print filling the top quarter page of the program for the school play for which she has the lead part. Her first name was the result of the color of her hair...she was born with a full head of hair that reflected in the sunlight like spun glass or a priceless Crystal. But the last name was an embarrassment!

It's bad enough that at school everyday she needs to endure the snide looks and name calling because of her height and hair color, but the teasing because of her last name drives her nuts. Some day she will change that name, that day can't come fast enough. Her dad is her rock and she doesn't want to hurt his feelings in regards to their last name, but having to write or say Grandcockski every day and bring attention to herself, has to end.

Frankly Crystal is surprised that her dad never changed his last name. He is a Captain in the Navy stationed at Naval Air Station Pensacola in Florida, but coming up the ranks, the teasing he went through, he admits did also drive him insane, but he also said it toughened his hide and made him the hard ass he is now. He wouldn't change a thing!

Growing up in Florida through grade 8 was a fun time for Crystal. She was an only child and the apple of her dad's eye. She went everywhere with her dad. She loved going to the base and going into the Control Room where there were many desks and men and women all busy, but taking the time to show her the telex machine and filing system and teaching her the phonetic alphabet. She became a regular around her dad's office and she learned how to sneak into forbidden areas. This is when Crystal learned and starting honing her skills as a mischievous sneak! When not with her dad, she loved to practice the piano. As she grew and her playing improved she loved to perform in the school concerts or take part in military talent shows. She was an all around kid with above average grades and a memory that did not allude her teachers or her parents. That memory got her the part of Dorothy in the Wizard of OZ because she had no problem remembering her lines. Just when all the stars were aligning and the people and activities in Crystal's life were showing growth and promise, her dad gets transfer orders. At 13 years old she thinks the military sucks. Having to go someplace else and put up with the same old crap about her height and hair color really stinks, but when everyone learns her name she wants to craw in a hole and hide. This is when her dad gets very busy and she can't be his constant shadow and her moms no help at all, she is just a shell of a woman, a real rag doll with no spine at all, no personal will power or the fortitude to stick up for herself. *In a way mom has been a great teacher to me for the past few years. I know exactly how I want not to be. Crystal thinks this often.*

Her dad, Captain Harold T. Grandcockski, had the respect of every person Crystal new. Her mom took second seat to her dad in everything that happened in their home and in their lives. She never back-talked her husband or ever disagreed with a decision he made. Their modest little house was run like a barracks and their meals were prepared with nutrition in mind and served punctually at 6pm. Never could she or would she even try to arrange an evening out, or heaven forbid a vacation. He laid out her duties and like a good military wife she obeyed orders. In other words, she had no life of her own. Crystal knew at a rather young age that she would be the opposite of her mom in every way. She loved her mom, but was not comfortable talking with her about things!

Surely, Rita Marie Dunski had dreams and wishes before she became Mrs. Grandcockski. Surely she defied her curfew to be out with the gang dancing and hanging out or just to be alone making-out with her current bow. The life of any teenage girl can't be that different no matter what year they're brought up in or decade for that matter. The heart wants what the heart wants, whether it be respect, wealth, romance or freedom. Every person, man or woman has the right to strive toward that goal. So why did Rita give up so freely or so fast. Crystal never knew her grandparents, so she had no idea how her mom grew up, her mom would never talk about her parents or her beginnings. Therefore, it was really hard for Crystal to bring her feelings and woe's to her mom.

Just two weeks before the last day of school, dad comes home with the news that he has gotten a duty change and they are moving to a base in Virginia. This is military life, orders are orders and they affect everyone. Now that they were moving, her world fell heavy on her shoulders because she could share with no-one. Her comfort was her bedroom, and that was being taken from her as well. Her dreams of high school and changing locations and meeting new people also changed, in a big way. She'd be meeting new kids alright. Maybe this was the time to change her attitude about her hair...maybe the color, maybe mom could help her! Her name, well that's a different story... she can blame her dad for that "short" coming and also her dad for her gargantuan height of 5 feet 9 inches to date, because he is also a tall man.

It took a few weeks for Crystal and her mom to pack-up the household belongings and in that time dad was away securing housing at the new base in Virginia. Crystal used these precious days to say goodbye to the friends she had made and collected addresses for future correspondence. The friends here in Florida were flighty...not close but reliable for a good time. She knew high school would be different with a different caliber of friends, but until now she didn't know they would be in another state. She is finding out the life of a military family. Maybe that was one of the reasons her mom was so aloof. Anything to help label her mom's behavior.

It is June 2nd ....and a cable arrives saying that dad will be home in three days and be prepared to move out on June 6. The next day a complete change came over mom, she sat me down and swore me to secrecy and laid out her plans. Sitting knee to knee in kitchen chairs with mom's hand on one of my knees she explains that she is not making the move with us. She has saved a bit of money and has made plans to travel alone to what she prays will be a better life. Mom is a wonderful cook and has been forced into the role of a great organizer, so using those skills, she has managed to get a position for a monthly salary (her own money, she beams with pride at this mention) at a place where she will finally be appreciated. She explains that she has crossed all of her t's and dotted all of her i's and with the exception of running out on me she can't wait to start her new life. "Honey" she says, "I've never been a good role model for you, for which I apologize, but life with your father prevented me from being so. You are old enough to know that Captain Harold T. Grandcockski is a hard man for me to love, but it gives me much love to know that you do. Me leaving you with him for the next few years does not fill me with fear for you but rather a fulfillment for both of you. You two will grow closer together with me out of the way. Crystal, you have many talents, a good heart and a beautiful body, use them wisely and in time we will reunite. My goal for you is to be happy in all of your pursuits and to prosper beyond your wildest dreams. Please don't look for me...I will find you when I feel the time is right. This is the most selfish thing I've ever dreamed of doing, but with all my plans in place, I'm not backing out now."

Crystal sat there in awe of her mom with tears running down her face. Finally she saw strength in her mom that she didn't know was there. Keeping her secret, and living without her wouldn't be too hard, because until now there was little respect or personal warmth between them. This surely was a lesson in growing up. Little did she know that this was the first of many secrets she would keep in her life.

The next day is the last day of school. No more grade school. Crystal leaves her house with mixed feelings to say goodbye to many people knowing this is the beginning of many changes. Next year, high school in a different state and once again meeting new people and putting up with the same old problems. Dad will be home today. That thought brings about stomach nausea when Crystal arrives home to find the house looking a little….different. She and her mom stacked items to be moved very strategically.., but now Crystal notices and remembers how much care her mom took in filling the dark tan suitcases and brown suit bags, three of them as well as two moving boxes with handles. These items were totally hers. She stacked them along the wall at the front door, now that area was empty. Two blue/green flowery living room chairs and a matted blue couch to match were ready to go as well as the tall-back wooden rocking chair. The living room rug of dark green was rolled and tied and set across the couch. This room looked packed-up and ready to go, moving these items out would leave this room nearly empty. Crystal's piano was the only other item still in the room. This piano had felt and witnessed nearly as many of Crystal's moods as her bedroom four walls had. She was glad to see it was making the trip with her! Standing in the same place, she turned around to view the kitchen. The same sight of moving boxes stacked three high running the length of the interior wall on which the other side was the dinning room, that room also empty. The kitchen table was pushed against the outside wall and was pilled with boxes filled with can goods, boxes of cereal, spaghetti, and all the dry goods from the kitchen cabinets. The dishes and pot and pans were also packed and ready to go. Just then Crystal nearly trips on a kitchen chair as she heads towards her room, but she stops and realizes that this was the exact chair she sat in as her mom said good-bye. The house is quiet, she is alone, Mom is gone.

The few steps into her room make her gasp, it is entirely empty. She can't think right now. A lot of things have changed and there are more changes to come.

Crystal remembers the exact minute her dad arrived home...3 minutes before 6pm. The house was as quiet as she had found it with no sign of food preparation for dinner, his body language implied he was not happy! Crystal watched him move from room to room as he assesses the packing and readiness for the move. He asked her if she packed-up her own closet and dresser as he looked at her totally empty room. She thought this was an odd question, as they were the only words he'd spoken since he got there. She pointed to two boxes on the kitchen floor and simply replied with "these are mine".

Without seeing a bed or head-board or mattress and box spring or a dresser that housed Crystal's belongings, he muttered "I guess she wanted you to have everything new at the new house, and this is her way of making sure you get it." He added, "she worked fast and hard to get rid of everything today before we both got here." Crystal just looked down to the floor with an immediate grin and thought...*damn mom, you're good, I really didn't know you at all.*

Taking the bull by the horns, Crystal said "it looks like you are taking me out for supper, there's no food in the house." She held her breath until he replied to the affirmative. There was not any mention that mom was no where to be found.

Chapter 2

Fast forward to 1945

igh school graduation was a week long process with class night and dinner at a swanky restaurant, the next day class ring and year-book distribution, the next day class trip and finally graduation practice.

Crystal looked forward to each and every event. Without realizing it, these were the happiest 4 years of her life. The move to Roanoke, Va and a fairly new three bedroom house, close to the navy base and attending a huge school mitigated all of the adolescences teasing that occurred in Florida. Her life flourished, her dad was ever present but not in a mingling way... and thoughts of her mom only occurred when she discussed them with Peter.

Peter just happened in Crystal's life one day after school in line at the ice cream pallor. He noticed her first because of her height. He didn't voice that fact immediately, that would have totally turned her off, but rather with a swift swish on her shoulder to push away a bee, he introduced himself. She turned and saw a smiling, embarrassed face trying to tell her he saved her from a bee sting. She smiled back and accepted his gesture as a 'pick-up' line! It was a fast friendship and they talked everyday after that.

This happened when Crystal was in the 10th grade. It was just about then that she was allowed to stay out a little later, her curfew extended to mid-night, spending more time with Peter became a thing. They hung out with a fun crowd but would always gravitate toward being alone. They talked about everything...no-holds-barred...Their thing was meeting at the ice cream pallor...with each meeting he hugged..he was a huger... he never bought...it was always dutch. They studied once a week in the library always on a Thursday and helped one another with geometry. They read the same books in English Literature and composed book reports that were easy and fun because they did it together. He suggested the movies and a burger every now and then... once again, it was always dutch. They had the same circle of friends, but found a fondness for each other beyond the circle. It was a comfortable relationship that they both needed in their life. He was the only one that she could confide in about her mom or her fathers toughened attitude as she grew older. She loved her dad but there was something missing in him, even at her tender age she could recognize this.

As the 10th grade turned into the 11th and now Crystal is a junior in high school, Peter is still the one who makes her think maybe there could be a future for them. He was always the one to put words to a situation to make her see it better and make her feel better. Peter believed that when you loved someone, you needed to let them go forward with their dreams even if it meant their leaving, as long as you left the door open for them to come back. Peters words always seem to make her feel better, that was the affect he had on her. She would often play back in her head some of the words or feelings that he used on her and it made her think that maybe he was trying to verbalize a way out of his own dilemma. He was such a cool guy with a level head, but she admitted she did most of the talking and complaining. He was her fixer, he very seldom hinted that he needed a good listener, he very seldom let his demons out.

Peter was her equal-plus in height at 6'1" and enjoyed walking side by side with her. He bolstered her confidence and belief in herself and broke her heart when he showed no interest in being more than friends. Their relationship remained platonic and friendly and never even got messy with kissing or petting or anything too personal, it just didn't feel right, it ended at the hug. They spent a lot of time together just talking and walking and watching the sun go down, This one night standing behind the ice cream pallor, just watching the sun go down Crystal asked him if she could ask him a personal yet male question.

He replied, of coarse we talk about everything else. So she got up the courage to ask him if it was true that the size of your hands, (his were huge) was an indication that your penis was also big, huge... or more so than a guy, lets say 5'10"? He laughed and said "let's see"..he dropped his pants, (no underwear) and wrapped her figures around his penis. He said, "you might have to work at it a bit, because you are not his sexual type."

Everything happened so fast she didn't have time to react until her hand was wrapped around his limp, soft penis. She gave it a quick look but her eyes flew to his face with questions she hadn't yet formed and a look of sheer panic started to cross her face. She didn't move, but neither did her hand. Peter helped her hand to pump his shaft and look at what she was doing. He knew she had never seen a naked man before, it came up in one of their conversations, so he gently wrapped his hand around hers and helped her in her pursuits to enlarge his penis. He told her to close her eyes and think about what it would feel like to have him (because he knows how she felt about him!!!) kneading her right breast while kissing her senselessly..and pressing her against the brick wall...now breathe hard and think of all those feelings, let your mind wander...Because I'll thinking about the tall center of the varsity basketball team all sweaty and looking 100% male, wishing it was his hand wound around my penis and willing it to grow! Still in shock, standing in the night air holding on the Peter's naked penis with him breathing hot air down her neck, she wished with all her mite she hadn't heard his last remark, but he made sense to her now...that quickly, alone in the dark, in nearly their favorite place, Peter comes out to her with his true sexually.

Peter stilled Crystal's hand, bent and pulled up his pants, kissed her on the cheek and walked her home in silence. Home a place of solace... Her piano sat in silence...beckoning her to use it, beat on it, abuse it, just take her mood out on it. Anything to move beyond her embarrassment of the last 20 minutes. That's all it was 20 minutes...just 20 minutes to wrap up and tie in a knot the last 3 years of coming on to Peter! She banged out a very soulful song. She played every sad song she could think of to reflect her mood. Her fingers flew across the keys so fast her father just stood and watched and listened to her play when he slipped in the front door to enjoy her playing until he realized the tension she was releasing with every key stroke. He'd always enjoyed listening to her play but he also knew this was one way she corralled all of her frustrations into one place and successfully put them to rest. He hoped that their dinner conversation would move her back to the here and now and they could discuss pleasant things. It's actually when she asked her dad's permission to go to the lake with friends during the summer. He was so happy her thoughts were on having a good time with girlfriends, he agreed to it readily.

Little did Crystal know that the Captain had 'looked into Peter'. Being that Crystal had spent so much time with this young man since moving here, he had to know about this guys motives, character, and family. First his impressions were, *my daughter is safe with him! Then, how many other fairy people is Crystal hanging out with? These guys make me sick! She's gonna take a lot of ribbing if the Operations Center staff finds out about him. Harr and Pierce better stay on my better side, or just stay away from me. There kind don't belong in the military! God help me, I can't let this attitude out!* Captain Harold T. Grandcockski had a sleepless night that night, his little girl was growing up!

The next day was Thursday and Crystal, like always headed to the library. When she went around the corner at the art history section, without hesitation she sat next to Peter at their favorite table. It took about 10 minutes or so, but then Crystal took has hand...held it up and starting examining it. He let this continue for a full minute and then assured her with a sensual smile that her suspensions were correct. Peter had already written Crystal a note that he slipped into her book bag on the sly.

Chapter 3

The summer before Crystal's senior year started her on a new path, one of exploration. She already had her fathers permission to go to the lake with a group of girl friends for a week and a part time job at the Operations Center on the base as a runner. She also set three goals for herself for these few weeks before school started again. One...to get laid...she needed to find a guy taller than her, more experienced than her and prove the theory of the large hand. Peter's note, the one that she found in her book bag two weeks after school let out, indicated that "handled properly and lovingly, by a person who wants to achieve sexual pleasure from the shaft, can grow it exponentially to nearly three times the length and thickness of a tall male's thumb. Using lubrication adds a pleasurable sensation to the 'handling'. She guessed that this was his full explanation to her examination of his hand in the library...Two..to sneak into the Control Center and remove or send or way-lay a piece of information that is sensitive and vital to personnel information. She felt just mischievous enough to try something harmless without hurting anyone. Three..to start an anonymous search into her mothers whereabouts!

The lake vacation was just what Crystal needed to both separate herself from Peter and to help her set her sights on a very tall, dark, and handsome man. Enticing this lucky guy would be no problem. At age 17 Crystal was a knock-out. Her hair the color of pale platinum, flowed off of her shoulders and fell down her long back to her belt loops. This long back was carried by a slender girl who stood 6' 1" tall. She'd be able to charm any unsuspecting, horny guy into bed.

The first weekend on the beach at the lake proved to be her testing ground. Stretched out on a dark blue beach towel, her hair glowed and caught the attention of everyone that happened by. That was her goal and she provocatively set her plan in motion. Norman was the forth guy to approach and say in a tone of voice that pleased her, that she was the most intoxicating amazon he had ever seen. He wasn't too bad himself, her equal at just above 6 feet, she could work with that! He begged for a corner of her towel and she liked the way he begged. Within minutes into their conversation he had persuaded her to wade into the water with him. It felt good, cool and refreshing and built goose bumps all over her body. They were particularly evident in the dimpling of her nipples. He reached out and tweaked her left one through the flimsy material of her bikini top. He said 'nice' and with the other hand reached inside the right side and fondled the heavy orb. Not quite satisfied with what he knew could be attained now... here…., he stopped his attention and walked Crystal in the water and dove shallowly and came up between her legs. He stood not inches from her body and slowing started kissed her lips until she responded. Still walking her deeper in the water, water nearly up to their chins now... his hands never stopped their exploration of her body, all hidden under water. First her breasts, material up and away and then one hand cupping her pussy under her skimpy bottoms with one finger exploring as deep as he could go, up into her vagina. Their eyes met, standing toe to toe and they saw mutual confirmation that this was just the beginning. One more kiss and he placed her hand on the swollen lump of his groin. Her figures moved and rubbed and grabbed that which she could without touching flesh. A look of surprise touched his face with the realization that this could be a first timer or an inexperienced school girl out for some jollies. In an instant, he made up his mind he was going to have her. At the same time, she figured,... he'd do.

Back up on the towel they made plans for later that night. Separating themselves from their friends, they made plans to meet at the Pizza Dome in the center of town around 8pm. That accomplished, Crystal was proud of herself for following through with her number one plan. So far it was easy, Norman was a good looking kid, about the right height and forward with all the right moves. She had to stop thinking about Peter and allow herself to be fondled, groped and deflowered by this stranger. But first she needed to get up the nerve to touch and handle and learn to enjoy that which she had never done before. She had heard, slam bang, thank-you Ma'am.. It would be easier this way, no ties. No matter how much she talked to herself, she was nervous.

Dressed in short-shorts and a colorful mid-drift gypsy, off the shoulders top, Crystal made her way to the Pizza Dome to meet Norman. No matter where she went she always got stares and whistles. Tonight was no different until Norman took her hand and walked her through the crowd saying "she's with me, morons, mind your manners." All of a sudden her heart filled with yearning, her breasts were tingling and the hand he was holding felt scorched. Once they cleared the crowd and were walking by the edge of the park, she stopped him and kissed him gently on the lips and said thank you. That simple gesture and the look in her eyes were his undoing. Their leisurely stroll turned into a romp into the wooded area of the park and ended in a roll in the very thick grass underfoot. The first kiss was hot and fast and exploratory as were their hands on each others body. His hands easily found her bra-less under the short top she had on. Her arms were wound around his neck holding the kisses and then coming back around to travel under his shirt with hands so soft and caressing to feel his warm back and then back to his hands, she traced his fingers touching her. She used her hands to push his hands down her torso and into her panties. At the maneuver, he gently pushed her to the ground as he shed his pants and underwear. Crystal's top was already on the ground so he then proceeded to strip her of her pants, planting kisses anywhere he could reach. Any inhibitions she had an hour ago were now gone, she loved the feeling of laying naked out in the night air, next to this guy who was making her feel things she'd never felt before. Norman could now feel Crystal's body relax and could tell she was enjoying being touched so when he led her hand to his warm hardened penis she complied without hesitation. He moved his hand away, but so did she. He led her back to the hairy area at the base of his shaft and helped her move her hand upward to the tip. Again he moved his hand away, but this time she wound her fingers around his penis and experimented with gentle pumping. His sigh of contentment was her undoing and she started the kissing again while still holding on to his equipment. Breathless they laid next to one another just letting their hands move at will. While cupping one of Crystal's breast, Norman turned her slightly, lifted her leg on to his and gently proceeded to insert his throbbing penis into her very wet, waiting pussy. She shifted and adjusted her hips to make his entry easier, all of her moves were right on like she'd done this before so without further ado, Norman filled her with a swift movement that struck to Crystal's core and brought her to tears. She stiffened immediately and he stopped any further action. Still nestled inside her, Normans arms immediately wound around her as a comforting gesture when she said I thought this was suppose to feel good not hurt. He assure her immediately that the next time it would feel better, he explained he just opened her up and broke the barriers for the first time. Without a pause she thanked him. Confused and not satisfied, his arms relaxed a bit and he started exploring her body again starting with rubbing her ass and crushing his hips toward her while pushing her towards him. In no time his penis was ready to go and attain the satisfaction he missed a few minutes ago. He counted with, thank you, you were deep enough to take my entire length, not all shorter girls are, I'll have to remember that!

With this encounter over, they dressed themselves and walked hand in hand from the park back to the pizza shop. The rest of the evening was spent with friends.

Crystal was inwardly proud of herself for conquering her first goal so quickly. She had 5 more days to enjoy the beach and any other tall guy that met her fancy. With her friends all busy and filling their dance cards with quests of their own, she was able to wander off and tease, entice and flirt to her hearts content. She found out she was good at it and enjoyed the playful power that it gave her. Sitting next to and teasing the shit out of, he said his name was Tom, with her hand on his bare knee and touching his chest at times for emphasis at a statement that was made, she watched him go from a pimply faced, trash mouth, wannabe to an embarrassed kid about 5'8" when he stood up!

Next she met her match at dusk on the 4th day and danced with Matt under the stars until the crowd thinned out and the evening turned breathless with quick kisses, unmistakable touches in all the right places and unspoken promises all made with the eyes, of more to come. Matt had an unruly head of thick, curly, blond hair, worn too long and it kept falling in his left eye. Once Crystal starting pushing it aside just to look at him more clearly, his objections stopped and his hands stared adoring the length of her hair. He played with it, pulled it to her front, circled his fits in it, smelled it, lifted it from her neck and nuzzled behind her ear. Matt was a sensual tease with a soft touch, she guessed much older than herself with much more experience, but oh... what he would feel like...he stood at least a half of foot taller than her...she wanted him! Norman said she accepted the length of him which was a delight for him. Matt...she thought, with pleasure... would more than fill her! Her own thoughts were enough to make her nipples harden and her panties wet. She is learning that anticipation was as much fun as concurring! She'd have to be careful her anticipation didn't get the best of her. After all this was her week of exploration, so way settle for less than she was looking for. She'd be careful!

Once the pavilion closed and the music stopped, and the short, little, stolen kisses stopped, Matt proceeded to walk Crystal to his beach house. The last hour had been filled with the agony of anticipation which caused her panties to be wet. This was a fairly new sensation and would need to be a trigger in the future. She was learning that she was very quick to 'want' and not bashful enough to be very forward. Once inside the beach house Crystal asked Matt if he preferred short or tall women. He said he loved all beautiful women and enjoyed their bodies and experienced different feelings and positions with each one. Standing toe to toe, Crystal became the aggressor and gently lifted Matt's shirt from his body and dropped his shorts to the floor. Not to be up staged, Matt returned the favor with stripping Crystal of every article of clothing while locking lips together and investigating the interior of her mouth. Once she had possession of her mouth again, and while massaging and prodding his mammoth penis, she asked him what was the tallest woman he had every been with. He thought this an odd question and wanted to know why she had an interest in that direction. She simply told him that with her height, she thought he could lose his length in her and wallow in sensations he'd never felt before.

He said, "you certainly are a forward one, and have a wonderful way with words so let's try out your hypnotist."

It was a short way to the bed but the trip made luxuriously sensual with Matt's hands running over Crystal's body from the tip of her hair down her back, to behind her knees and back up over the cheeks of her ass to the corners of her mouth where his tongue had taken residence. He now made way for his fingers to do more exploring in that hot wet mouth which sent shivers throughout Crystal's body. Matt could feel the sexual tremors he caused with each of his explorations and enjoyed immensely what he was doing to her. So while his feet never stopped moving ever so slowly toward the bed his body and it's language never stopped exploring every inch of Crystal's body. They now bumped into the bed and fell upon it with all of Matt's weight squarely on top of Crystal. It's where he wanted to be because it made it easy for him to slip his penis directly into Crystal's slippery, waiting vagina. This action as well as his fingers and tongue playing games in her mouth brought her hips up to meet him in the most urgent way. Once Crystal knew Matt had satisfied himself and collapsed on her, she shifted and slipped out from beneath him. She moved and looked at his face. He had the look of a happy, silly man. She needed to take advantage of that man and experience the length of him again. Crystal walked to the bathroom, ran the water until hot and soaked the face cloth. She then walked back to Matt. Using the very warm cloth she began to gently stroke and cleanse his penis, his groin and pubic hair. The warm sensation on his body, particularly in that area brought a huge smile to his face and immediate action to his penis. It was the beginning of Crystal becoming the aggressor. When Crystal was walking away from the cabin the next morning, just when the sun was coming up, she knew she had left Matt a weak and very satisfied man. Walking back to the camp she shared with her six friends, she knew she learned more and enjoyed more in this week than the others did. This week also taught her that sex could be a very valuable tool as well as a pleasurable past time.

Chapter 4

Once back home, she started her duties as the runner for Control, at the Operations Center. With this job she had access to desks, mail boxes and private communications. Time to get nosy and hone her skills at being sneaky and stealth. To date Crystal was a trusted person in this military community. Trust was earned and never getting caught was a way to keep that trust. She wanted to see if she could do it! She didn't want to get anyone in trouble, least of all herself, but you hear stories all the time of clandestine meetings that should never have taken place, people being where they don't belong, she wanted to live on the dark side and keep secrets of her own...she wanted to give it a try!

So, one afternoon when lawfully picking up a sealed communication from Sgt. M. T. Finnely's desk to be delivered three buildings down, she copied the pertinent information for use of the telex machine, it was lucky she was all alone in this area. This could be useful in the endeavor of finding her mother. She was always thinking about her and ways of finding her, but her resources were limited as were her contacts. She often wondered if her dad had looked for her or heard from her, they never talked about her. As Crystal was exiting the building with her mind miles away, she neglected to see Sgt. Finnely barreling into the doorway with arms stretched out to push the door open which she had already done, so his hands landed squarely one each on each of her boobs. They stopped in embarrassment until Chrystal said, "that was nice." but Finnely counted with "your place or mine." Crystal replied with "this is your place and there's no one home." With his hand still on Crystal's chest, they both stepped back inside the building where he put a lip lock on Crystal enough to curl her figures immediately around his manhood. He had her up against the wall and his hands up under her shirt before she could take a second breath. She searched, found, undid three buttons at his fly area and fondled until he filled her hand in size and in release. He was now trying to dry and cover himself while she examined his face to find it mildly attractive and older than she first thought. No further words were exchanged and she exited the building to deliver the package.

Her thoughts were all over the place. *How could I have let that happen? How old is he? Is he married? I think I liked it...a lot.* That thought made her smile. *Yes, very pleasurable!* With the package delivered, and no other errands to run, she headed home. Her mind was once again reeling with the knowledge that she has the ability to "undo" or "mess-with" or "down-right" sexually tease a guys penis or his mind into a sexual frenzy. And then, why not satisfy! This was the home she shared with her dad, a quarter mile off base and filled with new furniture when they moved from Florida. It was comfortable and attractive but she had no choice in its purchase or its placement within the walls of the house. It was just a fact, nothing she thought over critically, just a fact! Mostly her thoughts were, *some day I will have a say in what my house looks like or where I will live or how I want it to look.* Right now I am living in dad's house.

Summer wasn't quite over yet, so she went in pursuit of Peter. He wasn't hard to find. At days end he was always in the park at the basketball end sitting in the shade. He lit up when he saw her, they hadn't seen one another for 4 weeks. He was afraid their last encounter had scared her away. He didn't move much, but just enough for her to slip behind and hug him, that was usually his move, but not today. From there he pulled her to sit beside him. He said "are we good? Because this feels like old times".

"We're more than good...and thank you," she said. "I now know that you need to feel something for someone in order to get hurt." She looked up at him and continued with "you bastard, you hurt me good, but it was all my fault." He hugged her close and said, "Yes it was, now tell me all about the beach."

She never shut up, pulling up weeds, scuffing her feet in the sandy dirt, she diverted her attention away from Peter as she told him all about Norman and a mouth full plus more about the night with Matt. She was very descriptive about their physical attributes, because this is where her interest laid...yes she had found a couple tall ones, long ones, thick ones..he put his hand over her mouth to shut her up. He said, "do you forget, that's what I'm looking for too...you're killing me! At that they fell over in laughter and a hug. She felt the familiar male bulge in his pants. Right there she asked him if he would fuck her to get the curiosity out of the way. Besides I now know how and when the guy gets relief, but how about the woman? At that he sat them both up and tackled her second question first.

He said "honey, after everything you've told me about Matt, he didn't bring you to that brink of madness. To a point of uncontrollable body shakes or feelings of loosing control of your body or your mind?" Crystal just looked at him like he didn't know her at all. She said "have you forgotten who your talking to, I could never loose control like that!" "Now for your first question," he said "No I will not fuck you, now or ever, because I could never be the one to bring you to the brink or edge that you need to be taken to." She smiled at him and said "you do love me". At that they got up and walked to the ice cream pallor.

The rest of the summer flew by with Crystal busy at Control in one way or another...she preferred the other! After her second encounter with Sgt. Finnely, one she encouraged, arranged and thoroughly enjoyed, he asked her if she had any friends that were as "worldly" as her. He had friends off base that didn't enjoy the women at the base club and he too wanted to get off base every now and then. Crystal admitted to him that she also would enjoy someone else as long as they met her qualifications. He laughed and said I do? She said sure, "you are a male over 6 foot 3 inches tall.

As long as they are at least your height, you set them up for me and I'll talk to a few of my friends."

"You are a particular little wench, aren't you," he said while she was walking out.

It didn't take but 3 days after that conversation and Crystal had two dates for the up coming weekend. One was a double date with men unknown and one of her girlfriends and the other a solo date with 6'5...she couldn't wait! Going out with Carol was a struggle...she is a know-it-all...so watching and listening to her being put in her place by a good-looking, well spoken college junior warmed Crystal's heart (but she didn't show it). It's a good thing the movie was good because the entire night fell way short of a good time.

The next day Crystal made a point to talk to Sgt. Finnely about her solo for tonight. Making sure he was alone in the Center she asked "how old is he, by the way how old are you?" Finnely's face smiled and said "32, do I pass"...she smiled back and said "you're learning... tonight, how old is he"? "Your only qualification was tall, we got that... he is a friend of a friend...be careful, don't fall in love, I don't want to be done with you yet."

She checked all of the mail boxes for out-going messages and turned to him and said "I'm looking for the one to rock my world and put me over the edge, then I'll talk to you about love". And I'm always careful now when going through this door." With that she left.

Peter knew all about her date with Mr. Tall for tonight. The plan was cute, they were meeting at the ice cream pallor, each of them caring a blue umbrella. Like they needed a plan...they were both freaking tall!! But in he strolled, good looking, strong build (yum) straight looking and confident. (shit) Peter was thinking, Crystal may have met her match...this will be interesting! Then he saw her..no one can miss Crystal..that head of hair announcing her arrival every time. He ducked toward the men's room and out the back door. She'd kill him if she knew he was here! Sure enough the umbrellas did it. Crystal met Samuel James. Samuel remarked that the umbrella was a unique idea, but he had to go out and buy one. Crystal looked "up" at him and said she'd make it up to him. Theirs was an easy banter back-and-forth and the get-to-know-you conversation continued most of the night.

This was a real date, Crystal was thinking that she'd really never been out on one. He was a gentleman, opening the doors for her, pulling out her chair, helping her with her sweater. There was no groping, or snide sexual remarks or even side ways glances at other girls or women. He was a real gentleman. This is not what she expected. All that tallness and he was a gentleman! She found out his full name was Samuel Bartholomew James III, age 28 and widowed. It was a sad story, because death always is, but with his families support and no children, life goes on and he was looking to the future, the past was buried. When he found out she was only going to be a senior in high school, he was disappointed. He said he was looking for a real woman, one ready to make a future with him. He knew she wasn't. When Samuel Bartholomew James III walked Crystal to her front door and lightly touched his lips to hers, it was her turn to be very disappointed. Crystal couldn't sleep that night, dam M. T. Finnely.

Chrystal decided, no more dating. She enjoyed the dominance of being the aggressor and the woman dominated by the sheer size of a man, she had tasted sex, experienced closeness and those things were not present in dating. She liked things quick and lusty. Dating took too long to get to the good stuff, in that length of time one was apt to lose their heart to feelings. The good stuff...Peter said she hadn't experienced that yet.

The summer days just melted away with friends, her work at the Operating Center, and of course Peter. The Center was quite the draw for her because with the help of Sara Harding, her dad's secretary. She learned to type. Using her fingers to move on the keys of the typewriter was like a prep-piano exercise, because these keys were harder to push. But learn to type, she did. School started and all things seem to return to normal. No more work at the Center, no more time to try and find her mother, definitely no more dating, no more hook-ups with Finnely and no more sex, period. School was her dominatrix now, but thank goodness Peter was still there with her.

Chapter 5

I t's now graduation week and Crystal thinks back and realizes that this guy was her best friend, confidant and protector of her feelings, as needed. She wasn't sure what she did for him. Once he did tell her that he was the most honest with her than any one else in the world. He just held close to his chest, most of his feelings. He said his day would come and he'd surely think of her as he let all of his secretes just slip out. She could only think back on all of the wonderful, loving things he had said and taught her! As far as best friends go, she had one of the best!

Since she'd moved to Virginia with her dad four years ago, she'd seen very little of him. He was always gone in the morning when she got up, all day she was either at school, out with her friends, or working at the Center. When she was in the Operations Center, she rarely saw him...she'd actually need to be announced to enter his office. She did it often, just to have the father-daughter connection. Dinners were a free-for-all, never together, homework, then back to bed. She knew things were going to change with graduation, but she had no idea how. She'd made no plans, had no skills for employment and had no money. Her support and housing was totally her dad. All of a sudden these things weighed heavy on her mind. Her thoughts went back to last summer...the best weeks of her life...they were a free-for-all...all fun and sex. Quite the learning experience. She still hadn't experienced an organism, at least now Peter referred to it by name!

Chapter 6

Gathering in the outside garden on the back lawns of the school, lining up for the official graduation ceremony, Crystal spots a head taller than most in the crowd. She's always looking for height. Once her line is marched closer to his section, she now sees the face to go along with his height...(not nice...sex pops right back into her head) he's gorgeous with thick wavy dark hair, a rather wide mouth that seems to smile easily (he just licked his lips, she could taste that tongue!) and eyes that sparkled at what he was thinking about. Little did she know, he had just spotted her! She totally missed the way he was dressed, it just didn't register, she was so accustomed to seeing men in uniform. She turned her head to check out the other side of the lawn and saw her father, standing tall and proud, sharing a conversation with many of the people she saw daily in the Operations Center. The ceremony went forward without a hitch, there was no formal lining up to end the program……just a dismissal and a general meeting and congratulations and mingling on the lawns. Her dad was the first one to reach Crystal with a gigantic smile and big hug. "You make me proud, girl. You are smart, beautiful and level headed...your future is in front of you and I know you will do well." These words from her dad were so unexpected, they swelled her heart like nothing ever had. His show of affection also stumped her a bit, but she'd take what she could get. His arm slipped to encircle her waist and he leads her in the direction of Mr. tall, dark and handsome. Smiling and nodding to to several people they both knew along their short walk, Crystal was now face to face with Lieutenant Vincent Octavio Clear. Her dad presented him to her almost as a gift. The introduction was that clear... from him to her. It was odd, but Crystal and Vincent looked at each other like they were the only ones standing in the sunshine, in this beautiful green field with soft music playing all around them. Everyone around them just seemed to disappear. It was an intoxicating feeling that Crystal had never experienced before, her panties were wet. Vincent broke the 'spell' with saying how nice to finally meet the young woman that Harold, (with a nod of his head toward her dad) your dad is always raving about. So many nice things being said to her, about her, from her dad, from this perfect specimen of maleness! He was holding her hands. When did he do that?

The afternoon party and cook-outs were loud and turned into a drunken bash for many of the graduates as well as the invited quests. The afternoon turned into evening which turned into a very late night for many of the party goers. This just wasn't Crystal's scene, so early on she invited Vincent to accompany her to the Ice cream pallor. This was familiar ground with an acceptable noise level, she even thought maybe they'd run into Peter there. For some reason it seemed important for him to meet Vincent.

Sure enough, with arms out-stretched Peter was standing there watching them walk in. She spotted him immediately and rushed into his arms, pushed away quickly and introduced Vincent to Peter. Vincent was a good sport watching Crystal being hugged by another guy (but immediately his blood pressure shot up) Peter shook his hand at the introductions and winked at Crystal. After about thirty minutes of conversation and filling Vincent in about his and Crystal's past and sharing an ice cream in his company, Peter said his good-byes with good luck and be good.

Vincent didn't care, he was with her. He also didn't care to continue listening when Crystal went on and on about Peters fantastic and loving attributes. She tried to tell him that Peter had been her best friend for the past 4 years. She said she really didn't have a close relationship with any girls her age, Peter just fit the bill.

Vincent had no idea when Harold starting talking about Chrystal, months ago, that she was this raving beauty, a budding woman needing to be coveted with love, affection and sexual fantasies explored. He spoke of her as a child, his daughter who just seamed to grow up overnight! All day Vincent had been trying to reconcile in his head how to undress and touch and devour the "child" he came here today to meet. She was a woman, every move she made cried sex extraordinaire! He'd never been this enticed so quickly or entirely by anyone before. But after meeting Peter and then lost in his own thoughts, he missed the clues she had been dropping. He didn't catch on to the removing him from the large crowd, he enjoyed the stroll hand in hand as she lead him to the edge of the park, her perfume was enticing, her closeness was intoxicating, but he needed to get over her closeness to Peter. He either needed to believe Peter was 'just' her friend, or get on with his own perusal of her and see where the chips lay. He realized just then that he was talking to himself and missing every word she said, he realized that if he didn't wake up he'd blow the chance she seemed to offering him, she poked him in the ribs and said" are you listening to me"? That woke him up in a big way, so to be honest, he said "No, I've been trying to figure out when I could do this" at that, he turned her to him and kissed her quickly and then again tenderly and then merely said "this is not the way I want to have you." She was now on his wave length and listened to every word he said. She stood close to him, kissed him on every other word and encouraged his way of thinking. Her hands were inside his jacket, he was so hot. It was wonderful that she needed to reach up to unbutton his top button. She walked over to the stone wall and stepped up a little to reach out and touch the hair on his chest. Stepping up again, while untucking her blouse, she reached for him to step closer so she could nuzzle his face between her boobs. Her hands were busy, her moves were inviting, her panties were wet again! Vincent just kept his hands to himself and asked her if she was almost done. He said, "I am...if you keep this up there will be no need to move this to my bed at the Inn".

"I want to move this to your bed at the Inn she said, all night?" He challenged her and said she didn't have the stamina for all night.

Walking again, the warm night air did nothing to cool the sexual atmosphere that they carried with them. Their hands touching all the while, while walking, was the heating point at both of their bodies. This heat radiated from those points to every other part of the body. Standing in front of the door to his rented room at the Valley Point Inn, Vincent had trouble retrieving the key from his pocket, his bulge was in the way...trying to be so cool, had worked so far, the big man in uniform, but he was loosing it, fast! Crystal nearly undid him with her antics on the stone wall. His powers of personal refusal were nearly used up when she started her butterfly kisses during her failed attempt to seduce him into the park. Finally standing inside the bedroom, his libido was in over-drive, it took all of this manly strength to slow it down and remind himself they had all night. He stood in front of her, started at her shoulders and rubbed his hands slowly down her arms, once he was holding her hands he coaxed her to stand closer to him. On tip toes (the only way to possibility reach his lips....oh man!!!) she started to make her move, but he stopped her when he bent his head and gently cupped his mouth over hers. The powers of excitement were in overload as their tongues touched for the first time and he discovered just how much she helped him to delve deeper down her throat. The sensation for both of them told of the promise to come.

Crystal's body responded to his nearness, his touch, and his kisses like she has never responded to anyone before. She was in the arms of this man kissing her and holding her and making her feel like the world outside didn't exist. He was driving her insane with his nearness and his heady maleness. This is what she craved, but he was taking his time and making her want him all the more. He stilled her hands and her forwardness with gentle, silent looks of persuasion. She stood perfectly still while he took his time with each button, zipper or clasp that held her clothing in place. He saw the anxiousness in her eyes and willed her to be patience, using her technique of butterfly kisses. She had never been treated this like, almost revered with every touch and every look. She started whispering the way she felt, what is felt like to be touched in such a manner. He had not touched any portion of her skin as yet.. just pushed her blouse from her shoulders, watched as it hit the floor.

He then lifted her chemise over her head and again watched it hit the floor. Next he went to her skirt which was merely hanging off her hips, zipper and clasp already undone. Tugged just a bit and helped her step out of it where it fell on to the floor. Now finality his anxious hands were all over her body. Gently at first, both of his hands cupped both of her breasts. This was Crystal's undoing, she could stand still no longer. She moved ever so closely to him and kissed him with such reverence, it stilled both of them. It took a few seconds for that moment to pass and when it did nothing was off limits.

Vincent was already in love. Feeling as he did, he wanted this night to last forever. He wanted to bring her to such heights, heights she didn't know existed. Hoping he could take it slow and meaningful, he wanted to make sure she was as satisfied has he knew she'd be able to satisfy him. He thought, *she took me that deep with a kiss..her body was made for me, she'll bury me so deep, I won't ever what to pull out.* His head was full of crazy, loving thoughts. He wanted to be lost in her!

Slow it down, his head said to his heart. Finish undressing her!

After the kiss Crystal was still standing there in just her (wet) panties. Feeling free, she moved to Vincent and hurried him along with undressing. Once that was accomplished, she slid her panties down, took his hand and led him to the bed.

Bury him deep and often was the theme of their night. She proved she had the stamina to keep him erect and ready. He proved that he was still a young man. Just as the sun was coming up, Vincent rolled on top of her, again. He stroked her long legs, kissed each breast lovingly and injected her ever so slowly with his mammoth member. She awoke slowly and gladly, made her slightly used and tender and waiting vagina available for him to proceeded. He stoked and pumped, waited and stroked and pumped again...and... withdrew completely to let the tingle of want begin. He continued these repetitions until her hips reached up to him so he didn't completely withdraw...that was agony! He felt her responding with desire and want and tantalized her clitoris mercilessly with his fingers while stroking her ever so rhythmically. He felt her control slipping, her breathing increase, her fingers and hands searching for something to hold on to. He freed one of his hands, gathered hers together above her head and eagerly sucked each breast in turn. Her being bound above her head, having her torso weighed down by his, being suckled and impaled by the most wonderful piece of male she'd ever known drove her over the edge. Her mind could not comprehend, or compile all of these feelings all at once and she lost it. Her control was gone, her body took over with shakes as she'd never known and breath that wouldn't let any words out. Her body constricted and mussels she didn't know she had tightened around Vincent's penis and drove him to a release that took his breath away. He had never felt this way before. Crystal's body took on a control of it's own...or lack thereof is more like it...her labored breathing and body shakes led to unexplained tears and the words 'I love you" stuck in her throat.

This was Crystal's first organism, and although she didn't like the thought of loosing control...she loved it. Vincent had the magic touch to turn her into jelly, make her feel things she had never felt before and still treat her with reverence and respect after seeing her loose control. After breakfast and much thought on the subject. Crystal realized that Vincent's ability to drive her to an organism was his control over her. With his looks and his size and his moves, OK...they were good together. She craved his size. He filed her with not much room to spare or to move around, so when he did move or pulse, she felt every neon, it felt wonderful. She wanted this in her life! She wanted him in her life.

Vincent sipped his coffee at breakfast with absolute resolute that he didn't want to live another day without Crystal in his life. With Crystal sitting across from him he had no desire to be anywhere else except maybe back in bed with her. She took total control of him with her technique of kissing. Never before had he felt almost rapture from the touch of a tongue, then couple that with her simple sigh when she wrapped her arms around his neck for a closer kiss, it was almost enough for him to lose his control.

Their breakfast conversation touched on many subjects. But mostly he answered her questions. How old was he...how long had he been in the Navy, how did he know her father, when could they go back to bed? At this he smiled, took her hand and led her directly back to the Valley Point Inn.

Lieutenant Vincent Octavio Clear had made up his mind to marry this girl. She finished his life, made him happy and his days with her in them were worthwhile. He was stationed here now, so moving her out of her fathers house to one of his own should be relatively easy.

Chapter 7

Crystal C. Grandcockski was walking on air, playing the piano with such feelings, filling her fathers house with such happy vibes, he asked,"what are you thinking about that's got you so chipper, I haven't heard you play like this in a long time". She beamed at him and said "Mr. Clear, and if I play my cards right, I hope to be Crystal Clear." At this her dad beamed right back at her, he hadn't seen her this happy in a long time, so if Vincent could do that for her, he was all for them being together.

Crystal found out her dad had met Vincent a long time ago when he was stationed in Saratoga Springs NY and Vincent was just a little kid, without a dad. Vincent was very taken with Harold Grandcockski in his very sharp uniform and the way he talked, so every time Harold's company was in Saratoga Springs he'd make a point to see Vincent. Actually, truth be known, it was Vincent's mother that held Harold's fascination, but, regardless, Vincent was very taken with the man! It was Harold's uniform and influence that attracted Vincent and encouraged him to join the navy, just to find out that his dad, grandfather and uncles before him were all navy men. As a youngster the Navy was all Vincent remembered about Harold. Not his (Harold's attention to his mother), not until a few years ago when he came home on leave and found them having breakfast together. He remembered it was an interesting time home with his mom. It was his 21st birthday and Harold's unit was also on base. The three of them spent a good deal of time together, but Vincent would head back to base after supper, where

Harold stayed in the house with his mother. Two days later Harold was still at the house with his mother. They'd' stayed in touch ever since. That was two years ago.

This set Crystal to thinking about her mother...dad wasn't faithful.. he was a typical navy man, no wonder why mom left, it's a wonder she stuck around as long as she did. This saddened Crystal and prayed Vincent wasn't cut from the same clothe because she intended to marry that man. She'd be his 'enough' and he wouldn't need to look elsewhere. She was finally able and ready to get the 'I love you' out of her throat and share her feelings and thoughts with Vincent.

With that as her goal...One week later Crystal became Mrs. Vincent Octavio Clear. She loved her new name, Crystal C. Clear, it was so much better than Grandcockski! Life was grand now that, that name was gone. They had one whole week to spend together, decided to try a new hotel in NY City. Crystal was so excited, she'd never been to NY...she had never stayed in a hotel. Vincent didn't care where he was as long as Crystal was with him. The hotel was magnificent. New and exclusive and hosting every desire one could think of. Dress shops, barber shops, three dinning rooms, each one more glitzy than the other and a piano bar which Crystal preferred. One morning after leaving the Coffee Shop, Crystal wandered into the Piano Bar and sat at the piano. She played a happy festive tune that caught the attention of everyone present. This sort of thing had never happened before. Music only happened at night, this was delightful! One tune lead to another and soon she was playing to a small crowd of employees just arriving for work, cleaning crews finishing their nights work, or hotel staff arriving to man switch-boards or reservation desks. Patrons leaving the Coffee Shop were also meandering in to listen. Vincent was thrilled to see Crystal enjoying herself and proud to sit next to her or applaud with the others at the end of a selection. Not wanting to interrupt her current song, Mr. Clive Brentwhistle (his name tag said so) waited until she was done and asked to have a word with her. The show was now over and neither Crystal or Vincent knew the tone of voice his word was going to have. After escorting the couple into the Mangers Office with the name tag Clive Brentwhistle, in gold lettering, Mr.

Brentwhistle wanted to shake Vincent's hand and kiss Crystal on the cheek for a heart warming morning performance. Chrystal thought this payment enough with pride and Vincent wanted to knock the guy into next week for touching Crystal. Without another look in Vincent's direction he started talking to Crystal about tomorrow morning and the morning after that and meeting with the program director to make a proper schedule and payment plan. "My dear your playing was delightful and very entertaining. It's just what this corner of the hotel needs in the morning." Mr. Brentwhistle finally sat down and took a breathe. At this interval, Vincent spoke up 'sternly' to inform Mr. Brentwhistle that Crystal was not available to work at the hotel, but rather she, they were honeymoon guests with only four more days to enjoy their privacy. Privacy which is hard to come by when you are military personnel. At this burst of information, Clive stood back up with hand out to Vincent in apology saying, "lucky man, congratulations, she is both talented and beautiful. Let me offer you two (now he looked over at Crystal) the next four days on the house for two more mornings of songs in the Piano Bar." Vincent looked at Chrystal and saw the most brilliant smile beaming off of her blushing face. "Mr. Brentwhistle," Vincent started," my wife is a natural at the piano because she really enjoys it, if she wants to entertain here for a couple more mornings, it is entirely up to her because she knows I'll support anything that makes her happy."

At that Crystal hugged Vincent and said "I love you for that" and to Mr. Brentwhistle, she said, "throw in three dinners, one in each of your dinning rooms with the free rooms and I'll do three mornings". Brentwhistle loosened his tie, shook Crystal's hand and finished the conversation with "talented, beautiful and conniving, good luck Mr. Clear" as he opened his door to see them out.

After one whole week of being together in bed, out of bed, moving around the city, traveling in a horse drawn carriage through Central Park, back in bed, she never knew such happiness. She never knew that an organism was not loosing control, but rather controlling the sex to make sure an organism occurred! They leaned this together and learned to control each other with these occurrences. Life was Grand controlling a Cock like his! Now the words were fun, she'd tease him endlessly and threaten to change her name back. He'd threaten back by showing her his limp, hanging cock just waiting and needing her attention to grow it back to a Grand. She'd comply willingly.

One week was not enough. The following Monday, Vincent needed to report back to the base and be on duty for a 24 hour shift. That same Monday, Chrystal was back at the Operations Center, still as their runner. The only difference was at the end of the day Crystal had no where to go. In the week they'd spent as husband and wife enjoying all of the sexual positions and sexual marathons they could muster, they never got around to getting housing. They gave up their room at the Inn, so back to her fathers house is where she was thinking of going. With that in mind, she approached his secretary and asked for entrance to his office, she still needed to be announced. This meeting with him started off a little off-setting. He said no. "I don't want to talk here." With the quickness of their marriage and their attention elsewhere, he took it upon himself to rent a little house for them down on Bridge Road. He explained it wasn't much, but enough for them to get by in for the time being. Now she was listening through her tears as he explained that he also had her piano moved there and he'd miss the beautiful music she could make with it. He also made sure that Vincent was reclassified as married and that she would get her first allotment check in the next pay period. She was overwhelmed, just standing there with tears running down her cheeks, she didn't know how to say thank-you. So instead, she took his hands, looked deep into his eyes and said "what do we sleep on?" He replied with the same look of intensely "that train of thought will go away in a few years!" That broke the ice and he said, "lets go shopping". Laughing they left his office and the building for their shopping trip.

This was a side of her father Crystal had never seen, didn't know existed. He was a real person, out to please and he did. As a wedding gift he bought the bedroom set Crystal picked-out, but then apologized that Vincent couldn't be there to put his stamp of approval on it. At this she became a little quizzical...his approval? Why would she need that? After all, she had her own mind and she could make decisions.

She stood her ground and needed her fathers answer. "Well dad, why would I need his approval", she asked again. "Because he is the man of your house now, you can't go off half cocked and do as you please." There it is was again, that attitude that went up one side of her and down the other. She'd keep her mouth shut...he rented her a house paid for her bed, she was glad she didn't need to go back to his house She was learning day by day who she was and how she needed to be She cooled her temper and asked if he'd show her to her new home that's where the furniture was going to be delivered.

When she walked into 18 Bridge Road she was delightfully surprised. It was charming with a front porch big enough for two chairs for morning coffee, a sun-lit living room that now housed her piano.. only her piano, a large eat-in kitchen, that had a stove and ice-box, two bedrooms on either side of the kitchen and a large pantry with a washing machine in it and the bathroom at the back of the house. The pantry room also had the back door which lead to a small back yard that had a clothes line and an overgrown garden. "Dad, you did good, we'll be very happy living here" she said once she'd walked through the entire house. He was merely leaning against the kitchen wall and watching her walk around, not saying a word.. his face set with his "scowl". His mood had completely changed since their little encounter over the 'approval' situation. Her heart sank at his disposition now, he was back to 'normal'. His off-putting stance made her think twice and not hug him in thanks for all he'd done.

She stayed at the house waiting for the furniture delivery and let her emotions run rapid on the piano keys. Her thoughts went from her dad's moods to thoughts of her mother. She and Vincent were married so quickly and everything moved so fast, this was the first time she thought about her mom. *It's too bad mom couldn't have been with us. I think she would be pleased at my decision to marry Vincent. I also think she'd like him a lot.* Her dad left after she said thank-you and walked him back to the front of the house. He still hadn't recovered to his joyful side. Still tapping out a sorrow-filled song, the doorbell rang, the furniture had arrived. Praising her playing, two men proceeded to carry in a headboard, bed rails, box and spring mattresses. They setup the bed and went back outside to get the dresser. The store, finding out this bed was for military newly-weds, threw in the sheet set, on-the-house. She was pleased for that...they had nothing!

Chapter 8

Within a few days, Chrystal and Vincent had the little house all cleaned up with hanging curtains, a kitchen table, a few scattered rugs and a few pieces of furniture for the living room. Life was good and the sex was even better, until Vincent asked Crystal how many children she wanted and saw in their future. The question came out of the blue and nearly choked her. "None now, probably none later either, not with you traveling the globe...you're not leaving me fat with a swollen belly to tend to babies all by myself. It takes a lot of work to keep my figure the way it is! Besides, I'm still young, too young for babies" That nearly knocked the air out of Vincent...he said "I want children in my life, many God willing. I think you and I would make beautiful children." This subject had never come up before. He had thought about it, her never. Sex was definitely off the table for tonight. She slept great, him not so much. The next day was just as Crystal had said, Vincent got orders that would take him off of this base for the next 4 months, she was devastated! He leaves in 10 days. They both knew this could happen, but so soon...! The talk of babies was shelved for the time being and they resumed their sex life with vigor. The ten days went by so fast.

Vincent was away for two days before he called Crystal. Contacting her was relatively easy because she was in the Control Center daily and commutations there were better. Everyone in the Center was accustom to Crystal being there, looking at things there, opening drawers and mail boxes. No one watched her with a suspicious mind. No one questioned her motives for the things she did. To date she had never taken anything that didn't belong to her, or handle anything that could be classified as 'none of her business', but Vincent needed, and asked her to wire him some money. She didn't have the extra he was asking for so she'd improvise and 'invent' the means of getting it for him. With her access to all things, she put the name of Sabers, Reginald T. (totally made-up, she liked the sound of it) in the roster for $85 payable from the car-pool fund with instructions to be dispersed immediately to the Seattle field office. Next she needed to create Reginald T. Sabers, all back information, dates, Social Security number, rank and current assignment. She felt invigorated, sly and mischievous. It was fun, she was inventive and covered all angles. It would work and no one needed to know. No one looked over her shoulder and no one wondered what she was doing. Task completed she contacted Vincent and told him he needed to pick-up a package at the dispersing office in the morning for a visiting officer, Army Lt. Reginald T. Sabers arriving in town to attend a personal Christening. So far so good...she felt giddy at the concept that she could pull off such a thing! Her learning to type and how to use the Telex machine was paying off. Army was brilliant, not at all connected to this base or any of the personnel here!

Crystal slept fine that night, not a second thought about what she had done. Before the end of the next day she got a 'thanks babe' communication from her husband.

The next 4 months were dragging without Vincent. Once you've been introduced to sex, to 'good' sex it creeps up on you like a hunger, if not satisfied it's all you can think about. Crystal was keeping herself busy at the Operations Center, keeping her nose clean and out of trouble and avoiding Sgt. Finnely and the base bar. She'd just go home at night and read a book. She needed to be very selective in this regard as well. Everything she picked up at the base library screamed sex and she needed to return them the next day. Now she was picking only one book a day and making sure it was not going to send her into a sexual frenzy. She was also looking at 'everything', as to what she could do next that was just as simple and lucrative as her first 'indiscretion'! The 'thing' snuck up on her. It was a "Personal & Confidential" communication for her dad that she intercepted. Again no one saw, no one was even aware there was such a message. There was a time stamp so she needed to act fast if she was going to do anything. *"Think, Think"* she thought! Then it hit her...go to the ladies room...steam it open, read then decide how to act on the information.

It was from a woman, lightly scented, hand written on official letterhead and dated today, 9:30 am.

To: Captain Harold T. Grandcockski
From: Suzie H. Clear
Wonderful to know about the kids
Somehow you knew they would be a good fit
Arriving today BLV12-22 at 5:30pm
Think of a way because I'm determined to meet Crystal
Sorry Vincent is deployed, but maybe it's better this way
Love, Suzie

Crystal's head was spinning. *His mother??? Coming here??? To see Dad???*
Sounds personal...knows about us?? What to do??
She hurried, re-sealed, dried, tried to act normal and arrived at her father's office, looking to be announced. Sara Harding, his secretary informed her he was in meetings until 2 pm and couldn't be disturbed. The message sat on the corner of her desk!

Still, what to do? She went to the visitors lounge just to think. She often took her lunch in there, so it wasn't an oddity for her to be in there, but it was early.

She was thinking back to what Vincent told her when he was a little boy. Harold visited them as often as he could..he said so..Vincent liked dad's uniform, so he was a youngster, but saw dad often over the years right up to his 21st birthday when he and his mother were having breakfast together. Dad always eats his breakfast early, before signing in at the base...so they slept together and she made his breakfast?!! Was she conjuring up her own story or was he really cheating on her mother all these years?

Join the Navy and travel...just like a traveling salesman...We've all heard those stories! She needed to go home and play the piano, she needed to bang on something. It didn't solve anything, but it made her feel better...Not yet, she needed to contact Vincent...let him know...No she needed to think...she thought, *dad knew we would hit it off and be good together,* still thinking, *the way he introduced us, I was right, he was presenting me to him. How did dad get Vincent here for my graduation... did Vincent know of dad's plans...that bastard!!*

Feeling all alone... again...she couldn't wait to get home to bang on the piano. She was glad Vincent wasn't home right now...not feeling the way she did! She had no idea how she was going to act when meeting his mother.

With that thought still on her mind, she was about to find out. Her dad had arranged a dinner out for the three of them at Crystal's favorite restaurant, Telly Greens. Suzie Clear was no where near what Crystal had pictured her to be, but she started conversations very easily. The three of them sat down and ordered their choice of beverage. Crystal was still uncomfortable ordering a rum and coke in front of her dad, although she drank plenty of them on her honeymoon, she settled for a plain coke. Dad always drank beer and Suzie ordered a whiskey sour with a twist of lime. She was a woman of medium height, dark hair now gone salt and pepper and looking every day of her 50 years. With her hair severely pulled back and tied with a simple elastic, glasses with frames two big and too wide, she looked like a spinster librarian. This seemed to put Crystal's mind at ease. Naturally the conversation centered around Vincent, his likes, his temperament and his current location. Once Suzie noted that this was a very congenial restaurant, nicely decorated and very clean. Suzie thought Crystal was a knock-out and Vincent a very lucky man. *Did the woman ever shut up? When one subject was 'exhausted' she'd move on to another and then another, Crystal's mind was now wandering...*but never did the conversation circle back to her and her dad's relationship. Let sleeping dogs lie...and she did!

The next afternoon when she talked with Vincent, she had cooled... some, but she still needed answers. Was meeting her a 'set-up'? Did he know if his mom and her dad were together? Why was she here now, knowing he was deployed? "Can't you tell, I miss you, can't wait for you to get home." she said at long last and ended the call. Her answers would have to wait until he got home.

Crystal's life had changed little since she got married. Yes, she had her own house, shared with her husband when he was home, rather than with her father. Still 'reported' to the Operations Center and saw her father every day and carried out her duties as runner. Saw Peter occasionally as his schedule permitted. Since graduation, he was the #2 photographer for the Army Times being run out of the Army base 22 miles away. He was busy and happy and regarded Crystal as yesterday's memory, they now had so little in common. This is how Crystal's life had changed the most. She respected her marriage vows and stayed celibate and alone while Vincent was out of town. Boy, that was a loaded thought, he'd only been gone a little over 3 months, and she was horny as hell. They'd really have to have a talk about him making a career of the Navy...She didn't think she'd make a good military wife!

Chapter 9

Two weeks later Vincent was home. What a home coming...She made sure of it! Curtains drawn, table set for dinner, flowers and candle light, she even spirited the air with her perfume, he loved that fragrance. Even more than the aroma of the lasagna in the oven. But dinner could wait. There was a sexual appetite that needed to be satisfied first, hers!

Once he walked in the door her libido was met by his, there was an equal feeling of lust that needed to be slowed down. The looks in their eyes mirrored their need and hunger for one another. The unspoken gentle reach Vincent used to close the gap between their clothed bodies and the arms Crystal wrapped around Vincent's body were patient and carefully executed. They were acting like two strangers experimenting with feelings ignited by the heat in the room. After a sweet and deliberate kiss, Crystal held his face in her hands, looked deeply into his eyes and said, "until this moment I didn't realize how much I love you". With that a tear slid down her cheek. That was the undoing of Vincent..he carried her to the bedroom and they made love like it was the first time.

Once they made it back to the kitchen table they were both famished. The candles had burned down and were now a pool of green wax which left the area in darkness. Their bedroom romp lasted well past the diner hour, through the evening hours and left them sexually satiated at this midnight witching hour and ready to devour the lasagna still in the oven. After lighting a couple more candles, the lasagna tasted even better now that, that is what occupied their minds. The morning brought routine and order back into their lives. As much as Crystal wanted to address the questions his mother's visit brought to her mind, the sleeping dogs were still lying. So be it!

What she really wanted to know was, did he have any trouble with the cable to Reginald Sabers and collecting the money from the wire. She skimmed the top of the details when she explained to him how she did it, he was all ears. Bottom line, it was relatively easy, it didn't take long and next time, we'll try for more money. "As long as I maintain my position a the Operations Center, don't make any waves and loose my accountability, next time should be just as easy". She said this with the upmost certainty that there would be a next time. Vincent just went along, to go along, but his inners were nervous at the joy Crystal exhibited at getting away with it. She was too easy to look at and dream about 'the next' bedroom encounter to let the 'maybe' next time interfere with his daily activities. He'd go to base, do his 8 hours and come home to her and do her for the next 8 hours. He knew she had it in her! He knew he wanted it in her! *How the hell did I mange the last 4 months without her, her body fills my every thought. Next time I'm sent away...somehow she is coming with me!* With that, he left the house and reported to duty at the base. He was thinking *if she needs to work her magic, she can find a way to get a room, and be with me at my next assignment. Finance the trip and make arrangements for us to have more pocket money to enjoy the adventure. Stop...Stop...dangerous thinking!! But OH, what a military career she could make it!*

It was a really long day, Vincent was in and out of classroom activities nearly all day and Crystal was in and out the building doing messenger drop-offs nearly all day. It seemed each time Vincent changed rooms or was marched to a new exercise, Crystal was near-by and their eyes undressed each other to the unmistakable extent of lust in overload. The endorphins released from Vincent's body caused Crystal to lose her breathe at one of their close' encounters' moving through the hallway near the mess hall. She needed a quick explanation of her behavior to Pvt. Charles Pickins. As he thought he was going to have to pick-up a fainted woman. "It's the closed in aroma seeping out of the kitchen" she explained. Yup, really long day! The rest of the afternoon, Crystal huddled in the Control Center working on a 'private' project. She open up doors and files and cubbyholes in file rooms, items that hadn't been looked at for months and found a way of making Reginald T. Sabers a paid, Lt. in the Army transferred to the Army base in the next town to complete a project and immediately be transferred to Ft. George G. Meade in Maryland. Once he was in the monthly payroll roster, she figured accessing his account would be no problem and she and Vincent would have more money to play with and live on. *It really wasn't such a long day after all. This took a little more digging and moving of dates and assignments, but I know it will work….I can't wait to share this with Vincent.*

Crystal was sitting on the front porch waiting for Vincent to arrive home. He saw her. Threw her a kiss and ran the rest of the way. "Save some of that energy, sir" she cooed into his ear when he hugged her hello. "This is the best kind of a hug" he whispered right back at her when he felt she was bra less and totally unbuttoned waiting for his touch.

"I have some news for you" she said…"but I'm gonna make you pick between sex or money" *please pick sex…please, please…*

"You said sex first, so that's what I want right now". Crystal's smile couldn't have been any bigger or brighter, they made it in the front door and the clothes started disappearing. Sex, it was, long, hard and very satisfying. The after sex drink was cool, strong and lingering on their tongues when they shared a kiss standing at the kitchen sink. She tried to set the table for dinner, he decided another drink was in order, she turned the oven off, he continued to turn her on. Dinner was forgotten for another romp in bed. There was no way they could feel sorry or bad about their behavior, what they did to each other and for each other felt too good to be bad. "You get me pregnant and this will need to stop" she said breathlessly. "I'd much prefer you in my bed than one or two little ones sucking at my breasts, I think they were made for just for you."

At that moment he agreed, totally. Her rough, husky, throaty voice was really a turn on voice talking about her breast, while still stoking his penis and massaging his balls making his brain mush and his mouth hungry for those round, heavy breast she so loving teased around his mouth. "You know that ham we have in the oven…it's now going to be breakfast, because there is no way I want to leave the warmth and sex filled aroma we have built in this room. I think there might be room for more, please don't make me get up." He rolled her over and demonstrated what was 'up' in a most loving way. The night gave way to morning and she never had a chance to tell him about Reginald T. Sabers .

Vincent woke up to Crystal scrambling eggs with ham and drinking coffee and humming a tune he knows she has played on the piano before. He was happy and felt like a lucky man. Looking around he noticed the hooks and multicolored coffee cups dangling from them. The green and brown kitchen curtains featuring coffee pots and coffee beans floating in mid air. There was also a green table clothe with white threads running through it. He then noticed his feet weren't cold because he felt a rug beneath them. When Crystal turned from the counter and delivered his cup of coffee, she noticed a different/strange look on his face. "Are you OK" she asked with concern on her face. He smiled up at her and said "I love you so much, thank you for making this a home, our home".

Crystal was so pleased he noticed the little things she had done in the kitchen, she dared to ask him about the house he grew up in. "Did your mom decorate your house? Was it is a house or apartment, I know so little about you." Over breakfast Vincent told her all about his mom and the Welsh house he grew up in. "Mom was a really good cook after awhile. She learned it from my Nain (Grandmother, pronounced nine) my dad's mom. We lived in her house. One too big for her after my Taid (grandfather, pronounced tide) died. I remember him as a really, really big man. Jet black curly hair. Now Vincent was just looking skyward and letting some of his memories out. "He had hair all over. I remember wondering if I was going to have hair covering my chest and arms and legs the way he did. His voice fit him, deep and resonating, it made people listen! Ha, it made my dad listen, I remember all the stories Nain would tell me about my dad. I lost them both when I was about 11 years old. That's when mom packed us up and we moved in to the big house with Nain. That's when my mom really learned how to cook, to bake to entertain. Nain loved to play cards with her friends. She would bake up a storm to make sure there was always something to serve at their, she called it, half time. That's when my mom started baking...for Nain's card games. Then came really good suppers from Nain's tutoring and her recipes."

Crystal said, "she sounds like a lady I would have like to know, how old were you when she passed?"

"Oh, she's still baking and playing cards, that's probably why she didn't accompany Mom on her visit here. She's undoubtedly wants us to visit with her so she can meet you, just say the word and she'll start baking!" Vincent was smiling brightly at his memories and thoughts of going home to visit with her. "So what do you say we try to visit next time I get at least a three day weekend?" There was still time to linger over this breakfast before Vincent needed to rush off to base so Crystal dared to ask the question, the nagging questing that had been bothering her since his mother's visit.

"I get a sense that the last time our folks were together they sort of conspired to introduce us, to blind date us, if you will. What do you think, or were you in on it when you came to my graduation? Did my dad bribe you to come up here to meet me?" "No bribe was needed, he made an invitation for me to check-out his base, attend your graduation and yes meet you." Vincent's answer was so fast with wrinkles in his forehead, it made Crystal laugh. "Why would you think there was a 'conspiracy' underfoot for us to meet?" He was really confused by her question. "Only because when your mom was here, it was strictly to meet me. You were away, so it seemed like a strange time for her to come. She met me, seemed satisfied made a remark somewhat like.."you were right, they are good together'...and she left…..long pause...I guess I'm reading things into it. We should visit and see them." Again, Vincent smiled brightly, kissed her good-bye saying see you for supper. She still hadn't mentioned her shenanigans with the name Reginald T. Sabers.

Chapter 10

With nothing but love in her heart and silly, dangerous thoughts on how to play with Reginald today, Crystal also headed for the base to see how busy they were going to keep her today.

Once she arrived on base, just inside the west entry gates, she noticed all hell breaking loose. There were trucks being loaded with men and supplies, busses being loaded with men and a dozen or more helicopters heading for the landing field at the north side of the base. With heart palpitations she'd never experienced before, she made a dash for the Operations Center to find out what was going on.

There was a horrific storm that nearly took out Haiti and then slammed into Puerto Rico, flattening our base there and leaving over 200 service men and woman dead or missing. Half of all of the eastern sea-board military bases have been ordered to report to Puerto Rico for search and rescue, and clean-up for rebuilding. "It's a mess down there Finnely told her," when she finally arrived and found someone to talk to.

Now she was in a panic...Where was Vincent? Where to start looking, surely she'd get to see him if they were shipping out his unit. They couldn't just move personnel without prior notice, could they? She headed for her dad's office. Once permission was granted for her to enter, she pleaded her case to Captain Grandcockski to please help her find Vincent, now, on these grounds. Still pacing around his office, her dad softened a little for her sake, but made no promises. He was up to his ears in orders and moving people and moving supplies. All of this started before he arrived at the Base this morning and just seemed to snowball once he arrived, like he was superman and could move mountains in mere minutes. His head was spinning and his daughters request just added to his headache. "I'll do what I can, check back with Sara every 15 minutes. Without feeling much better Crystal made it outside before the tears started. Nope, military life was not for her, she needed more security in her life. This was for the birds. She took a deep breathe, went back inside and checked her board for assignments. None...now what...with everyone busy and their heads in turmoil, no one would pay her much mind so once again she was going to visit with Reginald.

Everything was in order, just as she had left it last night. 1st Lt Sabers was just finishing his 22nd month and due for review, new orders and possible deployment. With the crisis in the south, she didn't want his name associated with that mess and the possibility of moving men under his name, so she moved him to join a regiment in Spain for 4 months with off-shore pay and liberty with liberty pay after 1 week for the swift move. As per his request in writing, all of his payroll was to be held in a saving voucher and sent to APO Box 12, Roanoke, Va. This is the box she had rented last Thursday just for such matters. Once again her head was swelling with personal glee at the maneuvers she had accomplished in such a short amount of time.

She left the building and walked down every road that was lined with busses and trucks looking for Vincent or someone she knew or could talk to that would know him. The day was cool with a hint of rain by the humidity in the air and as she walked and kicked up dirt and dust, she thought about Vincent's possible departure and her lonely bed...again! He made her body crave him, the more she thought the hornier she got...*cut it out, she thought!!!* Her panties were wet. Just then, she looked up and saw him hanging out of a window in a bus headed for she didn't know where.....he yelled...south exit near PX and the bus rolled away.

In tears Crystal starting walking toward the PX in hopes of catching up with Vincent and finding out where he was headed and when. Not ten minutes later her dad happened by in a jeep driven by a Seaman and picked her up and drove her to the PX where she could find and talk with Vincent. This was an area she was not very familiar with so she was nervous when she was dropped off and left alone. There were so many men, so many vehicles and the noise was deafening. She felt in the middle of someplace she didn't belong. She needed to move away from the 'middle' and try to contact someone with knowledge of the operation so she could gauge her movements. The news she heard coming over the radios was devastating regarding lives lost and property damage and the need for help. Standing still and trying to wrap her mind around such devastation caused her to silently pray for the men and women here to be angels delivered to rescue and rebuild broken lives. She'd find Vincent and wish him great speed and good luck in helping in such a place. She also needed to see her dad in case he was also being relocated to that area. Her dad had left her many times in the past...her husband had left her not too long ago, orders. Never before had she had this fearful, empty, gut wrenching feeling of loss or lonesomeness. They'd come home with their heads full of sites and sounds they wish they had never seen or heard. This was their mission, she knew this intellectually, but as the one left behind, not so much! Stop thinking...find Vincent.

This turned out, not to be an easy chore. Every man in the same uniform, so many men moving around so many vehicles, each having a job to do, no one stopping to talk with her. One hour, two hours later, the light drizzle that started to fall that made everything uncomfortable to touch or sit on. That didn't help Crystal's state of mind or temperament. Finally her dad found her standing under a canopy at the fuel docks where most of the vehicles lined up for refueling. This was a short and tearful meeting, as he was next to fly out to that devastated area. She was told to stay put, that Vincent and his unit were two or three back in this very line. Forty minutes later, she finally had eyes on Vincent. Relief washed through her instantly, she couldn't wait to find out what was going on. Joyfully she was told, this unit and company J through M were being left behind to hold down this fort and resupply returning ships as needed.

For now that's all she needed to know, Vincent was not being shipped out and once again the tears started running down her cheeks. It took another 20 minutes before she was snugly in his arms being comforted and told he'd be home for supper. All this to cheers and jeers from his entire unit as they clung to one another! Her heart couldn't take too much more...no, she was not cut out to be a military wife. A ride back to Operations Center was easy. The wait for him to join her was harder, but she occupied herself playing again with Reginald. For the next four months his station was secure as was his monthly earnings, so she expanded her and Vincent's port folio to include savings bonds to be purchased on a regular basis with deductions for their purchase to be automatic from their new savings account being funded via the funds funneled from Reginald's earnings. A new automatic deposit into their personal checking account was also established, again from Reginald's earnings. Just for good measure she also included a deposit to their personal savings account to enable them to take little vacations or trips or long weekends such as the one they were planning to visit his mother and grandmother. It was getting so much easier and with very little worry each time she played with Reginald and it was also so lucrative! It was a great way to pass the time, as now, just waiting for Vincent so they could go home.

When Vincent joined Crystal at the main gate at the end of the day, it was with relief the way they hugged one another, just knowing he was not being sent south to the horrible conditions on the Islands. All the way home they talked about their safe lives here in the states. They could travel to NY or to his home town to visit with his mom and grandmother, freely without fear. Realizing just how lucky they were, how living in this country and serving this country supported their dreams made them rich in humility and thankful for their freedoms.

Chapter 11

It's so easy to fall into routines and forget about the other guy who is risking his life and living in conditions not fit for animals. Such as it were for Vincent and Crystal for the next 4 months being safe and living the life of Riley and enjoying their simple life of work on the base which was supply routine and evening meals at home. Their privacy at home was never invaded so they lived as honeymooners from 5pm to 6am. Crystal couldn't believe how much she was turned on by simply thinking about 4:45pm and reapplying her simple make-up and taking off her panties and removing her bra and unbuttoning her top three buttons. She looked in the mirror and added a thin cardigan over her shoulders to cover her undoings to look perfectly proper. Looks can be deceiving and she wanted to deceive...to a point. The way home, the 10 minutes it took to get there was torcher on Vincent when Crystal lost the cardigan and the undoings were flaunted in front of him. She was great at teasing, letting him know she was wet just thinking of touching him the minute they got home. You won't have to work to hard to undress me she'd whisper to him...I've no panties on! She'd dance in front of him to expose nearly a full boob with three buttons undone and then another letting the blouse fall off of one shoulder. She couldn't believe she was doing this on the open road, in total daylight for the world to see...but no one else was around, so she was safe, just a little crazy...crazy about Vincent. The four months of living on love and playing with sex and being carefree with bodily movements and positions and daily games around the base, treating it as a private backyard and not a military institution came to a screeching halt when they were caught naked playing with each others personal parts, sitting joined at their groins in the cloak room in the operations center. Crystal had her back to the petty officer who standing not two feet from them, kicked Vincent's foot to get their attention. Crystal instantly stilled her gyrations of sexual pleasure and fell forward to Vincent's' chest in embarrassment. The petty officer was also a bit tongue tied and simply informed them of the incoming, due in 20 minutes.

Their extended honeymoon was over. The work in putting the base back in order was back breaking and messy in the five days of rain and made all the worse by every military plane, train, ship or bus, carrying personnel or equipment using them as a stop-off for fuel and additional supplies. Day one was hectic after the quiet and almost serene atmosphere on the base for the last four months. Day two wasn't much better, but on day three Crystal saw her dad and his hug still made the rest of the world disappear. She didn't realized how pent-up her emotions were with him gone. He was still her rock. She loved Vincent, and she knew with every passing day he was becoming her rock of Gibraltar, but dad was still special. All things were now right in her world and that night she played her piano with joy and brightness. Vincent made a point of telling the Captain that...that he still played a major part in Crystal's well being. It made the Captain proud to hear it. There was still two days of rain and bustling activities on the base, but Vincent was back to his unit and busy and Crystal was kept hopping with carrying messages from one end of the base to the other. At the end of the 5 days of returning personnel, Crystal and Vincent returned home exhausted and run ragged.

Because of all of the extra activity Vincent put in for a long weekend and surprised Crystal with train tickets to Hopewell Junction to visit his grandmother and mom. What a marvelous idea...Crystal was delighted and not nervous at all about meeting his grandmother and seeing his mom again. He talked eagerly about the two of them. When Crystal could get a word in edge-wise, she told Vincent about Reginald and his duty station and his pay increases and their personal bank accounts linked to his name. Vincent sat perfectly still, just staring at

Chrystal during her telling of Reginald, asked how much money do we deposit on a monthly basis due to his existence and was shocked at the amount. Crystal explained that she may have over-done it, but done it was so she also opened an investment account to help grow the funds for future use. Once again Vincent was speechless, but a small smile stretched to a longer, wider smile and he rewarded her with a giant hug and passionate kiss. In the beginning of her telling Vincent of Reginald and the money, she almost stopped because of the look on his face.

The weekend arrived and they boarded their train to Grandmothers house. Because of their new found money, the three hour ride was taking place in their own car, being shared with no-one. So, being fondled in some very private places in a fairly public setting, she secretly warmed to all of his touches and reciprocated in kind. She was sure that this man was going to take her places and build memories with her that would last a lifetime. Being in his arms like this, feeling his strong arms hold her to his chest where their two hearts beat together, her mind wandered straight to a warn bed with crisp sheets where she could straddle his naked body with her own and make love to him until the cows come home. With this thought, she stilled Vincent's hand and asked if his grandmother had any cows. After a little explanation and a little laugh, she also asked him if there was a piano in her house. She had some lovely romantic tunes dancing in her head.

They were nearing their stop and the end of their train ride. It was a good thing, they needed to stretch their legs, readjust some clothing pieces and put some distance between their bodies. They were married a whole 8 months now and still couldn't keep their hands off of each other. Every other thought Crystal had was sexual. Vincent was so elated at the appearance of Crystal, it boosted his ego to be seen with her, to be near her to know she was his! His grandmother was going to love her.

The train station was crowded but her voice cut straight through the noise. Vincent looked left then right and sure enough there was his mother pushing her way to get to them. Vincent and Crystal were hard to miss with their height and mom was heading straight toward them. First Vincent hugged his mom, swung her around like a rag doll and laughed as he settled her back on her feet. Crystal bent and gently hugged her very quickly. Keeping mom between them, they headed for the street leaving the crowd behind. Next was a street car ride for 6 city blocks and then wagon ride to the farm. Yes, grandmother had cows! She also had chickens pecking the ground and a couple of dogs just lazing on the porch when they walked up. One dog in particular took a liking to Crystal's leg and sniffed and followed her straight into the kitchen. Grandma said "that's Dick, can't you tell, tell him to put it away and go lay down". Crystal chuckled, hugged the little lady and felt immediately at home. "Hey Vincent," she said, "I like your grandmother". It was the beginning of a wonderful visit. And eat… boy can these women cook and bake and put out a spread like the queen was coming. There had to be enough for them to take something home, and they just got there!

Vincent took their bags upstairs and looked around like he was still 12 years old. It felt strange to go to the big room at the end of the hall that had the biggest bed in it. He had never slept in that room, no one uses it now, it was there for the taking, clean sheets with pillows all fluffed for them. It felt good to be home, to bring Crystal there, where he remembered being happy. He rejoined the women in the kitchen and the eating began. Not too long after eating the card playing commenced. Grandma was a shark! It was a homey setting with people everyone was comfortable to be around. Vincent's mom Suzie ended the evening with, "you two be off to bed, you must be tiered after the afternoon of traveling and it's getting late, remember church in the morning."

Up stairs in their room Crystal nearly chocked on the word church! She hadn't been to church in years, if ever! Vincent merely said, "it's the cost of spending the night with my mom and Gram, so lets jump in bed and do things that we need to confess in church tomorrow." There had been a prelude to their love making for tonight. The entire afternoon and train ride had been filled with touchy-feely episodes and they were more than ready to continue their escapades, they knew morning would come too soon. Once Vincent was satisfied and rolled over to sleep, Crystal's mind was in over-drive. *Had her dad ever slept in this bed? Was he still in a relationship with Suzie? When was the last time he was here? Did Suzie make him go to church too? Did she have the gumption to ask Suzie these questions tomorrow or should she go home and ask her father these questions.* Sleep just wouldn't come, her mind just kept coming up with more questions. Some of her questions lead to her thinking about her mother. *Did she know about this place or Suzie or even Vincent? Where was she now? Is she happy. Is she safe? Has she made a comfortable place for herself and her work? What was she doing and where? Enough, Enough, Enough !!! sleep..start digging when we get home!!*

Church wasn't half bad...it was more like a meeting place for friends and family where everyone was happy to see you! Suzie was very well received and Grandma was almost revered! She met a lot of nice people who regarded her warmly as Vincent's wife. What a feeling, she had never really felt like this before. The coffee hour after the service was lively, informative with civic news as well as a bit of gossip. Once the word got around that Crystal was a seasoned pianist, she was urged to play right then and there in the church basement/function room. Happy to do so, Crystal played a few of her favorite tunes and that prompted a sing-along. Once back at the farmhouse for Sunday dinner, roast pork, potatoes and carrots with a side of spinach, all prepared before they left for church, the four of them collapsed to catch their breath. Dessert was to die for...fresh churned cream and fresh picked strawberries for strawberry short cake! It had been an impromptu party calibrated in fellowship with the parish faithful to recognize Crystal's talent and accept Chrystal and Vincent's marriage and visit. That's how Grandma explained the eruption of friendship. Crystal was a little baffled by the friendship and immediate offer of affection without any prior notion of expedience. There was nothing asked for in return except her piano playing, which to her was nothing. Crystal had never known the outreach of friendship or kinship offered by all of these people. She wasn't really questioning their motives because down deep she knew they harbored no ill will, but still she had never known such warmth, it wasn't in her past experience or family. The rest of the day was spent with food and conversation and the unexpected pleasure of family and stories of growing up. Crystal was delighted with Vincent's family and very happy they came for this visit. They were leaving the next day with a picnic basket full of berry preserves, pickles, smoked ham and fresh baked bread, Grandma wouldn't have it any other way.

The train ride home was quiet with both Crystal and Vincent deep in thought about the last two days.

Family was on both of their minds, but evoking totally different memories and feelings. Vincent was floating and wrapped in the warm memories of years past all culminating into this weekend with his new wife. Crystal reviewed the faces and the hugs and the immediate acceptance with a feeling of withdrawal. It wasn't really easy for her to be folded into those hugs and lead by the hand into the crowds of unknown people that really only wanted to befriend her. There was nothing in her past for here to draw on for comparison. She was very much a loner, both in her home and somewhat in her social circle. Strange that Vincent just rode the ribbon of kinship and didn't realize Crystal was having a hard time with it. They really didn't know that much about one another! She only knew for sure that she could keep and satisfy Vincent in her bed, there, they knew much about each other.

Chapter 12

Back on base the next morning Crystal realized that her explanation of Reginald was cut short by her man, who really didn't want to hear about the other man in her life while he was feeling her up and getting hard just touching that which he could. It was the rest he couldn't do in a public place that kept him hard and attentive and loving and denied. She'd go away with him anytime, sit next to him anytime just to be turned on like that. But damn it, her panties were wet, and it's Monday and she was in the Operations Center getting ready to deliver messages that didn't make any difference to her! She really needed to discuss Reginald with Vincent tonight after she reviews the accounts that have been set up for them with his money. Thinking about that and seeing the money grow is also a trigger to get her panties wet. She knows she's becoming a self indulgent woman and she likes it. Likes it a lot!

With the money on her mind as she travels to the other side of the base, to deliver other peoples messages, she is re-thinking her thoughts about a military life. As long as she has access to the Operations Center and the growing ease of communication and knowledge of things that are none of her business, this life could pay-off just fine, could pay them/her just fine. She is still thinking all the way back to the Center where she encounters her father and recognizes his foul mood. She also notices the type of paper in his hands and breaks out into a guilty sweat thinking she's been caught and this is notice of her thievery. Instantly she feels 8 years old again and awaits his angry wrath for her wrong doings. Can't be, all tracks were covered so well, there is no way she has been found out. There's not enough room in her head for all of these frightful thoughts or time to formulate a plan to stand up to her dad...he comes toward her slapping the message against his thigh and bellows. "she wants a divorce... now?" It's with instant relief that Crystal laughs and says, "that's wonderful news, we now know where she is."

Captain Harold T. Grandcockski, with murder in his eyes, stood before Crystal and calmly says (as he hands her the message) "you can see her if you'd like, it's your right, but I don't ever want to see her again." Crystal counters with "did you forget where I've been all weekend, who I saw, who I talked with and what we talked about? Either you tell me the whole sorted story about you and mom or you have no grounds to stand on being the jaded husband!" Crystal reread the message and made a mental note of the date of her mother's arrival, 4 days from now.

The Captains face lost its color but not his jaw set in anger. "You cook dinner, I'll be there at 6pm".

"Be happy to have you" Crystal whispered to her dad's re-treating back, as he walked away. *OH boy she thought...I don't know any more now, about them, then I did before we went to Hopewell Junction. My threat is bringing him to dinner. Good I guess now we get things out in the open and talk about it...no matter what...yes I want to see mom!*

Crystal was home early tiding the house and planning dinner when Vincent arrived home. He and Crystal discussed the Captain coming for dinner and let the matter lie until he gets there. Crystal went straight into the Reginald story again for Vincent's information for which, on the subject he had very little. Crystal needed him to know what she was doing and to the tune of how much. Vincent's attention was not really on Crystal's words or information but rather on her body language as she was talking. She was always moving, stepping forward to touch his arm, lay her hand on his chest, reach up and touch his cheek. She was talking but he only heard the sound of her voice, very soft with a hoarse rasp like she always needed to clear her throat combined with a touch of a southern drawl, he loved that! "Vincent, are you listening to me?" She was agitated, because she knew he was not paying attention. "I heard every word, you sound so sweet, can you please repeat what you were saying?" Vincent counted with his arms wrapped around her waist, facing her. She stepped away, grabbed the table clothe and started to set the table for supper. "You can be so infuriating, "she threw the words at him and started her Reginald tale again. This time, there was a little back and forth discussion about the funds routed to their accounts in their names. Vincent was again astonished at what Crystal was doing and how she was so far getting away with it. The worry was 'so far'..as he had put it! Crystal felt as long as she had access to the Operations Center and the communications that she had set in motion, and she didn't try to stretch the funds too much, all should be just fine. Reginald was just another guy in the Army! Smiles broke on both of their faces and they relaxed knowing they had money in the bank! Time to start thinking about another long weekend away...together.

Dad arrived for supper at 6pm sharp. The salad, fresh dinner rolls and cranberry sauce was on the table with the chicken and dumplings just simmering on the stove top, all was ready including Crystal's mood to have a meaningful discussion. He walked in with a small spring bouquet of flowers in his hands, scrunched up shoulders and a questioning look on his face that said..truce? Friends? Crystal flew into his arms with relief, things hadn't been well with them, not really good since he stormed out of this little house the afternoon he first brought her there. Their discussion started at the table with a couple of beers, rum cokes and civil tongues.

"So far so good? Can we talk about your mother now" The Captain just looked at the two of them, but mostly Crystal for permission to continue talking. Crystal was carrying the pot to the table then handed her dad the serving ladle. "You start serving dad while you talk, we need to get this meal consumed before we have another drink, besides this is when we always had our best discussions." With that plates were filled, rolls were pasted and eating began. "Your mother was a very sweet, very naive and quiet girl when we first met. We were in Florida and she was pregnant with you when her mom, who was in New York pasted away from complications after a routine gallbladder operation.

There was no time for her to visit with her mom for the last time. We traveled back to NY for her funeral services but that did something to your mom. We went back to Florida, you were born and I had base duty for the next year and a half. Your mom loved you, but she became even more reclusive, staying inside and at the house most of the time. We had a happy, but quiet life inside our own home. There were no social events that interested her or other people she could think of to invite for coffee or dinner or for the weekend. Other than spending time with you, she was always alone. Then over the next few years she turned cold, standoffish and running the house like a barracks. I was very seldom home, but you..looking straight at Crystal, were always clean, well fed doing great at school, had plenty of friends and took part in school activities, I guessed life was good." Except for the sounds of eating, the kitchen took on a quiet few minutes before anyone spoke again.

"So the next few years brought us up to the time you were transferred here and we packed and left Florida, right?" Crystal was looking straight at her dad waiting for some sort of acknowledgment. Finally there was a small yes movement of his head. Crystal continued with "okay let's talk about those few years that mom was standoffish and cold. Is that when you started seeing and getting warmed up by Vincent's mother Suzie?" Crystal threw that statement at him with daggers in her voice and in her eyes. "Mom found out, didn't she, but stayed with you because of me, didn't she? She set the rules and the time table in our house to keep you in line when you were there, didn't she?

She used the free time she had, that you allotted her when you were off on one your jaunts to better herself and prepare to leave you, no us, because of your behavior. Was Suzie the only one or were there others? (now Vincent really took notice and waited for an answer to that question) I don't care, wrong is wrong." Crystal was on a rant, but the serving dishes were empty, the dinner plates were being removed by Vincent, yellow cake with chocolate frosting was placed center on the table along with coffee and clean plates.

"When you're right you're right. I reacted very badly to whatever was making her unhappy in our home and I made it worse month after month finding comfort elsewhere, then deployment after deployment still seeking warmth in the arms of another woman until there was nothing left to salvage in my marriage. Meanwhile she was making advances in her life that had no room for either of us. So when the change orders to move here arrived, I guess she was really ready to move on without us. I don't think I was that surprised, just relived. I'm sorry we hurt you, bringing you up in our house with no love." These words from her father brought silent tears to Crystal's eyes. First, that he actually said them and second with sorrow, regret and meaning. Thinking back, she guessed mom had made about the same concessions that afternoon in the kitchen.

"OK dad enough. I know you love me, we've spent the last hour reviewing bad times and hurt feelings, whats past is past, but thank you for the apology. I love you too, Suzie is a great gal (at this she looked at Vincent who had been very silent and helpful) so I can't and won't question your feelings for her. I only hope that if she is still in your life or whomever you choose to be in your life, is comforting and loving." Now desert changed the conversation into happy, back and forth stories from Grandma's house when Vincent was just a kid and moving there with his mom. Vincent agreed that he noticed not much had changed when he and Crystal had visited. The old house still needed painting, the gardens were just as overgrown as he remembered them and the dogs still took residence on the front porch. With hope and questioning in his eyes, he posed the question mostly to the Captain, but looked sideways at Crystal when he said, "how about the three of us plan a long weekend at Gram's and tackle some of the chores. I can make arrangements with the locals to have the house painted and the gardens clean-up for the spring planting. This will give mom and Grandma time to cook for our arrival." The Captain was the first to jump for joy at the idea. "Yes, darling daughter, Suzie is still the woman in my life and her mother is a close second, so I'm all in on the idea." Crystal pushed back her chair and ran to her husband to land a giant hug to his body with "yes, yes let do it and soon".

Cleaning the kitchen and doing the dishes was a quick and easy chore with all hands on deck. The living room conversation that followed was a bit dicey because it revolved around Rita Grandcockski and her imminent visit to see Crystal and Vincent and to obtain the Captains signature on divorce papers. The divorce was just a legal means to their end. It had ended long ago. Crystal was excited to plan a meeting with her mom. Vincent had already made up his mind to meet her and make himself scare so Chrystal could privately get to know her and learn things from her.

The evening ended with hugs and a feeling of restored family ties.

In bed that evening Vincent said 'OK it looks like we're going to visit Mom and Gram again soon, are we going to have enough money put aside for that weekend?" "Now I know you don't listen to me, just before Dad arrived I was telling you about our new accounts complements of Reginald and how nicely they are accumulating...yes we are going to have enough money for that weekend and many more after that!" Crystal was snuggling his body and using a chastising tone of voice to try to get her point across. The snuggling had more effect on Vincent than the tone of voice. She also added that they'd have enough money to pay for some of the supplies and paint and workman to complete some of the jobs. At this Vincent said he'd pay more attention to the details of the Reginald accounts in the future and thanked her with a hardy and well earned organism!

The next morning at the Center, Crystal encountered a very chipper Captain as he walked through to his office. She smiled to herself and thought *that's more like it, he should be happy and content all the time.* But her smile was short lived when she picked up her out-going messages and read the board of company assignments for the next three days. Vincent was being reassigned again, this time a short stint at a base in NY. *I bet he is finding this out this morning to, she thought. No time like the present to plan another trip, I'll join him there.* Her head was reeling with ideas and making plans. Her mood was once again happy. She'd get it all worked out in her head and financially and present it to him tonight at supper. They'd make this a fun reassignment, one she could enjoy too.

By the end of the day Crystal had contacted Mr. Brentwhistle and made arrangements to play in the Piano Bar for 4 mornings, had a discounted room at the New Yorker Hotel and she was also getting payed for playing the piano. She was a happy girl and couldn't see any reason shy Vincent wouldn't go along with her arrangements. They could have dinner together every night while sleeping in the same city in different beds, it was the best she could do, maybe she could plan a sexy Saturday afternoon! Crystal was a happy girl all afternoon. She beat Vincent home and made a great roast beef dinner with homemade gravy for his favorite mashed potatoes. He was all in on her plans and didn't resent the reassignment to New York, it would be easy duty. She explained one little detour he'd need to make (donning an Army uniform with the name tag Reginald Sabers) to the bursars office at the Army base to collect this weeks pay. Not a problem, he'd done it before and it goes off without a hitch. Wonderful, all plans made for 5 days from now.

She was thinking...*it's gonna be a long five days* But the notion of having five long days went away first thing the next morning when her mother walked in the Operations Center. She was sure it was her mother, but this woman was totally put together! Every hair in place in an attractive modern due, a designer suit of red and white pin stripes on a navy blue jacket covering a soft white collared blouse and navy blue skirt, mid-way down her nylon legs. She turned every head in the Center when she asked for Captain Grandcockski. It only took another few seconds for Chrystal and her mother to make eye contact. It was a strange moment for both of them, Crystal seeing her accomplished mother for the first time and Rita seeing her adult daughter for the first time. Crystal made the first move in showing mom to dads office, making introductions and asking for an audience with him. His office door opened immediately and they both walked in. The Captain hugged Rita immediately and she in turn tried to hug Crystal, but Crystal backed away. The questions flooded into Crystal's brain and the longing for the mommy she never had struck her with such a fierce force, she needed to leave the room and do it fast! She was done for the day, she knew she couldn't recover steady knees here so she heaced home to seek comfort at the piano keys. Seeing her mother knocked the wind out of her...no...seeing the beautiful, confident woman that was now her mother knocked the wind out of her! Sitting at the piano and choosing to play the hardest and most confusing note worthy selections she could think of, gave her a boost and self pride that she could concur the keys and make the songs sultry and worth listening to. She had learned to do something right. Her making the piano speak, sadly, happily or reflective of her moods, spoke volumes of her magistracy. The piano helped. She realized now, that she had always been so wrong about her mother. I guess gladly so, Crystal decided she needed to learn about this woman and accept her as her mother. While Crystal was home licking her wounds and taking it out on the piano, her father signed Rita's papers, had a lovely lunch with her, learned superficially about her life for the past 7 years and closed that chapter of his life.

Poor Vincent, when he got home that night. He walked into a house of piano music that would wake the dead. The selections Crystal had chosen both shook the house and exhausted both the listeners and player. He knew at once she was trying to work something out. Rid herself of nasty thoughts or hurtful feelings. He cut up vegetables, sauteed sausage and started boiling water for pasta. Rubbing her shoulders and kneading the knots from her neck softened her next musical selection enough that he could ask her to STOP. "You've punished me enough into starting supper, so let's go finish it together while you tell me about this mood of yours." Vincent took her hand and led her into the kitchen.

After taking a long a deep breathe, Crystal merely said, "I met my mother today." Vincent said, "that must have something to do with this envelope your dad asked my to give to you." He reached inside his shirt pocket and handed Crystal a small card sized envelope. It was an invitation for Crystal to meet her mother tomorrow for lunch at Tweeds. Crystal hatted Tweeds, but for this occasion it would be good, no one would know them.

Guessing the clientele at Tweeds and the way her mother would be dressed, Crystal took great care with her makeup and her choice of dress for their lunch. Crystal still a knock-out and stunning woman with her hair of spun moonlight cascading over her shoulders and down her back over a ruby red fashionably tight knit top and tight jeans, still turned every head no matter where she went. Today was no different, but today she enjoyed it! Walking beside her mother and being seated by a nervous twenty-something year old young man, Crystal gave off the air of an actress or a countess or someone important. She was feeling confident and it showed in her posture. She needed her mother to know that she was her own person.

Rita ordered a drink and Crystal stuck to her rum and coke. Without either of them making eye contact yet, or willing to start a conversation, Crystal blurted out, "so where have you been since I saw you last?" Rita was looking down, examining her nails or the creases in the table clothe, anything not to look Crystal in the eyes. It was becoming an uncomfortable silence that stretched way to long. Finally Crystal cleared her throat and asked, "is what you've been doing for the past seven years as rewarding and exciting as you'd hope it would be? Better than being a stay at home mother and sharing in your teenage daughters life? I don't blame you for needing to leave him. I know he turned into quite a prick and cheated on you and lied to you and helped you turn into a cold and calculating woman, but you left me too!" Crystal stopped because she realized her voice had taken on more volume than intended and a tone more accusing than intended. At the same moment Rita's hand extended in the air (to the waiter standing behind Crystal) to indicate more drinks, but Crystal immediately misunderstood the gesture and grabbed at Rita's outstretched arm and hand in a way to protect herself from an oncoming slap. Both of them immediately realizing what had just happened pulled their hands in front of them folded them on the table and sat stoic for several seconds until their hands reached each for one and other and they breathed a sigh of relief, at that moment the second drink order arrived.

Rita started with an apology to Crystal for not being the mother Crystal needed, but Crystal stopped her with her own apology for sprouting hateful words reserved for spoiled brats, for which she was not. Before their lunch was over they both learned a lot about one another, their triumphs and failures for which the triumphs ruled! Crystal's best friend had turned out to be a gay man and she married the man of her dreams. Rita had excelled at her job of being the 'first lady' to the first lady of the United States. There were so many story's she could tell, but couldn't because of confidentiality! They ended their lunch with booze laden coffee and promises to stay in touch and try to become more familiar with each other and rebuild a family.

Rita had what she came to town to get, so having laid a foundation with her daughter and gotten the needed signature from the Captain, she left town on the 4p.m. train back to Washington and her 5 room apartment, a half a block from the White House.

Chapter 13

Poor Vincent couldn't get a word in edge-wise that night at supper. Crystal was so full of news of her mother and their lunch and her beginning feelings of dread being so wrong. Her mom was a wonderful, down to earth person with her head on straight and performing a job worthy of her talents and personality. "Plus she has learned so much, you should have seen the way she dresses, so professional!" Vincent just let her go on and on before reminding her that he never got to meet her. At that Crystal just stared at him for a moment and blurted, "We've never been to Washington DC., we'll need to plan a trip there so you can meet her. Remember, we have the funds, and I can play piano and earn more, you just need the time. The sky is the limit!" Crystal was in such a good mood. She reminded Vincent that she needed to be in NY by Thursday evening so she'd be available Friday morning in the Piano Bar, she was so excited.

Crystal's trip to NY was uneventful. The train ride was normal a little bumpy and a little noisy both things becoming common place after the first hour of so. The terminal in NY was as expected, crowded, busy and noisy. Once outside on the sidewalk, a bus to the New Yorker Hotel was easily noticeable and available. Everything in New York was big, huge! Last time she was here she was with Vincent, it felt strange being here alone. Once at the hotel she found Mr. Brentwhistle easy enough. He was delighted to see her and made plans to introduce her to a few bar managers, influential reservation and function mangers. He was making her feel important and talented beyond her own belief. She was just remembering what her mother had said; "Believe in yourself and others will believe in you as well." She felt wonderful. Mr. Brentwhistle walked with her to VIP reservations, introduced her to Katie Reynolds, the VIP room manger and handed her her room key to room 3108. Once settle in her room, she unpacked her few belongings, hung-up her outfits for her performances and stood and looked out of the triple wide window to the New York City view below her. Magnificent! She was a small town girl, a Navy brat, but here she was, ready to perform in a 5 star hotel. They call it performing, for which she will be paid. She calls it 'playing', because that is what she does for enjoyment. She plays!

She had a free night in NY City. Alone to explore and check-out a few places. Before heading out she remembered to dress down a bit, pull her hair back and were a baseball cap to hide most of her hair color. Besides being one of the tallest walking down the street, she blended in fairly well. The weather was fair and the temperature suitable for all the walking she did that night stopping into four sidewalk bars, a trendy clothing store and one higher class piano bar (for which she felt totally under dressed) but enjoyed the most and spent the most time in. Loosing the baseball cap and dropping the hair helped to dress-up her appearance for this establishment, but nursing her only cocktail brought more attention to herself than she wanted. Her body language and swaying to music in time said more about her to the pianist and his manager than she had intended. Not really being a paid performer in one of the most prestigious hotels in the city is something she wanted to expose. Hers was just a 'gig', she wasn't a head-liner with a following, she was just a gal with a little talent. That thought stayed with her during her walk back to the hotel. It's a good thing it was a fair night, she had walked further and stayed later at that bar than she had intended. But that one thought stayed with her...*do I want to be a head-liner with a following. If offered a job with a steady schedule and perks offered by the hotel, would I be in a position to accept and still be with Vincent?* The thought process made the walk shorter, but when she reached her room, she still didn't have an answer. A quick shower and off to bed...alone. Being a military wife, or taking a job at the hotel offered much the same...*me alone in a bed!*

Sitting at the piano at 9am, with a Silver Craft of coffee on a Silver Tray taking up room on the closed portion of her black Baby Grand, Crystal barely touched the keys to produce the loveliest sound of fleur-de-lis. Her hair, the same color of the white lights shinning down on her, which had been done in a french braid, trailed down her back over a black and silver-threaded turtle neck sweater. She made quite a picture sitting in the white light, absent of any color. The small poster announcement at the door, of music being available in the room from 9am to noon, brought in the curiously seekers as well as those guests enjoying their hotel supplied continental breakfast. The bagels, lox and cream cheese with assorted donuts and other pastries were offered on a back table also set with coffee, tea and juices. By 11m there was standing room only in the Piano Bar with applause and appreciation after each of Crystal's selections. At 12:15 when Mr. Clive Brentwhistle appeared at Crystal's back and waited for her to finish a sweet arrangement of Sentimental Journey, he praised her appearance and talent and thanked everyone for making her first weekend performance a success! Crystal was speechless and breathless by the way she felt. Brentwhistle sat beside her on the piano bench and just marveled at her beauty, talent and sweetness. She started to flirt with fleur-de-lis again as the people filed out of the room, smiling at them as they went. *Brentwhistle was thinking again that she doesn't know the extent of her talent or the draw she has on her audience or how much of a natural she is. She'd be easy to sell, he can't let her get away this time.*

"Excellent young lady, you filled the room. You do the piano and this room justice. I see you emptied the coffee craft, is there something else you'd prefer? I can make it happen for tomorrow morning." "Oh, no thank you, the coffee is wonderful and just what I like in the morning." Crystal happily answered. "This is amazing, I had a ball and they liked me". "What's not to like, you dressed the part and your smile is infectious, there seems to be nothing in-genuine about you." Mr. Brentwhistle was all smiles himself as he added, "I've lined up a few introductions for you after lunch if you don't mind, they're the managers I talked about yesterday. They have you at a disadvantage as they all snuck in here this morning and had a coffee and enjoyed at least one of your songs." "That will be great, I didn't know how I was going to occupy myself this afternoon until my husband can join me for dinner." Crystal was starry eyed and still caught-up in her excitement of the morning, but needed desperately to excuse herself to a bathroom...so much coffee!

Back in her room, she took care of her pressing business then *threw herself across the bed and just wondered what it would be like to headline her own show. Could she cut a prestigious enough deal by herself or should she have a manager or a second opinion. What would Vincent say about her line of thinking? Should she even be thinking about this, she was a married woman making life choices that didn't include Vincent...think... think. She'd made up her mind to discuss it with him over dinner tonight.*

Still wearing her knock-out black and silver sweater, she went into Sbarro's Italian Restaurant for lunch. She loved their strombolis. She had just enough time before needing to meet with Mr.

Brentwhistle and his other managers. She was excited at being treated like a big-wig! *Crystal's Piano Bar...she was still thinking!*

"Joanne Peese, please meet Crystal Clear, she'll be manning the piano in the Piano Bar for the next few mornings." Clive Brentwhistle presented Ms. Peese as the function director and manager of all of the outside rental activities. Crystal said, "Glad to meet you, but exactly what do you manager, what are outside rentals?" With a bit of a laugh, she said "please call me Joanne and to Clive she said, thanks you've caught me a real live nosy one!" At that Crystal blushed and apologized for asking too many questions. "Not at all sweetie, I love to show off the property and encourage people, couples especially to rent our dance halls, or banquet halls for their weddings or anniversary parties or bar mitzvah. The halls hold between 30 to 280 people, we have three different function rooms. We can rent with food and servers or you bring in your own food and clean-up afterwards. I meet so many different types of people. I love my job." Clive said "we are going down to meet The Baron next, wanna come"? "Not on your life whined Joanne, I'll eat his food, and I'll follow his directions but I don't have to like him, go without me...please". Snickering slightly and shaking his head Clive steered Chrystal toward the elevator again and explained, "The Baron is, yes he is titled from the government of Wales and England, The Baron Walter P. Maddox is our head chef for all of the food requirements. He hires managers for the different dinning rooms and chefs for the functions that Joanne books. Those two work closely together to make magic happen for their clients. We have the right people working here, it's not an accident we maintain five stars and have an excellent reputation."

Crystal's head was spinning, she has seen so much in such a short period of time. She loves the fact that she is associated with this hotel, these people, this level of professionalism. She can't wait for Vincent to get here tonight to share this with her, hold her and bring her back to reality. Now she is on the hunt for which dinning room for tonight.

After he threw his hat on the bed and threw himself on top of Crystal and filled his hands with tossed ample boobs, their necking lead to all sorts of clothes being stunned across the room and his boner filling her to both of their delight! Dinner could wait, it had been 48 hours since they had seen each other! Totally breathless she exclaimed, "these are the moments I live for." It took about two hours for them to satisfy their sexual needs and get hungry enough to even think about venturing out for dinner. Then Chrystal needed to dress. When she asked Vincent for help to secure the hooks on her bra she knew it would be his first undoing. She did it on purpose. But when she sat on the edge of the bed and worked those nylons up her long legs, inch by inch, making sure not to snag them, and then standing with her legs spread, one leg on the floor the other propped on the bed to do up the garter, showing scant red panties, she enjoyed knowing "she got him'! Once she had her shoes slipped on, she announced she was ready to go. Poor Vincent couldn't move. She walked over to him, cupped his groin and kissed him with enough passion to almost forget about dinner, but not quite. Let's go she said, we'll take care of that later. It was a very slow walk to the Terrance Room she had chosen for dinner.

Chapter 14

"I have so much to tell you, to talk to you about, it could be so exciting!" Crystal finally got the words out between the cocktails and bread sticks. Vincent just sat there with his left hand rubbing her upper thigh, beyond the garter holding her nylons and inching further up every now and then to test the wetness of her panties, while drinking his beer and hoping he was showing enough interest in what she was saying. If by chance she took a breathe between sentences, he would educate her on the wetness between her legs. He knew she was talking about playing the piano in the Piano Bar again, but his excitement only led to his disappointment in not being able to cup that which he could not reach! Dinner was merely to quench their meal-time hunger. Back up in their room they quenched that which they left unfinished earlier. It was a very lustful night for the both of them, but it needed to end soon. Vincent needed to be back at his post by 0600 and Chrystal needed to be sharp and beautifully put back together and sitting at the piano by 0900. Vincent thought he was going to get the shower first. No-way...Crystal was right in there behind him soaping and arousing the manhood that she used and delighted herself with all night. 'It' was a good sport, ready willing and able to play again, but this time for only 'Its' release. Hanging between his legs like a used, wrinkled, old hose Vincent stuffed his boys in tidy-whit-tees, finished dressing and promised to be back tonight for round two! Crystal was still naked and feeling very not satisfied with the last 'little' encounter. *Vincent got his rocks off, but I was merely getting started. Forget it! Get dressed and get coffee. These things happen. He had to get going. I should have never started anything. Dam, I don't ever want to feel 'not finished' ever again. I'm doing some personal shopping after my set this afternoon.*

Once again Crystal's performance filled the Piano Bar and thrilled not only herself, but everyone who had stayed and listened. She let the excitement of going to the "His and Hers" store after lunch show in her lively and demonstrative playing. She giggled and teased with her entertaining facial expressions, as well as bodily movements during what could be called arousing musical arrangements!

Very pleased with herself and the mornings entertainment, she was out of there in a flash and down the street with her personal purchase still on her mind. Lunch could wait. *Oh Vincent you've turned me into this horny, wanting, sexual being. I could feel your fingers lightly crawling up my legs the entire time my fingers were busy on the piano keys. I needed to keep them busy because I wanted to reach out to you, and help you find my sweet spot, but you weren't there! Now, still, walking down this street, the friction and rubbing caused by my every step is agony! I know my tiny, silk, black (OH..OH!!) panties are wet! Where did I see that store...ice-cream...think about ice-cream! There...*

Being inside the store certainly didn't help much! She wanted to buy one of everything! But for today she settled on an 8-inch (biggest they had!) dark purple penis that took batteries! Checking out at the counter the clerk also suggested lubricating cream and Crystal thought *maybe for later...but I don't need that now!*

Still skipping lunch, Crystal's attention was on getting back to her room and finishing what Vincent didn't have time to do this morning. *OK, I'm here...*swallowing hard, she opened her package, never having done this before, she handled it gently and with reverence, she washed the purple penis with soap and warm water, followed the directions to place the batteries the right way and turned the end to the on position. The immediate vibration thrilled her. *OK Vincent, here goes...*Without further ado the panties were on the floor and she walked to the desk chair and lifted her foot to it's seat. Closing her eyes she placed the 8 inches of purple on her wet, anxious vagina and then buried it and enjoyed the wiggling sensation. *I can take as long as I want.* Without removing the penis she found her way to the bed, legs spread and up on the headboard. *This could take a while, she thought as she pulled it out and redeposited it very slowly this time. Cool it she thought. We have all afternoon. What would Vincent think if he could see me now? He'd be jealous...*this thought made her crazy and she came immediately. Pulling the penis out of her throbbing vagina left her feeling robbed of additional pleasure, one that she fixed immediately, so back it in went! Picturing Vincent watching her drive herself crazy brought on more thrusting and groaning and tears. (she'd never cried when Vincent did it) Slowing the motion of in and nearly out only exasperated the longevity of the organism. The Control...OMG...she loved it. The vibration...she loved it...Oh Vincent...again!! Letting her legs down, she squeezed the penis at the top of her vagina and it rubbed the nub of her clitoris, instant orgasm! Clutching the penis in both of her hands she continued the rubbing motion on her clitoris and then plunging the penis again and again and again...bingo...orgasm!!! A few minutes later when almost normal breathing returned, Crystal's train of thought again returned to Vincent. This time with *I don't think I'll mention this to him. What could I say...I enjoyed it as much as with you.* Sitting on the edge of the bed, just thinking about Vincent and him joining her in this bed in just a few hours time, Crystal didn't even realize that she had Mr. Purple reinserted and she was working him in and out. And again, in and out with one hand while rubbing the clitoris with two fingers of the other hand, all to a tune in her head that had her near to organism again. Flinging herself backwards on to the bed, she let herself get lost in the orgasm with wild groans and kneading her pulsating breast with the hand she removed from her clitoris. Coming down from an organism was as excruciating as building up to one. Each with its own pleasure points that lasted and drove the body to extreme pleasure. In the act of relaxing, she positioned the wet, vibrating penis between her breasts and decided, this is heaven. A shower...I need a shower.

Slowly she got to her feet to realize that she was 'very' tender between the legs. Vincent had never left her feeling like that, either! *OMG...it's 4:30, he'll be here in 45 minutes. I did that all afternoon! It felt wonderful, I feel wonderful!...Mr. Purple, please join me in the shower, why not? With* hot steamy water running down her back and Mr. Purple pulsating deep inside her, again a tune was running through her mind that reminded her of her 'first time' and she smiled broadly. *OK Mr. Purple, this is our secret.* She retracted the fake penis, washed and dried him and wrapped him in a hand towel to stow away for later. She'd never be able to get ready for dinner in time! Wrapped in a towel, she spritzed the room and bed with her perfume, called down to the desk to leave a message for Vincent to come directly to the room before dinner.

With her skin feeling soft and warm from her shower, Crystal had her naked body stretched across the bed when Vincent arrived. "You've taken the picture I've had in my head all day and displayed it beautifully" Vincent said as he closed the door and crossed the room to her. Bending, he gently placed his 'cold' hands on her shoulders and kissed her waiting lips. Her breasts reacted to his cold hands by rippling up and aching to be sucked. Crystal stood by the edge of the bed and helped Vincent disrobe in between kisses and fondling. "I think I like being married" Crystal said. It's a lot easier knowing this behavior is inevitable and expected and wanted. It's great to know I can do it with someone that loves me and only me."

"I'm only doing it to you, because you do it back to me just fine. You are the only one I need. Now tell me in plain English exactly what 'it' is before we continue and do 'it' wrong."

"Well Mr. Clear, right now I am going to kiss you (as she bends closer to his mouth) until I can feel your penis reach for the ceiling. I'll be able to feel that sensation because I'll have my hand wrapped around you until I'm satisfied with it's length." And she nibbled his lips thrust her tongue in until he moaned in satisfaction. Coming up for air he whispered, "My dear wife, your English is a little broken, please explain exactly the length you want 'it' (that arbitrary word again) to achieve." "I'd love every inch over eight of your healthy male penis to penetrate my very female vagina and activate every nerve cell or feeling that your gyrating can activate! "Well Mrs. Clear, I don't know if you've noticed lately, but I have well over eight inches with which to start with!

And start he did. His thrust of penetration had Crystal, who was still on the brink of her afternoons organisms, climaxing and climbing his body and claiming all of his tender spots. Her 'enthusiasm' spurred his male libretto to new heights. When neither one of them could get a word out edge-wise or take a breath to express STOP, they clasped on one anther and laughed. "How can we bottle that and use it every time we come to New York?" Vincent said.

Neither one of them left the hotel room not satisfied heading down for dinner. Crystal's feelings of Vincent not living up to Mr. Purple were shot down in a big way. It was a wonderful feeling knowing she could enjoy both and not jeopardize the loving that Vincent injects into their feelings. Vincent had a skip to his step and a smile a mile wide...He was a happy and satisfied man.

Once Vincent starting drinking his beer and relaxing at the dinner table, he admitted he felt a lot better tonight than he did last night. "I feel this way in a big part because of you, dear wife." he said as he kissed the palm of her hand. "You are intoxicating and you know what I what (need) when I want it. And I love the way you explained what 'it' is. Please always remember that I love you and what you do to (for) me." Crystal's mind starting to go blank because she felt the familiar hand working up under her dress to the uncovered, panty-less crotch. "I love you too and all the ways and places you touch me to make me go mindless! Like now...she grinned! Please order another round of drinks, I need to keep my hands busy. The dinner conversation finally changed to their making plans to visit his mom and grandmother. They had two more nights here together in room 3108, two more mornings for Crystal to entertain in the Piano Bar and then back home. Once again traveling separately, this was the part she hated.

Chapter 15

Activities in the Operations Center had begun to get back to normal now that all the troupes had returned from Puerto Rico. Communications between the units had sprung back to life and Crystal's message board was once again full. She loved being busy, but it left her less time to play with Reginald. Dinners at home were full of stories Vincent came home with and relayed to her to keep her up to date with the guys she saw every day. She guessed this was normal, no fires to put out and Vincent's feet were firmly grounded here in Virginia. Just the right time to plan that trip to Grandma's house. That night at dinner Crystal dominated the conversation with just that idea. A trip to Grandma's with her dad in tow could mean maybe a day or two extended stay. Vincent was all in to the idea and would put in papers tomorrow for the time away. Crystal's job was to talk with her dad and schedule his days in with Vincent's. It's a go! Two weeks from this Saturday they had train tickets to New York.

Over barbecued steaks for dinner, Vincent complained (with a shit-eating-grin on his face) "that traveling by train to NY would be very boring this time in the company of your dad. I rather enjoyed the shenanigans of our last trip!" "Ya but, we'll be traveling alone on the way home...dad gets to stay three days longer than us. We'll get to 'play' then! I'm just thankful for the two days extra dad was able to pull for you. It's nice to know people in high places."

Crystal and Vincent got to spend 5 days at Grandma's house this time. The train, rail car, and wagon rides to get there were much the same as last time, only more reserved and talkative with the Captain along. Grandma was so happy to see us and Suzie was so thrilled to have dad there, she barely acknowledged us. As on our last visit, dinner was a big spread with everyone trying to talk at once. I just sat back and listened, with the dog at my feet. This was charming, it was family! There were differences in this visit. We were put in Vincent's old bedroom, Suzie and Dad got the big room in the front. With more time we were going to be able to travel around a bit and visit some of Vincent's old haunts, but first came Sunday and Sunday Service. This time Crystal didn't find it so scary. They sat in the forth pew back from the ministers podium and listened and sang their hearts out. Once again Crystal was asked to play the piano in the coffee room down stairs. Which she did so willingly. Having acted like mature adults on the trip here and falling dead asleep last night after traveling so long sex had been pretty much off the table. Even the last two days and nights at home were crazy busy taking their toll and sending them off to sleep immediately. So when Crystal's fingers starting playing Chattanooga Choo Choo her heart skipped a beat and her panties got wet. Looking a Vincent she was trying to figure out what in the world had just gotten into her. Sex must be imminent. To Vincent her smile and blush said it all. No more piano...less get out of here! To Crystal it was a puzzle... that feeling had happened to her before.

With Vincent holding her hand and saying farewells to all the good and faithful Sunday people, he couldn't wait to get her back home where they'd be alone for at least the next hour. It would take that long for Gram and the others to make it back for dinner.

"We're alone, we're naked, you're beautiful, what happened to you at the piano? Never mind, think on that later, right now just kiss me," as his hands were exploring all of the curves of her body. It didn't take long for his shaft to poke Crystal's legs apart and gently slide into her waiting, wet pussy. "You are always ready for me you little minx and I love it!" Both of them on their sides, she looked into his eyes and tried to explain, "It happened at the piano, when I started playing that song, I got wet! I felt …" She couldn't continue to explain without sounding crazy or like a wanton woman...she felt an unearned organism about to happen... wanting it to happen but yet trying to hold it back! She couldn't tell her husband that. "suddenly I felt sexy just looking at you, I'm glad you rushed us out of there. I'd much rather be here with you, so it's your turn, just kiss me."

With no time to spare, Vincent and Crystal's little sexual interlude concluded with time left to set the table for Sunday dinner before everyone arrived home. The Captain turned into Harold then Harry when Suzie spoke to him, Crystal had never, ever heard her him referred to as Harry! She loved it...it made him real. The rest of the afternoon sped by with family and visits from friends. The evening was fun filled with a bond-fire and songs. No one objected to early to bed...it was a welcome end to a fine day.

Everyone had other things on their minds!

Early Monday morning brought neighbors and friends with ladders, dressed to work. Even the women started scrapping the loose paint from the house while the men started painting right behind them. By noon half the house had a new, clean look. All of this thanks to Vincent. Once the plans were made to be here for the five days, he set to contacting neighbors and asking for help for his Grandmother. Everyone was more than willing to give a hand. The noon hour brought lunch to the forefront. Every neighbor who showed up with a ladder also came with his wife and many additions for the lunch feast. And feast it was. When something is unplanned and everyone pitches in, it turns out the best. All of Mondays lunch left overs were wrapped and enough for the next two days lunches. By Wednesday's supper time Grandma's house looked band new with white paint all around, a garden yielding potatoes that were last years plantings and prepared for supper with the garden soil turned for next year and weedless. Grandma and Suzie along with Crystal put together a barbecue supper for everyone that had worked so hard on the house and in the yard and gave thanks for all of their hard work.

Crystal sat next to an exhausted Vincent and just thought about the last few days in awe...she looked around at the other people eating, visiting, gossiping, relaxing, drinking, and thinking that this is the way Vincent grew up. Being part of a community that comes together to lend a helping hand. A good meal and a beer is all the thanks they need. She wanted to think she could get used to this, but did it fit with a big city and playing the piano in a bar? Conflicting wants, conflicting life styles. Even her dad look relaxed and Suzie looked happy. Was this the way he was going to retire? With her? She and Vincent had two more days to vacation, visit, relax and play. Play with each other and play house. She started to rub Vincent's thigh, the way she was leaning against him, it's all she could reach. She wanted to play with so much more. She shifted her body and softly said, "let's go". He understood the husky, little voice that said I'm horny.

A quick shower and a kiss goodnight would have been sufficient for Vincent this night, after the three days of fresh air, sunshine and constant work, but Crystal had other ideas. Her quick shower invigorated her and she wanted to organism at least three times tonight. Trying to keep it quiet and on the down low was a challenge she was up for. When she slipped into bed and spooned and fondled Vincent's balls, he made no movement toward her. She held him a minute or two longer and realized he was sound asleep. *Poor dear she thought, but what about me?* He was too tired to wake up, so she was thinking the next best thing. When she packed Mr. Purple she questioned the need. *Vincent was going to be with her, he'd satisfy her needs, why play with the act of maybe being found out? Maybe he'd laugh, maybe his reaction would be silly and dismissive. Why find out? She was still thinking these things when she slipped her wrapped toy in her robe pocket and headed out to the dark and now empty back yard.* She was not alone, Dick had followed her out the back door. So be it, when she sat in the recliner, he did as well. OK she'd use him. Once she had Mr. Purple properly lubricated she propped one leg up on Dick's body to give herself access to her waiting vagina. With the penis turned on it slipped into her easily. Enjoying the vibrating sensation it awarded her, she relaxed a bit and stared up at the stars. It was so dark she saw more stars than she even knew existed in the heavens. She felt free and uninhibited and the more she moved her hand and withdrew and then pushed full tilt again the closer she was coming to climax. Did she want these feelings to end so soon? She loved the feeling of being on the brink of loosing control. She had the power with her movements to quicken the feelings or retard them to controlled breathing and massage her breast and play with her pimply nipples. The night air felt so good moving up her bare leg and her bare beasts, no she didn't want to stop yet. So once again she found the swollen little nub of her clitoris and tweaked it while plunging Mr. Purple deep into her sexual chasm and enjoyed every sensation pulsing through her body. *"Oh Vincent I can feel you inside me, rubbing the walls of my vagina and finding that sweet spot...oh please don't stop...not now... don't stop...keep going...I'm coming...I'm coming"* Keeping her hand at a rhythm to insure a satisfactory organism, she schooled her enthusiasm to a low roar as to not wake the sleeping in the house. Now she knows why she packed Mr. Purple. She was about to change his name to Mr. Reliable...he doesn't sleep! Slipping back into bed with Vincent was easy. Dreaming about the two organisms that she missed out on tonight was another story.

Breakfast was another big meal at Grandma's house. Bacon or sausage or ham and eggs. Toast from your choice of three breads and homemade preserves from the peaches, apples and berries found on the farm. She gave up on biscuits and gravy because no-one seamed to like it! The coffee was strong but lighten by fresh cream every morning. This was the way to vacation...After breakfast Vincent announced that he wanted to take Crystal out beyond the pastures to the spring. Grandma just snorted and warned Crystal not to go because that is where she conceived Vincent's father! In unison Harold and Suzie both exclaimed "we thought that was out private place"! They looked at one another and Suzie finally said, while patting Vincent's cheek "you were conceived in a bed in Poughkeepsie. That's were you were born and lived until we moved here. Your dad introduced me to the springs on our first visit here...we thought we were sneaking away from the house, away from Grandma to 'our private spot', secluded and beautiful." Suzie finished her statement with a wishful look on her face. Crystal exclaimed, "Now I want to go...it sounds wonderful"

Vincent hooked his arms around Crystal's waist and said "It's a bit of a hike, but I know you'll think it worth it when we get there." Grandma counted with, while punching Vincent in the upper arm, "if she doesn't think it worth it, its your fault! Give me 10 minutes while I pack a picnic lunch for you to take along, that way there will be no need for you to rush back, you'll have the whole day" Vincent planted a kiss on Grams cheek and exclaimed "you're the best."

An hour and a half later, after strolling through the back yard and playing tag running through the pasture, and traversing an overgrown trail heading into the woods and also heading up hill, they finally reached a sunny, open meadow with a few trees at its most Northern edge. Their branches and leaves were cascading over a sparkling spring. Vincent just stopped and watched as Crystal wandered a few steps forward, spread her arms and did a slow pirouette in the sunshine. "This place is breathtaking she whispered," at first she had a hard time taking it all in. Vincent smiled his million dollar smile and beamed at the fact that it was still there and just as magnificent as he remembered. He knew he wanted to share this with her. Lay naked with her on the green grass in this sunshine and make love and make her groan and beg for more like she never had before. They could make this their 'special place'. He hadn't even finished his lusty thought when Crystal spun around and started making his plan fall into place. He knew what he wanted this afternoon to be like, so the clothes she saw on his body was all there was. So when she started tugging his shirt over his head, his raised nipples were the first thing she saw and couldn't resist. Her mouth plunged upon the right one as she finished pulling his shirt over his head. Her eyes eventually gazed up to find him grinning as she put her right hand down his pants to feel more than nine inches of penis leaking at the top. She only felt penis, no restrictions from underwear. Still grinning and liking the fact that he had shocked her a bit, he said "let me help you, as he stilled her hand and dropped his pants. Quickly he slipped out of his shoes and stepped away from his pants and stood, the perfect specimen of gorgeous male she had ever seen! The sunshine highlighting his thick black, curly hair was begging to be tossed with her long fingers before moving down his long body covered in all the right places with more curly black hair. Her fingers left his head and caressed his chest while she nibbled his nipples again. Once she was satisfied with his reaction there, she settled her mouth over his while continuing her movements with her hands to his back where she let her fingers and hands play with his mussel mass, all the way down to his slender hips and settled on his rounded ass. Cupping both cheeks in her hands, she pushed him forward into her, until she could feel his length pressing up against her clothed body. Vincent broke the kiss with a breathless, "my turn". Removing her hands from his body, he laid them straight down her sides. Unbuttoning her blouse and untying the rope belt from her skirt were easy. Removing them was equally as easy, she stepped away from the skirt and stood still in only her panties (they were wet) and her bra. The dam contraction of a thing! *How did she even do it up! It was so tight to her skin, it held her up beautifully, there was flesh popping out of the top of the big evenly spaced cups of light pink material. This excess was just asking to be touched, squeezed, licked, adored!* His mind had his hands frozen in place, covering her breasts with his fingers sliding up and down in the valley created between her voluminous breasts. In the daylight he couldn't get enough of the sight of them, always covered or hidden by clothes, he now wanted them uncovered so he could watch them move uninhibited by constraints. Knowing that his mind was wandering and he was having a hard time with her bra she put an end to his misery and undid the closures herself. Now standing next to him totally nude he covered her quickly with his body and took her fast and ferociously. There was no hands on, or mouth on or stroking foreplay here; there was just lust overload being released. The afternoon love making was glorious with the birds and bees and the surrounding nature learning a thing or two about noisy and continuous organisms.

Needing to replenish their energy, they devoured the picnic Grandma had packed for them. "She's a character," Vincent said as he pulled two towels out from the bottom of the basket." she actually thinks we're going to go in that cold spring water pool". Crystal thought that was a marvelous idea and started running in that direction. "It's really cold" Vincent yelled after her. But her long naked body in motion was too much of a draw for him, so he got up and followed her right to the waters edge. Holding hands they tip-toed into the water and they watched each others body change. Vincent's magnificent manly shaft shrunk to just the flesh it took to hang from his body, while Crystal's boobs filled and rose to new heights with excellent little pimply nubs rising on her darken, round nipples. Crystal pulled Vincent into her arms and kissed his lips gently at first and then more eagerly as he started returning the kiss and leaned into her to deepen the affection. With him still a little out of balance he started to say "Wow, what was that all about….when she pushed him and he fell, sprawled flat on his back in the frigid water. She giggle and said…"It was an up front apology for what I just did to you". The game was on and he was out of the water and covering her like a blanket before she could take another step…"cold, aren't I" he managed before plunging them both waist deep. Still holding on to her, he put a lip lock on her and together they stepped further into the water and began to enjoy the feelings of coolness where they had been so hot and used just a short time ago. "Do you swim?" Vincent asked Crystal, as he started swimming away from her. "You know, there are a great many things we still do not know about each other" she hollered as she swam after him. She caught up to him easily and started fondling anything she could get her hands on. "That feels really good right there" he purred as he put his body in a floating position on his back. "Your hands feel warm on my cooled skin, please don't stop. She had no intention of stopping, she enjoyed watching his face as she gently pumped his penis back to it's usable size. He looked comfortable and dreamy, but she had no immediate intention of using him just now…she wanted to make him come, like this, with him on his back and watch it squirt into the air, or just ooze out and slide down the shrinking penis. *What to watch…his face with a smile that could light up a room, or the penis do it's thing…reset itself and get wet.. while he licked his lips he exhaled to the point of loosing the perfect floating position.*

"You are good, my dear, that felt wonderful; I think I heated the water I was floating in. Believe me, I'm no longer cold and you have the warmest and most talented hands that I've ever had the pleasure of having set upon me." Crystal's heart was eating up the compliments and wanted to be near him and enjoy the water as long as they were in it. A quick swim around the perimeter of the shore line and out, it was as long as she could stand the cold water seeping into every orifice she had! Once her feet hit dry land, Vincent was standing beside her with the Grandma provided towels, wrapping her and rubbing her for warmth. Back at the picnic basket he gently laid her down on the green grass and again gently rubbed her arms and legs to warm her. To finish the job he laid his body on top of hers and again gently inserted his ready again penis into the now warmed and waiting vagina. This was the perfect ending to a most perfect day, in the sunshine. They made memories today, as long as that's all they made!

They dressed and slowly walked back toward the farm house. The picnic basket was not much lighter, it now contained damp/wet towels that came in mighty handy. Crystal's appearance was a mess, her hair needed a good brushing and was still damp when they arrived back at Grandma kitchen and her lips still had the puffy, swollen used look.. Her skin tone was still blushed pink which indicated good sex. Grandma was so happy to see them home before dark and in time for supper. She explained it was a light fare tonight, because every Sunday night it's cards at Nancy's house, so she'd be leaving soon. "I hope you made me a Great Grandma this afternoon" she crooned, as she set out platters of meat and cheese.

By the looks of things, when Grandma left, they had the house to themselves for the night, Dad and Suzie were no where in sight. Vincent asked Crystal to play a couple of tunes on the piano before they retired for the night. He inquired if she was keeping up with the new songs released by the big bands and getting a lot of play on the radio. She was proud to answer "yes, she liked a couple of them a lot and she immediately started with Star Dust and Paper Dolls. Then she jumped in to Chattanooga Choo Choo and let her body sway to the music until she felt her temperature rise, her panties get wet and her breathing accelerate to the point just before the organism groans begin escape the lips. Vincent sat in awe watching and listening to both Crystal's piano playing and her exhibition of unbridled lust escape from her limbs and her sweet lips. She didn't stop this time, she kept playing and let the tempo of the music guide her libretto to where it was going. By now Vincent is sitting beside her on the piano bench and aching to slide his hand between her legs...he knows she's wet and that dives him wild! He had seen the beginning of this behavior the last time she started playing this song and abruptly stopped. Now he knew why she stopped, but not the reason to the reaction it caused. She was wild with sexual endorphins and tonight, unwilling to stop the effect it was having on her. Vincent was also curious where and when this was going to stop and was enjoying every movement and sound she made toward that end. She had him turned so ON, he didn't know if he'd be able to wait her out. Every now and then, there was a melody that only needed her right hand to man the piano keys, so her left hand flew to her boobs and squeezed. That wasn't enough, the next time she freed her boobs by pulling down the front of her top and let the buttons pop off and fall to the floor. Her eyes were glassy, and she was licking her lips all the while as she continued to play that one segment of the song. The tempo grew harder, faster. This time she freed her hair and let it fall over her naked breasts, then continued with the rest of the song, letting her body continue to sway and bend at will. But by now Vincent was about to lose it so he did slide one hand up her skit and fondle one exposed breast with his other hand. Their eye contact was Crystal's undoing, she organismed and grabbed at Vincent's body, upper arms first for support then bear hugged him to try to control her gyrations. It felt so good it hurt. Vincent was at a loss as to what just happened, but on the whole he thoroughly enjoyed the last 15 minutes. This is a show he'd pay money to go and see, except this was his wife...what was going on with her, they both asked why this song? It's crazy! Having just exhibited totally abnormal behavior and having exerted that much energy, Crystal was exhausted. To bed they went without any further discussion. Vincent had that whole scene to play back in his mind and keep him company, spooning Crystal's body while she slipped off to sleep.

She should have been sleeping, but she was thinking about Peters explanation of an organism. She did it herself! Somehow she could arouse this sexual urge, this uncontrollable feeling of loosing control sexually and help it bridge the sense of reality. Having had Vincent's hands roaming over her, defiantly helped, but her thinking was, it was heading there without him! Also, having an audience helped...boy...

now she's an exhibitionist! *Peter, how did you sneak into my conscience? I hope you're well and happy.* Sleep finally took over. She woke next morning knowing it was their last day of 'vacation'.

When she stirred, Vincent was awake and waiting for her to roll over. "Good morning sleepy head, did you sleep well?" He asked this while stroking her face and gently rubbing his index finger over her lips. "You are beautiful" he murmured and then landed softy on her lips for a morning kiss. "Good morning to you too, handsome" she counted when he ended the kiss. "Where do you intend to take me today, functions manager?" she asked sincerely. "That's easy he drawled", as he dropped his underwear and climbed back into bed. "This beautiful woman I know introduced to a place where feelings are paramount and it doesn't take long to get there. Do you want to help me get there before we need to say good-bye to this peaceful place, again.?" Crystal just curled herself into his arms. Then stretched length wise to press her entire body to his. They touched and melted into one another perfectly. Vincent whispered, "I think you know the road to get there beautiful lady," then they dove into a deep, penetrating kiss that was the start to their all too swift end. Crystal's movements on the sheets, her twists to get to where she wanted to be, her arms reaching out and her hands touching and tugging at Vincent's hands and arms, all to settle on the mounds of his ass. Then moving to cup his balls, all while pressing her mouth to his nipples, groaning in delight. "You're too much this morning Mrs. Clear, but I love it" Hovering just above his eager mouth she asked, "am I on the right road to good feelings and bringing about tingly sensations?" She then proceeded to lightly tongue her way around his lips before sticking the tip of her finger in his mouth to entice him to suck on it. That brought about different feelings for both of them and they immediately proceeded to the main event. With her legs wrapped around his waist, he entered her with his entire length...once...then again...and now with her hands flat on his round buttocks, she pushed at him to enter her again, lifting her hips to meet thrust with as much force as they both could muster! She shuttered and cried out"...now, please...now...please don't stop...OH... go...more...harder..." With all of her direction Vincent pushed harder, then again and again...then stopped! Poor Crystal was convulsing into a heap of shaking, out of control organisms. Her rubbing, gyrating movements against his body made him come in waves of pleasure he can only give her credit for. She had turned into an amazing lover.

At 9:30 when they went down for breakfast, they found the kitchen empty with the aroma of breakfast long gone. Coffee was still hot and available, so they made do with that and thick bread with homemade jam.

Sitting across from each other at the kitchen table a sense of family, roots, and deep love came upon them in a wave of almost nostalgia. For Vincent he recognized where he came from, but for Crystal she feared she'd never feel like this again.... It was the perfect time and place to live out some sexual fantasies and to play. She had so enjoyed their afternoon together in the beautiful meadow and in the pool. They left nothing to the imagination in the freedom of their secret place. Unplanned adventures and experiences only happen once in a lifetime and she was fearing this was theirs and now it was in the past. It was like Vincent was reading her mind when reached across the table, took her hand and said, "we built some wonderful memories on this trip, we'll never be able to top the naked romp around the meadow and the green grass! Would it be so bad is we did start the beginning of a new generation under such a beautiful sky?" His voice was dreamy, exactly the way she felt, up until the last statement. There it was again...children.

"Vincent, I know you want children...but now is not a good time for me. If by chance we fertilized the beginning of a family yesterday, You'll make a wonderful Dad...Grandma will be so happy." *I've known since before my wild summer how to chart my period...I wouldn't have been naked in a beautiful field had there even been a chance of making him a dad this weekend, she thought!*

His smile was brilliant hanging on her words of 'by chance, family, wonderful Dad, happy', he squeezed her hand and asked, "what would you like to do today?" Happy to be off the subject she counted with "go shopping. The local down town shops, they'll have fashions and trinkets we don't have at home. We have a little extra money so we can splurge." she finished with a wink! After a quickly clean sweep through the kitchen and a note left for...whomever...they were off shopping, promising to be home for supper.

Crystal was amazed at the selection of woman's' tops! Her head quickly put them together with her skirts and dressy, wide leg pants for performing. Thrilled with her purchases, she'd built at least seven new outfits and felt giddy and naughty for dressing her body to 'attract'. Vincent loved most of what she'd bought, but wasn't sure about the gold and deeper gold with a neck so wide it would show off her breasts.

Crystal loved that one and had special plans for it. "You've seen me perform, you know that my wardrobe is important, I need to keep it fresh and updated. You also know that I'm not an exhibitionist, I do a family show." That topic exhausted, he pleaded, "Please do not play Chattanooga Choo Choo in public ever again. You need to keep it a family show." They looked at each other in understanding and agreed, for his eyes only...never in public! The shared an ice-cream cone sitting on a park bench...sitting by the waters edge and feeding the ducks. Once again, she had a memory of Peter.

Supper that night was loud and lively. Suzie and Harry (dad) announced their engagement and marriage plans for as soon as his divorce was final. Suzie had waited for this for a long time, she exclaimed "he was worth waiting for. All are invited to the wedding... when?...could be anytime...last minute...no plans...snow here in NY... the beach in VA...Be ready when we call and come if you can.....you know Crystal, fast..last minute...like you two! No, I'm not rubbing it in, I'm on a high that I've waited a long time for, that's all." Vincent immediately hugged his mom and outstretched his hand to the Captain. "OMG mom, are you really going to change your name... Grandcockski...really? Vincent announced each syllable and winched at the same time! It was a great meal and a fun evening after that.

Vincent and Crystal awoke the next morning to bacon frying and the rooster doing his thing in the back yard...early. "The food I'm going to miss Crystal exclaimed, but not these early morning wake-up calls."

"A quick...you know..then we need to be off to the train station." Vincent said looking toward the side window.

"A quick...you know...? We don't do anything quick, so don't expect it this morning" as she climbed on top of him, lifting her night-shirt over her head and leaving her arms stretched to the ceiling, creating a marvelous view of her breasts stretched upward and inviting! Sitting on his manhood, magnificent and tall, she wiggled to adjust the fit to just right! "Don't move too much, doll, or I'll be done before you know it!" Vincent whispered with alarm. "I am going to be easy this morning."

"The hell you are", she exclaimed and slid her body back off of her perch and started with a wet kiss in his mouth that finished with her index finger rubbing his gums and sliding down into and out of his slippery mouth. This energized him, he grabbed her and lay-ed her flat on the bed and mounted her swiftly and finally and brought her to an ending organism that should last until at least tonight!

Once she caught her breathe, she said "that was better...don't ever offer me a quick...you know, and expect me to be satisfied with deflating more than nine inches of macho man! I'm better than that!"

Feeling chastised and pleasantly used, he helped her to pack their belongings for the train ride home, complaining like any man, that they were leaving with more than than arrived with.

Crystal double checked and made sure that they had a private room in the coach on the way home. Being in the dinning room and mingling with people was going to be a strain on Vincent for this trip... She was going to see to it, wearing the gold on gold flouncy neck, fitted at the waist, glittery top! It's going to be a great, moving, showy item once I gather the neck to a 'proper' position above the cleavage and above the breast, but for today and tonight...Vincent...eat your heart out!

The family delivered them via horse wagon to the train station...they said their good-byes and heard their boarding call. Once in their cabin, after Crystal stowed away their bags, she claimed the long, low bench let her shawl fall to the bench. Vincent hadn't looked her way yet which was okay, they weren't underway as yet. She sat like a proper lady with her legs crossed at the ankles, shifted her upper body position to expose more of the color of her blouse and more skin below the proper line of her chin. Covering most of that with the book she produced for just that reason, Vincent took an interest in the title of her book, staring right where Crystal wanted him to as she started to hum the tune of Chattanooga Choo Choo.

"Oh lady, don't play with my like that, we're in almost a public place." Vincent went pail with desire and Crystal softly vowed to comp_y.

"Husband, here beside me, now…" Vincent sat immediate_y. "Husband how low can you pull this delicate gold, shimmery top of mine (Vincent's hands made a move toward her and she stilled them and pressed them into her nipples)while I lay back like this, and she lounged further back in a 'come & get me pose', facing the window as people walk by…with teeth! Remember, we are not exhibitionists nor are we trying to bring attention to ourselves. We are travelers and will see them for dinner in the dinning car. Please don't make a scene… just adore and satisfy me!" His hands fisted and starting kneading at her breast as she continued to hum the tune that would eventually drive her to gyrations that would make him loose a valuable squirt in his pants!

"You're a vixen Mrs. Clear and I love the way you entice me into these win, win situations. You win because I don't care what I look like to the outside world and you win because I can drive you wild at the drop of a hat or tune, this time! Go ahead, finish the song, I'm the only one here, but don't expect me to pull the shades down when you're dancing on the benches and shedding every stitch of clothing you have on. Your hands fist up and apply pressure to your love box and you cry out for satisfaction. You are such a turn on then, I don't know what is it about that song, but you can use it on me anytime you want! I'm ready…we have 3 and a-half hours to home. Please don't loose the blouse…It's as much a of a turn-of as you being naked!" True to his word he buried himself in her before they left the train station.

As promised, the dinning car was the ultimate turn-on. Lifting her arm to hail a waiter for a drink, exposed boob from the under-arm from the side…she made sure he saw it. Reaching in front of the elderly man sitting next to her to get a roll, caused the slooping neckline to sloop very low and expose an entire boob. No apologies necessary…he loved it. When she bent to the floor to retrieve her dropped napkin, the same gentleman bent with her to assist. They both came up smiling. She leaned over to Vincent and whispered in his ear, "we're never going to see these people again, what's the harm...this is fun" Half way through her meal Crystal brought attention to herself by dripping hot gravy down the front of her...on her flesh...She needed to immediately drag her napkin into the front of blouse and wipe away the hot sauce. In doing so, the entire front of her blouse was dragged to her waist, both breasts, shinny with grease were giggled as they were whipped clean. Fanning embarrassment, she retreated to her cabin with haste. Once again Vincent's lust was in overdrive and they organismed all the way home.

I love traveling with you Mr. Clear, Crystal proclaimed as they were dropped at their front door at home.

Chapter 16

Next day back at the base and the Operations Center...same old thing...Boring...boring, it was like they were never away. You really can't say things never change, they really do, but it rarely makes a difference. Crystal, enjoying the fact that they had ample funds to help-out Gram and splurge a bit while away, coaxed her to check-out the Reginald funds and her 'files'. Again everything is fine, which is great...but not exciting any more. Reginald is just an enlisted guy drawing a paycheck and earning over-seas and hazardous pay. Lucky, rich man...he spends very little of it! *Time to do it again?? It's exciting and Vincent doesn't seem to mind my messing around...I'll keep thinking on it.*

That evening at supper Vincent asked Crystal if she had heard the scuttle- buck about transfers or the shifting around of personnel? She admitted that she had encountered little groups all talking about our camp getting a clean-out. "Is that what you mean, is that what a clean-out is all about, transfers?

"Oh hell, I don't want to move do you? She asked Vincent. He merely said "that's military life, spend a few years here and then get moved to someplace else. As long as you are with me, you are my life, I don't care where I...we are! Anyway I think it's just some talk, nothing to get crazy about." They finished their meal and Crystal sat at the piano quite a few minutes before she started to play. Finally she started to play Take the "A" Train. Vincent hadn't heard her play this before, it was a new release from Ellington, getting a lot of play on the radio lately. Damn, she is good. A new song and she can let roll off her fingers like she's been playing it for years. *Would it be so bad if she did take the job at the New Yorker Hotel? She loves doing it, she dresses the part of an accomplished pianist, but that's easy for her, she's beautiful. I'm a selfish pig if I stand in her way of using her talent this way. But she was offered the weekends...I'm free, not working the weekends...I could go and stay with her...every weekend? Nah...Watch, she'll turn it down and I'll get transferred so far from New York she won't want to go or the Reginald money won't be enough for her to make the move with me...this shits, because I know I'm a selfish pig!* The tone of the piano changed and he knew Crystal was trying to release demons from her mind. She had started taking something out on the keys, striking at them rather than letting her hands and fingers glide over them to make their beautiful music...*her thoughts were running rampant...children, transfers, New York, Dad, Suzie, sex...dam he's good--great --gentle, giving, patience, smooth (!!)* ... a different song...Vincent looked in at her again and her head was gently swaying, then bent all the way back...she's playing Star Dust, very gently now and she was smiling and rubbing her tongue over her lips. *Oh-- don't do that while I'm looking at you, he thought... I can taste those lips...I want those lips, please sit back up straight...you're killing me...what are you thinking...your nipples...your breast---up so high...do you perform like that too? OH Crystal!*

When she relaxed her posture, she saw Vincent looking at her... watching her, and she liked what she saw in his eyes...it was love---she knew she'd go anywhere with him!

The next day at the Center was...the same as the day before and the day before that! She was bored, carrying messages from this building to the next and back again was not really a job, it was something to do to stay busy. *Knock it off, I need this 'job'. I need the excuse to be here every day to check 'my' files. OK, time to do something for myself, again.* One more message before lunch and she was done for the day, but no one needed to know that. She was actually going to enjoy her lunch today. She had some one to meet and to recruit!

Her lunch conversation was rather one sided, but that's what happens when you need to write an entire history and back story with parents and siblings, education and social security information and military experience on a new person. He really couldn't be a green recruit, they don't make enough money, so he needed to be of a rank befitting a monthly income to please her pocket-book. Name: Keith W. Rogers, born, Augusta, Maine, middle child of Anna and Wallingford Rogers, martial status: single. Rank: Command Master Chief Petty Officer: Ranger with the 52nd Squadron patrolling the borders between Russia and Armenia ----for his last three tours, equaling a total of 12 years drawing 'foreign soil' pay. A frugal man banking more than half of his earnings, now has a bank account in excess of $5500. *Wow, can I really make that happen..OK it will be a transfer from the Bank of Her Magistracy to a brand new account yet to be set up. Boy I've got a lot of work to do. That's a good beginning, he is going to be my private, special project kept under wraps. Reginald is the only one Vincent needs to know about.*

The rest of the afternoon, Crystal's attention and concentration was totally on her own project, and by 4:15pm the Command Master of the 52nd Squadron currently based in Armenia was fully vested and sharing command of 48 souls with Chief Petty Officer James P. Hardy. Their unit was self patrolled and under the oppresses of Third Fleet which kept them well supplied and well informed. While back at home she had two bank accounts with his name on them, each with healthy balances. Feeling very satisfied with what she had accomplished, heading home with Vincent and thinking about supper was just another happy segment to her day. Right at their front door she noticed the full mailbox. There went the good mood, these were all bills. But wait, one from New York addressed to her. Excited, she torn into it with a flurry. Vincent was waiting to hear what it was about and from whom. All smiles, she hugged the letter to her bossism, then handed it to Vincent, hesitantly. Her smile only waned a little as she watched him read her invitation to play at the new Crystal's Piano Showcase, days and hours (a minimum of 24 performing hours) to be arranged to justify the rooms new name and decor.

She was going to be a Headliner. Her own show, she danced around the kitchen on air! Naturally she would be getting paid, but they could work all that out later...Her Own Show! As much as she was smiling and feeling light headed with joy, Vincent was beginning to sweat and feel left out. Already he felt the lonely nights and weekends that she'd be not home. *Who was this not fair to…him for feeling left out or Crystal if he was the reason she didn't take this job! Awe shit…he knew the answer!* He opened the ice box and hauled out a few pork chops along with a head of lettuce. "Might as well start supper, looks like I'll be doing this a lot more in the future." They both just let the comment drop and started supper together. It wasn't until morning that Crystal dared to bring the subject up again. She hadn't slept that well last night, tossing and not touching, thinking and dreaming and wanting the chance to prove to herself. So she started, "I know we need to talk about the letter from New York and I know both of our feelings need to be weighed on this one sided opportunity, so please try to be objective and come up with your best argument and we'll hash it out tonight after supper. We'll grill steaks, have a drink and come to a decision. I'd like to respond to Mr. Brentwhistle by tomorrow." Her tone of voice was optimistic and she looked beautiful. *"Oh course she is going to do it, she'll do it with my blessings…I can't be that selfish, not out loud…not to her, I know she needs this, she wants this. I'm just afraid…* "OK, tonight, we'll have a great supper, we'll talk and I'll help you write the letter to your new boss and then you can sit on me…all of me!" With that she flung her arms around his neck and announced that they needed to leave for the base.

Chapter 17

Once at the gate to the base, they both went their separate ways. Posted on Crystal's board were many new messages as well as announcements to take special notice to the enclosures in this weeks pay folder. There were too many new changes to post publicly, therefore if there is a change that is pertinent to you, it will be in your folder. Read it carefully and proceed with it's directions. Crystal noticed there was a message for her to report to her dad at 9am. Sure, once again her heart hit the bottom of her stomach because of her activities yesterday. *It's a guilty conscience, I did the same things as with Reginald, followed the same foot-print of procedures, no... he can't know... no one can...I was careful!* She gathered up her messages, put them in order for delivery and proceeded to meet with her dad.

When she entered his office, his back was to her, standing at a big window reading, he didn't know she was standing there watching him. When he turned and saw her, he rushed to her with open arms and the hug of a dad. At first she panicked, his movement was so swift and unexpected, but the hug was nice, equally unexpected. I guess spending time with Suzie and family had had a good affect on him. "Sit, sit" he indicated the couch again the long wall and he sat as well. "I guess things are going to start moving pretty fast around here, there are some big changes happening and I mean soon." With a warm smile he said "first, Suzie and I are going to be married in the church we all went to last Sunday, then I am being transferred to Fort Worden, a military base in Port Townsend, Washington. Suzie is excited, it's going to be such a big change for both of us. And you my dear, are going to change your address to the Fort George G. Meade area in Maryland, because that is Vincent's new duty Station." Taking a big breathe he finished with "this all starts in two weeks."

Crystal's mind was racing in overtime..."dad do you have a map handy, I've news too, not confirmed but it's almost as big" The Captain moved to a side table, flipped through a number of large papers and asked "what area do you need to see?" Crystal moved to his side and they were looking at a large map of the eastern half of the US. "Great she said...moving her finger from MD to NY...dad help me see the distance from NY city to Gram's house...not bad…" she murmured after he measured and told her it was about 70 miles to Hopewell Junction. "What's going on in that white head of yours? "Well, I've been offered a job at the New Yorker Hotel...not just a job but a 'headlining' 25 hours a week playing piano in a redesigned room just for me!" The Captain stopped her there and congratulated her, it was big news and he could see she was beaming with pride at the offer. He questioned her about how Vincent was going to make out without her around all the time. She continued with," Vincent and I knew we were going to have to discuss the finer points to being apart, but now we are going to be apart in a closer proximity. Plus Gram is going to be alone when Suzie leaves and 70 miles is a lot closer than Md. So much to think about and so much figuring to do! Is Vincent going to get new orders with his pay folder on Friday like the notice says?" Crystal was breathless when she finished. "He is, and I also took the liberty of booking him off for the next two weeks to come to the weeding and scout around the Fort Meade area for housing or whatever you two are going to need." "Thanks dad, you're the greatest, now tonight when we (Vincent) and I sit down to write my acceptance letter we'll have other considerations to keep in mind.

Chapter 18

The wedding was a simple affair and quite lovely, then followed by a feast that was out of this world. Grandma was happy to have everyone back for the week, but we could see she'd be happy to see us all leave as well, she'd have her quiet home back! Fort Meade was about the same size as where they just left but with looser rules and not so many stripes on the shirts of the commanders. Getting to know people and getting to know your way around was way easier. Plus for Crystal, she didn't have to worry about running into her father! He had been good to them, she'd have to admit, but he had too many stripes on his shirt. Her maiden name and his stripes helped get the same type of job out of the Operations Center and it enabled her to be just as noisy and sneaky as she was before. Traveling to NY and staying at the New Yorker and playing in her own swanky room was a delight, not really a job! Coming home and loving Vincent, she was on top of the world. Vincent was bored and lonely!

Two years of marriage, a duty change, Crystal's job in New York City, their lives have seen a number of changes, not the least of which is traveling to Hopewell Junction frequently to visit and check up on Grandma. Crystal loved the challenge of always being on the go. Just in the last few months Vincent has had some traveling assignments where he'd be gone three or four weeks, home again for one and back off again for a few. When he was away, being in New York was great, she missed him terribly but made due with Mr. Purple as needed! When he was away she didn't need to think about scheduling him in. For the week he was home, no one was happy with her work schedule. Not Vincent and not Mr. Brentwhistle, it was different. It got so she would write down her work schedule and leave him a note to meet her on a given day at a certain time in her room, always 3108 at the hotel. It got so when they were in NY, only when in NY, he would wear an army uniform with the name tag R. Sabers and play games with her. She invented him, he played the part! They played as often as they could, with Reginald and with each other.

They both got used to the train terminal and all the people it handled on a daily basis, but on this day Vincent ran into a situation of a woman in distress. She had been knocked down and her personal property hitting the ground and strewn all over the place. He helped the woman to her feet and bent over and started picking up jewels, diamonds, many diamonds of all sizes and shapes. Once he stood up he was gently steered to an empty portion of wall by the most striking and alluring young woman he had every seen! There he met Oliver, Marie and their daughter Rhonda Tuffin. He was informed that Oliver and Marie were jewelers, actually diamond brokers and cutters and they needed to get out of this traffic asap. "Lt. Sabers," he heard Mr. Tuffin say, "I recognized your rank by the stripes on your shoulder and can call you by name by the pin over your pocket, so I do so with the utmost of gratitude in you helping Mrs. Tuffin back to her feet and with her possessions." But now we are late and must rush to the store. Noticing their hurry he offered to treat Rhonda to a drink at the cafe, if it would be alright with them. *In that instant he didn't know what got into him, but what the hay...he didn't need to meet Crystal for a few hours yet, why not?...* "Looking between her husband and her daughter who had blushed cheeks and twinkling eyes, Mrs. Tuffin spoke her permission as long as Rhonda was back to the store by five pm. Lt. Sabers promised that would be accomplished. Vincent had the most amazing afternoon of his life. He was playing Reginald to the hilt and enjoying the company of this adorable woman with the most stunning hair he had ever seen. At one point he asked if he could touch her hair! Rhonda just stared at him like he was crazy. "I hate my hair, I can never do anything with it...it has a mind of it's own. Bushy, curly and puffy all the time, long or short, it drives me crazy...go ahead and touch it if you want, I'm glad someone likes it" she bent a little forward and all of her hair was flowing toward the ground. In that moment he saw dark brown, light brown, strawberry blond, ash blond and red hairs just blowing in the breeze. He cupped his hands around her head and she lifted with him holding a top pony-tail. They both laughed and he let her hair fall naturally to her shoulders, then down her back. He checked his watch with what she perceived to be a little anxious movement, but he said getting her to the store by five was no problem because he had orders to fill back at the hotel, orders that were crystal clear and not to be ignored.

Leaving her in front of the store, he asked if he could see her again. "I've so enjoyed your company this afternoon, I'd like to do it again. Let's say dinner tomorrow night. Can I pick you up?" "Lt. I don't even know your first name, I need to know that before I answer." She took his hands in hers but that wasn't good enough for him. He gently wrapped his arms around her and said "Reginald Sabers at your service. Reginald Sabers feels just born because of you!" She planted a light kiss on his cheek and promised to meet him under the awning of the hotel tomorrow night at 6:30 pm.

What the hell am I doing...you fool...Crystal will skin me alive...no she can never know how stupid I just was. Rhonda is a good kid, we'll have dinner and I'll disappear from her life. Simple. Once back at the hotel in room 3108 Vincent met Crystal's libido with the same tempo as hers. It felt good to be back in her arms again. This amazon of a woman, all legs and the hair of an angel was his wife, his life, his release. "Slow down girl, not all the way down, just enough to have some left over for later tonight, I'm staying for your set and staying here with you tonight...if you'll have me?" Crystal was over the moon, he hadn't sat through one of her sets for weeks, and when he was in NY, he mostly went north to his Grandmothers house. "Oh I'm going to make you so happy you decided to play- stay with me tonight, You'll see." As she finished making him naked from the waist down and making herself comfortable sitting on him while he sat on the edge of the bed. "I won't move around too much right now to make this last, so just take your time in disrobing me, so I can dress later for my set." Between tiny gasps, he said "your teasing...right?," as he undid her bra strap across her back. Next he undid her buttons, one by agonizing one, as he sucked on her breasts in turn, first the left, then the right. "How can I not move when you move on me that way." She said as her hands went to his face to lift it from her breasts to trace his lips with her fingers...He caught her hands with his, held them together in mid-air and kissed her so passionately, they both lost it. While trying to catch her breath and still leaning heavily into his chest she whispered, "I'm going to think of this moment tonight while I'm playing 'Are you Lonely Tonight', so wait and listen and get ready... It'll probably be at my break time! No defiantly at break, I'll need you again by then!"

Crystal's Piano Showcase had transformed her from a bar girl hitting piano keys to this Golden Goddess sitting at this shinny, sleek, black baby grand piano hosting a golden tray with a crystal pitcher of ice water and one, tall, slender glass. The piano was up on a stage of sorts, four steps off the floor, in a corner sitting side-ways to the audience. The spot light above Crystal's head was the only light in the room when she was playing. The show-case was first-class as was everything associated with Crystal's show. The hotel had pitched the Piano Showcase and made Crystal a star. Vincent had to wrap his head around the fact that she was a sort after commodity and her income had begun to show that. There was now a cover charge to see her 8pm performance and two male waiters for the room wearing black tie tuxedos. As exciting as all this was, Crystal still felt no stage fright or showtime jitters, this was still just playing to her.

With Vincent sitting at the first table, up front near the piano, Crystal could just barely see his shadow, made from her spot light. Tonight he made her nervous, she wasn't sure why, but her inners hadn't relaxed yet and her hands were still clammy and aching to touch him, left over from the organism that was so expertly executed not 30 minutes ago. This is going to make for an interesting set...still turned on...all horny, and he's here...close enough to...nothing!!! I've got to work. The lights came up and she did her half pirouette, bent at the waist (hoped nothing fell out) and sent kisses into the crowd...

her opening song was '*Swan Lake*' and the applause started mid-say through. Swept away with her own music and the crowds appreciation after 95 minutes of continues playing, her next selection was 'Are You Lonely Tonight'. Her eyes immediately went to his table, but he wasn't there. She asked him to listen for it, to wait for it. She played, and played and anchored herself into the intermission sounds. She was excited and musically spent when she stood from the piano, swept the crowd with arms stretched wide and exited through her sparkly black curtain to her dressing room. The first thing she needed was a long drink of ice water and the second…Vincent sweeping her off her feet, lifting her off the ground, holding her in his arms and coaxing the longest most passionate kiss from her that he could muster. His efforts were not in vain, she responded with eager, hungry lips and her tongue working down his throat, just the way he likes it. "You weren't at your table…I thought you'd left.""NO way, I heard the beginning chord to your song and knew it was break time, my little sliver of time to be with you, alone with you. You know there aren't that many minutes that we can steal together any more, so I'll take what I can get. And for the next 18 minutes that's what he did. He hoped he gave as much as he took, because once when his hands and fingers felt their way through her hair starting from the top of her head and stroking all the way down her back, he pictured strawberry blond and golden highlights. He gasped and she laughed…I've got to get back to work anyway…but that felt great and I'm looking forward to what else you can do after mid-night!

Back at base in the morning Vincent was torn between two images, one he could have the other he wanted. *Stop…stop you stupid fool… OH Man…we're married…she gives great…she beautiful, and the way she moves…she moves me..she completes me…she's torn between her music and me…I'm not enough for her anymore…we are growing apart…I've got to get her pregnant…I can keep her that way, she can start our family, why hasn't that happened yet?* His head and his thoughts were his worse enemy today. He couldn't wait to get back to her tonight. His heart and his groin told him so! He had climaxed a number of times last night, but it wasn't enough…he needed more.

OMG… Rhonda…she's here…what the hell!!!…(Instant release)…..I've got to change my pants,(I thought only Crystal could do that to me!!!) before she sees me, before anyone can see me.. I've got civvies in Crystal's room, I hope I'm not seen. I forgot…dinner tonight with Rhonda…I forget to cancel. OMG…she looked so sweet, that hair…blowing in the breeze…I can't tease her because she hates it…I love it…what is it about her? Hurry you fool, she might leave, I don't know where to look for her…get cleaned up and hurry back to the front door.) Before he left Crystal's room he wrote her a note which included seeing her back at Fort Meade tomorrow night if he missed her here in the morning. Then he went back down to street level to see Rhonda.

Ten minutes later and arriving at the awning of the New Yorker to meet Rhonda for dinner, Vincent looked cool and collected in dark blue pants and a blue and white striped shirt. After taking a deep breathe and seeing that Rhonda was still there waiting for him, he proceeded to escort her into the most amazing dinning room she had ever seen. Dinner was wonderful and she turned into a chatty little doll, exposing sexual secrets of her mothers', unfavorable characteristics of her father and female admissions seldom discussed in mixed company. He was afraid he was going to shoot into his pants again at her direct and uncensored conversation. She also admitted a nasty falling out with her father before she left his apartment. *What a gal…I want her…she can't go back to that father of hers, she needs to escape and be free and…..*

The check arrived and she walked him to a bank of elevators and said, what floor? As surprised as he was, he managed… not yet, I need to do something first and walked her to the oval sitting room provided for guests waiting for a taxi…He ran to the reservations desk and got a room for the night. Returning to her he simply said, "there, we're saved, I got another key, I guess I lost my first one…."

On the way up to the room, he pushed the stop button, took her in his arms and solemnly said, "We need to make this an unforgettable night, I need to be back on base by 6pm tomorrow night. It's a long bus ride back." Once in his room, their room she put the moves on him to rock his world. She took his hands, mostly to stop them from any further forward movements, slid them down to his sides and took a giant step back from him. Looking straight into his eyes, she started to strip...untying her crisscrossed strings, then unbuttoning, ever so slowing the entire length of her dress. (Before leaving home, she stripped totally naked then dropped this dress over her head... doing this so when she started her advance on Reginald she wouldn't be able to chicken out) she let one shoulder free then the other...the dress fell to the floor exposing a totally naked Rhonda to Reginald. The only thing covering any part of her body was her long, wild, crazy beautifully colored hair flowing down her back. As she walked away from Reginald and climbed up on the king sized bed and beckoned him to join her, he noticed the triangle of colored hair just above her vagina. He wanted to be there! Outside of Crystal (*Crystal...OH shit... damn...how could I forget Crystal..she'll never know...she's busy..I wrote her a note...I'm covered...I'm OK)*

He'd never encountered a woman so free to be looked at totally naked. (*except...*) She was a total novice...his first virgin and he intended to treat her with kit cloves, respect and kindness. It didn't take him long to discard all of his clothing and show her, her first naked man. She was amazed, it showed on her face. She was excited, it showed by her flexing fingers and nubs growing on her upturned, pert , mouth sized breasts. Those few moments were all he could take...he wanted her and now and she could tell by his still growing penis and breathing. "Now...I want you too, but until now I wasn't sure what to do." She said this looking straight into his blurry, lustful eyes. Somehow that pleased him so he started his entry and she was wet, that also pleased him so he proceed to enter her and then enter her more and then push until he entered her fully and she screamed out. He Froze! "She said, Oh I thought this was suppose to feel good" as tears were sliding down her cheeks. Tears were always the undoing of Vinc….Reginald...he'd learned that about himself years ago. "He tried to explain that this first time broke a skin barrier in her vagina and it would feel better next time." "Then get on with it Army man, and make me feel better." She cooed and immediately impaled herself on him. "OMG, you are a big one aren't you sir" she said looking down at him, as she rode him, and rocked on him and slid up and down on him. All the while as he cupped her breasts and tweaked her nubbing nipples. Then he couldn't take it any more...stop..please stop or we'll need to nap before we can do this again. She stopped, she thought she was doing something wrong, she cried again. The next few minutes she was sitting in his lap, being hugged and rubbed and listening to him praise her initiative and efforts, no you're not doing anything wrong, but right and fast..too fast for me, once I'm spent, it will take a little time for me to get it up again. He tried to explain that once she learned to take it slow and wait for the feelings to reach her heart, she would move into a new realm and the feelings would be erratic and glorious and too short! She said, "you're talking about an organism, I know the word, I can't wait to experience one myself." He kissed her so gently, she responded in kind. For the next several hours they made love and slept. Rolled over and started again. By morning she had the experience of a lifetime with an organism that didn't want to quit, and it taught her patience and love and trust. Reginald was a keeper, she didn't want any other love in her life she wanted him!

During the night Rhonda had learned that good sex couldn't be rushed. So when Reginald let the sun in in the morning, she was up on his heels to cover the window and make the sun go away, she didn't want the night to end. As long as she was walking around the room naked and making no move to cover herself, he'd watch her until... now...she did it...he was UP and IT was begging for attention. She took notice, grinned and said "I can do something about that." And she proceeded to do just that. She crawled on hand and knees back to him sprawled on the bed and kept crawling until her mouth found his shaft and she licked at the dribble that had already escaped. Reginald was excited by this attention and delighted at her exploration. "Don't stop now" he instructed and helped her hand close around the base of his erection. This excited her and she slipped his penis in her mouth as far as it could go. Scrapping her teeth on him lightly she pulled her mouth back until she could repeat her words of a few hours ago. "You really are a big one, sir, you have the ability to fill me everywhere." Once again they were tangled up in each other unwilling to, but needing to, vacate this rented room.

When they left the hotel they walked down the street to the cafe where they had their first 'date'. Just when their coffee arrived and Rhonda was elaborating a little more about the rift she had with her dad the day before, her dad arrived. Rhonda stood to face him and he slapped her across the face saying I disown you and will never see you again. At this action Reginald was on his feet ready to...but Rhonda stopped him, with "I expected something like that, but my choice is still to be with you." Looking at Rhonda's pale face, very blotched where her dad had struck her, Reginald flatly said "finish your coffee, we have something we need to do before noon." Taking a minute to drink her coffee and relax after that scene with her dad, she asked, "What do we need to do, where are we going?" Instantly Reginald's tone of voice changed and he announced with pride that "If she will have me, I'm going to marry this woman here and now."

The entire morning crowd at that cafe started cheering and giving them directions to the court house.

A few hours after that, the new Mrs. Reginald Sabers, Lt. Reginald Sabers and Crystal Clear all had bus tickets on different busses going to the same place, Fort George G. Meade, Maryland.

Chapter 19

Crystal was making her way back to their nicely furnished 6 room apartment just off the base in Severn. Her head was spinning with news she couldn't wait to share with Vincent, an invitation to play in Las Vegas. She had read about the area. It's advertised as the adult playground of America with anybody that is somebody visiting, gambling and entertaining there. She worked too hard for her money, therefore had no interest in gambling and it wouldn't be her first place to pick for visiting, but entertaining there! *What a rush...All the celebrity magazines in New York are raving about the clubs and the arenas hosting top name entertainers. Yes, I entertain, it's fun and someday I'm going to record that tune I'm working on...can't wait to play it for Vincent.....not yet, it's not done. Las Vegas...me...it's been two years since I've seen dad... maybe, just maybe they can travel down while I'm there...I need a map to see how far it is...I need Vincent to help me maintain this high that I'm on. He'll be so proud of me, then of course he'll say he doesn't want me to go...it's too far, I'll be gone too long...he'll miss me, but then he'll hold me. I love the way he runs his fingers through my hair and most times down the length of it, then his hands come to a rest and caress my bottom and press me hard into his erection. He is predictable in that way and I love the way he loves me.* Feeling a bit turned on and a lot drowsy, she slept the rest of the way home with so many things filling her dreams!

Before leaving New York, Reginald Sabers had made living arrangement two blocks off base on Cooper Road in MD for himself and his new bride. This was also the first time he accessed the Reginald accounts Crystal had set up. If he was going to be leaving Rhonda alone in an apartment, he couldn't leave her with no money. So he helped himself. At the busy and crowded bus depot back at Fort Meade, Reginald found the happy and over-whelmed Rhonda just starring at all the people and all the men in different military uniforms. They made eye contact across two bus lanes of traffic, met in the middle and embraced like two love starved returning forces. Walking hand in hand they made their way to Cooper Road. He left her with money and sad words of, "For the next three days, I need to stay on base and finish a duty and report, before I can come home and be with you again." "So much for a honeymoon, she complained with a smile, don't worry I'll be fine, I have those days to turn this into a home. I'll be rested so watch-out when you get back. He left her with the money and without turning back, set his thoughts on Crystal!

Crystal was really hopping that Vincent would be able to meet her at the bus depot, but he knew which slip her bus would pull into and she didn't see him there. A little disappointed, she took a taxi for the 3 miles to their apartment, went in and immediately stripped and redressed in a bra-less mini-dress and house slippers. Now comfortable, she rummaged through the freezer for something for supper. Frozen wouldn't work...it was too late. Soup...no, more...Dinky's Beef Stew, now that'll, work with hot buttered rolls, that's a meal...Thank goodness for the dough-boy...always on hand and delicious. Vincent arrived home just as the rolls were heading into the oven. Just as Crystal was bending over to slide the tray into the oven. Just as her breasts were folding out of the top of her dress, with her hairless 'V' showing at the top of her legs, for him to see because she was bent forward to reach the oven. He helped her close the oven door, but wouldn't let her stand up...yet. It was the perfect opportunity to cup her from behind, feel the smoothness of her hairless crotch and insert three fingers, up as far as they would go. Enjoying the sensation and knowing they had 12 minutes to play, she let him continue playing until she needed something to touch and fondle as well. Vincent had worked himself up and he *needed Crystal..he needed her long legs wrapped around him, holding him firm and tight in her vagina, not moving, just promising ..*

bringing him to the edge of...and then gripping his ass and shoving it forward with whimpers of release and cries of almost anguish, the best kind of cries! He arrived home with all of these thoughts and feelings running through his mind, so to find her offering most of the best she has to offer, he was quick to take advantage. Supper was eaten and long forgotten when they awoke in the morning in each others arms.

The morning arrived with Vincent needing to report back to the base, but Crystal didn't need to be there until Wednesday. She was happy to say home, work on her arrangement, work out the finger work to make the cord changes easier and get it ready to play for Vincent, she wasn't playing it for anyone until she was happy with it.

First she started with doing a couple of loads of laundry, which included striping and remaking the bed, make a cake and had it ready for the oven with her pot roast and timing everything to be ready by 6. That gave Vincent about a half hour to relax and have a beer when he got home from 'work'. With everything under control for supper, she sat at the piano. When she was sitting at the piano, practicing old pieces, new pieces or fine tuning originals the time just flew. Right now she was playing her new song. She was quite happy with its composition and knew where it needed strength and cord copulation and where she needed to relax her fingers and let each key stand on its own. She had worked so hard on making it sound just right, she never heard him come into the living room. He was as quiet as a mouse and found himself swaying to the melody, and thinking her quite the performer. When she had finished playing, Vincent applauded softy and "complimented her on getting even better if, that was possible. That tune, you played it with so much feeling. I was picturing a moon lit sky above snow covered mountain peaks, a peaceful and serene place where lovers did not need to speak." He lifted his eye brows at her when she didn't speak, but rather, she just looked at him in AWE. After what seemed like an insufferable minute, she got up from her piano bench, went to him and gently kissed him on the lips. She said, "I hadn't even thought of a title for it yet. I've hummed it many times when playing, but had never put any words to the constructed lines, like sentences. You did better than that, you painted a picture! He could finally breathe, she liked his thoughts.

Over supper she let the cat out of the bag that, that was her own original piece of music. She had written it and arranged it's delivery with it's hard notes and soft music-box tones. With smiles all around, he was amazed and she felt proud. Using his complimentary mood she dropped the bomb about going to Las Vegas. She let him read her invitation with the dates, the accompanying performers the hotel/casino location, the accommodations with food and gambling chips, and the salary for 6 days, 3 shows a day...that is Friday, Saturday and Sunday the 14th, 15th, and 16th then the 21st, 22nd, and 23rd of September with shows at 7pm-10pm and 1am...this is the town that never sleeps. He was immediately just like she thought he would be. "NO way are you going to Vegas, I know you're good, but you and what security team is accompanying you? You're my wife, you can't just go across the country by yourself, play your piano for awhile and come back home! What makes you think that this is okay with me? New York was a stretch .. now you want to go even further away. This is your baby isn't it...you're own personal career to make flourish and grow like any well taken care of child...but it's yours, nothing we made together or share. You bitch Crystal, you selfish little bitch!" With that he stormed out the door ..

Her night was endless. She cried, but couldn't fall asleep. He was her world, she only wanted to fill it with sweet sounds. Sometimes they sounded even sweeter when she was paid to make them. *Am I really a bitch..sometimes he gets assignments that take him away for months at a time. He announced some time ago that he was a military man, in it for the long haul, a career. I don't think I'm being selfish wanting to take advantage of good things that come my way. This is only two weeks. New York is sometimes something that we share, and dam-it, we share well. I never got a chance to tell him that maybe when in Nevada there was a chance to maybe see the folks. It's been two years, that the longest I've ever gone without seeing my dad. I miss him...on that thought she cried again. I'm not back in New York until next weekend, when I'm there I need some help, maybe Mr. Brentwhistle can get me in touch with people or a contact or a company to help me produce my original piano piece. Vincent's words and the picture he painted about my song was beautiful, maybe I need a song writer to finish the song and we'll hire it out to be sung…who am I kidding, that's not how it's done…I wish I could write meaningful words to finish the song with style. If done right it could be a masterpiece.* With Vincent's white billowy clouds floating above her head and her music echoing in her ears, sleep finally won her over. But she was still alone in the morning.

Mornings are a horrible thing when you wake up alone. She was alone here at home and she hated it. Since she took the job in New York, she has had many lonely mornings. Her Choice, Vincent would remind her of that if she complained. He complains of the same thing and is fast to remind her that it is her fault. He married her to try and minimize his military lonely mornings when his feet were firmly grounded with her close. He would remind her that he has gotten used to frequent sex…good sex because they practiced together to make it that way and she was negligent in her wifely duties for not being around to exercise all that they had learned together. *Pigs ass! I like sex too. Last night you withheld a good go round with me because of your pigheadedness, I can still take Mr. Purple out of the draw (do I have any charged batteries).*

That was her last thought on her missing husband, she had better things to do. With a pot of coffee within arms reach, she sat down and starting writing a letter to her dad and Suzie. At first she needed to lie and say things were great, wonderful, but when it came to stating how much she missed them, was it the total truth. She went into a long story about her spotlight at Crystal's Piano Showcase and the wonderful suite they provide her at the hotel. Vincent has been a frequent guest in my room and audience member at my shows, but when he's not he has traveled a bit more North to visit with Grandma. We plan on getting her down to the hotel to see one of my shows very soon. She admits once she is here, she'll have a ball shopping and maybe having her hair done in the of the salons, it's the travel she afraid of. She'll only have to do it once, then we won't be able to keep her away. It would be good for her!

Now for my big news, I've been invited to perform in Las Vegas. The promoters have sent me an itinerary and are offering a whopping amount of money for nine shows each weekend for two weekends. Once I finalize the offer and know exactly the hotel I'll be performing in, I'll send you the information. Hopefully you can manage some time off to plan on having dinner with me and seeing one of my shows. My guest! Oh, How I love saying that!

Now more news, I've written a song that I think is beautiful. It even moved Vincent when he first heard it...I didn't know he was in the room, so it was still a practice exercise, but when I finished he said and I quote "I was picturing a moon lit sky above snow covered mountain peaks, a peaceful and serene place where lovers did not need to speak." I was speechless, its like he said what the notes were whispering and it painted a picture! He was moved! That's what music is suppose to do and I did it! I'm proud of my song...it will be in my repertoire once I announce it to the world.

She finished her letter, went on to paying the few bills that had piled up and then she was free for the day. She had to talk herself out of going to the base to poke around the Reginald and Keith Rogers files. It had only been a couple of weeks, things couldn't change much in that time. She'd look tomorrow. Being alone with not much to do now, she dressed in comfy jeans and a sweat shirt and set out for the Navy PX to shop for new jeans for both herself and Vincent for the next time they made it to Grandma house. She knew better not to shop in New York City, everything was so much more expensive. She was brought up shopping in the PX, having a little more money in her pockets wasn't going to change that! Poking around in New York was fun, but she was no fool. Find it in New York and look for it at the PX a month later. It was the best of all worlds! With one big bag of purchases, she made for home. One bag was enough to carry when you're walking. She has learned. Once back home she prepped her chicken and vegetables popped them in the oven for supper and spent the rest her time on the piano, just waiting for Vincent to come home. He'd better come home tonight, that way he'll sleep better and we can make our way to the base together in the morning.

He didn't say anything about this last night when he finally got home. Just waltzed in like there nothing wrong, bear hugged me, ate a mammoth supper, dozed while reading the paper and went to bed early. I guess sleeping on base in little, tiny beds with flat mattresses is not to his liking anymore. (Little did she know!...that the night before...)

Chapter 20

*H**aving a tiff with Crystal was almost unheard of, but shit happens.* Rhonda will be surprised when I show up. Moving into a 'furnished' apartment, all alone is the pits, I'm glad I'm on my way there. She'll be delighted to see this food, bath towels, two pillows and a blanket. *I hope she likes green.* He knocked on her door and the look of surprise on her face was priceless. "I thought you said you couldn't get back here tonight", she chocked out with tears running down her face. "I checked in at base and got permission to check back in at 0700 tomorrow morning, you've got me till then." he said inching his way in the door. When the door closed she leaped and wrapped her legs around his waist, cried and tried to explain how happy she was to see him. His bags of goodies hit and spilled out all over the floor. It took about ten minutes to get her relaxed and talking about what else she needed either for herself or the apartment. It was fun. She was like a child with a blank check just listing everything she would like to pick up at the store. "Where is the store you were telling me about, are you sure you/we can afford everything on this list?" She said almost breathless. "OK, here's the scoop, we need to get you your military id so you can shop on base at the PX. It's a huge food and general supply store, you'll love it, I'm sure it stocks everything on your list and in different colors too. We get paid every two weeks, it's not much, but we'll get by. As my wife you get an allotment, that's what we are using for rent, there's not much left over after rent but it'll buy a movie ticket, night-on-the-town once a month." She sheeked with joy. They looked around at what they did have in the apartment, had a sandwich supper and went to the corner department store to buy at least sheets for the double bed that was in their bedroom. On the walk back to the apartment, he ducked into a convenience store for a 6-pack of beer and she picked-up an oldie by Ellery Queen so she'd have something to read while he was at work. "I need to find a library as well," she said "I love to read, at least now I can read what I want rather than how to cut precious jewels."

"OK, so you like to read, what else do you like?" It was an honest question, they got married so fast, they didn't know much about one another. With a twinkle in her eye, "kids, I love kids and want a house full, can we start now?" This was said with each of them standing on opposite sides of the bed while trying to make the bed. Reginald stopped cold and vaulted across the bed, held her face in his two hands and looked at her seriously, "are you serious, kids, you want kids"? He kissed her silly, pulled her down on the bed with him and giggled "Kids, I can finally have kids." "OH yes, a house full and yes, we can start now. I'll help you make as many as you want." "Wonderful" she moaned between kisses, "and when we're done, you're gonna have to help me make this bed AGAIN. It was a wonderful night, one he'll long remember, they were sure they made a least one baby that night. But then morning came and real life needed to begin again.

Chapter 21

He was on time getting to base, had just enough time to hit the mess hall and grab a quick breakfast before grabbing his jeep and meeting his counter-part before drills started. He was exhausted, really dragging ass. Their first was, read ALL the directions and complete this mission in less than two hours. It was always something different, but always long, semi-dangerous and very strenuous. Alan, his counter-part yelled, "what's up man...pull you weight, I can't do it alone, times a clicking, damn-it...pull." Vincent was just not with it, but pull he did. They made it, just under two hours, but they were done! Alan was bullshit, he felt he had done it alone today, their time sucked, it was definitely not their best work. "What's up man?, no answer. "Well maybe your next partner, if they build teams in New Jersey can light a fire under your ass, because I certainly couldn't today!" "What do you mean New Jersey?" Vincent just started at him like he had three heads! "The board, didn't you see the board this morning?" Alan just shook his head and wandered away. The board is something Vincent never had to pay much attention to. With Crystal in and out of the Operations Center, she always made it her business to keep up with what was going on, especially with her father gone, and no longer keeping her informed daily, she checked the board once or twice and before leaving for the day, but with her not here yesterday things got posted that he was unaware about. He had it in his head to make sure he checked the board before leaving tonight. But as luck would have it, his mind was a million miles away when he went through the gate when leaving towards Rhonda's apartment, never thinking about the information board again. As was set up this morning, before Reginald left Rhonda, 'Vincent' changed out of his Navy work uniform into plain jeans and a t-shirt before leaving the base to meet Rhonda on the corner outside of her apartment building. He made sure she had all of her ID's, and marriage certificate, then they were heading to the Army Bursar's office to get Rhonda's Military ID, then over to the PX to get her acquainted with it's contents and prices. Things are always cheaper on a military base and her eyes popped with pleasure. "We can't linger too long right now, because, remember I told you, I have the 24-hour watch tonight starting at 6pm." Reginald repeated this to her again as he walked her home, but at least tomorrow she'd be able to get around with her ID. So true to form now, he was able to be home at Crystal's on time!

Chapter 22

Arriving home and hearing the piano long before he was at the front door, he could picture Crystal sitting straight in the middle of the piano bench, her arms reaching both left and right with her hands bent at the wrists and fingers reaching down and across and up to the black keys, all in a fluid movement that she made look so easy! Her hair would be down and not tied back at all, just hanging down her back and moving slightly with the tilt of her head at certain cord changes. Her head always reaches forward when the chord change is severe or tricky and her hair sometimes falls forward around her face. *She's a natural beauty and I'm lucky to have her. I hope I'm forgiven for my outburst the other day. I'll try and make it up to her tonight because now I know I really need her. We'll discuss Las Vegas again, I'm relenting, of course she will be going. That'll be my time with Rhonda, it will work out better. So far so good....*Vincent slipped in the front door, silently walked up behind Crystal and rubbed her neck while she was playing. She never missed a beat, just closed her eyes and rolled her neck and head to his message. *OH good, he's home her heart said to her head.*

While his hands were still on her body, she finished her song then swung around on the piano bench and hugged his middle torso while looking up at him. "Welcome home" she said to him with love in her eyes. He started with "Crystal I've been such a fool", but she cut him off swiftly. He lifted her to face him and they 'shared' a loving embrace and a kiss that said it all! After supper, while sitting in the living room together, Crystal told him of her day of walking to the PX and writing a letter to the folks in Washington. Vincent followed up on that subject with, "I hope when you're in Vegas, they can get time away and visit you and hear you play your own original arrangement." She was sitting in his lap and hugging his neck before he even finished his statement. She leaned back and looked at him, "It's been a difficult couple of days you know. I was angry, I was busy, I was selfish but never a bitch" "OK, so you want to discuss it now…You're damn right it's been a difficult couple of days. I was also angry, I've been sooo busy, I was more selfish than you and being the bastard that I am, I needed to strike out. There over and done with…can I make love to you now?"

And when tomorrow came she needed to change her mind about how quickly things can change. They'd been in Maryland for nearly two years and Vincent's duties hadn't taken him away too far or too often.. Down to Virginia for a two week stretch or up to New Hampshire for 4 weeks or New York many times for two weeks. The New York trips seemed like a gift…come the weekend they could spend the days and nights together. He had absolutely no grounds for hating her in New York, it was marvelous when he was there. But now look at that board. *And Dad is not here to warn me of changes like this, major changes. Vincent is being sent to Earle Navy Base in Colts Neck, NJ , Oh shit, this could change a lot of my/our plans. New York is going to be too far now and it puts Las Vegas in jeopardy. No, this can't be happening. I've got to get back to New York, talk to Mr. Brentwhistle, what's in New Jersey, He has connections everywhere, I know he can help me. We've got to book Las Vegas before that becomes just a dream as well. REGINALD I almost forgot about you, you and Keith Rogers have to come with me. I've got to start over someplace new. My head hurts, I need a piano.*

Crystal couldn't just stand there and stare at the board any longer, she had five messages to deliver. And with each stop she made to deliver a message, she tried to talk with someone and get more information on the upcoming personnel transfers. No one knew anything more than what was posted. Today was payday, hopefully there would be a notice in the folder explaining more about the move. She missed her dad and the stack of maps he had. She needed to find out about this

New Jersey base and where it is and how far it is to New York compared to here. She had just delivered her last message so she planned a trip to the library on her way home. She'd never been there before, had no idea how to go about finding what she needed but she had two and half hours before Vincent would be home for supper. With nervous excitement she headed off the base and into town on her mission to explore maps. What a great building...being accustomed to mostly military buildings of gray cement and cinder block or silver metal walls this was charming. Old red brick half covered with gorgeous green ivy climbing it's exterior, with only three steps leading up to doors at least 12 feet high with ornate carvings in their heavy oak construction. *I've got to get out more*, she thought as she opened the door. Inside was just as breath-taking with it's open feeling and ceiling heights of at least 40 feet. Books lining three walls extending up to the ceiling with two balconies circling it's entirety. The fourth wall consisting of a stair case with landings at the balconies and access to the other areas off the center. Their were also very neat, framed instructions in many places to get you where you needed to go. Easy-peasy, within minutes she was looking at maps, clean, crisp, no folded corner, maps. Not unlike her dads, but much better taken care of! She borrowed a ruler and like her dad, she could figure out the distance between all of her points of interest. Wow...thrilled, she made many notes, put the maps away and headed home. All the way home she was thinking...*I'm not a stupid woman, I know New Jersey is closer to New York than Maryland. I've got to stop freaking out over change and think! I've got to keep a clear mind and explain to Vincent what I want and where I want to play and even how often. That's stupid thinking again, fool. Wait until the change of duty stations is official and when. Things could be changing next week or not until the first of the year. Keep your feet on the ground Crystal, don't piss him off again with this anxiety.*

Making supper was a chore because she couldn't wait to share her news, her very good news about their upcoming new location and her travel destinations for her piano jobs. Vincent will be so pleased, New York is so much closer. Even visiting Grandma won't be such a hassle from New Jersey. Atlantic City, New Jersey. This new Eastern seaboard city rivals Vegas, on a much smaller scale, but it still features all the glitz and glamour, gaming, food and entertainment. When she saw the city on the map, bells rang in her head...she'd read about the entertainment and the headliners scheduled to play there. She was sure Mr. Brentwhistle would have some influence in helping her schedule a few shows there. Her immediate fears about a new home base were now gone. Sure, change is always hard, but this change could be a blessing for her. As long as she can establish herself in their Operations Center and maintain the civilian job title and responsibilities as their runner, she'd have it made. It wouldn't or shouldn't take her long to establish and bury Reginald and Keith and her inquiries into their monthly income and disbursing avenues. It's amazing how things have changed in the few years she had been poking around in an Operations Center. What she does and how she codes her work is facilitated, just like all the military records, by telex machines. They are still in use, but with the extended use of the telephone, and more telephone lines, the delivery of a telex is much faster. Just lately in New York she had noticed more cars on the roads. Even here at Fort Meade she has noticed more civilian vehicles. Yes, things are changing and the world is moving faster all the time.

OH Vincent, hurry up and get home. You used to like me all excited like this, so hurry up and come and settle me down. I'll know when you walk in the door if this is going to be a good move or not. If I can get you naked and playing immediately or if it's going to be a quiet supper and quiet evening. Just to get a jump on things, the bra came off so her nipples would show through the t-shirt and the jeans were replaced by a wraparound shirt that would show a panty-less woman, wanting and ready! She had changed just in the nick of time...Vincent came through the front door waving his pay folder with a smile from ear to ear. "Come here you horny woman...I can tell by the way you're dressed, you have a tell about ya, ya know that Mrs. Clear, besides that your nipples are asking for it!" With joy Crystal's entire body slammed into him. Her tongue working around in this mouth and her hands down his pants left no room for questions, he knew what she wanted. "Thank you, I'm very happy to be home and yes, you've made me want you too."

Chapter 23

For now, actually for the next few hours supper was forgotten. It's a good thing the stew pot burner was turned off when Crystal went into change, because it was delicious when they finally got to it. First things first, Crystal's needs came first, and fast, and wonderful and left her wanting more. It's OK, he was just as fast and wanting and eager. They agreed that if they smoked, they could enjoy a cigarette now, lay back for a moment and recoup...but they didn't smoke, so round two came so immediately and so vigorously their bodies just moved and curled around each other with limbs and tongue and penis and fingers touching and probing and hands reaching and touching until the climax built to the point of totally filling the pulsing, wet vagina with his penis so rock hard and huge it felt glorious to both of them. This is the way to build an organism, they both agreed! "I think I'm satiated for awhile, thank you sir" Crystal sighed as she slipped a short night gown over her head. "We're going to eat supper now, right?" Vincent whispered as he watched Crystal's hair nearly touch the floor and her right boob leave the front of her gown and her blond patch wink at him as she bent over to retrieve a slipper. "Yes, I'm starved, we just worked up my appetite." she answered...but he wasn't done yet. As she stood up and started adjusting her body to fit into her clothes, Vincent helped her immediately out of the gown and back onto the bed. In between kisses he tried to inform her that she can't flaunt her body parts and expose that which really turns him on without consequences. He tried to explain that he was barely down but the sight of her bending and letting her hair run wild and letting him barely peek without touching just did it to him again...Up and ready and needing entry back into that blond patch that entices him so! So once again they turned their immediate breathing area into a cloud of sexy, sweat laden aromas. Later, laying there together, giggling, they agreed they are really good together.

Helping himself to a second helping of stew, Vincent asked "what got you so turned on this afternoon?"

"You whore-monger you...you almost made me forget. Did you get a notice with your pay today, you should have...I saw it posted on the board in the Operations Center...tell me...tell me." "Well,.... you didn't see it all." He got up and retrieved the folder and handed her a folded piece of paper. It was a written commendation informing him he had attained the new rank of Lieutenant Commander to be awarded at review this coming Sunday at 1pm. This also means a decent pay increase. Yes, I also saw the up-coming change of duty stations...New Jersey...that's the pits!" "What do you mean...it's closer to everything. I went to the library and looked at maps. It is going to be so much better. It's closer to New York. That means closer to your grandmother. It might also mean another place for me to get a part-time job, in Atlantic City. Close just like New York. What do you mean it's the pits?" She looked in his folder and saw the personnel change order to take affect by October 1st. That gave them 5 weeks to give notice on this rental and go to New Jersey to find something else. The only saving grace is that the Navy picks up the costs of moving. A team comes in packs everything and moves it out. Everything will be shipped to New Jersey at the Navy's expense, brought right into their new living quarters. Once Crystal understood this, she was super excited. "When can we go to New Jersey to look around and rent something new?" Crystal was all questions, one after another after another and got on Vincent's nerves! "We can't do anything in the next five weeks." and he stressed the word WE. "You have New York next weekend, come home through New Jersey and look around. We have enough money for you to stay there awhile and scout it out. Rent something if it's to your liking and close to base. Are you going to try to wheedle your way into the Operations Center again?" "It sounds like you've given this some thought, she questioned "Sure I can look for a new apartment, but without you with me it won't be any fun. And yes, I still need Operations to continue to monitor my extra activities. That's how I'll have the money to stay in New Jersey without you, I can tap into a Reginald account." "You've been thinking about this all afternoon... you've already got yourself another job in your head...I can tell! After looking at those maps, you probably know where to look for an apartment as well! You're going to have a grand time in New Jersey, me, the job duties and responsibilities are going to suck, really suck and drain the shit out of me! I'll be staying on base a lot more than I do now. No I don't want to move. I'm going to bed." and he left her standing there wondering what the hell just happened?

Those last few minutes were a turning point in their relationship and she didn't know it yet. This move was taking him further away from his new wife and he hated it. Crystal's piano career had started taking her further away from him and he hated it.

Chapter 24

If she couldn't be in bed loving-up next to Vincent, the next best thing was playing the piano. She loved her time in New York. Mr. Clive Brentwhistle had become a major contact in her life and she respects him to the hilt. Her performing has improved because of him and all prospects or advancement avenues explored became a reality because of him. She once approached him with the offer of being her manager and doing it for a fee, but he rejected that and other ideas along the same line completely. He assured her that she made her own way, if he could help open some doors for her, that is what family is for. The respect ran both ways and they both felt richer for the association. If only Vincent could see the good in their relationship rather than thinking that Brentwhistle was maybe on the make for Crystal. That's what Vincent hated about New York, it was Brentwhistle, and now he was moving her closer to both!

The humidity in August in New York City is stifling. When Crystal got off the train she felt her clothes sticking to her in some of the most uncomfortable places, and she knew she looked like hell. Arriving at the air conditioned hotel with two suitcases in tow made her feel like she was coming home, that's how comfortable she had become in these surroundings. She looked around in awe that she actually belonged here. On her way to the reservations desk, she was saluted by two security persons and called to by name by Caroline, the convenience store clerk. Everything here had become familiar and she was made to feel very comfortable by the people she encountered and her surroundings.

Anna, the gal at the reservations counter just handed her her keys to room 3108 with a smile as she handled another incoming call.

Room 3108, her home away from home. It lacked only two things a piano and Vincent. When she was alone, like now she would think about Vincent. It's a good thing they are to good together, because those loving, hot and heavy bedroom memories keep her going. Certain songs she relied on in her routines were triggers of Vincent, as well. Still, that one song she can't play in public haunts her as to why it sends her into a sexual frenzy. Vincent loves her rendition of that song and the way she moves and halts and moves some more. *We have our moments,* she thought. *Vincent, he needs to get over his jealousy of Mr. Brentwhistle, I've seen it, I feel it. It's his problem. There is nothing to be jealous about. The man has helped me and he continues to help me, but from afar. We have a 'great' working relationship. OK enough…*Once unpacked she went in search of a piano.

On the 40th floor there was an elegant lounge and restaurant open to the public Thursday through Sunday 4pm to 2am. There was a piano on the stage that was hers for the taking…until 3:30…it's only 1:20, great. Playing to her hearts content, she was undisturbed for two hours, then the dinner band came in and started setting up. A very tall, dark haired man starting walking her way. She caught a glimpse of him from the corner of her eye and was thrilled that Vincent had found her so they could have dinner together. She finished her song and lazily and a little provocatively stretched from sitting so long, bent to touch the floor and when she stood up she was face to face with the most 'beautiful' man she had ever seen. "Oh, I beg your pardon, I thought you were my husband". She said this while covering her mouth with one hand in embarrassment. Mr. beautiful took her other hand to his mouth and kissed her palm very suggestively, with tongue. The hand that was covering her mouth was now striking him across the face for his forwardness. Unphased, he followed her to the door as she ran from the room.

Her heart was still beating in overtime when she reached her room. Who is he, how dare he? She looked at herself in the mirror to see a blush running across her cheeks and over her nose. He is a better looking version of Vincent. She'd never thought that of any man, but this one was! *Just being objective, it doesn't mean anything. She told herself...He has the same great black hair, just like Vincent, the broad shoulders and slender waist, just like Vincent, the mouth that looks like is wants to be kissed, just like Vincent's, just as tall as Vincent, so the slap fell perfectly across those rosy cheeks and brushed those piecing blue eyes. That's what it is...the eyes. Just beautiful!..OK, down girl, you've got a show to do. Stupid me, Vincent isn't here with me, of course that wasn't him!*

A quick bite to eat, she had learned the best places to eat, in the hotel and on the street. She had been dropping into some of the sidewalk cafes for a quick lunch every now and then and had learned the prices and quality of what was offered. She knew the ones to stay away from. This afternoon it was Karl's, they had best onion rings she'd ever tasted. That and an iced tea should hold her until after her show tonight. So now back to the hotel for a quick shower and to call for Sharon in the beauty salon on the 7th floor. Sharon loves to play with her hair and when she's done Crystal's hair looks like a million. Sharon can make it look like Crystal has a french braid a mile long. Or a twist that wraps around her head three times. No matter what she does the effect is dazzling with flowers or sparkle or sometimes jewelry. Crystal is a beautiful woman, her height gives her a regal posture, her smile lights up her face and her hair, no matter how it is styled is her crowning glory. Without a doubt, Sharon will work with the silk mauve colored tunic Crystal has chosen to were tonight and make her look like a magazine cover!

Crystal has come a long way since she first sat down at the piano in the empty piano bar in the a.m. a year ago. Her playing has improved with her sense of relaxing on stage. Her stage presents is almost automated with audience participation and her feminine appeal greatly enhanced by the clothing she now wears and the care with her hair. The changes didn't happen over night, but with each change a professional entertainer was born. She is a self made crowd pleaser and deserving of every compliment or applause that is awarded her. Mr. Brentwhistle often just stands in the back of the room in the shadows and admires the confidence that ripples off of Crystal and her performance. She never needs to know that it was his doing getting her the opportunity to play in Las Vegas. He knows she will be outstanding! But tonight he stands too close to the door and one emergency light gives him up as Crystal looks his was and spots him. She has a page get him a message that she needs to talk with him at break. It's only two songs away, so his staying is not a hardship at all, but rather a pleasure. He meets her back stage in a dressing room and she's all excited to tell him that they've, that Vincent, has been transferred to Colts Neck, New Jersey. In unison they both say "Atlantic City" and hug and dance around the room. When is the move Brentwhistle asks when they finally sit and catch their breathe. Then Crystal fills him in on the time line and the fact that she is stopping there on her way back to Maryland on Monday. "There's no grass growing under your feet, is there young lady?" Brentwhistle declares with her news. "Nope, and I plan on staying in that area until I find something. Not just something, but something really nice." Her facial expression and animated hand gestures told the whole story. Excitement overload! "Good for you, if you need to, you can use this job and me as a reference. Sometimes landlords don't like to rent to military personnel for fear of you leaving. So use this job as stability. Try to also use Atlantic City, show that this apartment is the greatest because it's in the middle. I know you can talk it up to your best advantage." Crystal just looked at him with amazement. "Better still he continued, stop by my office on Monday morning before you leave, I'll have something for you." Crystal could barely get, What??? Thank you, off her lips and Brentwhistle was out the door. The second half of her show was lively and very entertaining being lead by her excitement.

When her show was over she was still feeling the effects of the excitement and the additional adrenaline, so she proceeded to do something she rarely does. She barely ever looks in the mirror to see how 'Crystal' looks. She looks for color matching or hair styles, or make-up differences, but barely ever to judge 'her' appearance, But tonight after her show. She looked. She wanted to make sure she looked like a bomb shell about to explode. The hair was perfect, but she added a little make-up here and there, lost the printed scarf around her low neck line and added a simple gold chain that was lost between her boobs. Checked her front and profile to make sure she looked as great as she felt! She was off to the 40th floor to have a rum-coke and listen to some music. She was either going to apologize or get slapped back. She just wanted to make sure she looked her best either way.

She heard the music on her approach to the doorway, where she was stopped as an unescorted woman. Then she was recognized and allowed to enter. She made her way to the bar, turning every head in the place. It was late, she new she looked good so she ate up the attention. She sat, crossed her long legs, ordered her drink, and noticed Mr. Beautiful looking her way and nodding in appreciation. *By god Crystal what are you doing? Just what I intended to do. I've been married for more than two years and I haven't teased like this since high school. This is fun...I don't need to tease Vincent any more, he bulges just thinking about going after my gold chain.* So she sat there nursing her drink playing with the chain around her neck letting it slip in and out...in and out of sight. The music was really good, very good in fact. She understood why they were performing on the 40th floor in an elite dinning room getting the prices charged for the drinks and meals. Lost in her own thoughts, she didn't notice when the music stopped and he was sitting next to her at the bar. Not until her glass was disappearing and a fresh drink was deposited in front of her.

"I love the chain you're wearing around your neck, it catches the light and sparkles like your hair." Tonight she had gold drops here and there in her hair-do. "You made quite an entrance when you came in,... all alone" he continued, Crystal still hadn't said a word. "Are you alone?" Now Crystal said "No, married". With a little chuckle he counted with "That doesn't matter to me." Crystal still didn't say anything else, just titled her head a little and continued to look at him. "You have a mysterious way about you Crystal Clear. That husky, robust voice rather fits you." Crystal took a slow sip of her drink and asked "How do you know my name?" "Well, my ears are always tuned in to the good music. Awhile back I heard a music-box song coming out of a door way and peeked in. There I saw an angel with golden white hair wrapped in a golden gown accented with a light blue shawl, belt and slippers playing the piano and swaying to her own music. The spell you wove around me was broken only when the music stopped. The marquee at the door announced Crystal Clear, performing etc....."

"I had a music box with that song in it when I was a little girl. That's when I started practicing the melody on the piano in our living room." "too much information Crystal Clear, I just wanted to dance with you" as he lead her on to the dance floor. Crystal didn't even realize the band was still playing, playing without him. He had his arm around her in a very intimate way and his head bent down just a bit to kiss the lower part of her neck, two more kisses up her neck to her ear where he said, this is heaven, we fit together so well. She couldn't resist, she reached down to take his other hand in hers and stretched their arms out length wise. She then started playing with his fingers, folding each one into her hand and then pulled his hand in close to her heart. He backed away from her a bit just to say, "I know what you're thinking." She pulled him closer to whisper in his ear and reciprocated with "extraordinary, I love being tall, I'm deep enough for you to lose every... throbbing... inch.!" While the music was still playing she stepped away from him and walked out of the door. That was the only thing she did with decorum! Once she was away from him she ran to the elevators half laughing and half crying. She had worked herself up to quite the state of feeling alone and very, very horny!

Down in her own room, she needed to be alone...It's a good thing he didn't follow her, there was only 'A' door between them, all other barriers would have been stripped away easily. The cool, cold shower did work wonders. She had always heard that, now she knew for sure. After spending a rather restless night, Crystal left the hotel and walked in the delightful summer morning air to an outside cafe for her first cup of coffee. It was a cheerful place, a bit crowded, but the murmur of conversation was acceptable. Here she let her mind wonder..she let the what if's take over.

What if, he knows my name, I never got his. He doesn't care that I'm married...what does that say about him! I'm thinking this way...what does that say about me? What I did last night...such a tease...I did it on purpose...I was looking for it, then I ran away from it. I fixed my face,

I wore that necklace...I kept that cowl neck blouse on, barely on. I went looking for him. One more night, I wish I could go home now.. damn I don't have a piano I can go and beat on...I wonder if his band has a name? I'm going to buy a bathing suit and use the pool.

The walk did her good. Two stores later she had two bathing suits. She paid the New York prices, but what the hell. When in Rome..... Walking back to the hotel she was thinking, cursing herself... *I can't wear that black one here, too many people know me, damn, that's for Vincent's eyes only.* In her head she knew the little black piece wouldn't do...so that's why the green and yellow one was her second purchase. Once back at the hotel, she changed into the cute green suit with the one large yellow flower covering her left boob and it's stem running from the flower down to the hem at her right leg. Her mother would have been so proud! Now the pool beckons.

She skipped lunch and went straight to the hot tub adjacent to the pool, lounged there a bit then ordered a drink. With her body totally relaxed and her mind a little numbed by the drink and the effect of the hot water, her libido was acting up on her again. She reached up with one hand and let her hair down. For a blond or rather a woman with such light hair you'd not picture it as thick and heavy as it is. Next she sat up a little straighter, that allowed her to untie her straps and drop the suit into the water. When she stood up to leave the only thing you saw was the mane of hair half covering one breast and a large, hairy, pale 'v' just above her long legs. The rest of her hair touched the crack of her ass down her back as she walked away. The other people in the pool area had never seen her before and were too shocked at her total inhibition to walking around naked to either stop her or go after her. Her towel and bathing suit were left behind as she walked out of the pool area toward the elevators. Having arrived on the 31st floor with no identification, no room key and no clothes would have presented quite the problem had housekeeping not been currently in her room doing their daily clean-up. Without a care in the world or thought about her nakedness, Crystal acknowledged the two women cleaning in the bathroom and went to bed. Alice, the day manager of the housekeeping crew was alerted to Crystals odd behavior and she, out of concern for Crystal, reported it to personnel downstairs because she knew of Crystal's piano job with Mr. Brentwhistle. Alice said to her girls, "You see all kinds in here!"

Within minutes Mr. Brentwhistle was at Crystal's bed side waking her. "How much did you have to drink and when was the last time you ate?" Crystal sat with a start and her bed sheets dropped to her waist. Brentwhistle just looked at her (with lust, he is a man afterall). Half rubbing her eyes and then piling her hair on top of her head with both of her hands, with her arms lifted above her head... she just looked at Brentwhistle (from this height and angel, she could surely see the erection growing in his pants) and asked, "What time is it....?" in panic she started to pushed the sheets away and started to get out of bed, totally naked, thinking she was late for her show. *That's why Brentwhistle was here and showing irritation with me, she thought.* He firmly but carefully placed his hands on her shoulders and made her sit on the bed and re-cover her naked body. They both took a deep breathe to start over. Crystal was the first to speak and asked, "what time is it?" Mr. Brentwhistle calmly explained that it was Sunday afternoon about 1:30 and again asked "what and when did you eat last?" Crystal's poor head was so tied, she just wanted to sleep, so she lied. "Coffee and a bagel with cream cheese at a diner this morning. Then I went swimming...no, the hot tub at the pool, had one Rum-coke, can I sleep now?" She laid back down and was fast to sleep, but not before she heard him say he'd be back at 5pm to wake her and he'd bring supper. The room was dark and quiet and this time she slept good.

Her body felt so good, warm and languid after soaking in the hot tub, wrapped in loving arms so big his hands could rest just at the top of her rounded buttocks. The fingers of those hands were lightly scratching and pinching her skin, that's how she knew where they were. His warm breath was activating her tender nipples into raised, reaching peeks just begging to be sucked, so he did. Her inner thighs were also reacting and so she reached down and started tweaking the little nub at the opening of her vagina. With all tender spots getting attention, she was starting to react with batted breathe, arching her back, biting on the pillow and thrashing endlessly! Not wanting the sensations to stop, but still wishing they would, she reactivated the feelings by inserting two fingers into her vagina and continued teasing and rubbing and cupping then screaming and letting go and stopped. She opened her eyes and Vincent wasn't there. There was no man holding her or touching her, she was sweaty and spent. She laid there another minute to regroup and wake-up. It was 4:30 on Sunday afternoon, she had barely enough time to shower before Mr. Brentwhistle would be by with supper, she remembered that much.

Crystal sat there in jeans and a t-shirt with her hair, soaking wet hanging down her back eating a soup and sandwich supper with Mr. Brentwhistle. After thanking him a hundred times for supper and his concern and trying to convenience him that she was all right, Brentwhistle caved and wished her a good show, kissed her on the forehead and left her room. What the hell happened to me this afternoon? She wondered. I never drink in the afternoon, particularly on a work day...what the hell? I wish I weren't working tonight...but on the other hand, I guess I need to...I could really get into trouble with nothing else to do. I'd probably end up on the 40th floor again...is that who was holding and touching me in my sleep? At that she hastily grabbed a dark blue ensemble for tonight and headed down to Sharon so she could do her hair. Crystal was sitting in Sharon's chair with damp hair and no makeup, so the girls in the salon had a blank canvas to work with. Somehow Crystal didn't care, she was still feeling...out of sorts. The girls looked in the bag she carried in so they knew the tunic top zipped up the back...will not muss the hair. They knew the color pallet for her makeup and they knew how much time they had. Easy, when you begin with beauty, it's easy to make it shine. First things first...she needed to loose the t-shit, again not to muss the final hair do. So with it lost, they wrapped her in a salon robe and got to work. Actually it was like a party...Two other chairs were occupied for comb-outs and facials and no one felt over-worked. There was a radio playing the top songs of the day...Crystal was swaying to the music until...this one...what is this song, I've never heard it...Rum and Coca-Cola...I like it...it could be my song, it brought on giggles, but no one paid her much mind. Crystal had a knack for being able to hear a song once and put it to memory and play it on the piano. All of her songs were self taught, except the one...she wrote it! Some day, yes some day they'll be playing it on the radio as well.

Finally done, Sharon had worked miracles again. Crystal's hair was high atop her head all woven with royal blue ribbons the color of her dress for the evening. Her makeup was flawless and she felt glamorous as she left the salon and took her time getting to Crystal's Piano Showcase. Once she sat and started exercising her fingers with a simple tune she broke into her song with all of her might and finesse. That's what carried her mood for the first half of her show. It was fast paced, loud and exuberant. Tonight it's what her audience wanted and they showed her with applause and song requests. During her break she read the song requests and almost died...there it was, for the first time... Chattanooga Choo Choo...no she couldn't do it, wouldn't do it...forget it! Once back on her piano bench she acknowledged everyone kindness in the first half of her show and hoped to please as well in the second. She started with Boogie Woogie Bugle Boy and that became a sing-a-long and the party continued until her last selection where she invited everyone to crowd the dance floor and enjoy Sentimental Journey. She played the melody at least three times to give everyone their money's worth. When she finally closed the key lid and took a deep breathe, Mr. Beautiful slid beside her and congratulated her on being an excellent entertainer. She felt good, she felt satisfied that she delivered a good and enjoyable show. So her demeanor to her visitor was forward, almost inviting and cheerful. She turned in her seat, looked him in the eyes, smiled beautifully and stated a fact. "I need to at least know your name so I can greet you properly or (and she titled her head suggestively and widened her eyes) throw you the hell of my stage." He smiled just as suggestively, offered his hand in friendship and announced, "I am Johnathan Whelton, I hail from Detroit, Michigan, I am the violin player in our band called 'The Midnight Men'. Still holding his hand she admitted that she really enjoyed their music and hoped to catch their show again. He reached and held her other hand and asked her to keep talking because he loved the sound of her voice. He laughed and said she sounded like a troubled frog who couldn't clear her throat!

"I'm holding both of your hands so you don't hit me for that remark, but that's what I thought of when you started talking. I'd know your voice anywhere!" She let her head fall a bit so he wouldn't see her wide grim and a hair pin fell out. She lifted her head and a lone strand of hair was falling across her face. He let go of one hand, reached up and removed two, three, four more pins and her hair cascaded down to her shoulders and then down her back. With both of his hands he pushed what had fallen in her face aside and kissed her lips. "Married woman kiss the best" he whispered and left her sitting there alone as he walked out of the door.

Not at all surprised by Mr. Whelton's behavior, Crystal sat there another moment questioning her behavior and reaction to his kiss. *OK, I'm wet! It's not OK, she thought. I should be outraged! I'm married, is that a turn on for him? Is he married? How old is he? How tall is he? Are all men circumcised? Where did that come from? How different does it look if not? I wonder if it feels different? It must feel different, there is an additional 'slide', I bet!* Without even knowing it Crystal was at her door to room 3108. She let herself in and went directly into the bath room to look at herself in the mirror. *Yup, it's me...What am I turning into?* She let her clothing fall to the floor, gave her hair a quick brushing and let it fall naturally. Next she slipped into a pencil tight green skirt, ribbed black sweater, black slippers and went directly up to the 40th floor. Their show still had more than an hour to go. With a rum coke in her her hand, she turned her back to the bar, crossed her ankles and enjoyed the show. After a little discussion on stage the next song was 'Rum and Coca-Cola' and she got a knowing nod from the violin player. *How can just a look and a song do that?* Her panties were wet! She drank down her drink and returned to her room immediately.

Chapter 25

The next morning she had her wardrobe ready for the laundry and her travel clothes packed and ready to go. She'd take the bus to the train station, but this time her train ride was to Colts Neck, New Jersey. She was ready for a new adventure and to be alone. She needed to clear her head and not let Mr. Whelton take up any more room in it. It was time to plan her and Vincent's future and find a suitable and comfortable place to live. She went directly to the Colts Neck Navy base and asked directions to the Operations Center. She was informed by a very nice, very young petty officer that there wasn't 'one' Operations Center, but rather a Squad Room for each Division, "so where would you like to go?" he asked with a smile! She realized that she wasn't quite over her mood of last night, because she wanted to wipe that shit eating smile off of his face! So...she'd play...with her froggy voice low..."honey, what time do you get off, I can help you with that, (she smiled) by going any where you want to go." She walked past him to the PX and went directly to the information counter. The first piece of information she needed was where to find lockers for rent to stow her valise until further notice, not too long she hoped. That done, she got a map of down town, a local newspaper, a bus schedule then she bought a meat sandwich wrapped in white paper. Next she walked out to the flag pole in the center of the grassy yard that was surrounded by park benches. There she ate her lunch which was on the better side of good which was a pleasant surprise and read the for rent listings and checked the addresses against the map. After checking off three apartments in what looked like a close proximity to one another, she checked the bus schedule and was in luck. A ten minute walk back out to the main gate to the bus stop and then a bus would be expected 10 minutes later. So far so good. She also needed to find a hotel for the next few days, also in the same areas of the apartments or bus line.

Once on the bus, she knew she needed the Hampton Square stop, the driver told her about 10 minutes and he'd let her know. The further they got away from base the prettier the area got. Narrower streets, and more grass. They just pasted a hotel...she'll look better on the way back. Damn this bus makes more stops than..."Miss, Hampton next stop". Off the bus she looked around and rather liked what she saw. Many Large white houses. They looked to have at least three floors and many more rooms than just a single home. They all had a centered front door with six to eight windows on each side of it on the first floor. She was looking for 61 Hampton Square. Right here, the second white house. She went to the front door to learn it was an entry door to a 12 unit apartment house. She met the manager and was shown to a 4 room apartment on the second floor. She learned that it was formerly a boarding house for men only, returning from the war with no where else to go. With government funds the men were moved and housed elsewhere and these three dwelling were remodeled into apartments. Nice little place with a great view, but not for her. She asked for directions to Shelby Street where she hoped to find an apartment more to her liking.

Within walking distance, she took a left at the end of Hampton and Shelby was diagonally across the street from there. A pleasant walk brought her right to the end of the driveway of 637 Shelby. Wow, a long driveway leading to glorious white and brick, old colony house that mirrors some of the southern plantation houses. *Maybe the apartment manager lives here and this is the first stop, lets see.* Crystal walked up to the front door and was greeted by an elderly woman who had a terrible stoup, beautifully braided long salt and pepper blackish hair and youthful looking hands. When she open the door Crystal said "Hi, I'm Crystal and I'm inquiring about the apartment for rent." The woman said, "my aren't you a tall one, please step back I want to look at you." as she lifted a cane, pointed it toward Crystal in a way of making her back up. Next she beckoned Crystal inside and she closed the door. As first glance Crystal saw very shinny hardwood floors, braided rugs, and crisp clean white curtains in every window. "Your house takes my breath away" Crystal said to the woman as she was pointing with her cane to a coach for Crystal to sit. "Where do you hail from and why do you need an apartment? Is it just you or is there a husband and kids?" Crystal half laughed and answered "just me". The woman offered Crystal a drink of water or anything because her voice sounded so hoarse. Again Crystal laughed slightly and said "no thanks, that's just me." By now the older woman was sitting down and looked a little straighter in this position. She was a very attractive older woman and seamed as sharp as a tack. Crystal started again explaining that she was a military wife with a couple of side jobs and she traveled a bit for one of the jobs. She said how her husband would be stationed out of Colts Neck within the next 3 weeks that's why they were looking for an apartment. So you understand, being military, he could be deployed and gone for weeks at a time, so there again, no there are no kids. "Young folks like you should have kids, but because you don't let me tell you about the apartment.

'I'm so tied of having to sit down here in the front window and watch who ever walks to my front door. I've had quite of few inquiries into the rental ad, but no one I felt I could live with. At this Crystal's ears perked up, but she just let the woman talk, I'd much rather be up stairs in my own rooms and not have to bother with the stairs. It's not an apartment, it's this whole house that's for rent, minus of course my rooms on the back of the house upstairs." Crystal's mouth went dry, but managed, "you mean we'd be living with you, in this furnished house, but the ad said includes all utilities and is renting cheaply." "That's right, you live here, you entertain here, you make it your home. I have a cleaning service that comes in twice a month, washes floors, cleans bathrooms, dusts, changes my bed, washes windows, I certainly can't do those things. So you provide food, some laundry services for me and no pets." "I don't even know your name," Crystal said to her and "you are willing to have us, strangers living in your house?" The woman just stared at Crystal like she was waiting for more. Crystal continued with, "I go to New York about every other weekend for one job, I hope to have a part time job on base and I hope to be able to book a couple of shows in Atlantic City, I honestly don't know how much time I'll be spending here."...long pause... "And just what kind of a SHOW do you do in New York...I'll not have any riff-raft under my roof!" By now the older woman was sitting on the edge of her seat and those last few words were said with a shrill to her voice "OH, no, I'm sorry to miss lead you, I'm a pianist and I have my own show at the New Yorker hotel in the city and I'm hoping to be able to book some shows in Atlantic City as well." While Crystal was talking she could see the other woman starting to relax, she even dawned a slight smile, she was pretty when she smiled. "Well Crystal, my name is Elise and I want to show you something" she said while grabbing her cane and getting out of her chair. Your the first perspective tenant to see anything other than this room "Come with me this way and I'll show you around the house."

They had been sitting in the office which was a front room in the house. They left this room and went across the front hall entry to the left, slid large double wooden doors apart to reveal a large living room with a stone fireplace on the back wall, lovely couches and chairs in heavy brocade fabrics and wood set in inviting visiting arrangements, again on beautifully kept hard wood floors adorned with more braided rugs. Down the middle of the room there was a narrow table with lamps on either end and a beautiful 'Blue' Willow bowl centered with a white flower arrangement growing out of it. There were also two chairs, one on either end of the table facing the front wall which had the 'peseta-resistance' a baby grand piano and a harp. Now Elise was all smiles, like she was presenting these things to Crystal. Crystal's eyes went from Elise to the piano and her fingers were wiggling, she approached the piano, looked back at Elise and said "may I?" Elise shook her head in approval. Crystal walked to the piano and still standing played a few bars of Fleur-de-Lis and then she played a couple more.

Elise's smile widen, and her eyes became glassy, she hadn't heard anyone play that piano like that in a long time. Crystal's heart filled and her mind was busy with a million different thoughts. "I'm going to stop seeing applicants on the ad if you want to live here, but as soon as possible I'd like to meet your husband" The piano playing had made up Elise's mind. Crystal voiced her main concern… "what about the times you might be here alone, me in New York and Vincent deployed, I know you were trying to avoid the alone time." "That's very nice of you to be thinking about me, I knew I liked you, but I'll worry about that, so what do you say? Do you want to see your room?"

Crystal straighten up and walked away from the piano, not taken her eyes off of Elise. "Are you sure, I think this would be ideal for me, for us…yes, I'd love to see the rest of the house." They walked through the kitchen which was large and bright with windows on two sides, again with the crisp white curtains, and a stair case to the second floor. The dinning room which was massive and had a table that could seat 12 easily and a huge, high side board with large carved, ornate doors. Now they encountered a wide hall way which was about eighteen feet long witch had at least 4 four doorways off of it. They peeked into a bathroom, next a laundry room, across the hall a large bed room with an attached bathroom which was also accessible from the hall way. At the end of the hall was a door which opened up to a large screened-in porch which had access to the back yard and gardens. "Beautiful." said Crystal, "I could easily live here, Thank you very much." "Good, do you want to see up stairs now?" Elise was primping like a peacock at Crystal's expressions and impressions of the house. They walked back to the kitchen and went up the staircase Crystal had spotted earlier. "These first three rooms are my haven; my bedroom, sitting room and bathroom. I only need to go down stairs to eat, if I want to. The rest of up stairs is, (as the walked into a balcony area) the main staircase, many more bedrooms, and bathrooms and the library, another of my favorite rooms. As you can see there is plenty of room to entertain, have house guests or be private, we'll visit the 3rd floor another time… we are well off the road with very few neighbors. So when do you want to move in?"

"I, I, my head is reeling with everything you've just shown me and the real thought that I could actually live here, has not sunk in yet. First I need to find a hotel for the next two nights, find out about…" "No,

No… you stay here, no hotel. Sure go back to base and get your job, on your way back pick-up some cream for coffee and eggs for breakfast, that's all we'll need for the next couple of days." "Are you serious, you want me to stay here now?" Crystal's head had still not caught up yet. "Yes, of course, it's a lot cheaper than a hotel. A dozen eggs and a pint of cream, I'd say it the best deal in town, but there is a catch. I need to hear you play three of your best songs before we go to bed tonight!" "I'd say that is quite a good deal indeed, Miss Elise. I'm grateful and excited, I'd love to play that beautiful piano later today." Crystal then hugged the little lady and was starting to head out. "Wait just a minute I've got something for you." At that Elise handed Crystal a leather strap with a key on it. "Front door, dear". Crystal was now on her way to the bus stop, again.

This time she was headed back to the information desk to retrieve her personal items and inquire about the Central Operations Center or main intelligence office. Having gotten directions to the Bursa's Squad Room, she was told to start there. That office always had fires to put out or personnel to find and important messages to be delivered ASAP, it was the worse run office on base. Everyone in ear shot heard those words and started a giggle-fest! She looked around and remarked, "I think this would be a good place to work, you guys are fun." "Get to the bursa's office and see if they can use you, if not when you are permanently settled her in New Jersey, come back and talk to us, we'll get you something." So off to the Bursa's office she tried to go. Standing back at the flag pole where she ate her lunch, she got her bearings and knew it was quite a walk deeper into the base to find the bursa's office and she wondered and hoped that she could snag a ride when she saw the next jeep or truck go by. She was in luck, the jeep stopped and asked if he could be service. With a giant smile she hopped in, said thanks and asked for a ride to the bursa's office. Boy, was she happy for the ride, the building was the last one on the road, nope, she didn't want to work back here. Running messages from here to the front and back again, nope! She didn't even see anything of interest on the ride down here. A very neat base, nice grassy areas, well kept gardens, the PX, RX, mess hall and Information Center right after the main check in and then nothing to make you want to stay! *Vincent isn't going to be happy here unless there is more that didn't meet my eye. She thought* "Thanks for the ride" she said when he slowed to let her out. "I can wait for you if you's like, do you need a ride back to the main gate"? The driver made that offer when he saw the dissatisfied look on her face. "That would be great if you can give me 5, no 3 minutes to conclude my business," Crystal said as she was walking away. Once inside the Bursa's Squad Room all eyes fell on her. She talked with the first person she saw very briefly and explained she be available for any type of job they had here in about 3 weeks. Did they have civilian type duties? She was told, check back in 3 weeks, then they could talk. Two minutes and she was back in the jeep.

"Jim Davies at your service Ma'am, back to the main gate?" "Yes please" was all Crystal had to say. "You don't look very impressed by our base here Ma'am, would you like to see more, this is merely the boring side of where the paper work is held. The guts of our operation starts down the street a ways, wanna see it?" Crystal said, "sure as long as I can buy cream for my coffee along the way." "No problem, we'll take care of that on the way back, as long as you need to come back this way.' "I do actually, I need to catch the bus right at the main gate." "Alright then, be prepared to be impressed" he said, as they took a short ride straight ahead and then he took a short side road which opened up to a large area and she saw another Main gate. Once they passed through, what she saw was massive. They drove to the approach of two major roads with piers on each side which ran straight out into the ocean. They got wider as they stretched to their ends. She couldn't see the end of either of the gigantic roadways. There were ships moored along the side one of the piers and more on the other side. What a site, the air was filled with the smell of fish and oil. There were men everywhere, there were short trucks, long trucks all moving with purpose around the docks. "This is more like it," Crystal said. *A real Navy yard, I take it back, Vincent will be happy here!*

"Thanks Davies, you're right, I judged way to soon, this place looks amazing. Now that store you promised, ya think they'd have eggs too?' "Sure thing Ma'am, after that if you're not going far, I can drop you at home, that's why you need the bus, right?" Davies was now feeling proud of himself and of the Navy yard he was able to showoff. "I have the jeep signed out until 1700, so I should have plenty of time if it's rather close." "Thanks, you be the judge of that, after groceries I'm going to 637 Shelby."

Back on the road again, the store was rather close. Crystal splurged a bit and got donuts and ice cream as well as Miss Elise's cream and eggs. Back in the jeep, Davies said, "OK tell me the way." Crystal just giggled and said, "I rented there this afternoon, I don't know the way, the bus does.' Davies giggled now and merely said, "we'll find it, just watch for things that look familiar." They fell into an easy banter back and forth and Crystal's memory of things she remembered seeing from the bus was helpful. Then she remembered her little walk between rental places and arrived back at 637 Shelby in ample time for Davies to have the jeep back in time. "You rented this!" Davies voice was high with excitement at the look of this magnificent place. "Well, kinda, we'll be living in the house with the elderly woman who owns it. I pray it works out, we'll see. Thanks for the rides. My husband and I will be back in three weeks, full time, maybe we'll see you around." Crystal got out of the jeep with her luggage and store purchases, fished around for her key and went in the front door.

Miss Elise was indeed watching for Crystal's return, met her in the hall way at the front door. "Glad to see you didn't get lost, and found your way back OK". She took the shopping bag from Crystal as Crystal replied, I'm learning my way around." They both headed for the kitchen, Miss Elsie deposited her bag on the counter top and Crystal continued down to her room. Dropped her luggage on the floor and felt immediately 'at home'. *I certainly hope Vincent likes it here, I think it could work out fine as long as Miss Elise is taken care of and she likes us here. Crystal noticed the same crisp, white curtains in her windows. Charming.* Until morning when Crystal woke up to the sun shinning straight in eyes. *This must be the east side of the house, good morning sunshine, I'll have to remember that!* She showered, dressed and went to the kitchen to start breakfast. It was 6:45 and Miss Elise was sitting at the table reading the morning paper and enjoying her morning coffee.

"Thanks for getting the cream yesterday, I went two mornings without it and really missed my rich, light coffee. And thanks for entertaining me last night. You play like an angel one minute and then a woman possessed! I love the feelings you put into your music." Crystal blushed a little at the compliment, said "your welcome on both counts," helped herself to coffee and joined Miss Elsie at the table. "Did you sleep well?" Elise questioned. "Yes, very comfortable, I crashed...can't wait for Vincent to get here! So, how do you like your eggs?" Crystal asked. Miss Elise shook her head slowly, then said "No...no..no... I cook, you provide the food, but I always cook! We'll talk about it as we eat. How about French toast and sausage this morning?"

Chapter 26

It seamed as though she had just started to unpack and decide what to leave here and what to carry back to Maryland and Miss Elise was yelling ready. Crystal went back to the kitchen to find a stack of about 8 pieces of French toast on a plate and another plate full of sausage links, everything was steaming hot and smelling delectable. There were also full coffee cups at their places. "How'd you do this so fast? It looks wonderful" "Thank you, good...sit and eat and I'll explain how I'd like this to work."

Between bites Elise explained that she had been a cook, actually a chief most of her life. She started as a young girl cooking for the troupes in Kansas heading to Germany in the fall of 1918 to join in the fight of WW1, but fled that area when the Spanish influenza virus killed nearly everyone in Fort Riley. Over the next year this "Spanish Influenza" killed 20 million worldwide, so my family headed east. "I remember the move to Virginia, I was in my teens. It took months and I was scared most of the time. We stayed in VA for the next 20 years. I was married and worked there, always as a cook in some of the finest homes and even in the Governors mansion of Arlington. My husband, also a military man moved us to the New Jersey Army base of Fort Monmouth in Monmouth, NJ, very close to here, next town over, but he was shipped out almost immediately and I never saw him again. He died in 1943 in Germany. But I stayed on and cooked in some of the finest restaurants in this area. As a matter of fact as little as a year and half ago I was cooking for the governor in his summer home of Surf City. So you see, I cook! So, when you and your husband are living here, it would be helpful for you to put you dinner requests on a calendar also marking the days you won't be here. After you shop I'll put everything away, that way I'll know your requests are covered and I'll make a list of my own as well".

Crystal said, "you're amazing, when did you buy this house?" "Oh, that's a great story too. In my circle of friends and cooking colleges, I met the governor and his wife and his sister. Us three women became fast friends and co-conspirators. There was a death benefit when Charlie, my husband, died and Mary, the governor's sister was married to a big-shot lawyer and Penny, the governors wife was always on the look-out for the next best thing! So one sunny afternoon the three of us were looking at houses for sale or empty houses or come right down to it...something for me. Since Charlie died I was no longer 'military' and lost my allotment rights and the apartment because the benefit was being held up because of the war. We pasted this house, it needed work, but I loved it! For the next week, for the next several weeks I walked by this house every day. I had already sent my note of interest to the posted name on the front door and heard nothing. That's where the lawyer and the governor come in. Penny is brow beating her husband to do something to help me. He's the governor, she told him to push his weight around. He called his brother-in-law, Mary's husband to make a final offer on the house and enclose a deposit of goodwill. This offer was made with decreasing amounts of money being offered for each week that went by with no response. This little clause was missed or ignored when Harkness Realty finally responded with an acceptance of our offer. Their acceptance was returned with a friendly note 14 weeks after the offer letter was sent, still listing the original price. The deposit check having been cashed and the wording in the original offer being lawful and ambiguous and so-on-and-so-forth, the sale needed to go through at my offer minus $1400, the 14 weeks of waiting. So I used the $1400 on repairs and cleaning and I had enough to buy most of the contents of the house. It was definitely my gain, their loss! And I love it!

Crystal just sat there and listened, the account of Elise's story was fascinating. She was a very interesting woman. "OK, yes, you can cook, we'll buy the food, and now we need to know how much is the rent?"

After cleaning the kitchen and unpacking as much as she dared. Crystal bid farewell to Elise for now, she had a train to catch back to Maryland. Her head was spinning all the way home, dying to see Vincent but excited to get back to New Jersey and that house and piano. Living there is a steal… *how can she cover her expenses and property taxes on that little rent? That's my military allotment amount. That's our gain until she smartens up! But that's what she had charged her last people, that's was her advertised amount. I don't get it.*

This train ride was shorter, from New Jersey, she still had most of the afternoon and all evening to tell Vincent all about her adventure, because that is what is was. And she still had money in her pocket because Elise wouldn't take a rental deposit or the first months rent. "Pay it when you get here." Elise said. *Yes, fascinating woman.* Crystal went straight home to find the apartment empty. No sign of him at all. No cooking left-overs or any garbage. The bathroom sink and tub areas were dry, not showing any sign of use. *So much for getting home a day early she thought. OK use the time wisely. What stays and what gets ready to move?* She moved around the bedroom methodically and packed her things for next weekend in a New York pile, then started the New Jersey piles. Her bureau draws were empty, next the closet. Oh boy, one step at a time. By the time her stomach was telling her she was done, she needed to eat, and damn, it's after 7pm and Vincent isn't home. The surprise was on her, she was going to be alone tonight. She made herself a grilled ham and cheese sandwich, downed that with a rum coke and sat at the piano. Her own song always made her feel good. Maybe some day some words will come to her, because right now she only had Vincent's; <u>a moon lit sky above snow covered mountain peaks, a peaceful and serene place where lovers did not need to speak.</u> It can't get better than that!

I can't make believe I'm not disappointed Vincent's not home, or coming home, I didn't pack one little item yet...it's late, I need...need...just go get it before it gets any later. Mr. Purple was right where she had left it, Vincent need never know about his rival!

Chapter 27

The next morning, Monday morning, Crystal was back at the Operations Center, she'd told everyone to expect her Tuesday because of her trip to New jersey, but because of the great luck with the rental she was back a day early. That's probably why there was little- to- nothing for her to do...one message on her board. *Great I can visit with Reginald, oh heck, Keith too, then go find Vincent. No, get your work done first dummy!!* So she grabbed the message and headed out the door. She read the building number and smiled, now expecting to see Vincent in her travels, as it was his building she was going to. This put an extra bounce in her step, but when she got there she was confused, and again disappointed that Vincent hadn't logged in yet and wasn't expected. She found out that Friday afternoon before he left, he put in for two days to accompany his wife to New Jersey... he had the time coming so why not. Except! ... He wasn't with her in new Jersey...Where was he? She didn't want to see anyone, she didn't want anyone to question her about New Jersey because if she's here... where is Vincent? Weird, but now she was uncomfortable. *OK girl.. go check on your other two boys and get out of here.* Crystal hurried back to The Operations Center, plastered on a smile and made like there was nothing on her mind. She just nonchalantly got down to her own business. Again she smiled, Keith was just fine, accumulating money left and right...just as she had planned. Reginald...?impossible...how could he make withdraws...shit...what's going on?? Feeling guilty and sick to her stomach, she needed to get out of there fast. All the way home she was thinking.....*who found out about Reginald...how could they get into his account...stupid...I've got to check our own accounts linked with his! I should have never done that...I'll get caught for sure...Am I caught?...Oh Shit!!...Vincent is going to kill me...sorry love...where are you? Does Vincent know...Vincent, you lied, where are you.*

Two more hours before Vincent is excepted home. Do something...go play the piano, start supper...Miss Elise I sure could use you now...pack some more. Humming her song she opened Vincent's underwear draw, looked and decided no, three weeks until the move, he'd need these. Next draw, jeans, keep one pair out...pack 'em. Next, casual T-shirts, again keep one out...pack 'em. His shoes, confused, she was looking at one dress pair, only one pair of sneakers and no boots...what the hell? Her stomach wasn't much better, and now she was building a headache. After having such a delightful time in New Jersey, this homecoming was really a let down. Now rather than sitting on the edge of the bed, she laid down to rest her acing head.

She loved dreams like this. Strong, warm hands sliding up her shirt and fingers circling her nipples and cupping her breasts. The feeling of a man, a very tall man spooning her and pressing his bulge into her pelvic area. Not just pressing, but pulsing ever so suggestively. This is wonderful. He has three hands, one is now sliding down over my hip... oh yes, keep going...Mr. purple is no substitute for this. Keep going... right there. There's a slide, oh yes. One, two three fingers, slide right on in..right on down...OMG. Crystal woke up with a start! Vincent was spooning her and tantalizing her breasts. She turned to face him and knew she needed more. He knew it too.

Without a word they were stripping each other between kisses and touches and getting ready to, but not ready to yet. Shoes had to come off...he managed while watching Crystal's hands undoing the tie that was in her hair...hair now down, shoes now off...they just looked, reached---touched at arms length. Still not one word, just eyes locked on one another and hands traveling at will. They could both feel it..the sensation of lust, want, need, lack of self control, self depredation. They could read it in each others eyes, tilt of the head, tongue crossing their lips. One step forward...he moved her hair off of her breasts. She rubbed her wet figure across his lips. Control gone. Instant, mutual organism with him inserted so deep she thought she'd died and gone to heaven! "Only you, you are the only one that can do that to me," she groaned without letting him withdraw. "I'm glad" he whispered back. "We may not have been each others first, but we sure are special together," he continued on the same whispered breath. The way she was holding him, there was no way he could withdraw, he didn't want to anyway, the kiss said it all. First her tongue then his tongue and then the stirring started again as his penis began to revisit it's location and come to life again. This marathon was just what Crystal needed. All thoughts of Reginald or New Jersey were pushed so far away, Vincent filled her in every way! This seemed to be their natural diet, it always seamed to happen at supper time! So once again they were eating omelets at midnight. The hunger appetite satisfied and the sexual appetite satiated they agreed 6:30am showers were right around the corner, so back to bed they went. He never should have kissed her goodnight...not satiated at all...round two had just begun. She was more than happy to take her favorite seat when he was around. Straddling his form, legs beneath her carrying most of her weight but having his penis straight up into her vagina as high as he could make it grow...go! Before they knew it it was 2am, and dark, and tied and sleepy. Work in the morning, which was to soon to fathom! They agreed, at 6:30am that she could go first in the shower, it took longer to do her long hair. Agreed, but not for his penis, it knew the way and it followed her straight into the shower. This meant great sex and lots of it...but no breakfast, today they didn't care! 8am...On base, him in uniform, Crystal starring at her board, hoping there were NO messages!...She was wrong, it didn't pay to take a day off! There were plenty. Before she left the building, she checked Reginald again. She must be seeing things, 3 withdraws. She checked their holdings, all of them. One withdrawal from their joint account funded by way of the Reginald accounts. She took a deep breathe and needed to remember to talk to Vincent before jumping to the nerve-jumping, worry-sum conclusions that had her nearly sick yesterday. Thank goodness for Vincent ... and her dream...her panties were wet ... Get a-hold girl... She maintained her decorum for the rest of her day on base and enjoyed talking to and saying good-bye to nearly everyone she encountered.

This weekend she was away to New York and then the move was on! *Could she bring Vincent with her…OMG…what he did to her…sometimes Mr. Purple just wasn't enough!* She'd ask Vincent if he was available this weekend. Please come with me to New York. I need to work 8 hours in the 48 I'm away…just think of those 40 hours and what we could do… She'd make the plea and see what happens.

On the whole, the week was long…Crystal had other things on her mind. Finally Thursday night… Once she got home and started packing for the weekend, her weekends started Friday mornings when she left the house to catch the train. Finally Thursday night she planned a pot roast, potato, and carrot supper. One pot in the oven, juicy and delicious. She should have known better…Vincent knew she was leaving in the morning, but not without him all over her! So he was… all over her…in the living room when he got home…in the kitchen when she bent over to check the meat in the oven and finally in their bed…together, warm and cozy. This had to last her the long weekend, so she enjoyed and encouraged, and handled him with kit gloves to make him feel loved and cherished. Come Monday night when she was home…they could, no they would want to do it all again. Not bad, they had supper around 9pm.

With Crystal on her way to New York, Vincent had the weekend again to go 'home' to Rhonda. This was working out so well for Vincent. He could be supportive of Crystal's dreams and her being away to New York and even Las Vegas; that would be nearly two weeks. He'd really be able to enjoy Rhonda at that time. No time table or fear of being found out! Maybe he could encourage her to stay longer, visit with the folks, do some site seeing. He'd work on that when she got home next week. Right now he needed to get to base and be a good do-be! Rhonda was 5pm tonight until sometime on Sunday. She was a sweetie, all ready for him and giving him something no other woman ever had. He was looking forward to having her plump, pink lips curled around his penis and trying to swallow his length. It was a feeling that was indescribable, and he wanted it again! *Go to work fool, be good until you have to be 'better'...what a life...*

While riding on the train, Crystal was thinking about the train ride she had with Vincent up to his Grandmothers. She really should not have been thinking those thoughts...last night with Vincent was still very much in her mind and in her pants! He always got her wet! That train ride was reckless, tricky, rated 'R', showy in all right right places and damn near unforgettable! Like now, she was seeing it again in color and with a lot of feeling! Her train rides between New Jersey and New York will be shorter and maybe not as treacherous. *He's quite the man!* Finally in New York, she'd be busy and that would keep her mind off of 'him'. Once she checked in, her room 3108, there was a message for her to check in with Mr. Brentwhistle. He had good news for her. Las Vegas was in five weeks. She flew down to his office and wanted all the details, she was over the top excited. OK, Las Vegas at the Eldorado Club, a new hotel on Main Street. You'd be their first performer. A two week contract for Friday, Saturday and Sunday night shows 8pm till 1am with a 20 minute intermission. This was a renewable contract as long as the show pulled 75% admission seats, every 6 weeks with a 10% raise in fee or until renegotiated. Her head was spinning. She thinks she knows what all that means, but contracts were new to her. She needed to get through this weekend, then home to Vincent to discuss all this. Then they'd be moving their home base in two weeks, then Las Vegas two weeks after that!! That was a lot. Brentwhistle was beside himself with pride for her and smugness for himself in helping to pull this off! She was speechless and a bit nervous. Yes, she wanted this, but she also knew how Vincent was going to take this...*One day at a time...just get through this weekend, then tackle Vincent. Fuck his brain out until he agrees that this is good for me! He's a good fucker, I'll enjoy it!.. oh boy, here I go again..go find a piano!!*

Friday afternoon 1pm, up to the 40th floor she went...she had at least 2 1/2 hours to use the piano...Why did it seem like ages since she had sat on a piano bench, touched the piano keys, made her kind of music...packing, her piano, what is she going to do with it...she doesn't need it at the house in New Jersey, but the Navy will move it for free...that's worth a lot...be still my heart...so much to do. All this time talking to herself she was playing her song. When the song was finished, she had an audience. Johnathan had been standing there just listening and trying to place the tune...he couldn't. His giant smile and soft applause caused Crystal's heart to skip a beat. Was it him or his attention to her music that had that affect on her. She didn't want to examine the question to deeply. She smiled back at him and started another song. He took the smile as an invitation and joined her on the bench...she continued to play, a simple song that was soft and sweet. He knew that her attention was more on him than her music just now, therefore he knew he could start a conversation, or at least tell her what was on his mind. "I've been up here every day about this time wondering when you were coming back, I've missed you." She never missed a beat. He knew this song, so he went down an octave and with his right hand starting playing along side of her. Her smile grew even larger and wider, it made her ten times prettier and even more appealing. "What was the tune you were playing when I walked in" he asked, still playing beside her. She brought the song to an abrupt end and had to still his hand. That made contact, skin on skin. That made her hot. He felt it too. "I didn't know you could play the piano too" she remarked as she was turning on the bench to face him. (Big mistake!) "I can dabble on the piano, but don't play well. I dabble with a lot of things and strive to excel in a few, for instance" and he leaned closer and kissed her. Just a touching of their lips, but she didn't move so he deepened the kiss. He lingered and tasted her tongue and waited, then prodded just a bit until she relented and leaned toward him and returned the kiss with interest. With his mouth still on hers he needed clarification of a statement she made during their first dance. "Do you really think that you could bury every throbbing inch? I've not met a woman yet that could. You so intrigue me and I've been dreaming of that sensation ever since!" Just him saying the words, so close to her, made her panties wet, she was hot. He'd fill her alright, she knew it. Right now she needed Vincent. Neither one of them had made a move. They were still glued at the lips, hands holding tight to the edges of the piano seat, their upper bodies just barely touching, having learned into one another. "I'm 13 years old again, I can't move and I certainly can't stand up. I'm in agony. That's what you do to me. Such sweet agony!" he half whispered and 100% groaned all of this while leaning away from their kiss. "I'm a fully grown woman and I can't be in the same room with you without wondering the same thing. I knew I shouldn't have come up here, but I also knew why I did and what I wanted. She started to reach for her room key on the top of the piano and he mistook the movement to be something more personally intimate, so he capitalized on it and reached for her as well. This culminated in an embrace and kiss that rocked his world. She was sucking his tongue and had it as far down her throat as she could. The swallowing effect he felt on his tongue was...and she was doing that at the same time as holding him securely to her body with one arm while holding the side of his face to hers with the other hand and letting her fingers stroke rhythmically with the sucking of his tongue. "That's only a preview of the feeling of complete absorption!" she claimed when she released the hold she had on him. And holding him she was. She needed to feel the bodily connection he was perpetuating, so yes, she was going for her room key! The sound of her throaty voice, so warm and moist so near to his ear had the same effect on him as the hold she currently had on his face. He was soaring, she brought him to such heights as he had never experienced before. She did this in such a short time, he knew he had to had her. But when she opened her eyes and looked at the face she had been stroking and the lips that had kissed her silly, a feeling of almost...loss filled her. *I can't do this, I'm married, I can't lose Vincent by doing what I'm driving myself to doing right now. OMG this man feels so good...it's wrong, it's forbidden, it's here for the taking, Vincent would never know. He'd never forgive me.* At her sudden stiffness he knew...his heart fell to the floor as he released his arms from around her. He leaned back a bit, rested both his forearms on her shoulders and looked into her eyes. He saw the distance very clearly. "I can never see you again, I can never put either one of us through this again. I have a longing and I hurt very much and I am so very sorry for hurting you." These were her parting words, but as she was speaking he pulled his arms away and wiped a tear running down her cheek! He watched her leave the room without looking back. She was gone. Now he tried to breathe again.

Once out in the hallway she made a mad dash for the elevators, let the tears roll out of her eyes silently until she reached her room where she sobbed openly into the pillows on her bed for a good long time. Now she was asking herself why she was crying, she was playing a stupid game, one she let go too far, what did she expect. She wasn't 17 years old and playing with men at the beach. She was a married woman of 23 and she had the man of her dreams, he was just out of reach right now. She was starting to realize that she did this with her piano and her dreams that didn't include him. She had a show to do in one hour then she was telling Mr. Brentwhistle she was heading home and begging off of her show for tomorrow night. She was ill, down right sick and she needed get to the bottom of it! At what had become his habit, Brentwhistle stopped into her show at intermission and noticed the pale ash color of her cheeks. Not the rosy, happy look he was expecting. He accepted her skipping out for home in the morning and wished her well. Get better and we'll talk about Las Vegas after your move to New Jersey. He thanked her for finishing her set tonight, told her to sleep well, travel safely tomorrow, kissed her on the forehead and left. It was with relief that she knew she was leaving with his blessings.

She finished her set, but for the first time it felt like work. It was something she had to do, so she did. That night in her cold lonely bed she cried some more. Morning came and she headed to the train station early to catch the first train heading out rather than the afternoon one. Sunday morning and the terminal was packed. She bought her ticket but now she needed to get down to the proper track to get on the right train. She was carrying only one small suitcase as well as her hat. It was just too dam hot and she had too much hair to keep the hat on her head! Who said women needed to wear hats anyway!

Having maneuvered through the throngs of people, she made it to her proper track and waited. The air at the tracks was stifling and smelled. Maybe she was coming down with something, this never bothered her before. It took another twenty minutes before her train came to a stop and she was allowed to board. Agitated and hot she took her seat and willed herself to relax and enjoy the ride home. Home to where she was going to physically ride and love her husband until he asked her to stop. She smiled, *that will never happen!* A short time later, the train was only out of the station about 10 minutes and she felt an uncomfortable sensation in the pit of her stomach and in the small of her back.

Dam it to hell, menstrual cramps! She figured it was better than the alternative. But it made for a long ride home. Her mind was working in overtime. He wanted children, she wanted to play the piano, she was young and enjoyed her life. He said a house full of kids. She was denying him his god given rights to father children, but she loved to love. He loved to touch and love too, but not now. Not while she was on her period. He'd be disappointed she wasn't pregnant. She was disappointed that they'd have the week together without loving. *I could have had love and robust sex last night, but I turned it down. Stop thinking like that...it was with the wrong man.* Oh ya, the cramps were her punishment. She couldn't even nap. It was a long ride home.

She dragged herself into their lovely Maryland apartment at 12:40, three hours ahead of schedule, of course he wasn't home. She dropped her suitcase and noticed she didn't have her hat, good riddance. From there she wandered into their bedroom and was struck with a sense of sameness. The packing piles she had made the day before were the same. Nothing had changed. The bed hadn't been disturbed, her pile of skirts still on hangers, were still lying to one side the way they had slid. This was deja vue of last weekend when he wasn't home. *Why should he be, but over-night? Forget it, don't make waves, when he gets here he'll be happy to see me.* She moved her pile of skits and laid down. She had so much to discuss with him and to tell him, why wasn't he home? But it felt good to be home regardless, and she fell asleep.

Not too much later, it was still light out, she heard a noise at the front door. She jumped up to meet him in the living room and he looked like hell. She got her bearings, looked at the clock, of course it's light out...it's summer and only 7:10 and she was sure she didn't look much better. After a quick embrace and light kiss, he said "good, you're home early. I didn't miss supper did I?, because I've eaten. What

I really need is a shower and a good nights sleep." She followed him into their bedroom and replied to him with, "well that's what you'll get because I've got my period." He stopped and hugged her again and said "are you alright, I know how achy and tired and miserable to get when you get your period." She hugged him back and felt touched by his concern. He didn't have a smug remark about her not being pregnant, that was refreshing. She broke the embrace and told him she'd been home since about noon, but fell asleep. "I'll have a bite to eat while you're in the shower" she said "Then we can have a nice evening together and early to bed" "Sounds good to me" he offered and headed toward the bathroom. He needed to shower to wash off all the effects of Rhonda. He was still a young man, but she exhausted him! Such a great feeling! *Good Crystal's not available tonight, we can sleep. It's going to be a long week with her not available...dam it!*

Crystal had a quick soup and sandwich supper, changed into comfy PJ's for the night and was curled on the couch waiting for Vincent when he exited from the bathroom pink and squeaky clean. He sat next to her and leaned back into her chest. There they stayed for a long time just enjoying the intimacy of their privacy, holding hands and playing with each other fingers. She broke the silence with "last week did I tell you about Miss Elise and the house I've rented." With a little giggle and a lot of interest, he turned to her and said "do tell". Crystal probably talked for a full 30 minutes before Vincent hushed her with a kiss. "I can't be this close to you, smell your scent so close to me without wanting you. Is this going to be a problem at Miss Elise's house?" "I assure you, it will not, remember she lives upstairs. The only problem I see is what to do with my piano, she has a beautiful one. Do I leave mine here, I don't want to, it's mine." He got up and was looking down at her, it made her feel small when he said, "it all comes down to the piano again, doesn't it?" He left the room and went into the kitchen. She was near to tears, because he was right, but then he hollered. "You got the really good cookies, want a couple?"

He came back with two glasses of milk and the bag of oatmeal-raisin cookies, their favorites She smiled and accepted his snack. Their discussion continued with her news of the schedule of the Las Vegas show. She repeated as best she could everything Mr. Brentwhistle had told her about the dates and contracts and her earnings. He had left his mood in the kitchen, because he seamed genuinely interested and excited about her contract and her performing in Las Vegas. Good for you he repeated more than once. He also asked if she heard from the folks about them being able to visit with her. What a feather in your cap he said. She laughed and said she'd given up wearing hats!

Together, in much better moods, they moved their tired bodies and weary minds into bed. Vincent's head was full of Crystal being away and him being with Rhonda. Las Vegas was turning into a blessing for him. He'd encourage any portion of it, even her signing for longer if it meant he could be with Rhonda. She'll be thrilled with his unhurried time to spend with her. Crystal's head was filled with getting to the bottom of Reginald's withdraws and Vincent not coming home at night. She was also cramming thoughts of Vegas and not having children and not following through with Johnathan and wanting Vincent. She turned and spooned Vincent and placed her hand flat on his thigh just below his balls. She had her connection, she could sleep now.

Chapter 28

Things on base were a little different, when everyone knows your short, they tend to treat you differently, kinder, they are more helpful. They made arrangement for the movers, the apartment was piled the way they wanted it stacked in boxes for the move, unpacking would be easy if all went well. The piano was being moved and would be housed on base in a storage unit. They would be arriving on a Sunday and the belongings on the following Monday. Vincent had his orders and his company commanders name and building number where to report at 7am on Monday. Crystal would be going to base with him to inquire about a job and to see where the most likely spot would be to get nosy. Since Crystal saw the withdrawals in Reginald's account, there has been no security breech announced and no one looking for her. They'd be just about settling in and Crystal would be off to New York the following weekend. No rest for the wicked. They weren't wicked, just young enough to endure.

The Sunday of their arrival Miss Elise was so exciting. She was perched in a chair in the front window just waiting for them. They were due to arrive between noon and one and she started sitting at noon. At twelve twenty she saw Crystal's long hair waving in the breeze, as she walked up the walk with the most handsome man she'd ever seen. The contrast between the two was striking. Crystal with her very fair appearance and...and...oh ya, Vincent with his black hair and confidant swagger. As she remembered, all young men had that swagger! But, boy this guy carried himself and his height, oh my, all six and a half feet of it with an easy flare. She couldn't wait to meet him, Crystal spoke so highly of him, she hoped she wouldn't be disappointed. She went to the door and opened it for them just as they stepped up to it. Crystal immediately bent down and hugged her and stepped inside to let Miss Elise get a good look at Vincent. "My you're a big one" she exclaimed "Vincent I presume". "Yes, At your service." He bent way down and gave her a hug as well.

"Wonderful, just wonderful, I've been on pins and needles waiting for you two to get here. This is going to be fun. (she never stopped talking the whole time moving out of the door way, holding Vincent's arm and leading them straight down to the kitchen, where she sat down at the table) Now tell me all about your trip here what is expected of you tomorrow on base. I hope your hungry lunch will be ready in about 30 minutes. The coffee is hot if you need to wet you whistle until lunch is served. She was just so chipper and happy to have them there. "Take a breath" Vincent said. "We are going to live here and have a good amount of time to get to know one another. I agree, it will be fun!" "I'm so glad you agree" she beamed up at him. Crystal kept the conversation going by telling her all about the train ride and asking how long it's been since she-Miss Elise had been on a train. From the pantry, they heard a bell ring and Elsie announced lunch is ready. While she got the silverware from the draw she instructed Vincent to get the casserole from the oven and place it center on the table, she had a hot plate mat ready while telling Crystal which cabinet had the plates. They all met at the table, set and ready to eat. There was never a lull in the conversation, so when the casserole bowl was empty and the coffee pot was dry and all of their plates were whipped clean with the fresh bread that was on the table, lunch was over. Elise remarked about their healthy appetites and the fact that she was glad they were buying the food. Vincent heartily complemented her on the casserole and said if she feeds them like that all the time they'd gain weight and never want to leave. The three of them carried their own plates to the sink and Crystal cleared everything else. Without thinking or asking, Miss Elise took Vincent's arm again and walked him to the living room where she hoped Crystal would favor them with a song or two. She'd been looking forward to this for three weeks. "I promise, two songs please, and then I'll excuse myself to my rooms and leave the house to you." She was so cute when she said it, Crystal was happy to do it.

The next day Vincent needed to report to base but Crystal was able to stay at the house and wait for the movers to deliver their belongings. True to their word, they carried everything in and put things were Crystal indicated. Everything was delivered in good shape which was the second major concern, the first, they were on time. Next Crystal sat down with Miss Elise and discussed food. It was actually fun. Crystal named all the things they like to eat, steak, chops, french fries, spaghetti, burgers not hot dogs. Then Elsie finished the list with salad, vegetables, soup, stew, you know...just like your mother would cook, well rounded, healthy food! "OK, so you guys eat mostly anything, that makes it easy, I've already made the shopping list, you can take care of that tomorrow. Now lets discuss the days one or both of you will not be here." Crystal was impressed by Miss Elise's memory and dealing with details. "Wow you're on top of things, I'm impressed." Crystal said out loud.."I have to be, otherwise I will over cook and I don't want to live on left-overs" So now they sat down with a calendar and Crystal marked her days in New York and then asked for a pencil to mark the time in Las Vegas. That was subject to change...hence the pencil. Then she started to mark the time Vincent would be away but stopped, "we'll need to have his input with these days, I'm not sure."

"Wonderful, we've made a wonderful start, I need to start supper in about thirty minutes. That should give you enough time to play two songs for me, if you don't mind." Elise said this while getting up from the kitchen table and holding her hands in prayer mode for Crystal to see. On the way to the living room she told Crystal that her mother played the harpsichord and she remembered that from years ago, the instrument was in their house but she never had the knack for it but now she wished she had. Elise went on to say that she and her husband had enjoyed listening to music together. But he died young, so many years ago. She also remarked that she was a good listener and that's how she learned things. True to her word, two of Crystal's selections on the piano completed and Elise excused herself and went up to her rooms.

Crystal had just barely gotten warmed up, so she continued to play for the next two hours. She had intended to quite after her first two songs and get to the unpacking in their bedroom, but she lost tract of time and she got lost in her music.

All of a sudden she started tingling with a rhythm and cords that she'd never put together before. Then she did it again and the third time she up focused on the treble keys to give it a blues sound. She liked it. It was this kind of creativity that gave birth to her first original piece. An hour later she was still playing and practicing her show tunes, but she'd drift back to her 'blues' sound and add to it, think and then continue playing her show tunes. She was still sitting at the piano when Vincent came waltzing in the front door. Crystal was oblivious to his arrival until she felt the kiss on her neck. "Don't stop playing on my account, it sounded wonderful walking all the way down the walkway. And what is that scrumptious aroma coming from the kitchen?" He stood up from his kiss and sniffed in the direction of the kitchen. Now Crystal was very aware of everything. "It does smell tasty out there, I got carried away in here and hadn't really noticed...let's go set the table" "Not so fast..." he grabbed her around the waist and planted a lip lock on her that took her breathe away... then they set off in the direction of the kitchen where Miss Elise was thrilled to tell Crystal she so enjoyed cooking to the music.

Supper was again a wonderful meal and the conversation non-stop. With the kitchen clean everyone set off to their own rooms. Crystal took one foot into their room and sheeked and apologized for not organizing and putting away everything when it arrived. "If you help me I'll make it worth your while later" She said while taking off her sweater, she intended to work in bra, only! "I think we'll work faster this way, you on your draws and me on mine. I did have the movers put the boxes nearest to our dressers, that should help." "I'm going to need to work with my back to you if that's all you re going to wear, dam, now I'm carrying more around!" She looked at him and saw the bulge in his pants...Within ten minutes the dresser draw boxes were empty. He worked with his back to her the whole time...Vincent took it upon himself to tackle the bathroom boxes, alone, while Crystal emptied the garment bags and all of her clothes from on the bed into the closets. With the boxes thrown into the back yard to be broken up and tied into bundles they only had the bed to change again...it was clean last night, but boy not now, those boxes sure were dirty! They had this done in a jiffy so outside they went. Together they were cutting the cardboard boxes into a manageable sizes, stacking and tying them into bundles. Maybe twenty minutes into this exercise...with both of them out-side..Vincent approached Crystal and stripped her of her bra. It was just a forgotten item, didn't hinder either of them inside while they worked or out here either...until now...Vincent had been home long enough without the benefit of fondling or being fondled... this evenings air felt so good, no one was around, Crystal was so near, almost half naked, it wouldn't take much to finish the job. Once she looked around she was defiantly on the same page...Vincent had too much clothes on. She made fast work of getting him out of them, and laying him on the ground while she danced around him and took her time shedding the remainder of her clothes. With one finger in her mouth, and bending over to let Vincent have a suck as well, she undid the button on her long skit...she slid it down enough to show she had only skimpy panties on underneath. Vincent wasn't going to wait, he pulled the hem of the skirt and she had only to step away from it when it hit the ground. Now down she went to pinch his nubby round nipples and run her finger around in his mouth while she mounted the shaft reaching for the stars. They both loved being outside, little did they know Miss Elise also loved seeing them outside.

The next morning Vincent needed to report to base, he gripped about the new exercise planned for him and Alan again. He said he needed to do better today. Crystal's day was one of shopping. Miss Elise had made her list and Crystal was looking forward to the new store and poking around, knowing she had disposable money in her pocket. She was thinking she'd help Miss Elsie put the groceries away, that way she'd know where everything was kept. She was also thinking that she hoped they didn't have to move again too soon. Learning new routines and new stores and even new apartments really sucks. So far so good on this one, but in a 20 or more year military career, this could happen often. It's a good thing she loves Vincent. And tomorrow she still needed to land her part-time job on base in a position where she could build trust and camaraderie, then get nosy and work her magic. But until then, these groceries needed putting away. Back home Miss Elise was thrilled with the help. Crystal learned her way around the pantry and the kitchen. She also learned where all the preserves and canning of last years fruits and vegetables were. Boy! What a stock. She thought Grandma in New York had a good root cellar, hers was nothing to this. With the work done, Crystal gravitated toward piano. She sat and played just a simple song, too deep in thought to play anything too complicated. She knew she wasn't cut out to be like Miss Elise or Grandma. She didn't have it in her to plant a big garden, tend it for a season, keep it weed free and watered, fence it against critters and brag at county fairs. Then do all the stuff you need to do to can it or freeze it and in many cases, chase a few kids around the house! *Nope not me, sorry Vincent, I really hope you love me the way I am!*

The next morning Crystal went to the base with Vincent. He went his way and she wandered over to the information office. "The petty officer behind the counter spotted her and smiled with "three weeks must be over...you're back." Crystal smiled back and said "how can you remember that?" He walked to the front of the counter to be face to face with her and in a conspiratorial voice said, "please take a position in the Bursa's office, they need so much help, their organization really sucks and we need good gossip." Crystal's face must have really shown what she was thinking because he came right back with "They are great people but need direction. You know, in their work habits." now he put his head down a little and continued with "plus that's the office with the most intermarriage exchanging and cheating...we need to know more" Once again Crystal just grinned and shook her head and said, "it's the furthest unit from the main gate, I don't have a vehicle." He smiled at her again and said "no problem, we have shuttles running nearly all day because we are so spread out. You can go from here every morning and get on a shuttle nearly every hour to go anyway on base you need to go. These are the things you learn when you've been here a while." "So once again, how did you remember that I'd be back in a few weeks" she inquired with her shoulders raised in question. "Oh, anyone as beautiful as you is easy to remember, plus we marked 3 weeks on the calendar in hopes you'd be back and work down there." "Great, when is the next shuttle expected and where should I go to wait for it?" Crystal groaned and walked in the direction he was pointing.

The shuttle bus driver was an old man, working out his retirement because he had nothing else to do. A nice guy with no family left, so he made everyone who rode his shuttle his business! Within a week he knew Crystal's life story, had already made a point to meet Vincent and put his stamp of approval on him and wished he could meet her dad. He was impressed with Crystal's mom's position in Washington and was amazed with her being around here because of her talent and beauty.

Within that same week Crystal had started her job in the bursars unit, familiarized herself with the equipment, which was an updated version of everything she had worked with in Virginia and made friends with everyone she saw everyday. She also recognized the loose lips and flirtation which occurred nearly every minute of every day. What a den of cheating and lying and iniquity she landed herself into! She also recognized the insufficiency that could be corrected easily. For the past week she had visited with the personnel in the information office while waiting for the shuttle. She made friends with everyone she met, but up here they were only fishing for gossip, this whole place was a fish bowl of who was doing what to whom. It was worse than high school, but so far she was having a good time. Now that she knew the ground work and who would be looking over her shoulder, she knew how to cover her back and when, so it was time to visit Reginald and Keith and do updates as needed. She loved this equipment, it was much faster than what she was accustomed to, therefore her snooping didn't take as long, until…

Again, how? There were three withdrawals from Reginald's account. One she saw two months ago. She looked closer at the first…it was on a Monday. But now four more within two months, on a Friday. No one knows about these accounts, no one knows this name, where is this money going? Once again her heart had plummeted to her feet! She made notes of the dates and the amounts, felt weak in the knees. This was taking to long, who was around, who was looking at her. She had to get out of here. She'd need to talk with Vincent...he'd either freakout with her, be able to calm her or have an explanation. As calmly as she could, Crystal logged out of her current situation, signed out at the door and waited for the shuttle to pick her up and get her back to the main gate. She felt like she was wearing her guilt all over, but Pepere', the driver didn't let on at all. He was just as friendly and talkative as always.

Once Crystal got home, she went straight to the piano. She started gently at first, but that didn't address the feeling she had deep inside, so within the next heart beat she was beating out a tune that drew Miss Elise's attention and caused her concern. So much so that she stopped Crystal from playing to question her. When Crystal looked up and saw the concern in Elise's face, she apologized and told her that this is the way she works out her aggression or anger or things she can't control. "It usually helps and then Vincent works his magic and calms me down." With that Elsie left the room with, "I love your playing, just don't break the instrument." Crystal resumed her playing, but at a much more normal rate. She recognized the fact that she frightened Miss Elise. She'd have to watch out in the future. With that off her mind, she went back to her worries about the Reginald account. *What could she do? She had the amounts and the dates...she needed a calendar...*when she went racing through the kitchen on the way to her room, she stopped, hugged Miss Elise and thanked her for her concern. In her room she found the calendar with her dates for Las Vegas and thought, *this will do* She then looked at the dates of the last withdrawals that she had written down...looked at the calendar, they were Fridays. Four Fridays, consecutively with two weeks between them...these were pay days... *What the hell? Vincent was the only one who knew about these accounts. I'll kill him! That bastard! What is he doing! He lied to me once...I asked him about the first withdrawal when I saw it...he lied!*

Now she had a headache. What to do? Back to the piano, calmly this time she remembered Miss Elise needed them to mark the calendar when they'd be away from the house on a weekend. She'd ask Vincent to do this for Miss Elise and watch him somehow. These thoughts didn't help her headache any, but now she had the feeling that she couldn't trust him. She felt like shit! She needed proof. Tomorrow she'd dig deeper, look for a withdrawal slip and see who signed for the cash. *Now she's thinking...Relax, maybe is wasn't him...dam, if not him, I'm screwed...not so hard..relax the fingers, play nice or she'll be back, my song..play that song.* So over and over and over again she played her song. Each time she played with the intensity of some of the cords...it's getting better. Finally Vincent was home, just the sight of him smile at her made her relax. At supper Miss Elise told Vincent of Crystal's episode at the piano earlier and asked how often that happened, she was concerned. Crystal tried to explain it away, but Vincent knew better, he merely reassured Miss Elise he'd discuss it with her later. In the meantime Crystal brought up the subject of the weekend calendar for Miss Elise and she was grateful and put the calendar in front of Vincent. She explained for him to mark the weekends he would not be here because she didn't want to over cook and have too many leftovers. He looked over Crystal's weekends and only marked a two week absence toward the end of the month. He said sorry Crystal, I forgot to tell you about this until I saw the calendar, I'll tell you about it later. They said goodnight to Miss Elise and Vincent invited Crystal to walk with him outside for awhile. It was a beautiful night so she was eager to do so. They went out the back door and Miss Elise perched herself on her outside balcony to watch them. They walked out back to the garden and then the entire perimeter of the back yard. Hand in hand they discussed their day and Crystal admitted she had a disagreement with a person in the bursars unit, came home and took it out on the piano. "Poor Miss Elise got nervous at my agitation and burst of 'energy' and actually made me stop playing. I did my best to explain how I get and you can usually calm me down so she felt better. Now can you please tell me about the end of the month, where you are going and how long you'll be gone..." "I hate you not having a board to check on everything that is going on, I forget you don't and then I forget to tell you things, sorry. OK, at least a two week exercise of survival in up state New York. Right now they are saying two weeks, but if it is to be longer it will be posted in the information center, Plus with your connections, you can probably find things out anyway." "Thanks for that Crystal said. "Sure, if I know something is going on I can look, but I have to know something is going on first." Miss Elise heard most of what Crystal had said to Vincent and was satisfied that they were discussing it. Now she also knew Vincent was going to be away at the end of month. But that was it...No love scenes in the backyard tonight!

The next day Crystal was diligent at work making notes and checking the units scheduled activity and the duties of each person. Was it her business? Maybe if she could help the unit be more efficient, meet deadlines, be more productive and solve a few problems without stepping on anyone's toes and make enemies in the doing so, yes it was business. Some of these lacking areas were discussed when she signed on, so now after working there a few days, it was time to hopefully suggest a few changes for the better. If the suggestions worked out, maybe they'd be happy to have her there a little longer. She was hoping, because she needed to be there a little longer. She needed to be able to access her files without prying eyes every time she did. Like now, only three other people around, all busy and not paying her any mind. So once again she was in Reginald's files looking for those withdrawal signatures. Can't be...there is no Mrs. R. Sabers. There is only Reginald Sabers...where has this money gone? Who took it. *I guess if I can be crooked to put it in, someone can be crooked to take it out.*

This is going to drive me crazy until I get to the bottom of it. I also can't go on blaming Vincent for something he claims he has no knowledge, it hurts my heart to do so. I need to clear the air with him, I'm horny and going to New York for the weekend. That's not a good combination!

Before the end of the day Crystal messaged the bank in Maryland to forward to her by special courier, copies of the withdrawal slips. It's all she could think of to do!

The rest of the week pasted in marriage harmony with Crystal and Vincent enjoying each other and Miss Elise's home cooked meals. Miss Elise remembered Crystal's New York trips had her leaving on Thursday mornings, and she had prepared a goody box for Crystal to take with her on the train. She was really a sweet lady and they enjoyed living there. So Friday afternoon when Vincent got home, he apologized to

Miss Elise about not being here for the rest of the weekend when he left clean from the shower and carrying a duffel bag. She had already started supper for the two of them.

This was really the pits. It took three hours by train for Vincent to travel back to Maryland to be with Rhonda, but he knew she'd make it worth his while. He was excited to be going, he hadn't seen her in two weeks. His lie to Miss Elsie was no longer on his mind. At least he had the two weeks at the end of the month neatly wrapped up, he could put in for personal days and spend two fun filled weeks with Rhonda and Crystal wouldn't be the wiser. He'd handled that really well.

Crystal had her last visit to New York to make up for, canceling a show and leaving a day early is not good showmanship, she'd make up for it. Upon her arrival everyone was glad to see her. Mr. Brentwhistle especially was happy she was there. He had great news for her, the final schedule, the other performers also headlining, her earnings with the attendance percentages, her accommodations, and her travel information. He was busting at the seams to present all of this to her. So rather than wait for her to come to him, he joined her in her room as she was checking in. Crystal wasn't surprised to see him, but in her room, that was a surprise. At the far end of her room there were floor to ceiling windows at least 10 feet wide, and in front of those windows was a table with two wooden straight back chairs, more like kitchen chairs, He sat in one and invited her to sit in the other, now it was their desk. He dropped his black valise on the desk, unzipped it and started laying papers in a certain order, on the desk top. The whole while he was doing this he was asking about Vincent and their move to New Jersey and how they were settling in, just being totally friendly and comfortable. Crystal's eyes were on each piece of paper he laid out... she saw Las Vegas on a number of the papers and was getting excited. Finally Brentwhistle had everything in order and he was ready to get down to business.

"First" he said, paused and looked at her "this is etched in stone once you cash this." as he slid a check over to her face down. "Go ahead, look at it!" Crystal's face said it all when she saw the check. "OH, I want to cash it, but what's the catch"? She said breathlessly. "Once you cash that check, it's a down payment on the contracts that I have right here in from of me. Your signature on the check is better than and will get back to the producers faster than the contracts." Brentwhistle explained. "Got it, let me see the rest". Crystal looked at each piece of paper but concentrated more on the departure date and the arrival date in Las Vegas. "It's going to take that long to get there? With departure from New York, that means I need to take the train from New Jersey to here, then board the train to Vegas, can't I go direct from New Jersey?" Crystal's wheels were turning, she continued with "that means on my personal calendar I will be gone not two weeks for these performances, but including travel at least three weeks. That's going to be a hard sell to Vincent, (she smiled broadly) but I'll show him the check!"

This weekends performances were fun. She played like she was in Vegas, very up beat and showy. She was practicing being a performer, not only a piano player. It suited her, she was good at it, plus she figured she needed to be as good as Lena Horn and Mickey Rooney, they were playing Vegas her first weekend and Frank Sinatra the second. She would have loved to be a fly on the wall for these performers, but she had her own show to do. *Her own show, never in her wildest dreams had she ever thought she could rank among performers like them. I'm in New York, I play the piano...I'm a performer...I get paid to play the piano.* With this weekends work done, she once again boards the train for home. This time the ride will be consumed with reading her Las Vegas contracts and marking her personal calendar with the time and dates of her shows. Her boarding pass and train tickets are in the safe back at the hotel, too precious a commodity to travel with her to New Jersey and then back to New York...let them stay in New York. Now that there is a definite itinerary, Miss Elise can put it on her calendar, she can write to her dad again and she can pray Vincent doesn't hit the roof over her elongated visit to Las Vegas! With everything on her mind and the personal notes she needs to make and the letter she needs to write to her dad, the train ride wasn't quite long enough, but she got it all done. She was arriving home with longing for Vincent in her heart and excitement to share with him as well. Hopefully if Vegas goes well, she'll have a return engagement and Vincent could join her then.

Three weeks to go before the first...don't count the chickens before they hatch!!

It was late Sunday afternoon when Crystal finally made it home. She was exhausted and hungry. Miss Elise would take care of the hunger. . she was a great cook and Vincent could coax her into a sexual mood with just a look sometimes. Great sex and a good nights sleep, that's what she wanted. Vincent was only about ten minutes behind Crystal when he arrived home. He too was hungry and tied and looked it. "Do I look as bad as you?" Crystal questioned Vincent when he hugged her and collapsed into an upholster chair in the living room. "No you do not, you look like a refreshing drink of cool water. How was New York, it looks like it was good for you." Vincent was complimentary and said something nice about New York, it's about time. They had a great supper with Miss Elise and retired early, at least they started early. Crystal seemed much more in the mood tonight than Vincent, she was not going to sleep unsatisfied. Besides, Vincent liked it sometimes when she was the aggressor, it really got his juices going. He was easy, he was happy to oblige, he played back very well. Orgasm accomplished and it was still early. One more kiss, she spooned him and they were both happy to sleep. Crystal had so much on her mind. This was needed rest. Vincent played hard with Rhonda all weekend because he was blissfully happy, she was pregnant. His rest was heaven sent, for now.

Monday back on base was always crazy. Many men never left base on the weekends so a Monday was no big deal to them...they didn't get the 'readjusting' or 'settling-in' aspect to a Monday. These guys were almost more to put-up-with than weekenders! This Monday was no different...yes it was. Vincent was walking on air...he was going to be a Dad. But he couldn't talk about it. This was really the pits, one of the happiest feelings in his life and he couldn't share it. Crystal was back looking at the Reginald files and making herself sick...more money gone! Not much, but some. Last week she had requisitioned copies of the withdrawal slips to see who signed them...she should have those copies this week. That should shed some light on the mystery. Little did she know, this mystery was better left alone. She'd find out!

Chapter 29

Wednesday morning there was a special courier letter for Crystal. Thinking it was the copies of the withdrawal slips, she was anxious to ripe into it. Sure enough...one was signed by Reginald Sabers and three by Rhonda Sabers. "Who the hell is she?" Crystal exclaimed right out loud. Looking a little embarrassed for her out outburst, she ran to the ladies room and examined the copies more closely.

No mistaking Reginald's signature, but Rhonda's? *It was definitely a woman's signature, not Reginald just signing her name. This is getting more curious and curious! There is no one I can talk to about this...I've created a powder keg and it's going to blow up. Who knows? Accuse Reginald?...I can't do that, who's Rhonda? I need some time to figure this out...Look again, is there a location on the withdrawal slip? Ft Geo Meade, Army, Maryland...3:10pm...all the same location...all mid-afternoon.*

Dam, Reginald...what's going on? I'm going home.

Crystal was very careful when playing the piano...she kept an even tempo, was not banging, not assaulting the instrument, not wanting to alarm Miss Elise. She wanted to be herself but that always frightened Miss Elise. Dam, she needed to BANG out a tune! She really wanted to yell or bang on Vincent. *What was he doing with the Reginald money and who the hell is Rhonda? 5:15pm couldn't come fast enough, tonight was the night, she couldn't hold her tongue any longer!*

When Vincent walked in the front door, promptly at 5:15pm Crystal was playing her own arrangement. She was totally engrossed with her movements and applying gentle movements where the music warranted and heady, heavy, strong mechanics to the cords, leading to the melody. She was working on perfecting the total outcome of her first original arrangement. On any other day Crystal would have loved the feeling of Vincent's hands on her neck and shoulders, needing away the fatigue that had landed there. But not today, he was adding to it. So she abruptly stopped playing, turned on her seat and without any preamble blurted out "who the hell is Rhonda?' She was looking straight up into Vincent's face and watched it change. Slowing he shook his head, his lips turned inward which made his nose sniff and wrinkle between his eyes. His non blinking eyes bore straight into hers, but she didn't waver. He did first and looked away, backing away from her and scuffing his left foot back and forth on the floor and the back of his pants. She had seen him do this in the past when trying to avoid a situation. He was stuck in place, but his feet were moving. His hands were his give-away. He was wringing his fingers together about waist level, he'd stop and think better of reaching out to her and then start the finger action again. Now his entire body had lost its straight stature when he simply shrugged his shoulders and answered, "my wife." Earlier Crystal had gotten a whiff of supper making it's way to the living room, now the smell was turning her stomach and affecting her hearing...wife? She laughed, there was an emotion starting to swell in her but there was no identifying it. Now it was her turn to shake her head...in disbelief, in anger, in pain? She still hadn't taken her eyes off of him. Her head movements had released the scarf that was holding back her hair, so now it was gently moving, moving toward her face with each shake of her head. Her hair, that glorious mass that Vincent loved to touch, got him again. His movement toward her unglued her eyes and the tears started. His approach was gentle with one hand holding her hair back, while the other hand and arm circled her closer to him. She snuggled in and asked, "who are you?" His answer startled the hell out of her... she heard "right now your husband, and I- love- you, last weekend... Reginald." He felt her stiffen and slowly step away from him. He let his arm fall to his sides. Crystal was just standing there looking at him. Finally she said, "I have a million questions that I really don't want the answers to, but his one if you answer it honestly, will clear up quite a few of them. Three weeks ago and again this past weekend did you withdraw Reginald money?" Crystal's fingers were crossed against his truth… "Yes we did." was all he said. At that Crystal calmly told him to GET OUT, then she fled the room. Poor Miss Elise didn't know what was going on…a slamming from the door at the front of the house and a slammed bedroom door down the hall from the kitchen. Crystal just ran straight through, never looking at Miss Elise nor did she say one word! Miss Elise was left with a meatloaf, mashed potatoes and green bean supper, ready for the table, and no one to eat it. *I image this is like having a family of teenagers with hormones raging, but these two are adults with hormones in overdrive… Elise's* thoughts were all over the place… little did she know!

In the morning Crystal apologized to Miss Elise and then announced she was going to New York. "I can pick-up a show or two for Mr. Brentwhistle at the hotel and then I'm heading to Las Vegas for two weeks. So I probably won't be back here for three or four weeks or maybe more with the travel time." Elise could see a little light had gone out of Crystal, but refrained from saying anything more than 'knock 'em dead in Vegas honey when Crystal got up to leave the room. Twenty minutes later Crystal was heading out of the door with two big suitcases that nearly emptied her closet. She'd spent the night sorting and packing and straightening the room to leave it as neat and clean as possible. She'd written Miss Elise a short note leaving a months rent as well. Crystal just didn't know how to act..react to how Vincent was acting or the last words he'd said to her. *Rhonda his wife? That's ludicrous. That can't be true, that's criminal, a man can't have two wives. Wasn't I enough for him? Was I at least first? Was I second, is he divorced? I can't go to New York now…there is a bottom to all of this and I need to find it fast. His mom can't know this…can she, my dad?* She stopped, turned and ran back into the house.

Elise, my suitcases are at the front door, I'm not going yet, I'm heading to the base, (by now Elise was standing by her side and Crystal didn't need to yell anymore) maybe I'll see you for lunch and leave for the train station on a late afternoon trip. Elise tried to reach up to pat

Crystal's cheek, but even on tip toes, she couldn't reach. Crystal bent at the waist and hugged Elise saying, I'll be okay...Vincent is a jerk, I'll kick him in the ass for you!

Crystal arrived on base to the smiles and hello's from everyone. She announced I'm only here looking for Vincent, I'm not working today. Where should I start looking for him? She was directed to the ammunition depot where there was a great deal of activity she could see from this distance. As she approached, she could see Vincent heading her way. He told her straight away he only had ten minutes and needed to get back to work. She said fine..."when did you marry Rhonda?" This straight to the point, short question through him for a loop, he recovered quickly and answered, "three weeks ago when you were in New York, so was I, with my whole unit, remember? We were able to spend three nights together in the hotel and the next three you needed to work. As it turns out, I met, bedded and married Rhonda on the third day. I won't bore you with any of the details, just know that since that weekend, I have found out that she is pregnant with my child and we are both ecstatic about it. Crystal, she wants a house full of children, and so do I! You've known from the beginning that, that's what I wanted with you too."

Crystal's inners were turning and her head started to ache and she knew she was holding back tears and when she started to speak, Vincent took a step closer to her and spoke again before she could. " I know you don't believe that I love you very much...but since I found out Rhonda is pregnant, I love her as well. I've given this some thought in the last three weeks, so please don't hate me...I want you both.

Some day we'll have more than ten minutes to talk this threw, but just know that I need the Reginald money to keep this wife and this child like any father in a family. We are both, you and I, under the same proverbial barrel in that I have broken the law by being a bigamist and you have broken the law by stealing from the federal government. There is so much more to be said on these subjects, but now is not the time or the place, nor is there anyone else we can discuss this with, it stays under our own personal barrel." Once again Crystal could only stand there and absorb all of these words, these true words and feel... what? Helpless? Threatened? Discarded? Used?

Vincent was right, this was not the time or the place. There were no words for Crystal just yet so she merely said, as the tears were streaking down her cheeks, "I'm leaving for New York this afternoon and Vegas next Wednesday." She cupped him around the back of his neck with one hand and around his waist with the other pulling him even closer to her and kissed him soundly, passionately, and long with soft sounds of want and need escaping her throat. Before the kiss was done she felt his response pressing into her and when the kiss was done, his eyes held the same look of his physical response. Kiss over, with her hands by her sides, she walked away without looking back. They definitely shared a love and a flame that was easily kindled, but now threatened.

Back at the house, Crystal shared a light lunch with Miss Elise, played a couple of songs on the piano and headed for the train station to catch the 4:15 to New York. This train ride was not long enough to relax the demons in her mind or the anger and hurt in her heart. Without so much as a threat, Vincent had put her life and her lively hood in peril by pointing out her wrong doings, those that he was part-taking of and using to their fullest! He was right, they had one another over a barrel with their shared extra activities.

New York was what she needed. It was busier and more hectic than her mind. It was nosier and more unsettled than her thinking. It was a force stronger than her... to try to stay on track, because it succeeded in doing so. She needed to sit at a piano and steady her fingers to sooth her broken heart. She needed to stay her course and succeed in Las Vegas and prove to herself that she is that good and can ride the success train with the other headliners making the big bucks. She decided... that is what she wants. She wants and needs love, not children. She wants and needs Vincent, but not at the expense of her music and career. She backed him into a corner when she said no children, not now, she hadn't really thought of children in her life...*Right here and now, this minute I've decided to be number one. In Vincent's life in my career in my dad's heart and in all things I do, lawfully or not. Sure I can fund Reginald's life and family, but at a cost...to Vincent...he hasn't thought this through, but I'm beginning to. I may have created the barrel that we are now under. Him fathering children is his own doing but in the long run, he's making me pay for it. These children will never have his last name, I do. They'll never have a proper heritage. Let her have them, as long as I can still have him. And I will see to it that I do! When and where I want him. I may use him until IT falls off. The Hoop that I am going to make him jump through can be any size I say...from now on!*

Chapter 30

OH, New York!...That was the longest train ride of my life! I was reborn. A new and improved woman. I can now live-up to the ideals I've dreamed of for my career and my life. Vincent will have to learn to keep up with me and at times be my little puppet, because I have every intention of keeping him!

Standing under the marquee and awning at the front door of the New Yorker Hotel, Crystal just thought...Room 3108, here I come, be ready. Once inside she was instantly recognized and valeted up to her room. She unpacked only enough for four performances and 6 days, then it was off to Las Vegas. Before she even had the chance to pick-up the phone and announce her arrival, Mr. Brentwhistle was knocking on her door. "Come in, come in" was all she could get out...Mr. Brentwhistle folded her into a huge hug and muttered "You're a sight for sore eyes, I've...we've all missed you. Are you here until you leave for Vegas, I hope?" By now she had lead them over to the two chairs at the 'everything' table in front of the large windows. While reaching for the ice bucket, and backing toward the door she answered "yes, and I'm ready to do 4 shows here before I go, stay where you are, I'll be right back." When she returned, the coke and rum and two glasses were on the table, he anticipated her just right!

"The perks of having your own room...it can stay stocked," she said simply. They clinked glasses when their drinks were poured. She was happy to inform him that she'd heard back from her dad and he and his wife Suzie would be able to join her in Vegas for a one weeks stay. This would be their long over-due honeymoon and vacation. She was excited and really anxious for her dad to hear her own song as well as the blues tune she was working on. Once she took a breath and a long swig of her drink, Brentwhistle just looked at her and asked, "OK what's going on, or rather what's wrong? Vincent's not with you and you left him 6 days before you needed to and he's not accompanying you to Vegas? What gives?" Crystal was not ready for his questions, nor was she going to say anything about her current dilemma. "Let's just say I'm really excited about the trip and the exposure Vegas is going to afford me and what it could ultimately do for my career in the long run." Crystal said on a sigh. " It's this 'long run' that has Vincent's tidy-whit-tees climbing up his ass, isn't it? I think he's a little jealous of your success and afraid he's going to loose you to it or some adoring fan." Brentwhistle was choosing his word carefully while pouring the second rounds of drinks. "You and I both know that my music and Vincent share my front seat. I can't choose between the two and my going to Vegas without him was a very hard choice! Once he gave me his blessing, we both needed to remember that he is a military man and needs to remain true to his oath and serve out his remaining time. I am under no such obligation, just a vow to remain true to him no matter what I do or where I go, for me that's easy, I'm in love. (long pause, and then she just started to break out into a beautiful smile) You know...since I've said that out loud, I feel better." Crystal didn't know when she stood up and starting pacing the room while talking, but now she rejoined Brentwhistle at the table. She held both of his hands in hers, leaned down to kiss his forehead and said "you're such a good listener, have I ever told you about my best friend Peter?" Just that fleeting thought filled her with a yearning that needed fulfillment. "So your best friend was a guy...Vincent must love that! Have they met?" Brentwhistle's facial expression held merriment at his question. "I would have loved to be a fly on that wall...At that my fair lady...welcome back and I'll see you at your show tomorrow night." Crystal walked him to the door and latched it when he left. She leaned against it for a moment or two just thinking about Peter. What was he doing now, how was he and is he happy? The last being the burning question. She needed to find out.

The next few days were a blur to Crystal. She loved performing. Her days were filled with sleeping in late in the morning, having a leisurely... call it brunch. Going for a 'work-out' swim early afternoon, then a massage and having her hair done for her show in the evening. Just a light supper-snack would hold her until her night-cap after her show. It was all timed to her liking. Monday night when she returned to the piano after her break, she stood in her spotlight all smiles, filled with gratitude for the appreciative audience and as it had become her custom started reading the song requests for the next segment of her show. She also spoke a little about leaving for Vegas for the first time and working out her 'bugs' here in New York first. About into her fourth selection a new person entered the room and sat very left of her, he disappeared from her sight. But there was something about his gait or his height or his presents that bothered her. The show must go on, so she forget about it until she was playing her exit song and the house lights starting to come on just slightly. Then he appeared. Vincent stood at the end of her piano bench and held out his hand for her to come to him.

The touch of his hand was like magic. His closeness melted her knees when she was standing close to him. The light kiss he pressed to her lips became her total undoing. She folded her arms around him and he followed her lead with a full embrace of his own. Without a sound they wound up holding hands and heading to the center elevators, the fastest way to room 3108. Standing just inside the room he spoke for the first time. "I couldn't let you get on that train heading to Vegas without telling you again that I love you and to wish you luck in everything you do and hope to find." She turned her back to him in such a way to indicate that she needed help with her zipper that ran from her neck all the way down past the roundness of her ass. While making this turn she explained to him that she now knew she was living a new reality as his first wife. She repeated "first wife...Right?" She made him answer as he watched her slip the dress off of her shoulders and let it hit the floor. "Right?" she asked again. With no one to impress, she'd dress in elegance for her show and comfort for herself. So when the dress hit the floor, Vincent croaked out "Right" and saw all 6 foot 1 ½ inches of Crystal standing there naked and beautifully proportioned in all the right places. The longer he looked and the closer he looked he could see her perfect nipples start to pucker and dimple with desire. When she lifted her arms and started pulling pins from her hair and it cascaded down her body, his knees went weak and his desire could not be denied. His clothing soon became a pile on a chair and his body and hands were all over Crystal. With expediency and practice the bedspread laid on the floor and he laid on Crystal. There were no words spoken, just choreographed body movements and hand gestures and rubbing and guiding that spoke volumes of their practiced love making. No, she could not give this up, she'd just have to manipulate certain times to make this happen for her. With the heavy drapes pulled across the over-sized windows, blocking out the morning sunshine, the only indication that it was 9:20am was on the bedside alarm clock. "This is the way I've dreamed of waking every morning...in your arms." Crystal whispered. But that wasn't good enough for Vincent. He turned slightly enough to position and gently slide his engorged penis into her still wet and accepting vagina. "This is the way I'd like to wake every morning, you waiting for me, wet and willing." "Let's not talk...not now...we can still be us for a few more hours," Crystal groaned. "Exactly, that's why I came to New York last night. I'll savor and keep close to my heart the experience of the next few hours and then see you off when you board your train this afternoon. I needed to see you, feel you and love you before you left." Crystal loved hearing the words as he stroked her body with his strong hands and long fingers and pumped gently and rhythmically to reach and fill the very inside of her. Time had no meaning when they were together, but rather it disappeared too quickly when they were so entwined together.

They had never really ever said good-bye to each other in their short past. He'd be deployed to another place by military means, she'd take-off for New York for a week...but this...she'd be leaving to build a career and he'd be leaving and welcomed by another pair of loving arms. Another woman with kissable lips and loved filled nights and legs spread wide in the morning, waiting and wanting more! Their kiss standing on the boarding platform at the train station was bitter-sweet. Her tears didn't fall until she was well away from him.

Chapter 31

The train trip was an experience in itself. Long hours between stops at major cities, tolerable meals in the dinning car, good conversations with the other passengers and a thin, lumpy mattress to sleep on. The luxury of having a bathroom attached to your hotel room was not lost on Crystal after having to share and use the facilities on the train! *Vegas here I come, I hope it's worth it! I hope if it's offered again, I can forget about this discomfort and forge straight ahead!* With lunch finished on this final day, she knew Vegas was only hours away. Now her thoughts were nerve-jumping; what if...*she was not met at the terminal upon arrival? What if she needed to make her own way to the hotel, could she find it? Is she arriving on the right day? Does she have a room for tonight? What if this is a big mistake? What if she is a big flop?*

A gentle tap on her shoulder brought her back to the here and now. An older gentleman was standing at her table holding a Las Vegas paper. It was a complimentary paper just passed out to all passengers and he wanted to verify an item he just read. "This is you, right? As he was pointing to a picture of Crystal smiling, sitting at a piano. It's says your the opening act for the new opening of the Eldorado Casino this weekend. Is that right? He gushed, my wife and I have rooms reserved there for three nights, we love Vegas." Crystal picked up her own paper and turned to page three where sure enough, there was her picture and the article about the Eldorado. "I'm Henry, would you please autograph my paper for me." He put his paper down on Crystal's table with her picture starring up at them, and handed her a pen. Now it was Crystal's turn to turn pink and blush a little..."this is my first autograph" she admitted to Henry as she signed her name...Crystal. . with a flourish on the capital 'C'. Henry took his paper and started away, turned back and said "we'll be in your audience Saturday night'. The rest of the trip into Vegas was filled with all attention on Crystal, the item in the paper and her autographing everyone's copy.

True to her contract and introduction information, she was met at the train depot by a youngish man in a tuxedo holding a sign with her name on it. Feeling relieved with one hurdle conquered, she joined him, introduced herself and learned his name was Andrew. He shook her hand and looked up into her face. "I'm sorry, I don't mean to stare, but I've never met a woman as beautiful (he paused and blushed) and as tall as you. He giggled just a little but a little sneaked out of his mouth. Crystal stopped, looked at him and said, "what's so funny?" When he looked at her, she had a quizzical look on her face, he apologized again but added, "your voice, you're not a signer I hope". At that she needed to laugh with him. "No" she said, at his relief. But she asked him,' how long have you had this job?" With pride he answered, "today is my first day." Crystal then said, "I mean no offense, but in the future watch your tongue...what if I were a singer?" He stared at her with dread building on his face and body shrinkage. "Relax Andrew, I'm only saying for your future employment, be careful what you say to your charges. That's what we are you know. We are in your charge." At this he brightened and led the way to the trolley that would carry them the rest of the way to the Eldorado. When they arrived and he hauled her bags to the porter, she said "this is where you would get your tip for good service, but I already gave you a tip about watching your mouth, remember that, because it was priceless!" He wanted to kiss her, she could see it...but he knew better! The porter looked at her name and her badge and by-passed the reservations desk and when directly to the elevators and punched the 11th floor. She was room 1118, three doors down from the elevator, just right!. It had been a long four days, when she closed the door, her shoes were the first to come off. Then it was straight into the bathroom...A real bathroom, clean and just for her, thank goodness. Nice big area with a deep tub and shower behind shower curtains. The sink was recessed in a slab of black marble flecked with gold and yellow. All of the facilities were white with gold fixtures and the floor was black with gold fleck. All of the towels were black rimmed with gold. Very nice finishes. She took all of this in while sitting on the toilet, relaxed and alone! Next she ventured into the bedroom, it looked like a comfortable room, much like her room at the New Yorker, only larger. This room had a king size bed, the entire wall in front of it was a long dresser at one end, a safe behind a cabinet door, a desk section with a chair pushed under then more counter top to a wall. That wall was one side of the closet which finished filling that wall to the windows. The large windows looked down on Main Street, Vegas with all the neon lights and people filling the streets. Not unlike New York City. Crystal was thankful for the heavy material that the pull drapes were made out of, they blocked the light and noise.

With no more time to look around or unpack or just plain lounge, there was a knock on her door. She cautiously opened the door just a bit and there stood a tall, 40ish, balding man in an impeccable three piece suit. He threw out his hand in welcome with his introduction of Jerry P. Schaffer, a broad smile never leaving his mouth. Crystal opened the door in welcome and shook his hand heartily saying, 'It's so nice to finally meet you, your name was all over every document and contract that I received, now I can put a face to the name." She indicated a chair for him and they say facing one another. "I'd know you anywhere with that gorgeous head of hair you have, and even sitting down you're a tall one!" After Crystal's little giggle of embarrassment and soft thanks for the compliment, Mr. Schaffer went on to tell her about the Eldorado, the casino, the hotel, the restaurants and the Grand Theater. "I'm not going to keep you but another minute so you can kick-back and relax before dinner. Being that you just got here allow me to escort you to dinner, I'll pick you up here at 6:30. After that I'll show you around, introduce you to those you need to know and we'll peek into the Grand Theater." "Thanks so much, I'd love for you to be my guide and my protector in this far away city." "I can be that now, but actually I'm from back east myself" Mr. Schaffer offered as she was walking him to the door. "Yep, born and raised in a small town in Maryland, caught a beak in the hotel business and here I am. Oh here, he was reaching into his coat pocket, produced a business card and handed it to Crystal. This is a producer I know who might be able to help you with your original song. We can talk more at dinner, see you at 6:30" and he was out the door.

In the last few minutes she had learned so much. Kicking back and relaxing was just what she needed to do but her mind was spinning as she was trying to take everything in. She flopped back on the bed and read the card Mr. Schaffer had given her. Record producer, Jack Kapp, on the back hand written, handles Bing Crosby. Now that name she knew. *So Mr. Schaffer knows this guy, or can contact him.*

This could be a real lucky break for me she was thinking. I definitely want to pursue this. Not being able to sit still Crystal got up and started the task of unpacking. As she was doing so, she laid out the outfit she wanted for tonight's dinner with Mr. Schaffer. This finally accomplished she took that long hot shower, the one she'd been dreaming about on the train every night. Standing naked in the stream of wonderfully hot water, only one thing could make her feel 100% better was Vincent. *Dam she hadn't thought about him for at least 12 hours, Mr. purple wouldn't do now either! She was afraid nothing would do ever again. Stop it..stop it...get out, dry my hair, do the make-up thing and enjoy. That's the best advise I can give myself. I didn't do anything wrong, I didn't do anything wrong, dam Vincent you told me to pursue my dream. Stupid, I'm here and he's probably with her. I've given him all this time to be with her! I almost wish I wanted to be with someone else, but then I'd be like him... cheating. I don't think that's my style. Enough, enough, get dressed.*

Crystal did her own hair in a french braid and let it hang down her back. Her make-up was minimal with a little rouge and mascara and a touch of lip stick. She didn't know their destination for dinner so her trusty long black skirt with a slit up to her knee topped off with her gold cowl neck tunic top should do nicely. It was wonderful to know her wardrobe would be suitable here, no one here has ever seen her before. She could even wear her rings, there would be no piano playing tonight. It felt good to wear her wedding ring, monogram and pearl rings, she'd always loved them. The gold ban-go bracelets have always been among her favorites. This felt weird, like she was dressing for a date. She'd given that up years ago.

And then the knock on her door. True to his word, 6:30 on the dot. Mr. Schaffer was a complete gentleman all through dinner at the steak house that featured hand rubbed, grilled to perfection rib-eye. She had to admit that it was to die for, but while eating they discussed getting her a recording appointment with Mr. Jack Kapp. She was very excited at this prospect. A number of people stopped by their table and Crystal was introduced to the publicist handling her ads and marquee as well as the stage director who she'd be working with tomorrow. They made their appointment for 10am. Schaffer then announced this was the end of the meet and greets for tonight, it was time to explore. He wanted to escort her to some of the more interesting parts of the hotel. She found the casino fascinating, colorful and noisy. The Grand Theater scared the crap out of her! It was huge, seating hundreds and it was elegant. She'd practice there tomorrow, but tonight it gave her the woollies! This fact amused Mr. Schaffer, he'd forgotten Crystal was a novice, a great pianist, but she had only entertained in a small club for relatively very few people. So that's where he was taking her next, for some music and a night-cap, as he put it.

Crystal walked into the Monterrey Room on Mr. Schaffer's arm. He directed her to a tall, small round table for two. The music was excellent, something almost familiar to her. She was very comfortable with the rum coke, tapping her fingers and toes to the music. Unconsciously she was twirling her gold necklace with one hand and tapping to the music with the other. The crystal drops on the gold chain kept disappearing down into her blouse. "I'd know that posture and disappearing chain anywhere, hello beautiful." Startled as she was, she kept her composure because she knew that smooth voice and what he was talking about. She was thinking so hard... *Quickly, who is he, where do I know him from, do I dare look at him? He's looking down my blouse, he wants to touch the gold chain...the dawn!!* "Hello, 40th floor, you're a long way from home Johnathan." "Bravo, you remembered my name. Will you play with us tonight?

Let me introduce you and plug your show Saturday night." This time she did turn to face him, and touched his handsome face, ever so gently. She made the first move so he counted with lifting the gold chain off of her skin to let the crystal drops dangle and glitter in the soft light. He dropped it back down on to her skin and the drops disappeared into the folds of her cleavage and also into the material of her blouse. "You are seductive without even trying to be Mrs. Clear". At this Jerry Schaffer cleared his throat and asked if he was interrupting anything. Crystal immediately apologized for her rudeness and introduced Mr. Schaffer to Johnathan Whelton, the violinist of the band that was now playing. Schaffer and Whelton shook hands as Mr. Schaffer thought Crystal's playing tonight was a great idea. He monopolized the conversation for the next few minutes explaining who he was and how Crystal happened to be out with him tonight. He continued with thinking the exposure here would be good for her. The whole time he was talking, Crystal's attention was on Johnathan and his facial expessions and his good looks. Before she knew it, it was planned, she would be playing with the band in their next set. Johnathan smiled warmly, kissed her on the cheek and left their company saying 15 minutes, "wait for your intro."

Mr. Schaffer's attention was totally back on Crystal and her good luck in bumping into Johnathan and getting this opportunity to get into the spotlight. "In this town you are going to find out that everyone seems to know everybody. Thanks to you I now have the opportunity to engage Johnathan in conversation and possibly do business with him. You say he plays on the 40th floor of the New Yorker in the Velvet Room? That's big bucks up there." With a grin he finished with..."you were only on the first floor!"

Crystal wanted another drink before she was called away to play. With that thought, she removed her pearl and monogram rings and asked Mr. Schaffer to hold on to them for her. She choose to keep her wedding ring on, it felt right. She also removed her bracelets as they would be a distraction while she was playing. With a few butterflies in her belly, Crystal's name was now being called from the stage along with her introduction and publicizing her debut in the Grand Theater at the Eldorado Saturday night. The spotlight found her and followed her all the way to the stage.

It was fun, it was accelerating, it showed acceptance. Three tunes later she was back with Mr. Schaffer where they stayed through the end of this set, with another round of drinks and then left. That night Crystal slept like a baby. Being exhausted from her trip and having her talent validated tonight with the adrenaline rush and meeting Mr. Beautiful again, adding three rum cokes to her already heightened system, she now crashed. When she rolled over in the morning, her first thought was of the 'Grand Theater', her second was of Vincent. She felt she had cause for concern on both! The theater was mammoth, she'd never performed for so many. Vincent, it's Saturday morning, was he waking up in her arms this morning? She thinks they are married, of course he is.

After a quick breakfast and lots of coffee, Crystal was sitting at a beautiful, shinny, baby grand piano. If she looked straight ahead, or at her hands or focused on the crystal pitcher of water at her finger tips, she felt fine. It's when she looked out toward the audience her stomach betrayed her. *Come-on Crystal, be smart, look that way and smile, nod your head to the beat of your own music like it is taking you away, close your eyes and look back.* While playing her entrance song, she tried that, so far so good. Now while looking straight ahead, she thought, *sure that was easy, no one is sitting out there, it is quiet. What will it be like when the seats are full? I hope they will be full, shit something else to worry about.* With her eyes closed, she moved on to Rum and a Coke and had a great time playing it. After Take the "A" Train and Star Dust, she felt a presents of someone standing close and looking at her. She stopped mid stroke and said good morning, or is it afternoon now, Mr. Whelton? He didn't know how she knew, he was a quiet as a mouse, but at the recognition he took it upon himself to sit beside her on the bench. He started tinkling with a tune and Crystal joined in. Being very compatible they became very relaxed, took the tune to a faster beat, still faster, and again faster then broke into giggles. After a quick hug he said he stopped by to wish her good luck with tonight's opening. "We've still playing at the Monterrey Room so I won't be able to attend, I would have liked to." Johnathan confessed. "For me, tonight is a dry run for my real performance." Crystal confessed. She immediately explained that tomorrow night her dad and his wife, her mother-in-law were going to be in the audience, she hasn't seen her dad in more than two years. Plus she added "it's the first time he is going to hear my original, untitled arrangement." "That's right, you wrote a song, are you going to introduce it to the world here, tomorrow night?" Johnathan asked the question while getting up and stepping away from piano. "Yes, I've decided that's what I'd like to do. If I can come up with a title before tomorrow night, all the better, if not, so-be-it." Somehow Crystal found herself walking Johnathan to the door as he needed to get to the club for his practice session. This time Crystal kissed him on the cheek and thanked him for coming by. "Knock them dead sweet lady" Johnathan said as he walked away.

Curious saying, Crystal thought. *It's the same thing Miss Elise had said to her.*

Chapter 32

Opening night...the spot lights...the drum rolls...the red carpet...the FULL house. This was not the time for Crystal to get nervous or weak in the knees. Her intro was wonderful, compared to Liberace in high heels. A performance not to be missed or forgotten.

Her first set, thrilling to her and without a missed note to the audience! Stage fright gone and personality galore exhibited when she turned to the audience to introduce her own original instrumental called ' Meadow Memories'. Without her knowledge this selection was being recorded when she played it for the first time in a public arena. The audience acceptance was outstanding and having an on-cor going into break was unrepresented!

The second set was upbeat and full of applause. Crystal knew she was in the right place and for her at the right time. All other thoughts and problems disappeared and let her enjoy this one night, the first night of the rest of her public appearing nights. She started into her final, goodnight song and a note was delivered to her requesting that she repeat and play "Meadow Memories" one more time. Needing to take a deep breath and control the tears that threaten, she stood and faced her audience. With arms spread wide, she performed a little bow of thanks and verbally thanked everyone for their support. "Meadow Memories' was a big hit with the audience.

There was no sleeping tonight. Crystal's thoughts were all over the place. This place. Tonight's performance. Vincent..Vincent being with Rhonda. Seeing her dad tomorrow. Exploring a recording deal. Performing again tomorrow… Spending the week here and doing it all over again next week end! Being away for a whole week. Away from being able to check on Reginald. Not being in the office and rechecking on Reginald, his money and his security. My security, Vincent's safety in living on this money on a monthly basis with an entire Saber family. I hope and pray I'm as good as I think I am. But I'd really feel better if I could check. Vincent was really on her mind now. She thought that she needed him. In her arms, in her bed...the need was ebbing. Now it was more want. She'd always heard, you always want what you can't have...bullshit...I'll have him, when and where I want. I'll work around the picked-fence he is building for Rhonda's sake and she will always be my trump card in getting what I want!

True to her word, Crystal was at the reservations desk at 1pm the next day, pacing, waiting for her father. The Trailways bus just pulled up to the side-walk and she rushed to see the passengers dislodge. The fourth couple off were her dad and Suzie. Everyone all smiles, then tears and mostly hugs, turned into the meet and greet inside at the reservations counter while they signed it. They did cause a bit of a curiosity factor, one because of their height and two because of Crystal's show last night. "Well, the local paper has you as quite the celebrity, I guess you gave them a command performance last night!" Her dad preened. "Really, I haven't seen a paper or heard a review, do you still have the paper?" Crystal was all eyes when Suzie handed her the paper. "They handed this Vegas News out on my ride in as well." "Inside front page" Suzie offered.

After the Grandcockski's checked into their room, the three of them had plans to meet in the Bull-Run lounge for lunch. While the folks were busy checking in, Crystal had the opportunity to read the review that was in the Vegas News. Holding her breathe she turned to the inside front page and read the most faltering words she had ever heard or seen written about herself. After the paper raved about her appearance they raved about her performance and her style and her delivery. A star is born every day and Vegas had it's first last night at the Grand opening of the Eldorado. There was more but the happy tears in her eyes prevented her from reading on. She had the paper tucked under her arm when she strolled into the lounge a few minutes later.

Crystal ordered the first round of drinks and finished reading the review. When the folks joined her and they exhausted the conversation resulting from the review, naturally the conversation came around to Vincent and wasn't it a same he couldn't have come with Crystal. Suzie thought it would have been wonderful for him to be here with her for her first week and first show. Thank goodness for dad and his save, that Vincent is a military man and not always able to just take off on a whim. That topic over, now Crystal could relax and enjoy her visit. Summing up more than two years didn't take that long. Crystal explained working at the operations center in Maryland and taking the 4 plus hour train ride to New York every other week. Playing in the New Yorker and then the train ride back to Maryland. She explained how this had given her great exposure to entertaining and learning how to entertain. Vincent had been a good sport most of the time and even joined her in New York a few times. Then she explained about the move to New Jersey and the house they live in with Miss Elise. "She's really a hoot, a bit older than us, widowed, a chef and owns the wonderfully large house. Large being the operative word, that's why she advertisers for borders. We tell her what we like to eat, most times sit down and make a menu for the week, we buy the food. She puts everything away and she cooks. Together we make sure the kitchen is clean after meals. We are about a quarter mile from base where I am now working out of the bursa's building. The worse run, worse organized unit on base. It is tucked way inside on the last road on base. I need to take a shuttle to and fro every day. Oh, and Miss Elise's house has a great piano. Miss Elise loves to listen to me play. "You remember dad..., how I get when I'm worried or mad or upset? I need to 'bang' on something...the something being the piano. Well...it scares her...it's too loud and too aggressive, she thinks I'll break the 'instrument'! You guys need to meet her some day."

"I don't know where my next assignment will be, but there has been some scuttlebutt about personnel changes coming down the horn. And we don't know when yet either." Suzie added, "maybe the change will bring us back toward you and Vincent. That would be nice for a change" At that thought Crystal's stomach took a nasty turn. She covered with, "the house is plenty big enough or all of us if you do in fact make it back toward Maryland or New Jersey. But for now folks I need to rest a little before tonight and you need to play like vacationers." Their luncheon party broke up, but Crystal had already taken care of the tab, much to her fathers chagrin. "Remember, just say your name at the door tonight, I've already made arrangements for your table. I'll see you at my intermission. Have fun for the rest of the day." She hugged Suzie and her dad and left them in the main concourse of the Hotel/Casino. Back in her room, she really hoped Vincent's name wouldn't come up too often in their visit, she wasn't any good at side stepping her facts.

Rest, OK, she'd try. She couldn't. Four hours to show time. She was starting to get the jitters. Was it her dad? Something had her wanting to pace. She couldn't sit still. She also couldn't lay here on this bed and think of...nothing. Her thought process was nil. That's really strange, she was thinking of nothing! Not Vincent or Reginald, not Miss Elise or her dad...really nothing. Everything since last night had been fine. Shower time, wash away these creepy jitters and lay out your clothes for tonight. Doing something is better than doing nothing! Now she couldn't decide. A cool shower to snap her out of this fog or a hot shower to relax her tired muscles? Just do it...now she was a bundle of nerves...she couldn't even make a simple decision.

Very deliberately she walked into the bathroom, stripped and ran the water in the shower on hot. Just a few seconds standing in that hot steamy stream of water had her senses back. What in the hell had just gotten into her? She wasn't an old lady loosing her mind. She was a young woman who just lost her husband to another woman, another world, one in which she didn't belong. "Meadow Memories" was her baby. It still needed very careful tendering. Get it recorded and released, work on the blues piece and go find Rhonda! To what end she didn't know. But that was her plan and she was finally happy to have it!

Walking back stage in the Grand Theater, she was exhilarated! No nerves just really happy to be here. She walked to the piano and tested the scales. She was ready. With lights blinking the ready...Crystal sat in her spot light, dressed in a long black sleeveless dress, slit from her ankles to her knees on the left side and an equally interesting slit from her neckline just above her tight shoulder down to just cleavage level. Yes, she wore her silver chain. The one that plays peek-a-boo in material and skin. The spotlight caught the sliver comb she wore in her hair to keep it out of her eyes, as well as the silver loops that hung from her ears. With a deep breathe she began. This was just plain joy. She knew she had a full house and she knew everyone paid a pretty penny to sit and listen to her. But to her it was just plain joy. Joy she spruced up with body movements, flirtatious arm waves and accentuated piano movements. Yes, she was an entertainer, and a good one.

She found her dad and Suzie at intermission. The Captain was speechless, almost. He was busting with pride and couldn't believe that beautiful woman up there, playing her heart out and seemingly enjoying every minute of it, was his little girl! "Oh honey," he started "New York taught you so many things! You were ready for this!" "So right dad. Now, for the best part. The first song of my next set is my original piece. I've titled it "Meadow Memories". Some day it will have words and be recorded as a single by some magnificent singing voice, but right now it is my instrumental". Suzie took her hands and said, "we can't wait to hear it. Your program is excellent, and for us it will be over way too soon. You make it very enjoyable." The house lights started to blink and after promising to meet in her dressing room at the end of the show, they parted company.

The audience acceptance of her original song was stupendous. Once hour and ten minutes later, she was awarded with a standing ovation with shouts of 'more---more'. She obliged with her song first and two more songs to finish the night. Good to their word, the Major and Suzie were in her dressing room when she got there. "Excellent, wonderful, fun and worth every penny." her dad said. "I got you in free, you can pay for the next round of drinks." Crystal countered when he hugged her. "Suzie, you've turned him into another man, a hugging one. I like it." Crystal was smiling from ear to ear.

The next morning, or make it late morning they shared brunch and read every local paper for reviews of the local shows. Crystal's was by far the most complimentary and exorbitant and exciting. Everyone was talking about her own original song heading for recording. There was also a picture of her at the piano taken from a very precarious stance showing her very provocative choice of dress. Her first thought of the picture was...*I didn't see anyone that close to me to get that shot and then sheer bliss when she saw the name associated with the photo. It was Peter! She didn't see him there, she didn't see anyone on stage with her. Her mind was racing...is he still in town..where is he staying...how can she reach him...why didn't he call her.* By this time the Captain could tell Crystal's mind was totally somewhere else. "Hey girl, a penny for your thoughts" "Look dad, when she pointed to the name under the picture. It' Peter, he's here, I've got to find him. I want to see him." The Captains face went a little pale at this revelation.

"If he's here, he's busy and working, I wouldn't know where to inquire about him. Um, can you and I have a private minute, there is something I need to talk with you about." At the Captain's words, Suzie excused herself from the table. "I'm heading to the gift shop, you'll find me there", and she left them alone.

The Captain fortified himself with a big gulp of coffee and started. "Do you remember you had a funny feeling when you were first introduced to Vincent. Like I invited him 'just for you'. Well I kinda did. You were seeing way too much of Peter and I've been among boys, boys budding into men all of my life. I knew a long time ago that Peter, other than his height because that was a big thing for you, that he, Peter could never be the man that you would need in your life. At the time you had never encountered a great deal of what the world had to offer. That's why when I saw Vincent growing into a young man of morals, a military man, a man that loved his mother and a man heads taller than other men, I knew you two would hit it off. I'm so glad you did. So you see, you needed to stop chasing after Peter because he is chasing other men." The Captain held Crystal's attention the whole time he was talking. Now she just reached for his nervous hands, looked him in the eyes and confessed that she knew Peter was a queer since the 11th grade.

"Dad, he was my best friend, we talked about everything. I once made a romantic, sexual move toward him, but he told me that he'd only be interested if I were the tall center on the men's basketball team. Sure, I cried for four days, but it explained so many of the things we never did talk about. I did most of the talking back then in our relationship, you were seldom around and mom seamed to have little interest in me, so poor Peter got to know me pretty well. All the while he kept his secret closed up. He admitted in the 11th grade that I was the only one he had ever told, because he trusted me, he trusted our friendship and I had to know why he was not romantically interested in me!" The look on the Captain's face changed. He was relieved to know that his daughter knew the truth about Peter's sexuality. Happy to hear about their relationship and Peter's guarding of Crystal's feelings and young heart. With this new information his facial expression changed and he agreed, "OK, we need to find Peter."

Two days later, it took two whole days using Mr. Schaffer's contacts and Mr. Brentwhistle's connections to track down who Peter would be working for or with. It was a frustrating inquiry in a city that knows everybody but where nobody really comes from there. It's a city of thousands of visitors. Everyone checks in and then checks out...no one really stays. The employment turnover is seasonal or so it seems. It seems nearly every employee goes home with a few new lines for their resume and a story they tell over and over. Just like Crystal, there for two weeks, works a little and goes home with a great story and wonderful notoriety. But Peter could choose to be there for the long haul. Photography in this land of fast money and fast people kept him on the move and busy all hours of the day and night. He had his choice of assignments as he was his own boss. He had built up a portfolio that earned him a reputation of a see all, take pictures of all and carefully provide candor to this clients. Providing privacy in such a public place was worth every penny, or should we say dollar he charged. He knew Crystal was going to be in town and desperately wanted to see her. He also knew she was going to be in the company of her father and most likely her husband. He and his life style didn't fit with these people. He hadn't seen Crystal in nearly 4 years and didn't really know if she would want to see him or be seen with him.

It was Wednesday when she got a note delivered to her hotel mail box, it was from Peter. He requested her company for dinner Thursday night at the Boulder Club. She wasn't working and she'd be seeing her dad off at 4 in the afternoon so there was no reason why she couldn't meet him. It was signed...Hugs, Peter. Now that warmed her heart! She looked for more but that was it...no time or location at the club. She was excited! Her mind was working overtime. Her thoughts were everywhere. *She had a date with her best friend. What to wear? How to do her hair? It didn't matter...it was Peter. No...this is Vegas...it matters. This is the kind of news that's makes it back home before you get there. This is front page rag newspaper. It's the kind of stuff gossip circles love. But Brentwhistle told her a long time ago, it really doesn't matter what they say about you in the paper as long as they spell you name right! Any time your name was in the paper it is advertising and it is free! Oh was she really starting to think like that?? Things mattered to her. What she looked like, who she was with, The effect she had on people, it mattered to her. So many times lately she wished she was back in the little house on Bridge Road and her only worry was what to have for supper, because she knew Vincent would be along very soon and he could touch and fondle and love her worries away. Life was so much simpler then!*

(Little did she know how much simpler those days were compared to what was to come!)

Chapter 33

The farewells to Suzie and the Captain were bitter sweet. Crystal had turned into a sniveling, clinging vine when her dad tried a quick hug of goodbye. All of a sudden she felt like the men in her life were leaving her and she felt the crush of it. Trying to smooth over those uncomfortable moments she wholeheartedly invited them to the big house in New Jersey when they were on the Atlantic Ocean side again. Brushing away her tears, she smiled brightly on the outside, and watched them board their train. Feeling so alone and heart broken by their leaving, she walked around the corner (where they could no longer she her through the train windows) sat with her head in her hands resting with elbows on her knees. Very silently she let her tears run down her cheeks.

The pictures of her hugging her dad goodbye were touching, but the ones Peter just took of her sitting on the bench captured her sense of loss as he was able to catch the tears leaving her face, drifting downward and puddling in a stream of light. These images of Crystal were magnificent with the shadows of the train on the floor broken by hundreds of feet as well as the reflections of the train in the window just above Crystal's head. The shards of light shinny through the shadows were caught perfectly. All of these points of perfection would be uncovered later when Peter had a chance to develop his film. Right now, that he'd managed to snap a few shots of her, he wanted to sit near her, hold her and stop her tears. The sight of her like this was breaking his heart. First he sat next to her and let her know there was a body next to her. Then he gently, but with purpose landed his full hand on her shoulder and said, "I need a hug too"

She stilled immediately, his voice, so familiar, she never looked up but folded herself into his welcome arms and they hugged tightly for many moments. When he felt her body relaxing he pushed away from her just a bit and using his thumbs, whipped the tears from her eyes and pushed her hair back from her face. "You are still a beautiful woman, Cockski" he mumbled to her with their foreheads touching. She backed away from him so fast and laughed, laughed so hard she cried again! They walked arm in arm out of the train station, hailed a cab and went to the Boulder Club where Peter had a reservation. They talked and drank and talked some more, then ate and Crystal was brought up to date with everything Peter had been doing and the places he had been since the last time she had seen him. Sitting with Peter and talking was like old times. The minutes just ticked away into hours which lead to more drinking, then dancing and then when the lights went down and the spot lights starting bouncing off of Crystal's bountiful head of hair, recognition set in. This may be Thursday, but it's also Vegas. A woman such as Crystal can't hit town and stay hidden for long. The Boulder Club may not be on Main Street, but in Vegas any street is Main Street. The Boulder Club was happy to have Crystal's presents there and the notoriety it would bring to them both in the morning papers. A favorable quote from her as well as a song or two from her wouldn't hurt either. Crystal agreed to both as long as she could play her own arrangement. 'Meadow Memories'. Peter felt proud to be with Crystal and she made sure his name accompanied the photo that was taken and released for the morning papers. It was a totally unexpected fun filled afternoon and night for Crystal. A part of her heart will always belong to Peter. There is no other person that can make her feel the ways he does. It's more than love, it's trust, happiness and camaraderie. Knowing that he would never hurt her because their cards have always been face up on the table. There's is such a shared relationship of never having to say I'm sorry. What for..why..they owe each other nothing, but they give oh so much!

Crystal loved looking at the morning papers. Why not, she was pictured in nearly everyone of them lately. Last nights photo showed a girl out having fun. Peter is so good at capturing a moment and turning it into a story. There is always more to be said about his pictures. But tonight it's back to work, at least that's what her contract says, she still thinks she only 'playing'. The hard part is hanging around during the week waiting for the weekend and it's appointed show times. At least Sunday after her last encore she can ready herself for the train ride back home. She has a lot of work to do once she is back in New Jersey. After checking on her personal projects she needs to ready herself for a trip back to Maryland and visiting her pals in the Operations Center and learning her way around certain neighborhoods. Now that is what she calls work. All of this she needs do to alone.

Chapter 34

Sitting in her assigned train cabin ready to head home she is reflecting on the last couple of hours. Last nights show was bitter sweet in that it was her last! Her fantasy life is over. Once again she played to a full house with great praise in this mornings papers. She packed-up her room mostly yesterday, giving it a once over again this morning not wanting to forget anything. She had collected all of the newspapers with articles about her and she was bringing them home for Miss Elise. Peter had just seen her off with a big hug. She didn't know he was going to show up, that was sweet of him. And that brings us to now. With the engines running her thoughts went to, home. Her real life. The one in which she needs to share with Vincent. He'll probably not be happy to see her...now he needs to share Rhonda with her! This really sucks.

Crystal's next few days, that's how long, will be problematic at best. Her mind is working overtime to try to piece together time with Vincent, time to be in New York and time to relax at home, if she still has one at Miss Elise's. The agreement was to occupy the residence with her and eat with her and spend time at the house, not so much to keep her company as to make it look and feel lived in. The experience in Vegas was a great one and she would do it again in heart beat. The travel time was the problem with experience. She'd like to try for Atlantic city next. It was so much closer. She also needed to be in contact with the song producer to follow-up on the great lead. Her notes on things to do was growing, she was just fortunate enough to be able to afford her to do list!

Finally home, she was swept off her feet at the train station by Vincent pacing, waiting for the train to stop and Crystal to disembark and join him at the gate. He hugged her and swung her around and kissed her long and hard like he never expected to see her again. This greeting for Crystal was the perfect beginning to her homecoming. They both couldn't get their "I've missed you so much" words out between kisses fast enough. They arrived home together and Miss Elise was ecstatic to see them home together and all lovey-dovey toward one another. Dinner together, the three of them, was chatty about Vegas and untruths out of Vincent about his travels and mission for the last two weeks. Crystal knew every word out of his mouth was a lie, he did it so well. Him sitting here with her smiling, holding her hand, eating a mammoth dinner and helping to clear after dinner seamed like the Vincent Crystal knew, but was this just a facade? Just a false front and a mask to hide behind?

By breakfast time, Crystal had her answer. No one can lie that good. Oh No, that was her Vincent in her bed last night. There was no Rhonda in between them last night. It was like magic, he was like magic. His feather touches and anxious thrusts filled her and she held him with mussels that hadn't been used in a couple of weeks and the sensation thrilled him. With her body movements she could control his momentum and control the timing and thrill of their organisms. They happened frequently and laid the ground work and promises of more to come. Morning always came too soon for these two! Up and out early and off to the base for both of them.

With hoops and hollers and congratulations from everyone when they saw Crystal coming warmed her heart. They hollered "we saw the papers", "You were a hit"..."What's this about your own song" The voices and questions were coming from everywhere, she just waved and smiled and waited for her shuttle to take her to the bursars unit. Once there she had the means of communication she needed to complete nearly everything that was on her mind. First...the Reginald money was hit twice...two Fridays in a row...payroll money, Next, Crystal saw her withdrawal from the Keith Rogers file, it was still in tack and a secret. Next she sent a text to her dad and reinforced her invitation to stay at the 'big' house if they ever made it back to the east coast. Feeling a little better that she had accomplished a few things, her next chore was to contact the recording studio and try to get an appointment with Mr. Jack Kapp.

When all things happened like clockwork, as they should, it was a breathe of fresh air. Elise was thrilled to have them back in the house. Her appointment a the Kapp studio in New York was in two weeks on a Friday when she was due to be back at the New Yorker. Being with Vincent was like a second honeymoon, very loving. Each day they traveled to the base together, Crystal would be home earlier than Vincent, but each day she needed to practice then do laundry or go shopping, sit and pay bills or just be busy with every-day tasks. It felt good just to be normal. Each day supper with Elise was a gab fest and very enjoyable. Then Thursday night, the night before Crystal leaves for New York, her physic starts to work on her and she remembers when she's gone, so is Vincent. From now on, she has decided to return back to Jersey on Monday. The train ride isn't so bad, she can travel Friday stay until Monday morning and travel back. It's two weekends in a row away from Vincent, giving him free rein to do as he pleases. She tries not to think about that.

Her recording session goes off with out a hitch. She records one solo and one with accompaniment of harp, violin and trumpet. They both are wonderful, although she admits she loves the rich sounds of the other instruments. The next two months speed by in the blink of an uneventfully eye. Go to the base, check on everything important, eat some lunches, but always supper with Elise, make love with Vincent, get up with the alarm clock and repeat. There were major renovations happening in her corner of the New Yorker, so her weekends were postponed. Her professional life put on hold! Her personal life was in permanent interruption. This became very evident two months later when Vincent took two weeks leave to be with Rhonda and the birth of his son Russell. Naturally Crystal was the only one he could tell the absolute truth to for his leave, but Crystal being the loving person she was, backed him with his cock-a-mammy story on base. He returned to Elise's house a happy man, but Crystal put her foot down and told him straight out she didn't want blow by blow of his last two weeks. Neither did she want to hear him gloat about the beautiful baby boy Rhonda had birthed for him. That was Reginald's son and Reginald didn't live here!

Once the New Yorker had it's new face lift at it's main corridor and the entrance to Crystal's Piano Palace, Crystal was back to work. She loved the pace and she loved the work. She loved replacing the thoughts of Reginald with Rhonda or Russell in her head with thoughts of her song hitting the radio and selling like hot cakes and being requested whenever, wherever she played. She had taken on three appearances in the Madison Hotel in Atlantic City, and she always played to a sell-out crowd. New York and Atlantic City had been keeping her busy and giving Vincent ample time to spend with Rhonda. So much so, when they were finally together relaxing on this Monday night after a hectic weekend, Vincent casually announced that Rhonda was pregnant again. He also mentioned that his unit would be meeting up with another training unit in Virginia for four weeks around the first of November. This was too much! Now Crystal only heard noise, Vincent's voice, but only noise! Just when things were going so well, live was smooth, they were living together and things were smooth! C'est la vie, Crystal's heart was in turmoil again. At least he'd be four weeks away from Rhonda as well. That was a hateful thought! She couldn't help it!

It was the third Tuesday that Vincent had been away and Crystal received an "Important Message." at the Bursar's unit. Crystal's private number on the telex machine, only known by Vincent and herself, could only be accessed by a personal pin number. With her heart in her throat, so afraid something had happened to Vincent, she read her message. She read it again and with disbelief read it again.

Sorry Crystal, I've done it again.

I need the identity of Aspen Chambers, dob 7-1-1927

Captain, U.S. Navy, stationed Norfolk, VA

ASAP...We've done the deed, she's pregnant

hate me later, but please do this NOW

Crystal was too nervous and on the verge of tears to do anything else today. She left the unit at the back of the base and walked. When Pepere' picked her up, she couldn't even be cordial to him. He dropped her at the front gate and she walked all the way home. Yelled hello to Miss Elise and ran a hot tub and soaked. Soaked her sore feet and breathed between sobs of anguish.

For such as strong man, Vincent was such a little boy! He took what he wanted and thought about the consequences later, if at all. Crystal was such an enabler and working outside of the law, they both had major consequences to pay if caught. Their barrel was getting deeper, she hoped it could handle a little more turmoil.

Wednesday morning Crystal returned to the unit at the back of the base and worked her magic again to create the identity of Aspen Chambers. She had to smile, she liked the name. It fit him. He had another child on the way. Again this child would have no grandparents, no family tree or heaven forbid no bloodline to rely on in an emergency. Not her problem. *Stop thinking so much, fool. I am his only life line. I could bury him. Ya, well...he could do the same to me!*

It was that very weekend that Crystal's second original song was finished. Miss Elise titled it "Black Water Blues" Crystal had been toying with it for months, but her mood put it all together. Miss Elise hit the nail on the head with the title. Crystal pictured ocean waves churning in a storm, rolling frothy tops with angry black rolls.

Once again the holidays came and went. Lucky for Crystal the New Yorker was filled to capacity over the holidays and the shows must go on. Hers as well. This crazy schedule helped to keep her mind off of her home situation and where Vincent might be. There was little she knew about his newest heart throb, but what she did know was she was a rich kid, no living family and she was little. She has a little name, Amy and short bouncy blond hair. Much the opposite of Rhonda or for that matter herself. Vincent's taste in women must have changed and she must have said all the right things about family and having children. She knows her stand on having children is still a sore spot with him. But now there is no way in hell she'd have children with him. He should know that! There coming together is healthy exercise. The rhythm they have together is like good music. It's good, almost perfect even if there are outside currents trying to influence it's directive. There are just too many outside forces moving against her right now. But not really. New York is employing her just the way she likes it. Atlantic city is on the rise in the new year and her music, her original songs could eventually make her a wealthy woman. The next time she's in New York, the recording studio is setting her up with a young song writer just starting out. His specialty is more putting words to music. Just what Crystal needs. Maybe this could work out for both of them. She definitely has a picture in her head, so if he can put words to her thoughts, they'll have a winner! The only negativity in her life stems from Vincent. That is where the uncomfortable forces are coming from. If she could only make herself believe that she and her music are not the forces driving him away, she'd be happier with herself. *He has his career as first, not me, so I've put my music first, not him. Those thoughts drive her crazy!*

Crystal was going to use January to sort out her personal responsibilities, make sure the back story and all credentials were in place for Aspen Chambers, and just relax and try to enjoy being home with Miss Elise and Vincent. When Vincent was in New Jersey, he was all hers. She had his full attention. It was like he didn't want or need to be anywhere else. Their bedtime was lustful and satisfaction extraordinaire. The month of January had been good to Crystal's balance of military base work, the one weekend she spent in New York and Vincent taking off for Maryland and living with Vincent, totally as his wife. There was a skip in her step as she thought this is what their life should be like. (minus the Rhonda situation) So now February brings change orders to Vincent and half of his unit. They are needed back in Virginia to fix everything that has gone terribly wrong since they left. The only difference is that she, Crystal, will not be going with him. This moves Vincent further away from wife number two and puts him squarely in the arms of, going to be wife, number three! They have two weeks together before he moves on. Crystal clearly decides that she cannot go with him. Her dates in New York are firm, there is a new Vegas Contract in the works for two weeks in April and two weeks in

May. Between what contacts she now has and what Mr. Brentwhistle does, they have filled her off weekends in Atlantic City. This leaves her maybe one day a week to check into the bursars unit for a friendly coffee with the crew and a private peak into her personal affairs.

Before Vincent leaves, they sit with a calendar and review what dates are filled for Crystal and when they might see one another again. Before he can get back to New Jersey even for a conjugal visit, he will be married to Amy, and father to number two in Maryland with Rhonda. Just seeing these facts laid out in front of her in black and white, she can't believe this is her 'husbands' immediate future!

What Vincent isn't showing is his excitement in all of his upcoming changes. He acknowledges his beautiful wife sitting knee to knee with him and will love her with baited breathe until he leaves, but leaving doesn't hold loneliness or sex starved nights anymore. His son Russell will soon be a big brother and is learning to talk. Maybe by the time he gets there he'll say da-da!! And he'll have glorious months to spend with Amy. Maybe he'll be on hand for the birth of their first. Inwardly he is smiling and feeling the excitement. Crystal's life style would never give him these feelings! So leaving is not a sad occasion for him. Leaving the calendar to sit on the table with his future happiness, they retire to the bedroom. This is where her happiness lays, her in Vincent's arms and Vincent's bed and him nestled deep inside her for as long as she can hold him. But she now knows she cannot hold him the way she wants to, so enjoy now and whatever he gives her, she'll make do!

Before she knows it, she is finishing her April two weeks in Vegas and May is just around the corner. By now Vincent is the father of two in Maryland and has a new wife in Virginia, probably showing in her family way. The weeks are just going by too fast. Crystal will stay in New York until she returns to Vegas in two weeks and play in her Piano Bar at the New Yorker. Her meetings with young Brad, the song lyric writer are going well, fun. He is madly in love with her and she enjoys egging him on in simple ways. It gets his juices running when she paints a verbal picture of what she wants him to write the words to. She tries to tell him of her views or her feelings. She gets very dramatic with arm and finger movement, and again with feelings on the piano. He needs to be able to use words that will fit in the tempo and structure of the music...so far that is the problem. His words are wonderful, almost eloquent, he has painted the picture Crystal's song is trying to convey. His words are catching the movement of the music but they don't fit lengthwise or syllable wise. A little more time and it will be perfect. It has been time well spent. They both have learned a lot about their craft.

Once again her recording of 'Black Water Blues' has hit the radio by storm. It has also become one of the favorite songs in her show repertoire and is gaining popularity with other performers in their shows! Her dad even sent her a text...he heard it and loved it! In the text he also informed her that his orders have been changed again...he is headed back to the east coast next spring, location still not disclosed. Hearing from her dad always lightens her day and makes her smile. Him coming home is half good and half scary. She'd love him to be closer, come to dinner closer, but then there is the situation with Vincent. Once again...one day at a time.

Now back in Vegas, Crystal's name and marquee banners have changed and are all the rave about her new 'blues' song. They have her dressed in a long blue gown standing in black water with with ripples of blue simmering on the top of the water, with one blue tear coming down her cheek. Very illusive, eye catching and almost sexy...It is Crystal to a tee! She loves the effect. Everyone she comes in contact with congratulates her on her hit song and popularity. "You've found a home here in Vegas" is the general consensus. Her invitations to go out for a drink or out for dinner, have changed to written invitations to play at this club or another or another. Invitations to perform in other venues in the New York City area have also been flooding in to her attention at the New Yorker. Clive Brentwhistle has intercepted these messages and wants to have a heart to heart with her. To date he has been her unofficial manager for the Eldorado, only in Vegas. He knows things need to change. He's known from the beginning that Crystal would blossom and become bigger than life. She still doesn't know what her demands could be in negotiating show dates and times. His heart is full for her and her growth, but he is feeling like he is loosing his first child! Once back in New York at the end of May, Crystal decides to play New York for the month of June and return home to Miss Elise's for the rest of the summer. She's tired, she's lonely. It's time to think about a new song. She needs something to fill her mind if her arms and body cannot be filled!

Mr. Brentwhistle agrees that she needs a period of rest. It will do her good to get grounded with some old friends and family, he knows nothing of her situation with Vincent.

Once home, she makes sure she is still welcome at Miss Elise's. "Oh my dear child, I haven't had so much fun in years. You, You and Vincent, Vincent coming and going all the time. I never know and I really don't care. How long are you home for this time? Do I dare ask?" Crystal just hugged the little lady and shrugged. "The rest of the summer is what I am planning." A brilliant smile lit Miss Elise's face as she set about talking about supper.

Supper was just what Crystal needed. A home cooked meal and conversation all about her. But not just the music. About her childhood, she told of Peter (some facts) she talked about her mother. Her mother in her dad's house and her mother working in the real world with important people. She talked about her dad and Vincent's mother and maybe they'd be coming east from the State of Washington, still serving in the Navy. Miss Elise asked about Mr. Brentwhistle in New York, his role with Crystal now and maybe in the future. They sat so long in conversation, the dinner dishes were getting crusty and needed to be washed! The conversation continued over the pantry sink while they did the dishes. Crystal mentioned Vincent being home, hopefully around Labor Day for a couple of weeks before needing to return to Virginia. But during the next few weeks she intended to invite Mr. Brentwhistle here for a 'business' meeting. She also wanted to invite her mother here as well to just kick back, talk and get to know her better. Miss Elise listened to Crystal's stories and hopes and told her, whatever she wanted to do, just let her know and she'd cook up a storm! With that they retired to the living room where Crystal sat at the piano for the next 3 hours just playing her heart out!

This was Crystal's relaxing time...her thinking time and her time to let all of her demons escape threw her fingers. By the time she finished she had her summer mapped out and all the people she intended inviting here logged in her brain and she needed to write these things on the calendar. Then tomorrow she'd get busy with her invites and then go car shopping. Where did that come from?? She had enough money, why not! She could learn to drive and it would save so much time in her travels. Now that was a major, to-do, for her summer. Within the week Crystal had invited and confirmed her visit and pow-wow with Mr. Brentwhistle. She had also talked with and also confirmed her visit with her mom to visit as well. Mom sounded eager to come to New Jersey, like she had an agenda and this visit would fit very well. So be it, so far so good. More than good, in her daily treks to the base, she had been taking driving lessons from Jim Davies and having a ball. Jim was a good sport and had a lot of patience with Crystal. Shifting gears was the thing that gave Crystal the most trouble. Staying straight on the road, obeying the speed limit, learning the turn hand signals and using the mirrors were no problem. The dam stick on the floor didn't like cooperating with her left foot on the clutch! She stalled that dam jeep more times, she jerked her first gear starts every time, and had a hard time not rolling backwards on a hill from a stop to start!. Jim told her she needed to listen to the gears to be really good at all of these things before she could test drive a car off of a car lot. Then he remembered... the gear shift in cars was on the column, not on the floor. It would be a new learning curve for her all over again. He'd go with her naturally, but it was necessary for her to practice on a car before her shopping day and become become better at it. Besides, there weren't too many woman drivers these days, most men frown on it! He even guessed the car salesman wouldn't be comfortable selling a car to a woman, but for the money he would!

Mr. Brentwhistle was charmed by Elise and had a great visit with Crystal. He arrived completely prepared for his position in Crystal's career, recordings, recording studio personnel, choice and appointments with song writers or lyric writers. After prefacing that he loved her like a daughter, he quit! She was just too big for him now, she needed a real manager. Someone that knew the business and could get her the best deals. She knew this was coming, she had felt it in her stomach. He'd always be her best critic and best friend and she'd always want him in her life. He even offered to help her scout out the hiring of a good manager. That was a relief. Business over, now they could enjoy the rest of their visit, but on his fifth day, Crystal's mother arrived.

"Mom, your early, why didn't you send word, I, someone, could have met you." Crystal was opening the front door and helping her mother in with her bags and showing the taxi driver where to drop the others. The driver dismissed and bags all in, now it was time for hugs and introductions. "Mom, Rita Dunski, (even she had to rid herself of the name Grandcockski) please meet Clive Brentwhistle. And of course our hostess, the lady that owns this lovely house. Miss Elise. Rita hugged everyone and acknowledged she had heard their names before and was now pleased to put a face to those names.

At supper that evening Rita apologized for arriving early and maybe upsetting Mr. Brentwhistle's visit or business with Crystal. Rita explained she had the extra time because her boss, the President's wife was off campaigning with him. And no matter the results of the election in November, she'd be out of a job. So this was a well earned vacation. Nonsense, he made sure she could dismiss the interrupting notion, meeting her was almost the highlight of his visit so far. During coffee and desert Mr. Brentwhistle questioned Rita extensively about her work and what she'd be looking for next. It was like they had the kitchen table all to themselves, and he was conducting an interview. But the look in Mom's eyes was anything but business. Miss Elise and Crystal cleared the table and did the dishes in the pantry, making eyes at one-another, listening to the budding romance at the table. That is what it was, a total flirtatious conversation with them getting to know one another. Brentwhistle ran a few names past Rita, and she acknowledged she knew of them or worked with them on a few projects for Mrs. Roosevelt. Crystal whispered to Elise, "he's up to something...his brain is working over time. Mark my words, before lunch tomorrow he is going to announce a fool-proof scheme. I don't know if I'm the brunt of the scheme or is it Mom? Peak at her...her eyes are like watery sponges...taking in every word he says and measuring him and preserving him to memory."

"I failed miserably at one major job in my life, so I'll never put myself in that position again. My next failure was with Crystal, as her mother." Rita was answering a question Clive had just asked her, but Crystal missed most of the question. The answer was spoken with such raw emotion, Crystal wanted to go to her mother and sooth some of the rawness she just heard. But Elise caught her by the arm and halted her from doing so. "This is their conversation, let him handle her," Elise instructed.

The ease dropping had been fun up to that point. Now Crystal just wanted to assure her mother that as far as moms go, she wasn't the best, but when it comes to mothers, she was one of the best. It took guts to rise out of one bad situation and remake your life into a strong, trusting, person that can be leaned on. Rita had earned Crystal's respect by doing just that! Clive was learning where Crystal had gotten her drive and determination to go after what she wanted. Clive knew from the get go that Crystal would succeed in a big way just by her presents at the New Yorker. Now he knew from where that drive was fed. This woman sitting with him could teach him a thing or two if only he could tap into her strength. First of character and then determination, she's a keeper. *OMG...I've never had that thought before in my life...where did that come from.* Clive quickly covered both of Rita's hands with his and thanked her for a thought provoking conversation and great supper company. With that he left the table and wandered outside. Crystal felt the change in the room when Clive left the table. Rita was wringing her fingers together in a nervous manner and when Crystal approached her, she sighed heavily and said, "did I say something wrong? "No mom, you just gave him a lot to think about...he's never met a woman quite like you. I expect that tomorrow around noon he will explode with an idea or a proposition that will floor us. I got that feeling by some of the things he was asking you about. He's quite a character and a people and money mover. You'll see!"

Ten minutes and he was back in the kitchen asking Crystal to play for them. That's all the time he needed to compose himself and feel jovial and sociable again. He asked for 'Meadow Memories' and 'Black Water Blues' and whatever new material she was trying out. He wanted to be one of the first to hear it! The house was alive again with music and great people. Not more than 30 minutes later Crystal stopped the music and said, "listen up". Four bars later, and she repeated the four bars... she stopped and announced "that's all I've got, but I think it's enough for me to start working on a new tune. All smiles around the room when Crystal kissed her mother goodnight, hugged Mr. Brentwhistle and offered to walk Elise to her room. She knew the signs, she'd have her period by morning!

Crystal was restless in bed that night. Yup, period cramps and thoughts about 'not being pregnant' permeated her mind as well as thoughts about Vincent. He had what he wanted, just not from her. Her life was going to change again...Mr. Brentwhistle was giving up his post as her 'manager'. That is what he was...just never in writing or a paid position. Just in want and in love and in generous time spent on her career. She knew he was worn out. She knew he wanted better for her, but to date she was happy and satisfied with what he had provided. Changes again...with different people...she'd need to make sure Vincent had a place in her new plans. Vincent...4 weeks to Labor Day Weekend. Some days were longer than others and some nights were worse than others. Tonight she longed for Vincent's closeness and love. She'd have her period in four weeks...again...shit!!

Too many days had passed by, Crystal needed to get to the base today. At breakfast she offered a tour and introductions to her friends on base and in the Bursars Unit. Just a peak at her personal files would hold her if all things were in good order. Reginald's file always made her think of Vincent, but lately so did Aspen's. *Just as long as all the kids are all right.* That information wouldn't be in the files...why was she even thinking about that! *Because they were more a part of his life than me. They get more attention from him than I do. He thinks more about them than me...our lives have moved, divided now...his very much so! Stop the pity party...go to the base*

Inside the main gate, Crystal sat on the bench and invited her guests to do the same and wait for the shuttle and Pepere'. "He's an old man who drives the shuttle for something to do daily. He knows everyone and a lot about their business. He is very noisy..I relate that to him being a lonely old man. Here he comes". Mr. Brentwhistle had never been on a military base. He found this very exciting. Rita on the other hand was having a throw-back to her other life. She saw excitement in Crystal's posture and heard it in her voice. Crystal grew up on a military base, so this was like coming home to her. This was a major cause in Rita's marriage not working. It held no charm for her! Crystal and Pepere' pointed out the high-lights on the way back to the Bursar's Unit but informed them this was nothing compared to what they would see next. Crystal's introductions were quick as were her peeks at her personal files. No fires to put out, normal withdrawals and all deposits were safely where they belonged. Next Pepere' drove them down the street and onto the best part of the base. Now, even Rita was impressed. Mr. Brentwhistle sat at the edge of his seat...no matter where he looked, he couldn't get enough. Every way he turned there were ships, and destroyers, and tankers and even one aircraft carrier just being towed into the harbor. Never a dull moment!

Back at the house, Elise greeted them with afternoon coffee, tea and tiny cakes. Cakes of all sorts and flavors. Away from the base, Crystal could recognize the gleam in her mothers eyes. Just like last night, every time she looked at Clive Brentwhistle. It was nice listening to the radio and other people talking about their lives and their wants and their ambitions. It also took the pressure off of Crystal to entertain, so in this comfortable moment she let her mind wander. Mom was just reminiscing about Crystal as a teenager. Crystal's mind went to the beach where she was a virgin one day, but not the next and how much fun she had being a tease and a loose cannon. Mr. Brentwhistle was remembering Crystal's accidental audition when she played the piano for the first time in the empty, before hours of the piano bar. They were both talking about a Crystal that was very different from the one that sat with them today. Crystal's mind went to the way Vincent acted and reacted to Mr. Brentwhistle at their first meeting. He was a new husband and a macho man. The way he tenderly laid her in the green grass of the beautiful meadow. The way they learned how to synchronize their bodies to move and fit together perfectly. All of a sudden the room was quiet and all eyes were on her. Embarrassed, she said "what?"

Mr. Brentwhistle repeated, "do I have your permission to escort your mother to dinner tonight away from prying eyes?" "I don't pry," Crystal proclaimed and the same came from Miss Elise! "You most certainly do, both of you. If I want to hold Rita's hand, if I want to get her so stinkin' drunk she can't refuse me." "You won't have to go that far, I'll not refuse you, regardless of the location or situation." Rita retorted. So it was settled..Miss Elise didn't need to cook for them tonight!

Chrystal and Miss Elise had a quiet evening together playing scrabble after their supper of leftovers from the frig. It was nice to just stay home and relax for awhile and not have to entertain company. As much as they were 'family', they were still company. It was easy to go to bed early, it's not like they were waiting for teenagers to get home by curfew.

The morning breakfast was still just Crystal and Miss Elsie. The breakfast dishes done, the morning paper read, from front to back and the laundry nearly ready to be hung, greeted the two missing from breakfast just returning home from their dinner out last night. They both looked radiant with tired pink eyes, a slight blush to their cheeks and smiles from ear to ear. Mom's announcement of "after a shower and an afternoon nap, we'll see you for supper."…..long pause…. "If that's all right with you?" said Mr. Brentwhistle looking from Miss Elise to Crystal. Miss Elise.. "of course, that's what vacation is all about." After the two middle-aged teenagers left the kitchen, Crystal just whispered "who knew?"

There was absolutely no secret as to what was going on upstairs from the tell-tale footsteps from one room to the other, then all quiet. Not wanting to disturb her mom and Mr. Brentwhistle, Crystal knew there would be no piano playing this afternoon, so she headed over to the base and the bursa unit to be of help if she could, or raise hell if it were warranted and of course check her personal files if the corner was empty enough. Sitting alone in front of the key-board to the telex machine, Crystal's nerves and thought processes started to make her question everything she'd done to date. *Marring Vincent, that was easy, she loved him. He made her whole, he made her happier than she ever thought she could be. With him in her life and in her bed, she was Mrs.*

Clear. Doing what she did here…It started out…for the money. Now she did it for him. He needed these identifies and this money to … raise his families. She needed this money to continue to live her lifestyle as Mrs. Clear, but also as 'Crystal', the well paid performer, song writer, turning a blind eye to what her lover did when she was not with him. He was a military man always away on assignment and tired and horny when he made it home to her, just like any other military man. He'd never let her down, therefore, it was her job to never let him down. She played the odds in this office of never getting caught, she played the piano for a living and because she loved to do so and she played with a few men's hearts to a point, but never beyond the silly and the teasing and the flirtatious because she knew she could. She could be a dangerous woman on any dance floor or in any bar because that is where she spent most of her time, but she also knew how good it would be when Vincent got home and held her and filled her the way only he could! OK, time to go…three more weeks before Vincent is home.

Crystal said her good-byes to all in the office and waited for Pepere' to pick her up and get her back to the main gate. It was nearly supper time when she walked in the front door and she could immediately hear voices from the kitchen and the aroma of fresh baked bread. She made herself a rum-coke and joined her mom and Mr. Brentwhistle at the kitchen table. Miss Elise was busy between the pantry and the kitchen, but very much part of the conversation. Crystal loved living here and she could tell that her mom and Mr. Brentwhistle were very comfortable as well. Crystal just heard Miss Elise say, "I think that would be a wonderful solution and it would be good for her as well." Crystal jumped in with "good for who and what is the solution?"

At this Mr. Brentwhistle got to his feet and walked over to Crystal and put his hands on her shoulders, as much to hold her down as well as for comfort by his next words. "You know that I can no longer shoulder the responsibilities of being your manager, you're too big and too popular and you command too much money for your appearances. And you're too sort after for me to keep up with your…". Crystal turned to face him, with tears in her eyes, said "solution?" At this,

Crystal's mom joined the conversation with "to answer your question… good for you and the solution….may I be your manager?"

Miss Elise now took control of her kitchen and the conversation. "OK folks, freshen your drinks and please continue this conversation in the living room while I finish supper and set the table. We'll be ready to eat in about 20 minutes. I'll ring the bell.

Supper was wonderful, roast chicken, lots of fresh vegetables from the garden, tasty gravy over mashed potatoes and a new alliance between mother and daughter. Miss Elise couldn't be happier to have a new tenant in Rita, Crystal's new manager. Rita explained that with the election in November she'd be out of a job. All of her acquaintances were of a job related manner and they would cease to exist. Her rent was outlandish so without a job she couldn't afford it. This would be perfect if Crystal would have her and if Clive would help her get her feet wet with all of his acquaintances. Besides Rita went on, looking into her daughters tear filled eyes…"I'd like the chance to get to know the young woman you've grown into." Crystal was on her feet and hugging her mom like she had wanted to so many times in her younger life.

"Enough, enough for now…sit and eat before it gets cold…talk between bites, I don't want to miss a thing, you all are keeping me young." Elise started passing the potatoes around followed by the gravy. It was a festive meal and not lacking in conversation that lasted through pineapple upside-down cake for desert. Everyone had a hand in clearing the table and stacking the dishes to be washed. Rita insisted in hanging back and helping finish in the pantry while Crystal and Clive retired to the living room for more conversation. Elise was excited and so looking forward to the future.

Clive was ready for this alone time with Crystal because he had her bankbook with him, as well as a partial list of her expenditures and a list of incomes from a few of her shows. Crystal knew she had signed quite a few checks and had spent a lot of money on recording studios and song writers, but she never questioned anything Mr. Brentwhistle had done for her or arranged for her or set aside for her…she just didn't know. This was the time for her to find out. She was rich! It seemed like it happened overnight. "Where did all of this money come from" she quizzed him. 'We'll need to go over your books when we're back in New York. Let's just take this minute to talk about hiring your Mom. We talked about this scenario at length last night. With her connections and your talent, I believe it's a combination that can't fail. First she needs to sign a lease with Elise. That's her first expenditure out of what you are going to pay her as your full time manager. Her needs are going to be great so I'm thinking you start her at a percentage of whatever she books for you. The more she gets for a booking the more that goes in her pocket. Then if she is with you in Vegas, or were ever you go she needs lodging there. You'll need to negotiate with her who pays what and when. Transportation the same thing. To date you've done well, but your future is bright and she'll be able to sell you at a higher price than I did, because you've grown to stardom" Crystal just sat and listened to every word he said. She felt the same now as she did the first time she played at the New Yorker, like a kid with a new toy! "Crystal, say something. I've laid out a simple outline of what needs to be done, but it's not that simple. You'll need an attorney to draw up a contract so neither one of you gets burned in this agreement." "I've heard every word you said. And I'll do as you say. Will you help me with hiring an attorney and negotiating with my mom?" Crystal's tone of voice was soft and measured, like she had already asked him to do too much. "Of course I will...the three of us will sit together when we are back in New York and review all of your numbers to date. That will give her a giant leg up on your sale-ability and what she can be worth to you and how that will play out in her favor as well. This is such a weight off of my shoulders that you and your mom will be working together." Now Crystal really spoke up "How much do I owe you? All that you've done for me...you found me...you advertised me...you gave me my own room to play in at your hotel...you showed me off, to the world. I couldn't have done any of what I've done without you. I love you for all of that and I trust that you always have my best interests in mind." "Honey, I'm glad you play piano and didn't try a singing career, because even I couldn't do anything for you with a voice like yours!"

Mr. Brentwhistle hugged Crystal and said, "thanks for introducing me to your mom, that is payment enough. Please bring her to New York with you." With that, they went back to the kitchen.

Chapter 35

Friday morning came too fast. After the last three days of just sitting back and relaxing and actually making a vacation out of the last of their visit, Mr. Brentwhistle had tickets on the 10:15am train back to New York. They had discussed so much, covered so much ground and made some pretty spectacular decisions in such a short period of time, Rita's head was spinning. "Is your life always like this? I thought keeping up with the first lady and her appointment book was fast pace, but that was child's play compared to this! Brentwhistle just laughed, "you haven't seen anything yet...New York makes you dizzy! Just when you think all your t's are crossed, all of the dots fly off of the I's and you need to rearrange dates and times to fit in 'everyone's' schedules. It is management and people pleasing and getting paid handsomely to eventually get it right! I'll see you in New York in three weeks. Just ask Crystal, I'll leave the lights on...and he was gone.

The rest of the day, Rita shopped the PX with Crystal and bought so many non-sensible items she felt like a kid again. They both tried on and bought clothes sensible for riding on the bus and clothes sensible for walking the streets of New York City. Rita helped Crystal pick out a suit that would be just right for meeting with a lawyer in a big down town office building and was amazed at the size she needed to buy. Crystal learned a long time ago that she needed to buy long skirts because the skirt that came with the suit wouldn't even cover enough of her leg to be called appropriate, she was just too tall. So after mixing and matching and topping it all off with a white button down collar shirt, they finished Crystal's ensemble with a black velvet neck tie and did the food shopping for Miss Elise. Once home, the conversation moved on to driving lessons and buying a car. Riding the bus all the time was really getting old. Besides having a car would mean having so much more freedom.

In the morning and for the next consecutive four mornings, Crystal continued with her driving lessons and conquered her fear of staling when shifting. She had finally learned and relaxed and was ready to buy a car. Friday afternoon when Jim could leave the base and accompany Crystal to a dealership, they were off to test drive vehicles that Crystal had already scouted out and was interested in. Crystal found driving new cars was much easier than driving the four-wheel drive, heavy, old jeep Jim had taught her in. Now driving was a pleasure, she was really enjoying herself. Even Jim felt comfortable with her behind the wheel. "I guess I did a good job, you're a pretty good driver." Jim had told Crystal when she drove her 1941 Ford Super Deluxe Business Coupe on base to drop Jim then home to Miss Elise's.

Rita and Elise were really excited to see her arrive home in a shinny light blue, big car. Crystal went running in the house all excited repeating, "it's mine, it's all mine!" Within minutes the three women were back in the car going for their maiden ride and experiencing freedom and a supper out in a malt shoppe in the next town over. This was really a treat for all three of them and quite different from every other day of the week! When they arrived home, needing to park on the street in front of the house, was a really long, tiresome walk for Elise. This was half the reason she didn't get out much, walking any distance was difficult for her. So once in the house, she, Elise, plunked herself down in the living room ready to listen to Crystal's nightly 'practice'. For Elise it was the best part of the day.

Rita had also learned to relax and read in the living room and enjoy listening to Crystal's rendition of all the new major hits of the day. She had to admit, Crystal's talent was going to be easy to market and keep them both busy. For the next two weeks, Crystal and Rita made schedules and plans for their days in New York. They did this in between the visits from Brad, the song writer. This was also something

Rita found very interesting. To be a fly on the wall and witness the workings of how a song is born. Interesting, very interesting! She had so much to learn, and so far she enjoyed every part of it! Brad had come a long way from his first try at fitting words into the stanzas of Crystal's song. He had it pegged this time. Crystal was flying high and playing to her hearts content and humming his words as she played. He had the picture she had in her head laid out in words that pleased her beyond expression. Brad didn't have a great voice, but even he made the song feel like love lost and hearts riding those waves of loss. The story was one every person could relate to and recover from. This was a winner. Rita's mind was swept up in future exposure and seeing this recording go straight to the top! She now knew what her job was and with Clive's help how to make Crystal's music reach every home.

There was so much excitement in Clive's office when they reached New York. Crystal had her blues song worded and the recording schedules made. First to record the piano solo and then to record with voice, and 'some instrumental' back ground. Crystal wanted an unknown to sing the song. A want-to-be, so when it became a hit, they would both be 'discovered'! Clive thought a known talent would be better to get Crystal's career off the ground. Rita stepped forward and up. "This is where I come in" she interrupted all the chatter in the room. Now you could hear a pin drop. "We record Crystal's solo in one week. No problem. Then we take a break for Labor Day weekend and come back and have the studio at the end of September for one week rehearsals and record on the 27th. Let me line up some talent for background instrumentals and an unknown voice. We'll rehearse and make a decision. *Looking at the faces in the room, Rita was thinking she hadn't taken the bull by the horns like that in a long time. It worked by George, it worked. She had everyone's attention and she had applied her authority in all the right places.* Clive ended this meeting with "It looks like you've got yourself a manager there Crystal. She can start tomorrow...tonight she is having dinner with me."

Crystal felt very much at home at the New Yorker, back in her room and she knew nearly every employee in every department. Tomorrow night she would play in her Showcase room, but tonight she was on her own. Dressing very carefully and wearing her hair in a loose and fly-away manner she headed up to the 40th floor. She was no longer stopped at the door or given a snide, wanton-woman look, but rather a wide berth and escort to an empty table. At the nod of her head, her drink order was on it's way. Her table was a little off to the side and three deep, the spotlight on Johnathan's solo prevented him from seeing her entrance. For a whole set she could relax and just enjoy the show. But then her mind started to wander...*Background instruments for the vocal...piano of course, how about just a base fiddle and trumpet. The trumpet can be sultry at times and the fiddle can add depth..perfect! Rita's gonna love it!* With her mind totally off of her surroundings, the light kiss on her neck where he had pulled her hair away startled her back to the here and now! Feeling lightheaded and thrilled with her thought process and happy to see Johnathan, she planted a lip lock on him that curled his toes. "I'm happy to see you too, Mrs. Clear. Remember? That's who you are!" As he located and felt for her wedding band on her left hand. Sure enough, it was there. *Dam!* "How long are you back for?" he asked. "Long enough for you to meet my new manager, play a few sets in the Showcase and act like a silly teenager with you, like before I was Mrs. Clear." He drew her close for another kiss, pushed back just a bit and said "I'll take what I can get". He got up and went back to work, back up on the little stage. At 2:10, the end of his last set, Crystal was gone.

Back in her own room, Crystal was exhausted but sexually charged. *It's a good thing next weekend is Labor Day Weekend and Vincent is coming home she thought. I need a good romp in the hay. I need a whole day just to spend in bed with Vincent. Make up for lost time and some really good sex. He can usually rub my whole body and work the kinks out, I'm looking forward to that! For tonight Mr. Purple can work on my kinks...*

At 9:15 the following night, with Mr. Brentwhistle and Rita in attendance at her Piano Showcase, Crystal was just about to go into her intermission medley, when Johnathan jointed her at the piano. He started to slowing and lightly play the song they had played together once before. She joined him and gradually accelerated the tempo and they both played their parts in unison and with fun! When finished, she thanked him and introduced him and plugged his show on the 40th floor... for all of you who are still awake at midnight and need a night-cap! Together they went to her dressing room. "That was a nice surprise" she said. "What are you doing here? You're on in 30 minutes." " I need to do to you, that which you did to me last night." was all he said as he lifted her hair off the back of her neck, cupped her neck securely and held her still while he took her lips. He separated those lips with his tongue and plunged repeatedly, suggestively, sweetly until her knees let go and they were sprawled together across the only chair in the room. He righted himself and helped her to stand as well. "The only difference is that a teen age boy wouldn't stop now, goodnight Crystal." And he left.

It was hard, but Crystal went back to work. After her show, her mom and Clive both congratulated her on her showmanship with Johnathan and her easy way of working his show into his introduction. So now they suggested catching a set of his show before calling it a night. Crystal's first reaction was...No...but regained her composure and said "sure, let me change out of my stage clothes first."

With her long chain dangling between her boobs and the cowl neck of her gold sweater hanging dangerously low at times, Crystal was ready to visit Johnathan's set. Clive had seen the cowl neck before and didn't think anything of it...Rita on the other hand, swallowed hard and bit back her words when Crystal joined them. The Velvet Room was more of a night club with a dance floor with patrons coming and going all the time. So when Clive and Rita arrived with Crystal in tow, there was no commotion, just more customers arriving. The only difference, Crystal disappeared before the intermission and headed to Johnathan's dressing room. Clive and Rita called it a night and went back to there rooms. Crystal was sitting facing the mirror, brushing her long hair when Johnathan walked in. "I thought I saw you earlier, then you disappeared" Johnathan said as he walked up behind Crystal and lifted her hair to his face and smiled at her in the mirror. Crystal stood up and turned to him and said she needed to make sure there was a chair in his dressing room before he got there. Then she gently touched his lips with a tender kiss...he returned the kiss, it deepened, it became all consuming with hands busy in all directions. Mostly it was his hands inside the neck of her sweater, right where she wanted them. Her room key was nestled between her boobs. Once she was sure he had it, she ended the kiss, kept eye contact at all times, adjusted her collar suggestively and left the room. Johnathan still had two more hours left to his show, now what was she going to do? *You fool girl...you know you won't go through with it. Oh Vincent, you're the only man I want in my bed. Sorry Johnathan, I'm the only one that can PLAY with my body, I need love. I let you have too much. I let you believe I could do something I can't. I am that married woman I said I was. I can't think about my vows one minute and be 17, single and horny the next. I'm married, 23, horny, and waiting for my husband to fill me and please me in just a few weeks from now. I love that man, he's the one I want. Military life is not for the weak of heart or the straying unfit woman who can't control her needs. That's what they are NEEDS! And they haven't been met or satisfied lately! Cool it girl...tonight they must be controlled!*

At 2:10am Johnathan pulled his tie from around his neck and unbuttoned the top two buttons of his white shirt. While leaning against his dressing table he fingered and smelled her perfume on the note that he just lifted from his dressing mirror. The last two hours were agony in his pants but joy and excitement in his heart. He read the note and felt like that 17 year old teenager who should have known better then to ask out the prettiest girl in the room!

After having left notes for both her mom and Mr. Brentwhistle, Crystal was on the 8:25am train back to New Jersey. She was trying to escape from a situation she knew she couldn't run from, her own lack of self control and attraction to Johnathan. Time and distance. So this was the distance. She'd concentrate on her music for the next few weeks at home. *When Vincent gets home, Johnathan will be nothing more than a handsome face on anther stage. I will be that faithful military wife that loves her husband through thick and thin. What he does when he's gone is his and the governments business. Paid for by the government and kept separate from my life as a civilian. I ask no questions and he shares very little of his duties at other locations. Like any other military wife, I need to*

*make due with the time and love that we can make while we are together!
It's what I tell myself...now I have to make myself believe it!!*

Miss Elise was beside herself with joy when Crystal came walking through the back yard, but not speechless. "Good lord girl, what are you doing here? I've nothing for lunch or provisions to prepare a good one! Did you just get home and how long are you staying? Is your mom with you?" Crystal merely walked over to Miss Elise, bent over her chair, hugged her and invited her out for lunch and a ride in the car.

An hour and a half later, while sitting at a tiny table at the lunch counter in the PX, Crystal and Elise were remarking about the hassle that was just avoided and giggling over the bullshit to get this far. Because the People on base knew Crystal had recently bought a car, Jim Davies let everyone know. Their being stopped at the gate was merely to be informed that she needed to get an entrance sticker to put on the windshield of her car. Otherwise she would be stopped each time she wanted entrance to the base. Next at the information Center she was denied the sticker because she didn't have her military id on her. She was told she couldn't park on base, at the PX or anywhere without the sticker. With Elise in the car, her panic was stilled when the desk Lt. Issued her a temporary sticker...dated with an expiration date! He also slipped her a visitor pass so she could access the PX without a problem.

Now with lunch eaten, it was time to pick-up a few things, get home and relax. It was like pulling teeth when Crystal put the small wheel chair in their basket. She needed to get Elise to admit it would be easier for her to get to and fro from the car to the house. It was a quiet shopping experience after that and they didn't get half what Crystal thought they needed. She'd convince and show Elise the ease and the sense the chair makes. They'll be able to go out more often without so much strain on Elise. At the register she was quizzed about the visor pass... She'll never forget her id again.

When Crystal pulled to a stop at the top of the walkway to the house, she instructed Elsie to stay put for a minute while she opened the trunk and got the chair out. The disgruntled Miss Elise did as she was told and waited. Once she was seated in the chair, being pushed to the house was much easier on her body (she realized) but it hurt her self-esteem terribly. With a "thank you for the ride", she walked up the three front steps and said "I can walk into my own house". She unlocked the door and did just that! Crystal took a deep breathe and went back for the shopping bags. It was a rather quiet afternoon, then supper for just the two of them. Miss Elise didn't come alive with conversation or appreciation until after they had retired to the living room for piano practice. While Crystal was playing 'Meadow Memories', Miss Elise lounged in her chair, said quietly, "I love you living here" and proceeded to fall asleep where she sat. Being home was good for Crystal. Three days of pampering herself with long bubble baths, piano time anytime she wanted to, always wonderful balanced meals, quick runs to the bursars unit (the car made that so much easier) helping there when she could but always accessing her private files. This was a part of her military life. Making sure #1 she didn't get caught...but always making sure Vincent and his kids were taken care of. His advance in rank, therefore in pay as well, were stalled now that the war was over and because every minute that was coming to him in time off or that which could be switched with other personnel was taken advantage of. It was noticed that he was not as gong-ho with his assignments or volunteering like in the past. It was calked up to his beautiful, successful wife and wanting to get home to her all the time. Little did anyone know...he was rushing home to wives, that had his attention these days!

Labor Day was right around the corner...Elise had the grandest barbecue planned. Mr. Brentwhistle and Rita were going to be home for only the long weekend. Brad and three studio buddies were also going to be on hand, as well as a half-dozen friends and staff from the base. Yes, Pepere was also going to be here! And best of all, Vincent would be home on Thursday, two days before anyone else arrived. Glory days! Crystal felt as thou she had been holding her breathe for this day to arrive. Elise could feel the atmosphere filled with endorphins waiting to explode. Finally Thursday, 2:20 pm, the train pulls in from Va. She doesn't know how he did it, but Vincent was the first one to exit from the train. In uniform, all smiles and looking ten feel tall, he stopped, no froze when he saw Crystal not 15 feet away dressed in a red top, hair tied back with a blue ribbon, long white skirt that made her look ten feet tall as well, just starring at him and watching his every move. He advanced slowly in her direction, her feet were glued to the ground. By the time he had his arms around her, she was in tears, realizing that he was really here. Really holding her. She had had such a fear that he would have gone home to one of the other wives. Not wanting to confess those fears to him, it was easy to convince him that these were happy tears. Breaking out of the comfort of Vincent arms, she grabbed at his smallest bag while Vincent wondered why they were handling his bags and not hailing for a for taxi. You'll see she said smugly, when she opened the truck to her light blue car, threw his bag in and exclaimed…"it's mine…all mine." (she loved saying that!)

When Crystal got behind the wheel, in the drivers seat, Vincent was concerned. "It's one thing to own a car, but you need to know how to drive one to sit there sweetie" he said nervously looking straight into Crystal's eyes. "Oh but I do…relax and enjoy the ride, we'll be home in a jiffy. She hadn't written him at all about her driving lessons or buying a car. She wanted it to be a surprise! Surprise it was! It was one more giant step of independence and her not needing him any more. He was deflated! They greeted Elise happily and immediately went to their room. Door closed, Vincent put the moves on Crystal so fast, you'd thought he was a teenage boy! Feeling like she was stuffed into a box with no air, Crystal said "a kiss would be nice to warm me up before you get all grabby" Knowing he took that like a slap in the face, she came back with, "that came out wrong. I'm sorry, I've missed you so much and I've looked so forward to having you home." Crystal's arms were now traveling up Vincent's chest, just so she could be close to him. "Rather than slam-bang-thank-you-mama, I'd love slow and tender, heart palpitating, no, you can't have it yet..excruciating orgasms! You are so good at that, that's what I've been dreaming of!" Vincent just looked at her, held her hands close to his heart and confessed feeling chastised and embarrassed and like a heel. "I love you, and what you do to me and how you make me feel is like a gift. That's what I come home for. Believe it or not, Rhonda or Amy.."

"STOP…" Crystal's dander was up now. She felt she needed to get it all out… now. Looking him straight in the eyes, she dropped her hands to her sides, took a step back and calmly said "That's your other life…I don't want them here. Do they know about me?...Don't answer…I don't care. But, if they are coming to bed with us-----long silence---- I can' believe I'm saying this, you can leave now. I know I'm sharing you, that's pretty big of me! I bet they don't know…they think they have you all to themselves. It's a bed we've both made. Please no more threats about being under a barrel that neither one of us can lawfully get out from under. You are here and I still love you, whole heartily, I love you… so I'll be using you for sex. Good, long, healthy, carefully executed marriage sex. Just so you know…you are the only one enjoying my sexual appetite, I still believe in a monogamist marriage! Just for need, I've come close, but I've found out…I can't cheat! So if you've come here to my home to be with me and only me, welcome home." At that, Crystal collapsed on the bed in tears and welcomed the body that joined her and the arms that wrapped around her in…. consolation. That feeling was soon turned into a soothing, loving, warm hand down her bare back and into her panties. The kiss that accompanied was the touch and feeling that she'd been yearning for since their last togetherness.

"My dear Crystal, that was love. Bare and essential, the gift we give to each other. Just you and I alone…just the two of us. I love you for that. We've missed many a supper, choosing love first, but I'm starved now…can we eat?" All of the hostility and anger and separation frustrations were now over and done with. She remembered thinking supper smelled wonderful, but that was hours ago. "Yes of course we can eat now, I'm sure Elise left something really great for us. She'll be happy to have you back as well, I can get pretty testy when you've been gone too long!"

The weekenders all arrived and the festivities were wonderful. Pepere brought a shuttle full of young men for the barbecue and Brad arrived with fellow musicians and want-to-be song writers. Vincent was the other old man of the group, but he could drink them all under the table. Pepere was careful to have only one beer, knowing he needed to drive everyone back to base, safely! The piano never stopped, if Crystal wasn't playing, one of Brad's friends was at it. At one point they had two guitars, a trumpet and a clarinet to play along with the piano. The jam produced some great music and a fun time. Elise was a wonder in the kitchen and the prep work for the grill, which Vincent manned mostly and effortlessly, truth be known. The house was made for a party. Open in the middle, top and bottom with rooms, many of them skirting along the sides of the house. Most of the music started in the living room, moved to the center room-hall in front of the kitchen and moved to the back yard with night fall. By now there were neighbors and neighbors friends and a full blown band which included an accordion and a violin and another clarinet. Two of the neighbor girls could really carry a tune and encouraged more songs, particularly show tunes. It was really entertaining and fun. At four in the morning, Crystal and Vincent with Brad and his buddies were the last ones still able and were cleaning up most of the mess. Leaving whatever else needed to be done for later morning, they all retired to bedrooms. Around noon the next day Crystal and Vincent were joined by Brad and company at the kitchen table looking like something the cat dragged in. Miss Elise came bounding in from the back yard with her great smile and enthusiastic nature and informed them that Karen and Ruth had returned to the back yard about 10am to finish cleaning up the mess. They also washed all the cooking utensils and serving platters that were used and tidied the pantry. Now there was nothing to do except prepare lunch. Vincent reached out to hold Elise's hand in thanks and asked, "Who are Karen and Ruth?" "They are the two nieces of the Gadder's who live next door and were the girls singing last night. Nice girls and pretty too. Now get out of my kitchen and come back in 30 minutes and we'll have a nice luncheon.

When it came to food, Crystal knew not to argue with this lady!

With Crystal at the piano and the rest of the gang all stretched-out and lounging in the living room, she started one handed with the melody of "Black Water Blues". Brad said Gary, Al want to tell her now? Ben jumped up and produced a wrinkled piece of paper from his back pocket and joined Jack on the couch. Jack said, "sure I can sing but I can't eat lunch...last night's beer is still sloshing around in my stomach." Vincent said, "sing what"? And Brad simply said "the words for Black Water. We think we've painted the picture from Crystal's mind." He used the words Crystal had said about what the words should do. Without further ado, Brad removed Crystal from the piano and she went and sat nearest to Vincent. Vincent hugged her from behind and held her very close, he didn't know what was coming. Brad sat and softly touched the piano keys and gave the intro to the song. Jacks voice was horse and harsh describing the rocks that were being battered by the salt laden waves of tears washing over them. The endless beating was being delivered by the goddess of the sun lacking the energy to bestow the light of love or the warmth of forgiveness on the cruelty of mankind. A Crack in the sky (which was delivered in the living-room by Al hitting a glass with a spoon) revealed the hand of God who over-road the goddess and brightened the sky with colors of blue and pink and gold and bright light to cover all those who needed to shed the Black Water Blues. The boys added a choir of ...the light of love...the warmth of forgiveness..the hand of God...and the melody repeated the endless beatings delivered by the lack of energy caused by the Black Water Blues. Jack stopped singing and the room was silent. The piano had stopped already. All eyes were on Crystal. She was as still as a stone with tears running down her face and a heart that was so full of gratitude that they got her! The words did indeed paint the picture better than even she had imagined. "Oh Brad, Jack, guys you did it" she gushed. Now everyone could breathe! This was only Saturday morning, the weekend had just barely begun. Rita and Mr. Brentwhistle were still to arrive.

Vincent was so proud of his wife. He knew she was talented, but to this extent..he didn't know. He felt like such a heel when he thought of the times he didn't want her to go to New York, or certainly not to Vegas. He used the entire weekend to try to make up in a small way his trying to suffocate her talent or put it on the back burner because it was her thing and not his. This was very important to her and she had finality made him see it. His validation of her made him such an attentive lover all weekend. He was out to please and please he did.

His leaving on Tuesday afternoon was such a heart break for Crystal. He had left on other occasions, but watching him get on the train this day affected her in a way his leaving had never done before. She thought back to just this morning when he'd held her so close and so affectionately, not rushing, just sweet loving touches and a happy ending that lasted so deliciously long. If orgasms could be bottled and sold this one would be on the shelf and marked priceless! He left with her heart, that was the problem because now she felt empty and scared that this mornings euphoria would never be duplicated again, he was going back to them. She hadn't thought about them all weekend. Her body knew she needed these loved filled days and nights, therefore her period didn't start until the train pulled into the station to carry Vincent away.

Friday night back in her Showcase was the best place she could be. Before she left New Jersey, once again she checked...all things were where they belonged and she felt confident leaving the accounts alone. Some were holding Vincent's children's future. For each one of them after they were born, Crystal created in their names, accounts with monthly deposits for their college education. Military pay isn't much, so this was the best she could do for them, for him.

The Showcase was packed, they were happy to have her back. These were the prelude weekends before the holidays. She had learned that hotel life no matter where, was made for the holidays, and they started right around now! Two more weekends here then off to Vegas again. But before she left New York, she had recording times booked with Brad and an appointment up town with a high priced lawyer to make sure mom's position was a legal position in Crystal's newly formed company. One that paid mom benefits and help to secure retirement funds as well. One that would also own the rights to Crystal's holdings from all venues. When and if Black Water Blues ever earned her a Grammy...That she figures could be hers, selfishly hers! Clearly Entertaining, a play on words and a play on Crystal's name was a legal and an expensive venture. A play on her profession was now one which was being developed as the entity that would handle her recordings and a record label on which to distribute them. Her head needed the

Showcase tonight, this was like coming home and practicing in front of people...no sweat!

Vegas was not as it was before...she couldn't walk down the street without being recognized. The prices on her shows have gone up. She never looked at this before, but now it was brought to her attention by her new manager, and all the seats were still filled. Her marques were more elaborate and the stage had more 'crystals' hanging around! This wasn't just 'playing' anymore...it was a job! There was a plateau to be met and she never let anyone down. She just did it naturally.

Chapter 36

Five more original recordings, dates in New York, Vegas and Atlantic City. Life is never boring. Rita cracks the whip in a most lucrative way, we are always making money. Vincent, or should we say, Aspen now with 6 children in Massachusetts and Reginald 6 children in Maryland all with savings accounts compliments of Uncle Sam and Crystal's handy work. Each wife still living the life of a military wife and supporting their families with love and PX shopping, looking forward to some freedom when their youngest is in school. *I don't know how he does it. He loves me like there is no tomorrow. He is as frisky and limber and playful as our first times. In my mind I'm still that 21 year old wanting and willing and fearful and scared that I'm not as desirable as his other lovers, but he still comes back. Is it more what I do in the back room of the bursars office or in our king size bed at home? My body is still tight, taunt, limber and playful. Probably more so than a women that has givin' birth 6 times and maybe fearful of doing so again, but still, it's been years and I wonder! I've been so busy with my own life, building my career, where he was building families. I wonder now, has he been on vacations with these families? Has he wined and dined these wives or lavished them with jewels or furs or fancy cars? I've provided the money for their lively hood, what has he provided?*

Something different...this will be fun...vacation time with his two oldest boys. Thinking even more, she said... "Self, remember those hoops of desire you were going to make him jump through? It starts now!..It's not too late, let him show these two boys what a good time can be!"

It's been a long time since I've written a letter to Vincent, so here goes. I've got to make sure he has the money to do this so I'll give him a months head start. Besides the weather in New England will be grand for what I have in mind.

Dear Vincent,

Can you remember the last time I've written you a letter? I've been thinking, it's time to do something different, so I'm starting by writing it all down. I need a vacation, and I want to vacation with you. I want to love you at night like there is no tomorrow, swim in the ocean and enjoy the sunlight during the day and then do it all again in a different bed the next night. I do realize you have different responsibilities than I do so I've written an itinerary for you to follow with your two oldest boys Russell and Rockwell. They were the ones missing from your last visit to Maryland so I thought I could combine two special occasions into one. There is a vacation allowance in next months check, so use it wisely.

<u>First</u>, I don't care what time you leave, but on Saturday, July 30th meet me in Albany, NY -----I'll be at the Spring Water Motel, Exit 42 off Route 87, in Albany, I'll leave a note at the desk so you'll know you are in the right place. Meet me at 11pm in my room....Don't be late.

<u>Second,</u> the next day travel to Wolfboro, NH...lake Winnipesaukee, get lodging at the Willies Cabin Motel..off Route 9. Two nights...I'll find you. Then we can talk about what's next.

I've got the whole week planned, your boys will love it. It will also build a new relationship between you guys. Just thinking about the week I have planned, I'm getting excited just writing you about it, they say planning a vacation is half of the excitement and I believe it. I'm excited just thinking about having you to myself at least some of the time on this vacation.

I've made reservations at the Cracker Barrel on route 20, en route to Hampton Beach for Monday morning...it's on me so enjoy it! I will see you there and give you the name of your next motel. I'm still working on the next jaunt, but I'm thinking the Old Sturbridge Village in Massachusetts, as we turn south and start working our way back to home but still seeing the sights. I'm really excited, we've never been on vacation together before!

By the time you get your boys back home to Towson, you'll be their new hero and best friend. It's a no fail situation. So get ready to entertain you boys while loving and thrilling very part of me.
Love,
Your 1st Wife Crystal

Once she had written and re-written a few of the lines of the letter, Crystal drove to the Bursar's Unit, visited with the crew and handled a few of the outgoing messages that were waiting for her. Then she saw to her own business at mischievously increasing Vincent's next pay check for his vacation expenses. Still with a giggle in her heart she sent telegrams to both Rita and Mr. Brentwhistle informing them of her vacation dates with Vincent for next month. Now that her calendar was all set, she could enjoy her long weekend home, and dream about Vincent's attention and going back to work next week. Vincent was still stationed out of this base in Colts Neck so it was easy to slip the letter into his personal mail box. It just so happened that he was due back tomorrow from VA (again) so they'd have one day together before she headed down to Atlantic City. As far as she knew, he'd be in New Jersey until something else came up and he was told to leave. Her thinking was dangerous...checking the calendar again she was scheming to get him down to Atlantic City two weekends from now!

Rita did keep her busy, the month of June after Memorial Day weekend which she spent in New York, was now being spent in Atlantic City. Crystal found this to be a fun place to be and where she learned to gamble. With time on her hands and money in her pocket, the roulette table was quite the draw and sometimes very good to her. Atlantic City was more of a stop and go kind of city rather than actually making a week long reservation for a vacation. Crystal enjoyed talking with the housewives who wore jeans and T-shirts and stood at the table at 10:30 in the morning with their coffee cups and played one dollar at a time on their favorite numbers. These were real women with kids in school and husbands in factories just stopping by for one day either on their way home from vacation or on their way to vacation at the popular Myrtle Beach in South Carolina. They didn't know her and she knew she would never she them again so they could talk about anything, If Crystal weren't a pianist or entertainer, she'd write a book about what these women would talk about or confide in her about. The 'table talk' was fantastic, quick and over with, very entertaining! But she failed, Vincent would not be joining her next weekend. With the up-coming vacation that was planned for him, he was using Crystal's not being home, to travel to Maryland in his free time. Elise was none the wiser, he was a busy military man, not able to be at home! Besides it would be another two weeks before he could see his infant daughter Abby..

So he took the long ride to Towson. He used the long ride to cleared his head of Crystal. To help clear his head of Amy's repeated request for a bigger house, on the same beautiful apple orchard lot in Grafton, but bigger to house their every growing family of 6 kids. Little did he know that when they visited Grafton years before, because she, Amy was the only living relative of Martin Samson, and going to receive his award posthumously, for his invention of an epoxy that won him that Noble prize, used daily and exclusively by the military at Wymar-Gordons in Worcester, Ma and now at their new facility in Grafton, that his (Vincent's) commute would now be Maryland to New Jersey to Massachusetts. New Jersey is where Crystal calls home, all because of me, based here. He loved his role as dad, but the picket fence that he pictured so many years ago in Maryland needed repair or rebuilding around a bigger house that he couldn't afford. Amy would get her dream house, he'd see to it, using her money. But there was no extra money for Rhonda's bigger house for six kids. She was a real doll who never complained, just moved things around to make sure everything and everybody fit! Crystal turned out to be a real fairy godmother, with her gifts in the kids name when they turn 18. Whats a little more of Uncle Sam's money being used for the good of children! In just those quick thoughts, all was fine. The kids, all 12 of them were healthy...*don't think of them that way fool. Saying 6 here and six there is bad enough. Maybe*

Crystal did get me. In her way she gave me what I wanted! Almost there and I'll give Rhonda what she wants most in this world...Me!

For the next two weeks Crystal's Showcase was her home away from home and work helped to keep her mind off of her upcoming vacation. Her days were filled with either sleeping in late, or piano practice or shopping for vacation. She'd practice up on the 40th floor because she knew Johnathan was not performing there. His presents in her close proximity upset her equilibrium. When she hadn't had Vincent for a few weeks, she needed to remind herself that she was a married woman, especially around Johnathan. Rita stayed out of her hair, mostly. They'd have lunch every now and then, discuss business or an upcoming engagement, but mostly they did their own thing. Crystal's was the piano, Rita's was Mr. Brentwhistle. It was more evident every day.

A quick stop home to pack, to let Elise know she was off for vacation with Vincent, stop off at the Bursar's Unit to <u>check</u> on things, a stop at the Operations center to pick-up a few maps and away she goes...At last...on her way!

It was a pleasurable ride on this gorgeous, sunny day. Crystal had never driven this far or this fast for that matter. Just thinking about having Vincent all to herself, in her bed for a few hours daily for the next few days...her panties were wet! Her giddy insides were making her feel like a kid again. Never having done this before was also like being a kid again, a new adventure with 'his' kids. Now her mind was wandering. She knew the kids names and their birthdays and their ages, but she had no idea what they looked like. She never wanted to know. Seeing them would make them real. Real human beings that he helped to create. Him and another woman, not her. *This was your idea Crystal,* she thought. *All these years and he was the only one I could talk to about this...I was the only one he could talk to about this, no wonder why I'm talking to myself...things will be fine...I will see them, learn things about them, they'll never see me, the real me...I'll just be a face in the crowd. Vincent and I will have other things to talk about...if I want to talk about his kids! I'm hungry, time for a drink.*

Her mind wandering had made the miles go by fast. After getting off the highway someplace in NY, Crystal enjoyed a wonderful broiled, seafood dinner. Her rum coke was delicious as well, just what she needed. Sitting back and relaxing she let her mind rewind some of the old memories. The day she sat in the kitchen chair with her mom, the only home she remembered with both her mom and dad. That pivotal day when her mom shared with her, her monumental secret. While downing her second rum and coke she explored more of her memories. *Boy, my life has been full of secrets, I've learned to keep them well. If I were to strip my life of all of those secrets and lies and unlawful acts; what would my life really be like? I'd probably be a bored housewife with three kids giving piano lessons. Even now, I can't imagine it! I just couldn't give up being me. I love you Vincent, but I guess not that much. The next few days are really going to be interesting.*

Needing to clear her head of both the thoughts and the booze, Crystal chose to walk around the Five & Dime she saw across the street. She found it to be a great store. It packed into it's small interior everything and more than the PX, the prices were great too. She needed to get out more. These little stores in these little towns were the heart of America. She needed to remember that and it was driven home to her in a big way when she saw her own Black Water Blues on black vinyl being paid for and stuffed into a little paper bag. That was her first experience with actually seeing someone buying her music. It was on the tip of her tongue to ask if they'd like it autographed, but in this little store, who was she really? She let that moment pass.

Chapter 37

The Spring Water Motel in Albany was...the truckers raved about it! Needing to eat again, it had been nearly seven hours since that succulent seafood dinner, she braved the dinner that shared the motel lot. The greasy spoon, as they are fondly referred to, was excellent! Her chicken parm and home-made garlic bread rated an A-1. Who would have guessed. Her bed in the cinder block square of a room was clean and firm, just as she liked them. The room, nearly sound proof because of its construction, was pleasant with dark green painted walls, dark green painted floors with many tan rugs scattered around. The headboard of the bed, night stand and dresser were of light tan wood. The two pictures nailed to walls were also tan framed and pleasant to look at. The only window had an air conditioner and tan drapes. The bathroom was functional. The two lamps on the dresser came on with the light switch and the clock on the night stand had the right time. She didn't think the bible in the top draw of the night stand had ever been looked at.

Two and a half hours later Vincent gets here. The little Five and Dime was a gem. Crystal had picked up three paper backs. She loved to read and was generally entertained by her books. The beach and sunshine solitude would allow her to enjoy these books, she'd start one now. Deep into the pages of one of Agatha Christie's mystery's, she almost missed Vincent and his sons walking across to the dinner. *They're so tall, just like their dad. How tall should boys 9 and 12 be? I don't know anything about kids, I hope this week isn't a mistake.* She had a hard time going back to her book so she readied herself for Vincent's arrival. At first using the bathroom was uncomfortable for Crystal, but she found it to be very clean, just like the rest of her surroundings. Shocking red, sheer, over the shoulders, open in the front dressing gown purchased at the Five and Dime (really cheap) was all she chose to wear. This mornings perfume had already worn off, so a little dab under each breast should be enough to tantalize.

Ready and waiting, she worked herself into a sexual frenzy. Mr. Purple would be next if Vincent didn't get there pretty soon! *I'm getting bad,* she thought! And then he arrived. Without preamble or foreplay she was down his throat and down his pants before the door even clicked closed. With his two hands firmly clasping over her soft, firm breasts with nipples aching to be sucked, on his way down to do so, "such a wonderful greeting, thank you, he mumbled, so nice to see you too." Words of greeting weren't necessary. Light off and in bed was the order of business. He'd see the red thing some other time.

They were like synchronized musicians together. Each having their own part to play, with entrances and crescendos to be mastered. They mastered them well! This really wasn't the time to think such things, but how could Rhonda or Amy do to him the things I do, or make him move the way I make him move? We are more than practiced, we have created our own magic and excel because it is performed with love. "You're right, Crystal. We do move together in love." "Oh my god, did I say those things out loud?" Crystal was mortified!

"I'll see you tomorrow, I need to get back to the boys" One more kiss and one more long stroke along her long body and he was gone.

Crystal had a very long and fitful night after Vincent left. Her words in their love bed, her bringing up his wives names was dreadful. The way he made her feel, just like the first time...wonderful, special, alive, wanted, loved. How could he do that to those women as well? I'm not special. He closes his eye and uses the women under him...Damn!!!

Crystal checked out of the motel and left before Vincent and the boys even thought about waking up. She needed to put some distance between them. It was another long drive to Lake Winnipesaukee, but she needed to follow her own itinerary. Driving was good for her mood.

She could talk to herself...yell, curse and get over it. She had gotten 'over-it' many times in the past few years, what's one more time! After all she had no one to talk to about this situation...this was man made between her and Vincent! Cracker Barrel here we come...

Again following her own itinerary, she was the first to arrive at the restaurant. She loved this place and would come to this restaurant in any state any time she could. She loved their chicken fried steak. Sounds funny, but it's really good. This day it's only breakfast though. She had some shenanigans to pull off and really piss him off. The boys had seen her a few times, but didn't know who she was. She needed to be careful not to pop up in too many places and become familiar. That would really piss him off. She ate her eggs over easy with one stack of small pancakes, loaded with syrup. Coffee finished her off and she was ready to play with Vincent. True to the plan, they showed up all happy and starving. Once they had eaten their fill, dad gave them money for the gift shop and it was her turn to occupy Vincent. He was heading to the men's room and she way laid him by wet-floor cones at the ladies room entrance. She shuffled him inside the room, flattened him against the wall, unzipped his pants, no need to tease his joint into action, he was ready. She lifted herself enough to insert his penis into her wet waiting vagina. Using gyrating hip actions and gently pumping and riding him, ejaculation was his mornings delight.. Naturally once she had him by the balls, he was a willing participate. Anything of hers that needed pinching or sucking or teasing would have to wait until tonight. Needless to say, this was quick! He was shocked. He was used. She was satisfied! All clothes back in place, he met his kids outside while they were taking pictures. Crystal walked to her car and drove away.

Okay guys...we're off again but this time the ride shouldn't be as long. Have you ever seen the ocean. Has mom every taken you to the beach..I'm a navy guy, I should have before now, but we're going now...the No's...never, mom never has was echoed by both boys.

Hampton Beach was a party scene for all ages. She was glad she had planned two nights here. The motel was once again family friendly and she was pleased. She checked-in and took a nap. When she awoke she was famished. The boardwalk was loaded with fast food vendors but that isn't what she wanted. She strolled until she came upon a 'family style restaurant' serving 11am to 11pm. *I hope it's good*, she thought. *It's the beach...who knows...*

When Vincent and the boys arrived she was making friends with the people in the adjacent motel units. They had plans for the beach in the afternoon and a cookout back here for supper. She watched as Vincent and the boys arrived, unpacked a bit and headed for the beach. Vincent stood next to his boys and you could tell they were a family. The boys had thick black hair like their dad. They were gangly tall because they were just kids. Give them another 10 years and they would be handsome young men! Their looks pulled at her heart strings...Not her kids, only his.

Crystal spent her afternoon in the sun at the motel reading her book. The relaxation was wonderful and rejuvenating, she needed that. She did work hard and this was vacation.! Lots of people, booze, beer and kids. Russell and Rockwell fit in just fine. Vincent handled the horseshoes like a pro and she helped out with the barbecue. It was fun for all. Crystal got a little personal with Russel at one point, kissed him on the cheek, handed him a beer and told him to get lost for awhile. When he got up, she patted him on his ass! He turned with red face and hid behind the next tree with the other guy she handed a beer to. This is fun she thought. Vincent is going to kill me! I want to make sure these guys remember this vacation. The evening progressed with these new friends. Together with the beach activities, the cookout activities and the fresh air, the boys crashed the minute their heads hit the pillow. No TV tonight, they were too tired. That being the case, Vincent couldn't wait to get to Crystal's tonight. She had been flaunting her long legs and loose boobs all evening. He needed to exercise his rights as husband and corral those body parts under him. To install his member in it's rightful place and rest for awhile. Crystal had exhausted him and his will to be a good by-stander while she teased, and danced and willed him to stop her! Now was the time...she continued her strip tease just for him. As much as he said he was exhausted and needed to get some sleep, it had been a long drive and a long day, she cajoled him into an exercise of twisting and reaching and tonguing his way down her body and back up to land his right hand cupping her jewels, his left hand cupping her left boob and his tongue teasing hers before his fingers on his right hand drove into her for an endless organism. That action speared his penis into action. Once that happened there was no stopping him from inserting that throbbing member deep into her vagina and bringing that orgasm to a screaming, biting, tearful stop. Crystal always cried when she got that carried away! He was exhausted!! "Goodnight love, we should vacation like this more often" and he left.

The next morning Vincent walked the boardwalk with his boys, found a great breakfast place and planned their day outside. Crystal was content to lounge in the sun, read her book, and find the good food restaurant one block behind the boardwalk. Home cooked meals, not fried or already bagged, but made to order and delivered on a hot plate with a smile. This is a great place for the kids…The water is safe… you need to walk a mile for any depth., and right now it's too cold to stay in too long. It's not great for surfing…no waves. The boardwalk is marvelous…again great for the kids…a money pit for the dads. The arcade, skeet ball, real bowling, roller skating, water slides. If the kids will like it, it's here and it costs money to enjoy. Boy, we're in the wrong business.

The boys. Since the day they were born Crystal didn't want anything to do with them. All the kids. She had never seen pictures of any of them. As much as Vincent would try to engage her in conversation about them when they were born or the first time they said Dada or their first day of school, she was stead-fast in her refusal to be dragged into conversations and learning about them. If she gave an inch, he would take a mile and never shut up about them. Every time he came home he'd have new stories about them. That was his life, not hers. They were born, they had names, she arranged for a savings account for each one, the end. But now, she can no longer think of them as infants or toddlers. They're teenagers! Little miniatures of their Dad. She has her head out of sand now and wants to know if they are good students, play football or baseball. With their height, maybe high school baseball is in their future. Maybe college or the military like their dad. Because of their dad, maybe they'll be smarter and pick college! Oh god, now she's wants to know what their mom is like? *How stupid!...She's Vincent's other wife...I don't want to know that bad.*

The day was great, Crystal finished one book and started another. She had spent the afternoon in the grassy area behind the motel, in a lounge chair, under a beach umbrella reading and drinking Rum Cokes. The occupants of the other motel units were all on the beach or enjoying all that Hampton Beach had to offer. That was until now. Two families had returned. One mom was hanging their bathing suits on the lines provided along the back decks and the kids were all playing around the tennis courts behind her. The quiet was now gone, with her books closed, she rested holding her drink in her hands. Not a minute later her attention went to Rockwell just stepping into the three sided, creaky door, outside shower. It was built against the back of their motel unit. He came well supplied, she could tell. When he opened the door he hung a fishnet type bag on the hook inside of the shower. She saw a bottle of shampoo and a white bar of soap. He closed the door and hung a dry towel over the door, hanging both inside and out. Next came his pants, also flung over the shower wall near the towel. Even with the noisy kids behind her, she could hear Rockwell singing in the shower. It made her smile. He is a cute kid, as far as kids go. It made her curious and pay attention when she noticed the three oldest girls from the end motel unit quietly giggling and sneaking up to the shower. One of the girls grabbed and pulled to the ground Rockwell's towel and pants. He hollered blaming Russell for the gag while the other two girls flung open his door and the three of them proceeded to spray him with colorful streams of string, sticky string, sticking to whatever it hit! Poor Rockwell just stood inside his enclosure mortified, trying to cover himself with his hands. Vincent happened on the scene just as the girls starting spraying. He got between them and Rockwell, confiscated their cans, and with a calm, military boom of a voice instructed the girls to stand where they were with their eyes closed, and slowly count to twenty... out loud. He quickly retrieved Rockwell's towel and pants, told him he had until they got to twenty, handed him their cans and said, have at it young man! By now Crystal was holding her breath not knowing what was going to happen. So far everything had happened so fast! She didn't want to laugh out loud and bring attention to herself, if the boys had seen her, she was just another vacationer, but she was splitting a gut...she needed to breathe. When Rockwell started his assault on the girls, it was hilarious. He was madder than a hatter spraying each one up and down and everywhere and they were running and crying and afraid of more retribution. The whole scene lasted not more than three minutes, but it was the funniest thing she had ever witnessed. She thought Vincent did a good job. Quick thinking on his part and with little effort, let his son know that it was okay for him to have his turn, they started it! Vincent spotted her, winked and corralled Rockwell back into the motel. She would have loved to be a fly on the wall when Rockwell emptied his ice-tea over Russel's head in the dinning tent. I guess he was still feeling his Wheaties after the incident and being teased about it didn't sit well with him. Vincent told her all about it later that night, still re-living the shower incident.

"See vacationing together is fun. You get to bond with your sons during the day and bond with me at night. There isn't much about this week that you can't go home and tell your wife. The kids are taking their pictures and they'll have tails to tell and retell when the film is developed. It's a memory they'll have for a lifetime and you provided it for them. It's what being a parent is all about. Aren't you glad you had the opportunity to share this with them?" "Are you going to talk all night?" Was all he said when he mounted her and filled one wet cavity with his anxious penis and her other wet, tasting like rum, with his eager tongue. He whispered between kisses, "this vacation is on the short side now, I'd rather be with you like this than listen to you talk about my kids and my parenting. I have two other women that like nothing more than to exhaust those subjects. Please exhaust my body, use and miss-use, just a little, all my moving parts that please you so well. It's been fun being with you. I've been shocked by, but rather enjoyed all of your antics. You do know how to please. Thank You"

The next morning is when Crystal's vacation itinerary fell apart. The drive toward Massachusetts was uneventful; however, the Old Sturbridge Village being closed put a monkey wrench in her plans.

This is when she lost tract of Vincent. There was no communication with him when he drove away from the closed attraction. Closed until further notice due to a water damage from broken pipes. *Dam it to hell,* she thought. *Here he is in Massachusetts with his Maryland kids, doesn't that just take the cake. Now what?*

She couldn't just drive around and hope to see his car...nope. Vacation over! Just as luck would have it, when she pulled out of the parking lot of the Village there was a State Police Station just across the street. New brainstorm...Crystal parked her car in a visitors spot in the side lot of the Police Station and went inside for information. After making inquiries and requesting maps and directions to NYC she was recognized. Crystal had made eye contact with a middle aged woman sitting at a desk with a very large microphone. She wore a headpiece that had one ear covered, but was ready and eager to abandon her post to run to Crystal and engage her in conversation.

"You are 'that' Crystal...the pianist...aren't you? My husband and I saw your show at the New Yorker 3 months ago...you were great! May I have your autograph, please! Wait 'till I tell Frank that I met you. We'll be back at the New Yorker in November for the Thanksgiving Day Parade and I want to catch your show again." The woman never stopped talking. "So what brings you to Massachusetts? Can I point out our points of interest or attractions on the maps for you?" Crystal merely smiled and asked for a piece of paper. "What's your name" as Crystal wrote "Please admit Carol and Frank to my Showcase during the month of November...Compliments of Crystal", as she signed it with a huge flourish! Carol accepted the invitation and gushed her many thanks. Crystal padded her hand, said thank you in return for the compliments and left with her maps.

Sitting in the police parking lot quiet and alone, she examined her options. Head straight back to her room in New York, her playing with Vincent seems to have come to an abrupt end or get nosy around the town of Grafton. According to the map, she was only about 20 miles away and she knew she'd never have an opportunity to be this nosy and in Vincent's business again! Did she care...did she dare? She convinced herself that this excursion was just an extension of her vacation. A couple of hours wouldn't hurt. She could still make NY by bedtime.

It was a pretty drive through the small towns in central Massachusetts. A two lane road all the way from Sturbridge into Grafton. She knew the name of the street she wanted, just didn't quite know how to get there. *Apple orchard...look for a hill and an apple orchard. Yea right! Grafton didn't look this big on the map..No street names on this map. A hill, up we go...pretty but no apple trees. This is stunning, quaint and lovely...the center of Grafton...green and grassy, a beautiful gazebo ... park benches...a couple of churches, a library, an old Inn, a post office and a country store... around the rotary...oh good, Howard Johnson's...coffee time...I'll get directions.* The coffee stop was just what Crystal needed. Very friendly with talkative people. She got a turn by, go straight, turn to get to where she wanted to go. Sure enough apple orchard on the right...water tower as well. She crept up the hill slowly wanting to take it all in. At the top, she turned around where many had before her, by the farm that dead-ended this street. Heading back down the street the Chambers mail box was at the end of their driveway next house down on the right. *Aspen Chambers, her Vincent, living here with Amy and a growing family. Where is everybody...no one in the tire swing or playing basketball. Are they dark haired like Russell and Rockwell...and him? He's not heading here...no he can't be. Risk running into his other family...he's not that foolish.* Oh look!..kids...tall, Aaron, Andrea...t h a t must be Amy. *Get out of here...now. I've seen too much.* Crystal drove down the hill and straight out of Grafton. She didn't know that Vincent was in the orchard with Russell and Rockwell just playing, picking and eating apples when she left the area.

Her drive to NY wasn't terribly long or boring, she had a lot on her mind to keep her busy. She'd always been one to talk to herself, so doing so today was not out of the ordinary. She was just glad there were no listening devices in the car to hear her one way conversation. Today she used this solitude for confession. It was good for her soul to rid herself of the building guilt she sometimes felt for bilking the government to support the Sabers and the Chambers and all their children. The government had a lot of money...she was using it for a good cause. She rarely thinks about it now-a-days, only when she thinks she is caught. Someone will say something or she'll read something that seams to point a finger at what she is doing. It's never her mess that comes to light but someday...she quickly puts that thought out of her mind, she's not doing anything to hurt anyone! Next she thinks about the times she dresses to tease. Shows up with lust on her mind, tingling through-out her body but never cheating in her heart; she backs down and feels miserable about her desires and bringing that poor man to the brink of loosing it! *I've got to knock that off. One of these days Johnathan won't let me leave with my humility in tack! If it comes to that, if will be my own fault and I won't be any better than Vincent...cheating in my marriage! Sorry Vincent, there is a certain draw, but I won't cheat! There dam long rides, I paid extra for a radio in the car, but can't hold a station for more than a few miles. Vincent's daughter has beautiful hair...dark with highlights of a reddish color...she's gonna be a tall one. These are things that I still can't talk with Vincent about...never wanted to, can't start now... never should have driven through Grafton.*

The map was easy to read and follow and Crystal made it into New York City in less than 4 hours. There was a good feeling of 'I'm home' when she pulled into the parking garage of the New Yorker at 6:45 pm. Without knowing it, Mr and Mrs Clear were only 10 minutes apart in their arrival at the hotel. Vincent had put on his thinking cap while traipsing around in the orchard and came up with a trip to the Statue of Liberty for tomorrow. Since Crystal's plans had seemed to fizzle and she was now a no show since early this morning, he was on his own. His plans meant spending the night in NY. Naturally the New Yorker Hotel sprang to mind immediately and was the solution. His boys were ecstatic, everything in NY was so big and fast, he was happy to share this with them. Given a little bit of time and choices, they used the indoor pool on the 9th floor first then went down and had dinner.

It was when Crystal was walking by the Rustlers Steak House that she noticed Russell. Sure enough, there they were having dinner. She quickly walked by and stood by the Bull at the door and just watched them for a moment. She was out of their site, but she could see them clearly. *OK Mr. Clear, you've given me one more night and I'm going to use it to the fullest, at my convenience!* Crystal then went to the desk and wrote a note to Vincent and slipped it into a hotel envelope along with her room key. She had given him exact instructions as to how she wanted him dressed when he arrived for her pleasure, just one item that could be slipped off his shoulders easily leaving nothing in her way for further exploration. Then she asked the clerk to deliver the note to Vincent's room around 10pm. He didn't know she knew, he was here. This is going to be fun she thought. In preparation of his arrival Crystal, returned to her room, took a shower and adorned that RED Five and Dime next- to- nothing, covering not much of anything! A little spritz of her perfume, the one he loved, turned down the bed and sat at the dressing mirror and bushed her long hair.

Precisely at 11pm there was a light rap at her door and Vincent, handsome, poised, wearing only the hotel bathrobe (completely open in the front and completely turned on) Vincent stood in her room just looking. The little RED thing had the perfect effect on him. There were no words needed, none could be spoken, they were both overtaken by the moment. They came together gently, his hands moving down her body and holding her still by the cheeks of her ass, while her hands were traveling up his taunt, muscled chest, to his face where she gently cupped his cheeks while kissing his lips. It was a long, sensual kiss leaving them both breathless. Still, standing toe to toe, Crystal was overtaken by such a strong wave of love and want and need, she cried. Vincent felt the same tug of need and cherishment at the same moment and felt helpless toward Crystal's tears. For the next several minutes they clung to one another like never before. It was with weak knees and shaky legs that they walked one-another to the bed and made love like it was the first time. There was no control and no holds bared! They moved together then apart then to the floor and back to the bed. There wasn't but one orgasmic explosion that continued into the shower and back to the bed before exhaustion led them to laying flat on their backs holding hands and giggling! It wasn't until 3 in the morning that Vincent kissed Crystal good-bye and said he'd see her at home in two weeks. Totally spent, alone in her own room, Crystal slept soundly until 10 the next morning. That was unheard of for her!

Back in the shower, Crystal replayed the night before with Vincent. It was perfect. She hatted to see him go, it made her feel empty. This place, this room had become as much as a home to her as New Jersey. Miss Elise had been really good to them and their coming and going. Vincent forgot, Vegas was next for Crystal, he wouldn't see her in two weeks! Well he and the boys are already on their way to Ellis Island, I'll go to the pier after lunch and wave good-bye then. Nearly one whole week and she hadn't even touched a piano! Leaving her room, she went to the 40th floor and longed to sit at that long, beautiful piano and make it make music. She was in luck, no one around. For the next three hours Crystal played that piano to her hearts content. In that time, she had acquired an audience. Bar staff and cleaning personal got to enjoy her music as they worked. The linen service collected bags to be laundered and dropped off clean linens to be put away. The food delivery was of interest to Crystal as she hadn't eaten since last night. She got nosy as it was being put in the stand-up refrigerators and freezers. The bread and rolls made her mouth water, so when the service exited the premises, she helped herself to a couple rolls and left-over meatballs she saw in the frig. Hunger satisfied, she played a few more selections and went back to her room. It was nearly time to walk to the pier and wait for the fairy to re-dock returning from Ellis Island.

The day was gorgeous, sunny and bright with a slight breeze. However, that breeze down by the water could get pretty gusty so she grabbed her colorful, silk Italian scarf, the one Vincent had brought her from his first deployment after they were married. The colors in the scarf looked really great tied lightly around her neck resting on a white short-sleeve sweater. Crystal had learned the art of dressing smartly on and off of the stage. These lessons were those of hard knocks and trial and error. Her mom was no help in the department. When Crystal was growing up she often heard her mother say "she wished Crystal was in a school that subscribed to the dress code of uniforms." Crystal never remembered clothes shopping with her mom or discussing prints not worn with plaids or stripes vertically vs. horizontally. Fashions were never a topic of conversation between them. Now look at her, a pillar of decorum and style. Oh well, things and people change. *OK, get going girl. I won't get to kiss him good-bye, but he'll be glad to see me regardless.* Crystal's appearance on the dock was not appreciated by Vincent as she had hoped. He spotted her scarf first and her second as she was pulling it up to contain her hair and Rockwell snapped a picture exactly in her direction. The boys had not seen her here yet, but when the pictures come back they are sure to recognize her as being familiar at the beach, at the cookout and now here...strange coincidence! Crystal caught Vincent's aggravated hustle to get the boys moving off of the dock and in the direction of the parking area. He gave her a nervous smile and a little salute of farewell.

Chapter 38

Crystal's life for the next two weeks was crazy busy. Between her appointments with the boys writing the words to her songs and the recording studio, she also had to meet with her attorney to seal the deals on her newly incorporated company. <u>Clearly Entertaining</u> needed it's name trademarked. She also needed to meet with the scouts for talent who would record on her new record label of the same name. Really it was her mom, her manager who arranged for and worked with the scouts, but Crystal made sure she had the final decision if she chose to exercise it. These were her busy days, but she was also doing six engagements in her Showcase in the next two weeks. Being busy made her feel alive. Keeping her mind busy and occupied help to keep Vincent off of her mind which helped her sleep better at night. When they were apart, he had his life and she had hers. She is building memories that she loves to share with Miss Elise, the people at the Bursa Unit, her dad and anyone else that will listen. Poor Vincent can't share his memories but with only a few. Only his Maryland family and friends and very separately only his Massachusetts family and friends. And of course Crystal if she chose to or wanted to listen. Vegas was very busy and profitable for her. She really enjoyed spending time there, because she knew in her down time she'd get to see Peter. They had grown close again, not so much like high school, but close never-the-less. He had taken up residence in Paradise, a township just outside of the busy 'strip'. He had been there long enough and met plenty of people in the 'know' and of 'power' to earn or amass certain privilege that help him build a good personal and business reputation. That reputation also helped him build a small house that he called home on a great piece of real estate which also housed his studio. When ever Crystal was in Vegas, her non working hours were spent out on his property. This was really vacation and relaxing time, nothing like the week she had spent with Vincent and his boys. His house had everything she needed except a piano. Some day, if she was still working Vegas as she is now, she'd ask Peter if she could ship 'her' piano out here, the one in storage back in New Jersey. If that ever happened, he'd never get rid of her!

The two weeks in Vegas flew by. With the time she'd spent in NY it had been 4 weeks since she'd been back home to New Jersey. Crystal has a weekend in Atlantic City scheduled and then she can take an at-home breather and relax a bit. Miss Elise is always happy when someone is home with her. Daily, Crystal's routine is checking in at the Bursar's Unit, the post office and shopping. No matter what Crystal buys for food at the house, Elise whips up the most tasty and appealing meals, it's home cooking but with a flare! She and her dad have become semi-regular pen-pals. She keeps him abreast of all of her travels and adventures and new song titles while he shows great interest in everything she has to say. He also knows that he and Suzy will be back on the east coast in the not too distance future, but his orders haven't come down yet. The Unit has had a change in a few of the daily personnel. All things change, but when they change when Crystal is away, she feels the difference and that difference layers another degree of her not belonging.

These have been longer intervals of her not checking the files she has sent up for Vincent's families and their own personal savings account. Yes, in the not to distance future she'll need to change things so that Reginald and Aspen age, have retirement dates and benefits. She'll need to move the phony personal accounts in her and Vincent's names out of the government system and sever all personal matters. It changed the camaraderie and all around friendships that had formed there. The new guys really don't understand the need for Crystal's assistance and have a hard time tolerating her use of the equipment in their office. Since her dad's transfer to the west coast and Vincent's transfer to here out of

Maryland, the people around her have changed. Her dad is no longer the head honcho on base and she is no longer his little gopher, so why do they need to tolerate her on base, in a Unit and being so familiar to have her using military equipment? Since the war ended, there has been a push to clean-up the military bases at home. There are more men home and available to man the factory's and do manual labor like before. This means the women can go back home to their homes and providing warmth and stability. Also since the end of the war there has been a need to form more government agencies to protect and investigate and govern more closely the workings of all paid positions in the government. Crystal's days are numbered now on base. She can feel the daggers in her back.

It had been four weeks since Crystal had seen Vincent, he was expected home this weekend. A whole three days with him, no work for either one of them, hooray! Miss Elise had a wonderful prime rib dinner with mashed potatoes and mushroom gravy ready the minute Vincent walked through the door. Whenever he arrived home he was famished! Miss Elise knew the two of them had vacationed together a few weeks back and they shared a few of the memorable highlights with her while eating. After dinner, as was the usual, they all retired to the living room to listen to Crystal's newest original tunes. Once again Vincent was blown away at Crystal's talent and loved her new songs. This evening was delightful even with the dreadful news Vincent shared with Crystal once they were together in their own room.

He explained that the morning after arriving home to Maryland with the boys, Rockwell was in the back yard with his best friend Kevin, climbing trees and mimicking scouting the seas for pirate ships, like in the movie TREASURE ISLAND, they'd just seen, when Kevin fell out of the tree. "Wait, wait wait" Crystal exclaimed. "when did they see the movie?" "Well," Vincent continued. "When we couldn't get in to the Old Sturbridge Village because of their water problems, we stayed on the same road, route 20 I think, on our way homewards. That's when I lost tract of you and knew I was on my own and needed to occupy the boys for the day. We came upon a movie theater sign in a parking lot of a few stores and the boys were intrigued. I thought why not, the first showing of the day was scheduled fifteen minutes from when we saw the sign so we bought the tickets and waited for the show. The boys had never been to a big screen theater show and the movie was really entertaining so the excursion was a big hit." All the while Vincent was taking, Crystal's hands were busy unbuttoning his shirt, un- buckling his belt, unbuttoning his trousers and generally stripping him of every garment he had on. His story was interesting, and she could picture the boys and feel their excitement. But having him this close, and feeling his warmness, the end of his tale could wait. She had a better idea. She could tell by his readiness that he was happy to be home! It didn't take him long to be quite aware that she had him at a disadvantage and he needed to step up his game to get her as naked.

Now with her hands moving, moving down his broad chest, his hand were busy undoing the rope knot in the belt around her waist. With that undone, he merely tugged twice and her long shirt laid on the floor at their feet. With her long fingers wounded around his penis and stroking him gently he needed to work quickly to undo the buttons on her blouse and release the hooks of her bra and begrudgingly move her hands from his prize to slip these last coverings from her body. As he released her hands she stepped closer to him and slipped that eager penis between her legs. No underpants were hindering her advance. She hadn't worn any, waiting for his homecoming!

In the morning over their 3rd cup of coffee when Elise excused herself to shower, Vincent finished his story of Kevin falling out of the tree and breaking his leg. This is the fact that was not mentioned last night, and really the end of the story. Now Crystal took up the conversation in telling Vincent about the advances in technology and computers that could be the major factor in phasing out her ability to access and manipulate government files. Also there were many personnel changes that caused and limited her ability in accessing personnel files. Crystal's mind started wandering and she was playing with her coffee cup when she said, "I think my days of being everyone's fairy godmother are coming to an end. We, you and I are very well off, especially with my music, recordings and new business venture. I hope the Sabers and the Chambers have been able to sock a little away for a rainy day. The storm might be coming very soon." Vincent looked very concerned at this revelation. "The Chambers will be just fine. " he responded immediately. "Amy has family money that she is not afraid to spend on her, our family. The Sabers however, might need to tighten their budget a bit. I'll need to tell Rhonda that the extra assignment pool is drying up. I won't be able to work the extra details for extra money. She's a good kid and will make due until she can get that part-time job at the jewelers down town that she is always talking about. She loves the kids, but I think she misses adult company." Vincent took Crystal's hand and looked her straight in the eyes and thanked her for all of her efforts on his behalf over the past several years. He went on to say he knew at first her playing with the office equipment and creating the two additional persons and putting one over on the government was her own personal way of kissing the proverbial big guys ass! But he said he also knew how much of a watch dog she was over the files both for her own sake but also for him and his families. He said "I know I've asked a lot of you over the years and a really do appreciate all you've done and how much you've risked in keeping it up. I knew at some point it would all end."

"Hey, wait a minute, It's not over yet. I think the storm came and went without blowing everything up. We were both out of town and didn't even know about the change-over. Everything in the Bursa's Unit has been updated and to date all things are running smoothly. If my two names and our extra accounts raised no flags with the switch-over and new equipment, the end of things need to be natural. I mean, Reginald and Aspen (she almost messed up and included Keith) need to age out and retire. All with proper retirement pensions and full service men benefits. I was very careful in their creation. I mean birth dates, family back stories, social security numbers and service ID numbers, there were no red flags to be caught. If all goes according to plan, all the kids will still be eligible to apply for all military college scholarships and programs. I think if I attempt to pull out now or delete these names and accounts it would cause more of a stir. So the Sabers should be just fine going forward." Vincent stood up and reached for her and held her for a long time. Miss Elise returned to the kitchen just in time to witness the embrace. Clearing her throat, she offered choices for the evening meal and the tender moment was over.

Chapter 39

1960ish

This was the 30th or was it the 50th time Crystal had been to Vegas. It was the town that never slept, therefore it earned it's nick name of 'Sin City". The papers were still raving about her shows and always about her talent, next to a headline of rape or murder in a casino further down the strip. People from all over the country swarmed to the strip to buy their tickets to see Frank Sinatra or Lena Horn. A younger generation also visited the clubs where a newcomer with a totally different sound was making some waves in the music industry. Elvis's Vegas debut was in 1956, he didn't take the city by storm but he definitely left his mark and was an expensive headliner by now. Vacationers or visitors to the city would stay up all night and try their luck in the always growing number of casinos that are popping up everywhere. Those who bought tickets for the Liberace show also bought a ticket for Crystal's show to see how close the talent or entertainment factor was. The papers were always comparing the two shows or drawing comparisons between the two. Crystal's notoriety and popularity was equal to or surpassing many of the stars that had made their name in Vegas. Was all of this leading to the fact that Crystal is tired? You bet! That's another thing you don't say around here, people will bet on anything!

Her home coming after these two weeks was more than welcome. She gave her mother/manager instructions that she was off limits and not performing for the next four weeks. She had seen her schedule and it was free of appointments. She wanted to keep it that way. It's going to be the first time in almost 5 years that she and Vincent are going to spend an entire week together. She has four days to relax and polish three new songs she has been working on. This love in her life is satisfying and thrills her each time she hears her recordings on the radio. Money is no longer a concern in their lives or livelihood, they can do or have anything they want or can dream up. Her concerns now are Miss Elise's health and her dad's up-coming retirement. He had relocated to the East coast five years ago, but to a base in Maine. Now with retirement imminent he and Suzie are moving down here to New Jersey and taking up residence in this house. Crystal's mom comes and goes out of this house, but really lives in New York with Clive, Mr. Brentwhistle. They live primarily in a suite in the New Yorker, why buy and furnish something else when they always land back at the New Yorker after all of their travels. That's where Crystal stays when playing the New Yorker now...no more room 3108. Over the years, things had changed but in a normal progression type of way. All good things come to people who work hard and hard work pays off. So far Crystal knows she works hard but really, really enjoys every minute. Her songs are an extension of her, maybe that's why they go together so easily. Sometimes it's the mood that dictates how the song will go. With her talent she can almost make the piano sound like a bird in the song Meadow Memories. And in Black water blues the piano sounds like water crashing over rocks. *OK, time to make magic on a few new one's she thinks. Vincent, loving, handsome, tireless Vincent will be here in four days and I don't want to think about songs undone. I want to concentrate on doing Vincent. Running my fingers through his not so black thick curly hair (now all over his body) and enjoying him running his fingers or his tongue over my body anywhere he chooses. Oh, that tongue!* Her panties were wet!

That man never seemed to age (except for a few more gray hairs) or tire of his rat race schedule. How could he still appear and act like a 30 year old. He works a Navy job five or six days a week as scheduled, travels New Jersey to Maryland or New Jersey to Massachusetts, has fathered twelve children, (I guess he has spent a lot of time in bed) has added on to a house and nearly refinished it from top to bottom and still comes home to me and ravishes me like he is still 30 years old! I love the ravishing parts, but I'm content to stay close to home and not try to travel the North East like we did 10 years ago with his two sons, Rockwell and Russel in tow. Or driving home from Vegas together 5 years ago. Again stopping at flea bitten motels and eating sloppy- joes and dry burgers thinking we wanted to see the 'country'. I'm done with that. Give me good food, clean comfortable bedding and his warm and wonderful body to keep me company at night and I'm a happy girl.

I guess I'm getting old, I now enjoy hearing his tales of his children. Russell graduated from school (finally) happy to have his mother off of his back. Poor Rhonda for two years trying to keep Russell in school and studying enough to at least graduate. Always being shown-up by his kid brother, Rockwell, the brainy-ac, now a freshman at Rensselaer Technical Institute in New York. But Russell teamed up with talented and stable guys in carpentry and is now a sort after carpenter. Rhonda herself used her studies and gifts of memory and self-teaching to stay up to date with metal-lurgy and fine jewels and precious stones to land a job as an appraiser with the jewelers downtown. Although she hadn't had any contact with or heard from her family since she couldn't remember when, her dad's name went a long way in the precious stone industry and she used it to her best advance. Rhonda was able to expertly function at her part time job away from home because her daughter Rachel, who was such a great help with the younger ones, was still at home. Vincent (Reginald in Maryland) had many times remarked that his daughter Rachel resembled his daughter Andrea (in Massachusetts)...just saying. Many times over the years Vincent had gone back to Rockwell's friend Kevin, the one with the broken leg and his medical troubles that included Rockwell's giving him (Kevin) through a surgical procedure, Rockwell's stem cell from his blood because he was a match to Kevin's Blood type. Well. I guess all turned out Okay because the two boys are in New York in college together. Crystal remembered Vincent's anxiety over these procedures and these boys, so she decided to take a ride.

Now her memory was in over-dive. She remembered a few years back, when she took a weekend and drove to Rensselaer Institute, she was already in NY so she figured, what the hell. She knew Rockwell's schedule as well as his address where he lived. She remembered thinking that she loved her new car, it rode so much smoother than her other one. And once on the way, how much better the roads were to travel on. A lot more traffic than before but the roads seemed wider and straighter. She remembered thinking that the school was huge, the buildings impressive with their ivy covered walls and flags blowing in the breeze. It didn't take long, a turn here and a conversation with a group of 'wanna-bees' and soon she had eyes on him. She followed Rockwell and she assumed Kevin to the Rec Center. After ease dropping for about an hour she decided...yup...definitely Vincent's son! Handsome, quick witted, and intelligent. He had nicely filled out since she saw him last on the pier in NY. With a bit of a sick heart that she couldn't share any of this with Vincent, she left and headed to Massachusetts. No way would she tell Vincent that she scouted out his families, just to lay eyes on them, just to feel more part of his life. All in the same weekend, she now had eyes on a yard full of kids trying to play basketball. The bunch of them were around 11 years old. She knew at least two were Vincent's (Aspen's) kids. Andrea was probably around 15 years old and Aaron 16 or 17 but not home or in the house, just not visible right now. The two youngest, just came out of the house with their mother. Abby perched on Mom's (Amy's) hip and Adam trying desperately trying to get mom's attention. Crystal knew their names, but not another thing about them. She wanted desperately to put eyes on Andrea and Aaron before she headed back to NY. She came all this way to see Vincent's children and wanted be able to put faces to their names when he spoke of them. Yep, she had definitely softened over the years. She had accepted the fact that he shared with another woman, two other women, that which she wouldn't share with him! She was their fairy godmother and major benefactor but they didn't know a thing about her or that she even existed. To date she and Vincent had done a good job of keeping many secrets and hiding many lies. But she still didn't want to head home until she had seen the two oldest kids. Crystal drove back down the hill and parked in the orchard in a turn-off on the right. It was late afternoon and the weather was still fine, she took a walk up the hill staying in the orchard. There weren't too many cars that traveled the road that ran parallel to the orchard where she was but one in particular caught her attention. It went up the street but she didn't see it come back down. It was a dark blue sedan and now she saw it parked in the Chambers driveway. From her vantage point in the orchard, just barely behind the Chambers house, she saw a gorgeous teenage girl get out of the car. She had long dark hair and even from where she stood, she saw striking eyes. She knew that she was looking at Andrea...Vincent always remarked about her eyes. Yup, a young beauty. That left Aaron...how long would she need to hang around before he made an appearance? Too long. It was getting dark and she needed to get out of the orchard and start heading home. Someday she'd take a ride to Maryland to see the rest of Vincent's (Reginald's) family. But this day ended with her heart filled with having seen the two college students, Reginald's Rockwell as an adult and his growing family in Massachusetts. She remembered thinking that she was just thankful they were all healthy and now seeing them, the lot of them looked very much like him!

Crystal had just finished an afternoon tea with Miss Elise and was heading back to the piano in the living room. They had just spent more than an hour thinking back and talking about when Crystal had first come to the house. That was a long time ago...a lot of things have happened and changed in those almost 18 years. They remembered when she first got her drivers license and first car. How many times she and Vincent would come and go. When her career first started and all the people both Crystal and Vincent had invited to stay in this house. Elise said again how much she loved Crystal and was a little lonely when she wasn't at home, but no one was gone long enough for her to be bothered with the loneliness. Elise was thrilled that Crystal and Vincent had made it their home and enjoyed entertaining family and friends here. *It's a good thing I don't mind being alone, Crystal was thinking.. Looking back, I've spent a good amount of time alone. Traveling back and forth to NY and then traveling to Vegas. And taking long rides to anywhere just to ease my sense of curiosity. I guess I was born with a wander lust and the ability to enjoy my own company. I've never really been lonely, just alone a lot. OK girl get off of this memory trip.* Get to work. *'Hands Down'. That's it...that really works...I like it. It's gonna be easy how.*

Ten minutes later Miss Elise was standing close to the piano, all smiles...knowing smiles. "You've got it don't you? I can tell by the way you are playing that song. It swings a little differently now. It has a slapping sound in many places. Share...what's it's title? Crystal was in her element now. Sitting straight at the piano, head bobbing, fingers lifting high and striking the keys heavily in places and softly at other times. Smiling back at Miss Elise she said, "yup...got it". She finished her new song with a flourish and shared the title. "Hands Down". Crystal told Elise that the package that had arrived here last week was from the boys (when Crystal referred to the boys, they were the guys from New York, the ones that were supplying her with song words) "I shouldn't refer to them as the boys anymore, Brad now works for me and still jams and writes with his buddies. You remember, they've been here, they loved your cooking. When I looked at the sets, one set really worked with the music you just heard. I love writing music, it comes easy to me. The cords and the fingers just move together and they wind up making sense. It's not until I feel the bridge forming, then it feels like it has a beginning and finally a proper end. The bridge works it's magic to tie it all together. When there are words, I really start to feel it fitting all together. I often go back and create a hook when there are words, I swear that's what sells the song! I feel I've learned so much! There, one down and two to go and I still have nearly four days to do it!

OK, I'm talking too much, but sitting here really helps to keep my mind off of Vincent and what I'll be doing when he does get here." Miss Elise just blushed and said "I can remember those days, you just enjoy your young man and keep doing what you're doing with your music because it is working."

But sit there she did, just remembering and thinking. Starting many years ago she felt unwanted around the Bursa's unit and unable to 'do' anything with the Reginald, Aspen or Keith files. Crystal was merely a visitor and a seldom one at that around the base these days. She was feeling less and less like a military brat and it made her feel almost homeless. She'd always been welcome on any base her dad was assigned to or Vincent's as well. Her identify now was as an entertainer, celebrity, not the pest with the long legs and long hair. Somewhere along the way she had grown up and out of an identity that was familiar to her. She never thought she'd look back and miss some of those days. Still feeling nostalgic and thinking about Vincent her thoughts brought her back to the weekend she drove forever and ended up in Grafton, Massachusetts.

The apple orchard was familiar to her as was the Chambers house, but what was different was that Vincent was there and she saw him with Amy. Amy was of average height with short bouncy blond hair. Vincent said she always wore it short to help show off her eyes which were a magnificent green glittering with nearly white neon. What Vincent didn't tell her was the woman had breasts the size of watermelons. Good God, now she knew Vincent's attraction to this one! Andrea had inherited those eyes and a figure that one day would also sport large breasts. Crystal saw Andrea as a young beauty. She saw Vincent (Aspen) planting a garden in the back yard with the help of a couple of his younger kids. She got a good look at Andi that day and felt now, as she did then, a little heart sick at that which she couldn't bring herself to do and that was, have children. She realized that this was the reason why she was looking for his families. She wanted to see him enjoy what she could not give him. After that weekend, Crystal made a point to take a drive to Maryland to find Lost Road in Towson. Reginald's kids were almost mirror images of Aspen's in Massachusetts, it was almost eerie. Rachel was indeed another beautiful daughter having the looks of Andrea almost down to a T. The boys all had very dark hair like their dads. Crystal had forgotten he had twin girls in this family, they favored their mom a bit with dark hair infused with red highlights. All the girls wore their hair long. Rhonda was a rare beauty herself. A slender woman with a straight posture which made her look taller than she was with long, very long natural curly hair with a mind of it's own. To say her hair was brown is not right, not red or even straw-berry blond...blend them all together and that was the look of Rhonda, very striking! Very different from Amy in Massachusetts and different from Crystal. Vincent's taste in woman was very much like his lifestyle, different! Getting close to Reginald's house was tricky because is was the last on a dead-end road. Crystal remembered tying her hair up and covering it with a ball cap, driving down toward the house slowly and stopping nearly at the side door. She spotted all the kids in the back yard playing badminton, hollowing and yelling and having a good time. She remembered thinking that Vincent (Reginald) must have put that net up. Having sat there long enough to get an eye full of Reginald's children without being caught she turned her car around and headed back toward the paved road just ahead. Pulling away from where she had parked she noticed a man entering the house on her left. There 'I've seen him before, I know who that is' feeling came over her so swiftly and so strong, but...can't be. She'd never been here before! Driving away, not being able to pull in a radio station without static, didn't help her mind settle away from that man. Somehow she'd get a name. She'd question Vincent about his neighbors in Grafton someday when he's talking about Russell or Rockwell or the kid that got hurt. Surely she'd get a name somehow.

Wow, memories...I never did pursue getting that name. That was a long time ago. I wonder if Vincent knows him? Thinking about it now...maybe in the next week I can work Grafton into a conversation and get his name.

The next four days flew by...Crystal continued to work on her music and she knew getting Vincent to talk about Grafton would be an easy thing. He loved to talk about his families. It had been five months since Crystal had seen, had felt, had loved Vincent. The Navy intervened again, sending him away to Portsmouth Navel base in New Hampshire to scout out and guard incoming 'hot rods' for nuclear inclusion for some of our subs. In this time he has gotten to see his mom and my dad while Crystal played Vegas and New York. It was definitely time to see him! This had been their lives for the past 16 years. He loved the Navy and she loved playing the piano. The places he has seen in his life was amazing. All to know how good he has it right here in the good US of A. Although he has been to many Naval bases throughout our country, he is always happy to come home to the east coast. Since Crystal had been a kid and moving bases with her dad and now moving bases with Vincent and traveling Atlantic City to New York and Vegas, she could consider herself fairly well traveled seeing a bit of Florida to Nevada, New England and Maryland. Her notoriety as a pianist paid her well and opened many doors for her.

One night in Vegas on the arm of Johnathan, he brought her to an after-hour club and introduced her to this guy named...only... Elvis. She knew the name because he was beginning to make a quick stir and commotion with the young women who went to see him. His music was very unlike Crystal's. Loud, fast and different. He told her outside of the church bible hymns, on which he had put his own twist, it was the only type of music that really moved him. He wanted to make his own mark in the music world and he was doing just that!

Another time she was with Peter just witnessing a photo shoot and had a wonderful conversation with a black man named Fats Domino. Crystal had met a lot of characters in her career and travels but this guy intrigued her. He loved her music but claimed he also was a pianist and song writer but not happy with others singing his songs. His was a fast tempo with almost a honky-tonk sound but he was hell bent on making it. Later that same day she had lunch with this very interesting gal named Patti Page. It seemed everyone wanted to break into a glamours career of singing or movies. Patti made it! A lot of what was happening in New York or Vegas or Hollywood was who you knew or who could you could get close to. Crystal was lucky she had Clive Brentwhistle in her corner. In the who do you know department...Clive's kid sister was married to a set designer on the hit move "Citizen Kane by Orson Welles. These were very close knit groups of people who ate together, traveled together and worked only together. Needing help during the war, Clive was able to supply the acting troop with shelter and food on occasion at the hotel and fell into favor with the production company. It was after he'd met Crystal that he contacted his brother-in-law and pleaded for an introduction on Crystal's behalf to a higher up in the production company. These people and many more names opened many doors. That's the beginning of the story, but Crystal's talent led the success story all the way to her own recording label of today. One introduction opened so many doors.

Chapter 40

He's home, at last, five months is a long time. Crystal met him at the front door at preciously 3:10pm on Sunday with open arms. They clung to one another like love starved kids. That part of their relationship had never changed. After Crystal unglued herself from Vincent's embrace he was able to undo his top button and ask for a beer. "Nice to be home" he said smiling his undeniable sweetest smile while walking with Crystal to the kitchen to get that beer. From there they walked together into their bedroom where Vincent wanted to get out of the 'monkey suit' as he referred to his travel uniform. Vincent undoing his shirt and belt buckle and stepping our of his pants just about undid Crystal's ability to keep her hands to herself. Five months is a long time to be celibate and have what you want in front of you for the taking, so she did. Tired and hungry but that could wait... Crystal felt too good to him to deny her these tantalizing approaches of long fingers down his chest to find and caress and stroke to it's full length and thickness his prize penis. He loved the way she rubbed the tip to wetness and abandoned it completely to two handedly capture his balls and softly juggle their looseness while knowingly bringing him nearly to the brink of loosing it with her tongue searching his mouth and slowly sliding down his throat. All the while she is filling all of her senses with him, he is touching and rubbing and pinching and sucking and making sure she knows he is doing to her that which she is doing to him. When she retreats and exits his mouth she uses her tongue between his fingers and then sucks one and then another finger until he mourns and mounts her swiftly. She stills him immediately not wanting the moment and fullness she feels to end so soon. At this rate the end would come much too fast, she wanted this feeling to last just a little bit longer, but nature was just about to take over. So with a gentle kiss that ignited the pulsating of tongue in and deeper so started the hips thrusts of penis in and deeper and again deeper until all human reasoning had obliterated into carnal lust and want. Their mutual need of each other had once again been spent and now they rested in each others arms. "Have I told you lately Mrs. Clear how much I love you?" "Have I told you lately Mr. Clear how much I've missed you?" "You didn't need to utter a word Mrs. Clear, I felt and shared your feelings."

"It's 6:15, do you suppose we could get up now and I could drink that beer that is probably warm and flat now, then eat some dinner and resume these activities later?" After hearing his stomach growl not once but many times, Crystal needed to swallow her negative remark and 'happily' escort Vincent to the table for a meal fit for a king. Elsie had prepared his favorite meal of roast beef, gravy and mashed potatoes with broccoli smothered in cheese sauce and held dinner for them until they emerged from their love bed.

Elise was beside herself with joy to have them both sitting at the table having dinner with her. The dinner conversation ran from Vincent's travels and some of the duties he could talk about to Crystal's new songs and contacts both in New York and Vegas. Crystal was excited about her record company, and her moms management of every aspect of their operations. They talked about Crystal's mom and Mr. Brentwhistle and Vincent's mom and Crystal's dad. They'd all been to this house at one time or another so Elise was not left out in the cold during these conversations. In fact, the conversation turned to the fact that Harold and Suzie Grandcockski would be relocating to New Jersey and this house quite soon. Crystal and Vincent exchanged looks of 'concern' that Elise totally missed while her expression was one of exuberance! "Who's going to do the cooking when they are here?" Vincent asked...eyes glued to Elise for a reply. "Of course I am," she quickly cut in. "I don't care how much of a good cook she champions herself to be, it's my kitchen." There were chuckles and then strawberry shortcake for desert.

The conversation lingered at the table long after the dishes were done and Elise excused herself to her rooms. Vincent and Crystal had a lot of catching up do do. He was elated to be able to talk to Crystal about his kids, she showed an interest these days and he was thrilled! After the review of the Massachusetts goings on, he moved to the gang in Maryland. The pride with which he spoke of his kids was heartwarming even to her. He mentioned that he wished he could have added on to the little house on Lost Road, but Rhonda said she liked it just the way it was. Now that the conversation was in that neighborhood, Crystal's thoughts went back to the man she'd seen in the house next door. Choosing her words carefully she inquired the name of the people that lived in the houses on that short road. "How many families lived on that road?" "Vincent said that's easy, just two, us and the Schaffers, you know Rockwell's best bud, Kevin Schaffer". The minute Vincent said Kevin Schaffer, Crystal's face cracked, the memories of Rockwell's friend and the man who had escorted her around Vegas the first times came rushing back to her.. Vincent continued with "it's a great area...to our right is a large corn field and the Remmey's house faces the paved road on the right hand corner. But on our road it's only us in the back and the Schaffers in front of us on the left with their yard stretching to the paved road.. Crystal asked how much Vincent knew about Kevin's dad. His job or his personality? "These are strange questions Crystal, what are you getting at or looking for?" "What is Mr. Schaffer's first name?" Crystal asked very calmly. "He's Jerry and a great guy. Ya know, he was in your line of business a number of years ago but gave it up because it was too much of a draw on his heart. He was diagnosed with a heart murmur and high blood pressure caused by his job. Now he sells insurance and is home every night with his family. What's going on, why the questions?" "I met him. He was my first contact in Vegas all those years ago, he was my lead in to Jack Kapp at the Recording Production Company. We had dinner my first night there and we visited a night club after dinner where I played with the band. My first exposure to a Vegas audience." Vincent was shocked silent at first. "How do you know it's the same guy?" "Truth…about 5 years ago I took a ride. First to Rockwell's college where I put eyes on him as a good looking young man. Prior to that my memory was of a scroungy dark haired little boy. That same day I headed to Maryland and found Lost Road. I saw a bunch of kids playing badminton in the back yard and had a pang of love/loss/quilt…I knew you put up that net for them. When driving away I saw Jerry, knew he was familiar, but couldn't place him until now." "Oh Crystal, did he see you? He'd know you anywhere!!" "No, my hair was up and covered and I had on dark glasses. I know he saw the car, how many band new cars with NJ plates go down your road?" Vincent got up and got another beer. Crystal asked him to mix her a rum and coke, a strong one. Do you want the rest she asked? There's more he questioned? When he sat down she finished with her Massachusetts story of that long ride she took. She finished with "You have very beautiful daughters and handsome sons, you should be proud." He was spell-bound! Speechless. Smiling from ear to ear and happy to know she showed that much of an interest to scout them out! Stretching out in the kitchen chair he sighed, "Mrs. Clear, we are two fucked-up people with the strangest habits and interests. I can't thank you enough for allowing me the gifts of my 12 beautiful children, You can't say you didn't have anything to do with that, because without you, I would never have been able to do it! And You. You've bent every rule, enabled me to live a life no other man has ever dreamed about and are still my bride of almost 20 years ago. If you say it, I will believe you, but can you still say you've stayed celebrate all these years?" "I sowed my wild oats before I married you, without an organism. That magical feat that you can perform on me is the reason why you are my only one. Still to this day, my only one. Only my love for you will permit you to make me loose control like that. In that regard, you are the only one who has ever had my body, the only one I've ever loved enough to trust!" That realization made her feel sad. He had misused that trust, flaunted it in her face, counted on it but she was rewarded for it every time he touched her. She knew the reason why she was feeling sad, in a way it was a way of life for her just brought to the surface every time he excelled in honoring her with that glorious organism! They finished their drinks and retired to their bedroom. With Vincent now based back here in Colts Neck she hoped their daily life and night time sexual appetite would return to their 'normal' and not rule her life! Having only two weeks to go having Vincent home on a mini-vacation, Crystal was determined to shake this feeling that had come over her. Spooning him in the middle of this warm bed felt right. He was comfortable and snoring within minutes.

The next day started early with the sunshine streaming straight through the clean, white curtained window. The birds singing also had something to do with that, as did the aroma of coffee from the kitchen. She didn't know who moved first, but that kiss coupled with his ready-to-go penis pressing her legs apart in search of her wet, waiting, chasm was exactly the right way to start any morning. With him nestled and pulsing ever so slowing deep inside her, her hands could not cover enough of his body to satisfy herself. Feeling him everywhere, deep inside her and his tongue deep inside her, her nipples strained to rub against his bare chest. Her fingers rode up his back to his face and once inserted into his mouth played havoc with wet tongue and lips. The pulsing actions she did with her fingers mimicked his hip action which produced instant organismic eruptions. Both of them laying on their backs trying to catch their breath was the best way to say "good morning".

The shower sex was next with hot, soapy water and hands rubbing and washing everything they could reach. This lasted as long as the hot water did, but then there was the chore of dressing. 'It's harder to suck on a pimply nipple when it's covered", so he pleaded..."please don't cover them". She in turn asked him to please leave that pulsing shaft available after he finished putting on his socks. With the items requested available, once Crystal was sitting on that wonderful specimen of his shaft, she was close enough for him to tweak and pinch and bite or nibble on her nipples while handling and rubbing her ample breasts. "The years have been good to you Mrs. Clear, these (he gently bounced one breast, then the other) have grown and are still beautiful just like you. I'm a very lucky man to have had you all these years." "Your dam right you are, but you're not done pleasing me yet...we still have thirteen days to go,"and she meant it. "Can we have coffee next, I promise to discuss this further after coffee!" Vincent pleaded.

Elise was sitting at the kitchen table reading her morning paper and enjoying her second cup of coffee when Crystal and Vincent joined her, she looked up, smiled brightly but then the unspeakable happened. Elise's head fell forward to the table and she died instantly. This fact was confirmed 12 minutes later when the cornier from the base signed her death certificate, death by heart attack.

The next six days were the pits! Within 36 hours the house was full. It only took Rita and Mr. Brentwhistle 5 hours to arrive, ready to stay indefinitely. It only took Harold and Suzie 12 hours to arrive, ready to stay indefinitely. Brad and his three side-kick song writers showed up the next day. The funeral arrangements were made for Wednesday at 10am from St. Crux's Cathedral, downtown. These were Elise's arrangements made years ago to also be buried next to her husband's stone in the cemetery across the street from the church. Little did anyone know that these instructions as well as a newly added white envelope addressed to Crystal was added to the manila envelope being held by the Gadder's next door. They'd been Elise's neighbors since she moved in and she trusted them to hold this envelope for her marked, "in case of my demise". The funeral brought together everyone from their street and half of the base personnel, having met and enjoyed barbecues and other outings at Miss Elise's over the years. So a very solemn occasion was brought to life through all the tears and joys of having known such a lovely and giving person. They showed up with enough food to feed the gathering for days. Being a military gathering it also provided enough beer to float a boat. Those who arrived in the base shuttle bus were the first to leave. Hours later the base personnel left one by one as did the neighborhood friends. Vincent turned out to be the best host and pillar of strength for Crystal, and organizer of everyone who stayed at the house for two more days. Friday at noon Vincent drove Rita and Mr. Brentwhistle and also Brad and the rest of his merry song writers to the bus station for their way back to NY.

When Vincent arrived back to the house he was greeted by Mr. Gadder from next door sitting with Crystal and her dad and Suzie.

He (Mr. Gadder) apologized for intruding again, but wanted to hand over the white envelope addressed to Crystal that was also in the manila envelope left in his care by Elise. Whatever the contents of this envelope he felt could wait until Crystal had a day or two to relax. He'd hoped he wasn't mistaken. In his presents, Crystal opened the envelope to find a tiny diamond ring and wedding band with a note in Elise's handwriting bequeathing to Crystal her earthly treasurers.

My jewelry and my house.

Chapter 41

Having lost Elise, their 'mother of the house' did something to both Crystal and Vincent. Rita sensed that Crystal was going through a period of mourning and backed off of traveling her for a few weeks. Even Vincent was home straight at 5:15 every-day. Some days remembering the way Crystal would greet him on the road or be waiting for him on the front porch all unbuttoned with wet panties. Neither one of them had much of a sex drive these days, they were just waiting for 'normal' to kick in again. Crystal, even waking up with her period, on day one of the third week bothered neither one of them. Two days later, Thursday evening having a cocktail with Vincent, Crystal encouraged him to go and visit with his kids...it would do him a world of good and make him feel better. He kissed her soundly and headed to the phone to call Amy. Crystal couldn't hear him talking but the look on his smiling face said it all. They had an early to bed, because Vincent wanted an early out in the morning.

Crystal watched him drive away, the house was so quiet. It was an eerie feeling knowing that he was off to visit with and sleep with Amy before she saw him again and she prompted him to do so. That was the one thing that could make him feel better, now she needed one for herself. She had no desire to sleep with anyone, so she headed for the piano and exercised her fingers and let her mind wander into the future. So far uncontested, because the note was in Elise's handwriting and she had no heirs to fight it, Crystal's lawyers were just and quick to title the property in her name which should happen by the end of next week.

Her House. She sat there all alone and didn't like it. Would she like it better with her dad and Suzie in residence all the time? She'd find out in four months when they'd be back to enjoy dad's retirement. Would it be any different than living with Miss Elise? She guessed only time would tell. At least someone would be there when she was in New York or Vegas or Atlantic City. She supposed Vincent would have the same question. Living with his mom again? With her fingers still moving across the keyboard, Crystal was determined to stop brooding and get up and do sometime constructive. With that thought the front door bell rang. *Not more company, not now...please.*

She opened the door to find Peter standing there. She was instantly racked with sobbing tears into his shoulder as he hugged her. Not letting go of him, walking him into the living room she thought *this is MY feeling better!* "Boy you're a sight for sore eyes" she blubbered as she let him sit down and sat down next to him. "It's been ages since I've seen you, what are you doing here?" she continued between sobs. "I haven't seen you in ages either and I knew where you lived and that you just lost someone close to you, so here I am." Peter was still holding her hands and looked like a million! Is Vincent here he asked. "NO, no he'sssss, (deep breath) working on a project on base for the next few days, it happens occasionally." "When is that man going to retire or you too, when are you going to retire?" Now, she was laughing. "join me in the kitchen, I'll make more coffee." Without letting go of his hand, they walked together.

Twenty seconds of busy work and they were sitting together at the kitchen table. Another twenty seconds of silence ensued before either one of them spoke again. She giggled and said I don't know where to begin. "almost twenty years...I can't believe it. Do you still live in the desert near Vegas?"

"Yep, been there almost 20 years now. I've built it up a lot with a studio and full dark and finishing rooms and turned it into a bit of a horse farm. If I'm not working I'm riding. I have a good and happy life Crystal. How about you? Do you love what you do?" She got up and poured the coffee. She remembered he took his black and the sugar was on the table so just the cream needed to be gotten. Back in her seat she said "love it... Besides Vincent, my music is my life. Performing is fun and exciting some times but hearing my own songs on the radio, knowing they were written by me and recorded by my own recording studio is most rewarding. Did you know my mother is my business manager?" He just stared at her...speechless. "HA... gotcha!" she wailed...you're never speechless!

OK girl, you've got a whole lot of story to tell and get me caught-up." While making lunch she was only up to leaving Virginia for Maryland and just having met Clive Brentwhistle and her Showcase days. Most of this he already knew, but not some of the finer details so it was fun to tell. After lunch in the backyard she got through the horrible train rides from Maryland to New York and then her first few trips to Vegas by Bus. Those were horrible rides she remembered. He agreed and admitted that that was most of the reason he stayed in Vegas. That and the money he made...more than any place else. "Plus I'm accepted there, no questions asked, there are people who live there with different or stranger life styles than me," he added.

" I loved Vegas at first Crystal said, most of the people, the rush of performing, feeling like a big wig even though I was still only me, but it really made me feel alone and the train...what a bore. Once I had a 'name', NY was home to me. Just like Vegas, people needed to pay to see my show." Now inside while making dinner, because she insisted, she brought Peter through the recording days with Brad and his 'merry men', but all kidding aside, they were great guys and loved working here opposed to NY, which made is easier for Crystal. All the while, almost fifteen years worth, still checking into base. Now she explained she was at in the Bursa's unit, learning all the technical equipment, using her finger exercises on their keyboards and still learning every day. It's what she did way back when she was with her dad back in VA and really she explained she never quite learned to quit. When Vincent was transferred to Colts Neck and I found this house, we've been here ever since. It's a breeze getting into NY from here and I loved

Miss Elise. Conversation with Peter had always been easy and this day brought that right back to them.

The conversation over their simple diner never stopped. Sitting in the living room after dinner with their brandy laden coffee, Crystal shared with Peter her scrap books of her early years of piano playing and her stage and publicity books of pictures. Whenever Crystal's name or picture was in a paper she would bring the paper home. Rita also kept an eagle eye out for publicity shots of Crystal and compiled quite a pile of information. With all of this Elise and Rita complied the scrap books Crystal was now sharing with Peter. Peter showed quite an interest in her books because he was able to add that the Vegas pictures were his handy work...not all, but a lot of the pictures had his tag on them. He said he had followed her growth over the years and was sorry she never took him up at staying out on his ranch when she was in Vegas, what he had built would have been such a surprise and restful place for her.

The hour was growing late and Peter had still not shared his 'sad' news or dropped the name Crystal was sure to know. So when she gathered her books together and walked them to the center table just for someplace to drop them, Peter changed the subject to other people that they both knew in common. Then he said it..."sorry to tell you girl, but Johnathan Whelton also died this week. I knew you two had this 'play with me but don't touch me relationship' that went one for years, but I also know you hadn't seen him lately." Crystal's entire body went limp. Her tears were instant. Peter went to her and walked her to the couch where they sat together in silence for the next many minutes. Crystal was the first to speak asking how, when and where? Peter replied with "the facts are easy. Heart attack, died instantly on Wednesday in Florida at the Palms Hotel just jamming with his old band. You remember the gang, the other three of them. Jimmy, Walt and Tanner arranged this week's get together as an anniversary, their 20th as the Midnight men. I guess the four of them arrived on Monday and occupied an empty area with a piano and just jammed. Sounds familiar doesn't it?" Now Crystal just smiled at the memory and could picture the four of them, a little grayer, with what they had left for hair, not standing as straight as they once had and not caring a bit! "I guess it being off season, they did a gig at the hotel for old times sake. Tanner, the youngest of the group is a friend of mine and called me with this information.

"Yea, Johnathan was quite the man." There was a far away look on Crystal's face when she continued with, "he was just my type, just the right size. Tried to kiss the pants off of me and had hands as smooth and warm and playful as I would allow them to be. That poor man put up with many years of teasing and foreplay and hoping I'd change my mind, but my pants only came off when I was alone in my own room. Like I told my husband, I have been celibate and only his our entire marriage. It's a conversation Vincent and I have had a few times with all the traveling we both do."

Peter felt the visit had wound down to its end and promised to try and stay in touch. Crystal walked him to the door where they shared a huge hug before Peter opened the door and walked away. He had refused staying the night even though Crystal insisted there would be no reprisals at being alone with her. Crystal closed the door on the best friend she had ever had with a feeling of love and renewed friendship. Turning off all the lights while walking back toward the kitchen and closing up the house for the night she was deep in thought as the past twenty years filled her head. When the thoughts landed on Johnathan, they filled her heart and her eyes welled up in tears. *I can't go to bed right now, I'd never sleep, I'm wound-up too tight with thoughts and feelings that need to be put to rest.* With that in mind, Crystal left the light on over the sink as well as her night light at her bed side and headed out the back door. Dropping into a chaise lounge under the tiny moon so high up in the sky, her thoughts ran a-muck between her meadow memories and the feelings Vincent could so instantly invoke with a touch or a word or a kiss over to Johnathan. Johnathan standing so close she could almost feel her resolve melting just by the way he looked at her. The few kisses they shared with his warm hands on her bare skin at the nap of her neck or the top of her arms or the heat that radiated through her clothing when he hugged her with his palms spread across her back and fingers dancing to a tune in his head. *The shear magnitude of that man and the plain strength and self control that we both exhibited...tears again! New thought!!! Twelve kids! And I was afraid of hurting him! Handsome kids...beautiful daughters smart boys that look like him...I guess... good women who made wonderful homes for their families. Why did he do so much for one and not much for the other? His Massachusetts house was mammoth and new and up to date where his Maryland house was small. Neat but barely large enough for all those people! I never wanted to know...I wouldn't let him talk about his other lives. There were so many 'people' in those lives, he could have gone on and on for hours. He could have told me tails of first steps, the tooth fairy, shone me class pictures, complained about crying babies or the boys first hair cuts. Giving his kids driving lessons or teaching them how to swim. Was I a fool? Was he ever there for my firsts... my NY solo show or my first Vegas show of my first Atlantic City show. Was he there for any of my firsts? Is this our house or my house. Outside of hotel rooms and military base housing, this has been our home for the past 15 years and no other soul that stays here knows anything about us! We are both unlawful and sneaky. He is responsible for so many and I am alone. I'm going to bed now...alone.*

Even going to bed did not shut off the stream of thoughts running through her head. How lucky he was to have twin girls...she remembered years ago seeing a back yard full of kids playing and maybe putting eyes on two girls about 9 ears old with jet black hair just flying around their head helter-sketler showing some reddish highlights.! Vincent had said Rhonda's hair was naturally curly and unruly at times. Rachel was not afflicted with that unruly hair, she remembered Rachel with long lovely tresses of dark brown bouncing on her shoulders. All those trees in their back yard...we don't have trees like that around here. *Enough, enough...now I'm thinking about trees!!* That was Reginald's family, why did he need more? Aspen's Andrea looked just like Rachael...did he ever make that connection? Is that one of the things he would have talked to me about, but I shut him down. I wasn't enough for him but neither was Rhonda. What is wrong with him? *Boy that is the first time I've asked THAT question or even had that thought!* Now with other things to occupy her mind she slowly drifted off to sleep.

Chapter 42

So Thursday night he made the call to Massachusetts and told Amy he'd be there late morning. She was ecstatic and he was in 7th heaven knowing he'd see his pregnant wife in just a few hours. He thought pregnant woman were beautiful especially when they were his.

The whole ride into Massachusetts was thought filled intoxication. The weather was perfect, the car was running good, and Amy was going to be his bright spot in this entire week. He hated being apart from his kids so long, they grow and change so fast. His kids filled his head the whole time he was driving. Aaron was such a clumsy kid. Too tall for his age, all legs and no balance. He was always the first one to be picked for a basketball team, but he couldn't sink that baseball for all the tea in china. Now whenever he heads out with his sister Andrea in tow, they form a little crowd. She is a beauty and all of his friends want to be the first to ask her out. Being his little sister and always being surrounded by boys has taught her how to take care of herself. Now he saw her as a big sister because she loved the twins so much. What he wouldn't give to be able to spend more time with them, especially with another on the way, soon, really soon. *I guess it's one of the things Crystal doesn't know about yet, telling her I have a new baby on the way isn't something she enjoys hearing. But she's such a good sport. Once the baby is here he'll/ she will have her/his own savings account. Just thinking back, she did that for all my kids. I love her...I can't believe she told me to take this ride!*

When Aspen arrived on Speer Street, Amy looked like a breath of fresh air. She was a beautiful woman of medium everything(except her gorgeous, ample, no.. huge Breasts) with gorgeous eyes. It was easy to pick her up but he swung her around carefully and in pure pleasure to be home with her and the kids. Thinking of which..."where is everybody?" There was still coffee on the burner, so she quickly prepared a couple of ham and egg sandwiches, sat down with him over coffee and filled him in on the most recent goings on. "Remember, this is Friday and a school day. Today is Aaron's class picture day, he should be home early. It's also Aaron's senior ball tomorrow night and I'm thrilled you'll be there to see them off." Now she told him the part about his monkey suit and the tie, but she was sure all young men went through that! "Andrea will wait for Adam and they will walk up the hill together around 2:30." "Do Andy and Adam know I'm home," he asked. (Andi being his pet name for Andrea) I'll pick them up, I'd love to surprise them". "Great, we have until 11:30 to get to the Grafton Country School to pick-up the twins, they don't know you are home either." In the meantime Aspen and Amy just sat at the kitchen table and got caught up on everything.

He loved being here at the top of the street and the top of the orchard, it was so quiet and peaceful and beautiful. It was a great place to raise kids. His were happy and healthy and he loved them to bits. Amy was a wonderful mother and liked being pregnant. It's a good thing, number six was due in two months. She now had the house the way she liked it, with all the kids in their own rooms and the nursery waiting next to their bedroom. Alex and Alley each had their own rooms, but didn't like not being together. Most nights you'd find Alex on the foot of Alley's bed of vise-a-versa, they were each others best friends.

This was not your typical military family in that Amy had a huge inheritance and spent what she wanted on their house and her families needs or to a limit, 'wants'. What she wanted was Aspen home more often with her, but she knew his military responsibilities were there before her and she married him anyway. He was a good provider and loved his kids and they loved him back. That's what meant the most!

With everyone home for dinner Friday night, Aaron talked about the dance tomorrow night, Andi laughed at his hair cut, she thought it was too short. Guys are wearing their hair longer these days. Adam asked his dad a million questions about the Navy and the twins just ate and talked to each other. Aspen was a good sport and answered all the questions but took a special interest in the twins behavior. He hadn't noticed their absolute focus on each other before or that they had a language all their own and pet names for one another. He was glad that Alley's hair had grown and could be worn in pony-tails with pretty little ribbons now. She looked like a girl and he could finally tell the twins apart. Before her long hair, only their eyes were different. Alex inherited his mothers beautiful green, neon lighted eyes, where Alley had dark almost black eyes. Both beautiful children, but as toddlers, identical, he needed to see their eyes to tell the apart. To date only Andrea and Alex had their mothers eyes, time would tell with the baby. (*Vincent sat in his own thoughts about the kids around this table and how different but yet with definite similarities to his kids in Maryland. They definitely could pass as siblings, but they would never know one another! I think that is a thought that will bother me now that I've come to that realization…how could I have created such beauty and life and have it be so taboo??*) "Hey dad, you look like you're on another planet" Adam said. "Hey dad, how many planets are there?" Alex wanted to know. And so the evening went, each trying to get dad's attention.

10:20pm and all is well. Aaron is out with girlfriend Sandy, Andie is in her room with her best-friend Lynn, who will be spending the night and the twins are fast asleep in Alley's room. "What do you say Mrs. Chambers, our turn to hit the hay?" My *head and my body has been in bed with with you since you arrived home! Wonderful, it's even a little early, he usually likes to watch the 11 o'clock news.* I'll check in on Andrea while you check on the twins then I'll meet you in the shower. Amy's reply was swift, happy and informative. He was excited! Ten minutes later they stood face to face under the spray of a wonderfully welcomed spray of hot water. Staring down at her beautiful round stomach, he was almost shy. She took his hands and placed them on either side of her roundness and stepped closer to him. When she initiated the kiss and held him in her arms, not letting him let go of her roundness, the baby kicked! They giggled and all of the shyness was gone. He held her to his hard penis and kissed her the way she liked it, tongue down her throat and hands cradling the baby she held in her body. After the quick body wash they took their time and were gentle with drying each other thoroughly. Touching every part of each others body, bringing tantalizing feelings to the surface and not letting a sigh or a goose bump go unnoticed or unkissed. The steam in the bathroom did wonders mixed with their heat! "Having the bathroom so close to the bedroom was a wonderful idea Mrs. Chambers" as he opened the bathroom door and carried Amy to the bed. "So glad you built it that way Mr. Chambers." The change in air temperature filled both of their bodies with goose bumps and they were quick to go under the covers. Aspens hands and mouth found Amy's swollen pregnant breasts and giggled at their goose bumpy feelings. I like you like this, he crooned with a mouth full. Traveling up to fill her mouth with a kiss he said he'd keep her pregnant all the time to enjoy breast like these. "Are you sure we're OK to do this" he said breathlessly after the kiss. "Good god yes," she nearly shouted, "I've been waiting all day to have you inside me" she said as she was maneuvering him into a position to mount her. The belly not being a problem, he slipped into her with ease and her Ah of pleasure said it all! He rolled to his side, taking her with him staying very deep inside her. In this position he could see the smile on her face and rub her belly. All was well with their world! Their hands explored and touched. Her breasts being the other object of his attention. But when he stared to push her to him and lift his hips to push harder into her the flame of passion ignited and the tender moment turned into an organism that couldn't be denied. The belly was forgotten and the flame intensified into groans of pleasure and body movements of twisting and stretching and hanging on and then giving up. "I need to breath" she said. "OK, you do that while I do this." and he maneuvered them back to the side position and he slid that ready again penis right back where it was warm and comfortable. "I miss you when you aren't here" she said. "I miss this when you're not here" she repeated. He liked the sound of her voice when she was spent and breathless. All the while he was stroking her breast gently and rubbing her belly. He wanted to feel the baby kick again. There was something magical about thinking that there was a real baby just the other side of her skin, so close to his hands. These thoughts turned him to mush and he exhaled with an Ah...of his own.

The twins had him hanging a tire swing right after breakfast while Amy and Andie worked on the laundry. This was family life and the sounds and smells reminded him of his grandmothers. That was another thing he couldn't speak of here. These kids didn't know they had grandparents, even a great grandmother. He could only share family moments with Crystal, but she was such a witch about it, those moments were off limit! She would say "that's the bed you made, now you alone lie in it!" He has heard the words before, so now he needed to change his train of thought and enjoy his kids.

Aaron was nervous about the dance tonight, his dad had never meet Sandy before. *What if he didn't like her? What's not to like...she's a knock-out and her height compliments mine. She well spoken and polite. He's gotta like her!* It was mid afternoon and Aaron took off for the florist to pick-up Sandy's corsage. It was a large gardenia adorned with white pearls on light blue ribbons and baby's breath. It was lovely and should compliment her dress, according to Andie. When the time came, dad did the honors of tying his tie and complimenting his oldest son on his attire. "I can't wait to meet her" he said. I bet you guys make a great looking couple. Then he got solemn and said softly, "I'm not here enough for you guys to grow up this fast." Aaron heard him and threw back. Just one day at a time dad, just one day at a time. It was coming up on to Saturday night, this weekend was going by way too fast, he needed to leave by 4pm tomorrow to make it back in time to get a good nights sleep and be on base Monday morning by 7am, vacation over.

Amy noticed a change in his demeanor and knew he was thinking about the fact he needed to leave tomorrow. She had seen the look and heard the tone of voice many times over the years. Now it was her job to liven him up, screw his brains out tonight, follow him into the shower in the morning and back to bed after that. Her chin was up and she was looking forward to the next 24 hours. She'd have a talk with Andrea about getting breakfast for the twins in the morning, dressed and out to play.

Aaron's was a dinner dance tonight, so he wouldn't be home for barbecue. He promised he'd stop home so dad could meet Sandy and mom could take pictures. "You're making such a big deal out of this, stop, mom, please don't embarrass me!" Aaron looked pleadingly at his mother. Aspen almost used his military voice when he next spoke to his son, but toned it down to a dad level. "Be proud boy, that your mother wants to share in some way your growing up and putting a young woman on your arm. These pictures will be treasurers some day." (Vincent thought...where did that come from?!!) Amy stood closer to Aspen, smiled and took his arm.

Aspen was out back manning the grill when Aaron pulled back into the driveway. The sound of the car returning had everyone racing to see Sandy, Aaron stopped the car, went around and opened the door for Sandy to get out. She was indeed lovely. Her ash brown hair was in a do high on her head with light blue ribbons twisted in and out throughout the hair. Amy said, "Sandy, you look beautiful" Aaron followed up with Sandy's introduction to his dad. "Nice to finally meet you Mr. Chambers, Aaron has told me so many things about you." She did need to look up at him a bit and she giggled when she said, "you are bigger than life." That's the way Aaron talks about your sometimes." It was Sandy that embarrassed him but it made Aspen proud. "Okay, let your mom take a few pictures and you two go off and have a lovely evening." Sandy had completely taken over the picture taking time, with posing and placement standing with Aaron and hamming it up and being serious. *OK, I like her. I hope they don't break each other's hearts.*

Once again dinner was eaten, baths taken, kids bedtimes arrived and the house was theirs alone, once again. "We can go to bed early if you'd like Mr. Chambers." "I'd like that very much Mrs. Chambers, if you'd allow me to have you more than once, being it is an early hour." "I'm not going to count, but I bet four times is not out of the question before the sun comes up and by then, you'll be up and ready again, I'm sure!" Holding hands they headed for their bedroom and he whispered..."four times...I like that Mrs. Chambers, you're feisty!... I can't wait to watch you breast feed again!"

Amy was different from the other women in Vincent's life. Crystal, tall, equally proportioned med-section to legs, the classic hour glass shape with nice, very nice large breasts. She is very strong. Rhonda, tall, all legs like a dancer, breasts... wonderfully round and squishy that held their size and shape and didn't need a bra and very slender to have breasts that size! Amy...rather short in height, very small waist with short legs that had the strength of any man. Tiny in stature one would say with a killer bod flaunting that tiny waist and those huge boobs!. Vincent would definitely have labeled himself a boob man. Loved to look at them, juggle them, suck on them and bury his penis between them. Yes he was a boob man! Amy was now the one holding his hand (and his heart) and heading him to bed to play with her boobs. She loved the feeling of his long wide, slippery, because she got it long and wide when she lathered it with cream, penis being massaged between her breasts. Lying on her back with him straddling her and her hands being held by his, holding tight her boobs surrounding his prize, she'd sometimes try to do a sit-up and lick the cream from the tip of his penis. He'd get even more excited at these attempts, but she couldn't quite reach. *Dam, this feels great, but I really wish she could reach!* He loved watching her try and imagining how great it would feel, like when Rhonda does it! These thoughts and the way she is now also touching his penis with her fingers is driving him nuts so he announces "this is number one Mrs. Chambers" as he shifts downward and inserts that very ready penis into her waiting vagina then fills her hot mouth with a kiss that finishes them both off! Not staying atop of her very long, he rolls to his side and lays his hands on her round belly. He is immediately presented with a swift kick that makes both of them laugh. Having caught their breath, she rolls on top of him and plays with his nipples, nibbles a little and curls his chest hairs around her fingers and finds pubic hairs and does the same thing then starts gently pumping his penis and rubbing the inside of his thigh and handling his balls and getting all of the results she was hoping for. "Ready for number two Mr. Chambers" as she lifts herself up and sits on his shaft with an audible "how wonderful, you're huge, I feel you up to...) but she couldn't finish. She moved once, then again and again and stopped.

"I don't think I've ever felt you quit like this before. You are rubbing on and poking....oh my god, please. Help. me. Finish.. this...not so fast..oh my ...I want this ...now...now. As he sat up a bit and helped her to bounce on him, slowly, more...not done yet...slow again... their eyes met, she cried and he held her until her breathing slowed and he felt the baby kick. Now he could breath. She'd never..never, like that before. "Aspen, thank you." She took a deep breathe and said "can you leave that here with me so I can use it again when you're gone?" He head the words, but the tone of voice, so pleading and so unlike her, made them both laugh. This last episode was exhausting and sleep came easily.

But it was just a nap! Aspen sleeps primarily on his back so with a little stimulation, activating his penis is easy. When he's this tired he thinks he's sleeping and having Amy mount him again is a pleasant dream. She is so slight, she can do this initially without waking him. But she screwed up, it wasn't a dream and she felt so good to him, he grew too immediately mammoth and he didn't want to miss a thing. There were two beautiful breasts so close to his hands, he couldn't resist. So he touched and massaged and licked his lips. There was a warm, tight wonderful feeling in his groin and it was growing his penis to maximum everything bumping into walls of wet, warm woman. He knew one move and it would be more than a wet dream. It was his turn to say "not yet...stay still...enjoy me for another minute. Let me get caught-up, you started before me." "You bet I did" as she tried to reach his mouth for a kiss, but she was too short. He bent forward, held her and delivered the kiss she was hoping for. The wet, warm, delicious experience happening in his mouth activated the wet, warm feelings surrounding his penis and he couldn't, didn't want to stop the wonderful, crazy, throbbing, now thrashing feelings happening to the rest of his body. It was so delirious, he didn't realize Amy was on the same ride he has on! This time Amy rode him until he was still. When she dismounted his shrunken, used penis and bent forward, his arms wrapped around her and they slept.

Of course, all too soon the sun was shinning threw their windows. "I wasn't dreaming was I, Mrs. Chambers?" "Oh, no, you weren't Mr.

Chambers… so can you?" "Hmm…I'm terribly sorry but I must take it with me as soon as I pack it away." "Well under those circumstances I know just the place you can pack it, if you'd like I can help you with that." "Well, I don't think it's quite ready yet, it rather likes it here." "Knowing and understanding how hospitable I can be. I bet I can find a more comfortable and dark place for him to be." "Yes then please help to your hearts desire" Before those final words were spoken Amy had her hands wrapped around, one, his penis, the other, his balls. Growing the former was her specialty. Warming the second made him hum. When he felt her about to move and straddle him, he flattered her on the bed, put his face between her breasts and his knees between her legs. "Not so fast this morning Mrs. Chambers. You know that makes me come too fast, I can count, this is only number four and I need it to last longer than three or four of your bounces. What your breasts to do me when you do that…well…you know…it's all over!" She smiled and said, "You're right, it's only number four…we'll have the morning one left to savor. So have your way with me and we can finish in the shower, later." That set hands and tongue and breasts and penis into action. She couldn't get enough of his penis and he couldn't get enough of her breasts. Kisses landed on necks, shoulders, nipples and lips, with his hands under her ass holding her up to meet his penis, it reached into the depths of her. He couldn't go any further, she accepted every inch of him! Still tucked deep inside her, he moved his hands first to her breasts, just for one more feel, then to her back to pull her up to him in a hug and for one more kiss. It was the kiss that always did it, just like like last night…orgasm overload!

A few minutes latter she said, "you realize, if I weren't already pregnant, I would be by now!" "Not yet, you can't be…we still need to take a shower!" He said with a giant smile. "A shower, of course that'll do it, meet you there. It works every time…look at me!" Standing under a wonderful spray of hot water, with his hands resting on her hips he went back to her last comment and said "I am looking at you, the most beautiful pregnant woman in the world!" Kissed her, finished a quick wash and exited the shower. "Hey you, get back here, we didn't finish" she whined. He yelled back, you will slip and fall, I'm done."

In a huff she finished a quick wash and having no clothes, not even a robe stormed into the bedroom naked and damp. Laying naked on the bed he was waiting for her, "You can't fall here….OMG, you are so beautiful, that belly and those breasts," He couldn't get out of bed fast enough to rush to her and softy touch and stroke all of the places that were hidden to him in the dark. They felt different in the daylight. Bigger, more alive, more special, radiant! He couldn't pull his eyes away from her body. His hands moved over her like he'd never felt her before. She helped him to feel lower than her belly, laying his hand on her pubic hair. He made a move like he didn't belong there. She led him back to the bed holding both of his hands, then placing them one on each of her breasts. He asked her softly, "I didn't hurt you did I?" "Aspen, what is it? Of course not, I loved everyone of your touches and the way you made love to me. Please do it again before you leave." She said this imploringly, almost like he wouldn't! "OMG, you are so beautiful and so tiny, I'm afraid I'll hurt you." "Good god Aspen, it's daylight, open your eyes. It's me…feel me. Love me and make me squeal with lusty anguish, please, one more time before you leave." They laid together in bed for many minutes before either one of them made a move. Finally Amy got on her hands and knees and let her breasts and belly rest on Aspen while she gently cupped his face with her hands and kissed him like a woman in love. He felt the passion radiate through her from that kiss and responded in kind. Now his hands were all over her and you'd think he was a young teenager who couldn't get enough fast enough. "Slow down Mr. Chambers, this is number …morning shower…remember, the last one you get for this visit." "I can't get enough of you this morning, it seems like there isn't enough of you to go around. You are carrying that baby and you are so tiny. Are you sure we can do it again?" "We need to do it again, Mr. Chambers, I'm wet and horny and want you to bury yourself deep inside me, again. Just when cyou feel warm and comfortable and are getting lost in me, that's when it will happen. That wonderful, crazy feeling of loosing control. Feel free to kiss me any time now so we can make it happen." It was when she starting saying we need to do it again, Mr. Chambers, he followed her directions and slipped deep inside her. With his eyes closed and his hands busy on her breasts, listening to her ask for a kiss, he did...long and hard. This time he knew it was the last time for awhile so he stoked her with his penis ever so slowly and softened the kiss to try and make these wonderful feelings last. But he messed-up...he was stroking her mouth with his tongue with the same tempo as that of his probing penis and those movements led to their immediate sexual explosion. Clawing at the bed-sheets and twisting and hugging onto his body and trying to breathe and groaning with delight and doing whatever else he said she does...she did! He told her, with pleasure a few minutes later when they were both able to speak normally. He also added a thank you Mrs. Chambers for that sexy goodbye followed by another kiss that he wanted to take with him.

Chapter 43

Over the years updates had been made to the Elise's house with input and money from Crystal's bank accounts. TV reception had improved with cable and telephone service installed throughout the house. The washer and dryer, a new kitchen stove and built in ovens had enhanced and quickened meal prep and Elise was all for that. True to her word Elise had a cleaning service in the house every other week for all of this time. Her back yard garden became smaller and was now non-existent, so Crystal had a three car driveway paved in the back of the house using much of the garden area. This made carrying groceries in the back door to the kitchen so much easier. The grass and flower gardens beyond the driveway and around the back areas and the front of the house remained untouched and were maintained seasonally by a lawn company. Many of the improvements to the house and the yard were made possible by Crystal's money and it made Elise and Crystal both proud of their home. It's no wonder Elise made sure Crystal became owner by her death, she deserved it. With Vincent away more than home Crystal had the chore of making sure the house was occupied and maintained and remained a home that was busy and loved. That's what a home is...four walls that contain love.

OK...dad and Suzie will be back in four months. They'll have Elise's quarters to themselves and be here full time. They know Vincent and I have crazy schedules and will be in and out all of the time. When I am here for any amount of time, I'm likely to fill two of the upstairs bedrooms with lyric writers or mom and Clive. That still leaves the 'left wing' empty. I need to do some brainstorming to use this house to it's fullest. Elise was happy to have just us and a party or huge barbecue every now and then, but I need to do more with the property. With this and many other things on her mind Crystal welcomed Vincent home three days later and they just sat and relaxed in their back yard with cocktails and soft music. This was not the two week vacation that either of them had thought to have. One week was gone, sometimes life or death gets in the way. They knew they were getting older, but thought it would take longer to feel this tied and feel their age! Crystal's stage appearances were getting fewer and fewer by her choice as well as a change in the music that was selling these days. She was taking more of an interest in the recording studio and record label her mother had managed and grown, but these activities were in New York. Although they had her name all over them, she wanted to stay closer to home these days. Vincent was still a military man based here at Colts Neck and with fingers crossed that's where he'd stay for a good long time. He needed to stay active because that is what gave Crystal access to the base and strategic informational areas to keep in the loop of her 'personal files', which to date were still, active, healthy and growing, invisible to unknowing eyes.

Still sitting in the back yard, not wanting to do anything more strenuous than think, Vincent brought up the subject of Peter's visit of just the other day, again. Crystal was happy to talk about Peter and his success and the fact that he had built quite a business for himself all contained on his own property on the outskirts of Vegas. She went on to mention that beside his home, he had built a horse ranch and his own photography studio. When Crystal went quiet and then sat up straight, then got up and began to pace at the foot of Vincent's chair, Vincent chuckled. "What great and very expensive idea just burst in that brain of yours?" "Oh Vincent, look at this house. It's huge and we could do so much with it, but I just thought what I WANT to do with it!" Now Vincent sat up straight and needed to pay attention because her tone of voice was laced with excitement, such that he hadn't heard in many days, weeks! "OK love, so what are we going to do with this house?" Crystal was beyond excited, first because she knew it could work and second because Vincent said we. "We, my dear husband, are going to live and work here. We are going to turn some portion of this huge house into a recording studio and run the New York operations here. Even with your mom and my dad moving in here permanently, you and I having our rooms that still leaves ample room on the second floor and an untouched third floor. My mom and Clive use one of each of the bedrooms and bathroom sometimes but that still leaves rooms empty...and that's on the right side of the stair case. The entire left side is still empty! OH, please can we please talk about this seriously?" Just to keep up with Crystal's pacing, Vincent was now standing. He reached out to still her and caught her in his arms at her last words and saw, even with the dim moonlight, hope and determination in her wishful eyes. After all of that Vincent came back with..."My mom is really gonna live with us?!" Crystal just collapsed into his arms and sighed. They wandered back into the house to refill their drinks and walk through the house just talking about the possibilities.

The upstairs was in fact huge and empty and begging to be used, but even in their excitement had no experience with building or remodeling or the first idea of how to start. She reminded him that he had undertaken a big project in Massachusetts, but he remaindered her that he was just the pick'em-up and hand it over or the guy who maned a hammer every now and then, the CB's framed and finished most of that house. So that night they decided how they were going to finish their next week of vacation. A call in the morning to Clive and they were off and running. He had over-seen the building of the New Yorker almost twenty years ago and still had contacts and more know-how then the two of them. Her mom was the one to put together the who and what would be needed once a game plan was in place. But that didn't take long. By Monday night, Crystal and her mom were walking through the house and discussing Crystal's needs with Barry Frank, the producer at the recording studio (who just arrived) to nail down all of the requirements for a sound room, sound-proof room, room for mixing boards, at least a six piece band area,(if there was that much room, you could always squeeze more instruments in) possibly two electrical boxes to handle the electrical needs and microphones that would function without feed-back, which was a room and placement ordeal. The house offered the room but designing the optimum use of the room was the order of business. The grounds also came into play at this becoming a working studio. The need for parking was discussed as well as a redesign of the yard.

Vincent had taken some time last week to clear his head and be cheered-up by his kids in Massachusetts, so this time it was Crystal's turn to fill her mind and brain with different activities and be happy. Whatever she did with the house was okay with him, he'd live in whatever grand space Crystal came up with designing. So he figured, not being that interested in the planning stages he'd leave her to be busy with her 'baby' and he'd take off to visit with the rest of his babies in Maryland. When he mentioned it, she tilted her head at his suggestion but smiled and agreed that was a good idea.

So the morning after, Vincent was off to Maryland but not before pleasing Crystal's libido for over an hour and in many different postilions. *God, we're good together! I can't believe that I'm not enough for him and I know he'll be in Rhonda's bed in just a little while.* The thought lifted Crystal to turn Vincent to lay on his back and she sat on him, straddled him with his penis reaching high and straight into her very used vagina. The entire movement was a little rougher than she had intended, but got the reaction she hoped for. Vincent in turn groped for her breasts and pulled her down to his mouth for the kiss she could only deliver with her long, wet, swollen tongue down his throat and delivering the final blow for his ejaculation, again! His hands fell away from her breasts and he sucked back at her tongue with ecstasy. When she straightened up and rolled off of him she knew she was the only one in bed with him just now!

Chapter 44

Driving out of NJ to Maryland, Vincent's head was full of thoughts. So many thoughts that he had a hard time keeping them in order. Rhonda doesn't know he is coming...she'll be so surprised. When the twins see him they instantly want to go out for ice cream, they are so cute. *Crystal must really be looking forward to her new project to be okay with me taking this ride so soon after lasts weeks jaunt to Massachusetts. It's the first time she doesn't bark at me spending so much time with my kids!! I'm really tired but I wouldn't have gotten any rest at home. Where did the years go..we've lived in that house for nearly 15 years. Crystal has accomplished so much and she loved Elise. Will having my mom around full time change things in the house? Neither one of us have lived with our folks for a long time...it will be weird! How am I going to explain my time away...away to be with Rhonda and away to be with Amy. How blessed I've been all of these years to have a wife like Crystal to bend the rules and put up with my antics and,* at his Vincent felt heart sick and needed to pull over and compose himself.

It was like the first time he had thought about what Crystal had gone through for him to be the 'beast' that he was! He loved Rhonda and Amy and he wouldn't have had the kids he did without them, and that was Crystal's fault, he'd spent years telling himself that! But he almost denied her her career in his selfishness of wanting her all to himself while he had other women.. She has such a talent and he almost stunted her opportunity to grow that talent and become the strong, independent performer and woman that she is today. The way their life had gone in the last fifteen years was almost a miracle. His wishes, his wants his spontaneous actions, all made her jump threw hoops to accomplish stunts to insure that there be a tomorrow for everyone involved! The love she had for him was finally registering with him! The side of the road on which he sat was very lonely. It became very quiet in his head as he watched the cars go by and he realized he had no one to talk to about any of this. It was that proverbial barrel that they didn't talk about any more. But now it was making him sick to think about Crystal's feelings in all of this. Her feelings never entered into his conscientious. When he saw something he wanted, he took it without consequences! Now he knew he was a piece of shit! How could he go to Rhonda? She thought she was his one and only...He was learning he was a bigger piece of shit than he knew...Amy thought she was his one and only!! These things never dawned on him before. The facts were always there but he didn't think..it didn't matter! He sat there on the side of the road for a few more minutes, put his 4-way blinkers on, got out and vomited over the guard rail. He, all of a sudden, became human and hated some of his actions. With all of these thoughts and more he proceeded the next hour and a-half into Maryland. The hour and a-half made him realize his kids had no lineage. The names Sabers and Chambers were made-up, fictitious. They had no background or history or factual blood line behind them. His kids had no grandparents or cousins. He had all of that as a kid. When he was with Crystal or his mom he loved to talk about them and remember them. His grandmother was a big part of his life and he couldn't wait to introduce her to Crystal. I guess his kids never having this, won't miss it. That was the only solace he had to lean on. So now thinking about his kids and Rhonda he needed to snap out of his mood and go and be the best husband and dad he could be.

When Vincent parked at 5 Lost Road he was greeted by two of the most beautiful 9 year olds, with long natural curly black hair. With their and whoops and hollers, you'd think Santa just arrived with the Easter Bunny. But maybe they had! "Daddy, daddy, we knew you'd come, now it will be perfect. Mommy, mom, dad's here. Come see!!" Rhonda walked out of the side door of the house and just stared.

Without moving she said "How do you always do that? Arrive and be the hero, make their dreams come true and save the day?" She was shaking her head in disbelief.

Reginald got out of the car, ruffled the girls heads, kissed them both on the forehead and headed toward Rhonda. He was greeted with a big hug and an "I wasn't expecting you" whispered in his ear. Before he broke the hug he said "I can't even properly kiss you hello, my mouth experienced an irruption about 100 miles ago, I need to brush my teeth." They walked into the house all smiles and he headed toward the bathroom. In the next few minutes while he and Rhonda enjoyed their coffee at the kitchen table, Ruby and Rose bombarded him with "You're here for the carnival right? Can we go now or should we wait until it's dark outside? Can we buy hot dogs there or have super at home first? If we eat at home, can we have cotton candy instead of ice cream...we always have ice cream." The two girls were talking in unison or finishing each others sentences while shifting from one leg to the other the whole time talking to their dad. Reginald just looked at Rhonda with raised eye brows as if...he looked back at the girls and said "did I know about this carnival? Rose said "I don't know," Ruby said "you do now". Rachel walked into the room, sat on her fathers lap and planted a kiss on his cheek and said "I'll hold their hands while Riley sits on your shoulders and we'll all have cotton candy." The twins ran outside yelling...we're going, it's settled...we're going!

Rachel leaned closer to Reginald's shirt collar and mouth and said "you stink, do you feel OK?" "Hi to you too, no I don't. But I guess we'll be eating cotton candy." "Good I'll go next door and get Riley and tell him you're home and we're all going out later." Rachel left her father's lap and headed out the same door that the twins just ran through.

Before sitting down to a quick hot dog super, Reginald discarded the shirt he had on, washed his face and neck, bushed his teeth again and pulled on a clean t-shirt. While helping Rhonda with the place settings on the table, he had the opportunity to grab her hands and place them on his chest to still her long enough to plant the 'hello' kiss that had been missing. Not skipping a beat she returned that kiss with reverence and now all things were well in her world. She longed for and waited for his kisses, sometimes his visits were too far apart. Conversation at super was all about the carnival and the fact that dad had arrived during their first week of summer vacation. No more school until after the summer. Okay if it's vacation where are Russel and Rockwell. Reginald hadn't thought about that, now he'd have more time to spend with his kids. Rhonda spoke up and said the two older boys had left this morning to go camping with the Schaffers. "You remember Rockwell's friend Kevin, well his family own a cabin/camp on Lake Roland and they'll be gone until Sunday, you might miss them entirely." Then she said she wasn't going to the carnival. "This was going to be a father with his children outing." She announced that it was her turn for some deserved alone time to relax in the tub and finish the last chapter in the book she started weeks ago. She reminded everyone that Reginald said he didn't feel up to par and that he needed everyone to be good and not to keep him out too late. "So get ready to go out while dad and I clean up the kitchen." In the blink of an eye the kitchen was childless.

"Rhonda" he said, "we have a great bunch of kids and I owe it all to you. The parent in charge and the parent in control. I don't tell you often enough how much I appreciate you and your love for our children." When she looked at him he had a single tear ready to fall. She stepped toward him, whipped the tear and gently kissed his lips. "What's this all about?" she asked. "It's just the way I get sometimes when I think about you and the kids." "Strong men do cry" she countered immediately. "Someone should write a song with that title." (his mind was somersaulting and he couldn't explain to her why!)

The carnival with the kids was exhausting but they had such a good time. It was definitely a memory maker. Rachel was like a second mother to the twins and they followed her lead to the letter. Riley was just in heaven riding a top of dad's shoulders seeing above the crowd for a change. The rides and the animals and the games were exciting. Everything was noisy and colorful, it drew quite a crowd. This was night one of five and once Reginald had his gang sitting all in one place everyone eating cotton candy he announced that even though the carnival was here again tomorrow, they were not coming again.

The groans were audible but shushed with just a look! Once back home the twins fell into bed easily and Rachel helped Riley with his PJ's and then dad tucked him in. He thanked Rachel for all of her help and promised a driving lesson for tomorrow afternoon. She headed to her room a happy girl.

"It's an easy crowd to please" he said to Rhonda when he joined her in their bedroom. "Yea, they are good kids. Thanks for the evening off" she purred as she wrapped her nearly naked self around him.

His large hands swept down her back and cupped her behind and lifted her up to be kissed senselessly. He carried her to the bed this way and laid her down so gently, just to step away long enough to shed his own clothing and disappear into the shower. He was tired but now very horny, she had that effect on him. When he emerged from the bathroom exhibiting his penis 9+ inches long wagging, with each step he took, Rhonda asked him to walk around the room so she could memorize, for future reference, how big he was. When she asked him to step to the side of the bed he complied eagerly knowing and remembering how her mouth felt when she slipped him in so deep his knees would buckle. A small price to pay for the feeling of tongue and wet and warm sensations being sucked upon the 9 inches while her hands juggled and pinched his balls until he could stand no longer. The removal of the now wet and throbbing member needed another wet and warm place to slid into to feel at home again. With a swift roll-a-bout on the bed, he was nestled deep inside her vagina just the way she liked it. "Oh, you smell so good, how did your book end? "I'm following her recipe for good sex right now, she made out pretty well. How am I doing?" "It's quite clear you follow directions very well," he whispered into her ear. Without much more kissing or finger sucking or hip action they were both sucking air and thrashing around on the bed enjoying each other and this organism until it worked itself out. "What a sad thing to have that energy die", Reginald murmured. "I love the way your body twists and turns and climbs on me and the way your hands find mine and moves me. The way your mouth lands on maybe my hip or latches on to one of my nipples or moves to suck on my ear lobe. Your inhibition moves me to new heights and to have those moments die, is sad!" "All the more reason for you to continue to touch me like that", as he handles in turn each of her breasts with loving care. "Or maybe find someplace warm to smother that needy prick of yours, it's not doing anything right now."..so he lifts her atop of him and she impales his penis easily deep inside her. "Oh...that feels so good", she says with a heavenly sigh and he heartily agrees. One kiss, with her tongue probing around his mouth and her bouncing on his hips and muscles tightening on his penis is all it takes for the explosion of sex extraordinaire! "There it was again" he says a few minutes later. "There what was" she lazily asks. "The perfect show of inhibition that never lasts long enough but can be reenacted with the price of a kiss." "You do that to me Mr. husband, you're the only one that can do that to me." "Goodnight Mrs. Sabers, that was part one, we will resume this in the morning when I have my strength back". Those were the final words for the night. The house was now quiet with sleep.

The mornings in this house were always pretty much the same. The twins had learned to take care of themselves, cold cereal, a piece of fruit and cartoons on channel 9. Riley would drag his blanket either to Rachel's room or on the floor in front of TV with the girls. This morning that's exactly how Rhonda found her three babies, eating in front of the TV watching cartoons. She peeked out from a cracked open bedroom door, was satisfied with their quietness and snuck back in bed with Reginald. He had felt the movement and was very ready for her when she returned to bed. "Ready for part two Mrs. Sabers?" he whispered. "Who are you kidding? I stole that about 2am...this is part 3," She came back with that so quickly it set him to wonder...the game was on. He came at her so fast with tickling fingers she couldn't get away. She squirmed and had arms flailing and gulping giggles, trying to do sit-ups and hands holding her head or hands holding back her hair and counter attacks to his body or anything she could get her hands, but with both of her hands at her head he took advantage and held her hands and arms straight above her head. They both quit, "I love the way you look right now, head held high with your magnificent, full breasts glistening with beads of sweat looking so perfect and round, I can't resist." She felt so weak from his constant playful attack to her body, she surrendered to him laying her flat on her back. One of his hands found and fondled one breast while the other was sucked into her mouth one finger at a time with eagerness. He rolled and laid beside her and said "you are ticklish in all of the right places, I love the way your body moves when I do that to you."

These days with his family were great, just what he needed to reset his tranquility. The driving lessons with Rachel were good for him, because she showed him that she was a cautious and careful driver, doing all things correctly. Building a fort with Riley and Rose showed him another big sister in the making the way she taught and played with Riley, and Riley loved dad's attention. Ruby was in the kitchen baking brownies with mom because they were daddy's favorites. He missed his two oldest boys, but that is what happened in a growing family. This was family life, the little piece that was missing in his life with Crystal, but it would be coming to an end really quickly mid Sunday afternoon when he needed to head back to NJ and the base. That was tomorrow, he still had one more night to camp fire in the back yard with his kids and one more night to enjoy his penis being sucked by that beautiful, lusty, almost strawberry blond with the rusty hair sitting next to him holding his hand. It was nearly the kids bedtime and getting closer to that time he could be alone with Rhonda. It's a good thing because the smoky night air with Rhonda sitting so close to him drawing circles in his hand and rubbing her foot up and down his leg made sitting uncomfortable for him in more than one way. First his pants were now too tight with his penis full size busting to get out and his thoughts about the things he could do with it once it was! *Down boy he thought, 30 more minutes and then we have all night!*

Rhonda's thoughts were running in the same directions because she didn't need more than twenty minutes with Reginald's help to get the twins and Riley in bed and Rachel settled in front of TV for the Saturday Night Movie. "Nite all" Rachel said happily to be left alone with her bowl of popcorn. In their bedroom Reginald and Rhonda wasted no time. She was plastered against the door the moment it was closed. Reginald had her pinned there, penis inserted nicely into her hot, wet, sex box and tongue down her throat before she could reach for the light switch. When he ended the kiss he thanked her for being panty-less and added that he loved these wrap around skirts, it made access so easy. "You whipped that thing out pretty fast there partner, are we glued to this wall or can we get a little more comfortable?" He had her feet off the ground with her legs wrapped around his hips. They were still connected! Keeping that position he carried her to the bed and proceeded to rid her of her blouse. There he found her second surprise...no bra! "when did you...?" she didn't let him finish and kissed him silly. "When I walked behind you into this room, it's on the floor someplace" They were both on the bed with him totally dressed with his thing still inserted in her and his pants around his hips. "I'll unlock my muscles and my legs and let you withdraw and strip if you promise to put it right rack when you're naked." "I've a better idea" he said. "Do you still have your boy-toy, I can work that in and out of you, kneed your gorgeous breasts, lick your delightful nipples if you suck my dick before I put it back where it is?" Just his words had her salivating and pumping her hips and wanting to play that game, but she'd have to let him go to get the toy. He didn't need a verbal answer to his suggestion. Her hip action and the tightening of her hands said it all, but she stopped, straightened her legs, and leaned him off of her so she could put her feet on the floor. Before she was back on the bed he was beautifully naked and stroking his own penis, he said to keep it warm! That action made her hotter than she thought she could ever be and she wrapped her mouth around it without preamble. That sudden action also stirred him into action. Groans of pure pleasure were escaping from both of them. Her with her mouth busy around his penis and her hands juggling his balls and rubbing anything she could touch. While he sucked alternately on the left and then the right breast while stroking her vagina with the fake penis with one hand and teasing her clitoris with the other. "Slow down he suggested to her, I don't want to come this way. I want to fuck you the right way." She slowed, he slowed, and they just enjoyed being filled by one-another this way for a few more minutes. His hands were exploring her entire body while hers were fondling more gently now and reaching up to pinch his nipples. He must have found a nerve or a spot that hadn't been rubbed yet because her breathing changed along with some hip action that wasn't there before and her mouth started to cry out when it wasn't down to his pubic hairs impaling his penis so deep into her mouth he thought he'd died and gone to heaven. But wait, she was climaxing through and gyrating and wiggling. He loved to listen to her and watch her when she lost control like this, but he needed to slow her down...HE didn't want to come like this. She was easy, he'd get her back this way... it wouldn't take long...or he could..he did let her continue a minute or two longer and enjoyed the show and sound effects. "Hey baby, slow down a bit, I'm not ready." He slid the boy out of her ,and lifted her body to his and held her as she came down. "I love it when you do that, I almost came, but you were stuffed with something that wasn't me." "Hurry up, fill me again, I love that felling and I want it back quickly." She crooned! His unspent, huge, pulsing penis penetrated her to the hilt and she started again. This time he couldn't hold back and they groaned through the kiss and came together in uncontrolled sex.

When morning came he hated to get out of bed because he knew this was the end of their lovemaking. But it was already late, 8:30, the kids have probably been up for a least an hour and they needed breakfast. Rhonda hollered to him, ready, and he was up and all set to eat. He hated last days, they went by so fast. The kids would play and disappear but he wanted to see them every minute before he left. That was the selfish side of him and he knew it! It was Sunday and mom always made something special for breakfast, today was no different. Fried dough with powered sugar and scrambled eggs. Everyone but the boys were there and they were missed. The kids ate and were ready to go out and play. Kitchen clean-up was just the two of them, Rachel was in the shower getting ready to out for the day with girlfriends. More coffee and conversation just sitting around the kitchen table for the next hour and they hated the thought of him leaving. "Life here is so simple" he said, "so quiet with no one expecting anything from you, so few rules to follow and just us leaning on each other." "Are you saying you are tired of your Navel community and it's rules and needing to kiss ass to the upper ranks? Are you ready to retire and come home for good?" "Boy, it almost sounded like that didn't it...but no,

I I just love you and being here with you and the kids, that's all... not yet. I still need to advance one more rank for a better retirement and I won't be ready for that for a few more years. Sorry love, this is our life until then." Reginald reached for her hand and held it threw most of that statement. From the kitchen table they moved their relaxation to the back yard and watched and played with the kids. The day just evaporated and it was time for him to leave. He never did get to see Russel or Rockwell during this trip and that was definitely unusual. He missed them. Hugs and kisses and he was back on the road again.

Crystal really is a good sport for allowing me these few days with this family. They were just what I needed. The thought was instant when he drove away from 5 Lost Road.

Chapter 45

The ride home wasn't so bad, he had Rhonda's kiss still on his lips and he was instantly thinking of Crystal's attentions when he got home. *It's a grand life I lead* he thought to himself, no more reprisals about being a bastard!

It was late Sunday night when he arrived home to New Jersey. There were night lights on, which made the house welcoming and cozy and a note on the counter near the sink that read:

Mom and Clive are upstairs in their room, I'm in our room waiting for you. Hope your had a great weekend. I can't wait to feel you...Love Crystal

The word 'feel' went straight to his groin, *she certainly has a way with words, that wife of mine. She said waiting...I hope that means she's as naked as I want her to be.* That's what he saw when he opened the door, he stripped naked where he stood, at the door as he entered. That wife of mine. The sound of it rang around in his head many times before he laid eyes on the beauty laying on her back with her head, center on the pillow and her golden, sparkling crystal hair flowing from her head and falling to the floor. He entered the room quietly and she only stirred a little, shifting her waiting, naked self to her side. This action laid her generous, gorgeous breasts on the sheets and she spread her legs a little more to support that position. *She's not only beautiful but moving in such a way to make it easy for me to fill her from the back. Once I'm on my side of the bed, that's exactly what I'll do.*

I'll start by spooning her. I started thinking of this the minute I left Maryland. This is perfect. Please don't wake up, I want you filled with me and moaning and I want my hands full of those voluminous breasts until you turn around and I can fill my mouth with their pimpled nipples. That did it, I'm ready...slow boy, take it easy, sit gently on the bed, lie down slowly and touch her softly. Touch her hair, she likes it when I do that. Lift it from her neck and lick a little, now see if I can gently squeeze my penis between her cheeks and gain entrance. Not yet, check to see if she is wet. One finger, gently...deeper...two fingers...yep, almost...a little groan...stop...let the fingers feel, move, slide deeper, slip out, now try the penis. OH...heavens. Don't move, she'll wake...just a little push, a little more...stop...that's it, do that some more... oh god, her hips are moving. She just leaned back at me a bit, I slipped in a little deeper, I can reach one boob, it'll filled my hand. She is so warm and moving more now.

He moved his other hand to her clitoris and fingered it's tip until she uttered a soft groan. It took all of his will power not to move his hips... to let her continue to dream her sleeping sex dream. So far so good. She felt so good and was responding as slowly and as womanly as he had hoped. This was a first and he was enjoying waking an unexplored, sexually buried gene she didn't know she had. He wanted to hear her and see her and feel her come alive in that uncensored, uncontrollable frenzy of a super orgasm. He'd take part, but later when she wanted him. Right now she didn't need him, she was taking control and leading her feelings right where she wanted them. He was merely her pond right now, moving at her pace and keeping herself on tract. She was making him feeling marvelous!!

Her breathing was slow and deep with sleep. Every now and then, like now, she'd stutter and groan lightly, back into him further and settle to sleep. *Ohhhh...there's not much more room up in there. I've filled her, she's squeezing me, she's wetter, oh yes, nubby pumps on her nipple, she's enjoying this! Oh-oh..so am I..slowly boy...we can do this together..now..yes..now...still nice and slow...this is excruciating!! Ahah*

Neither one of them moved until the sun was shinning in their eyes with morning light. He moved slightly and a sorry looking 'little penis' lying on his upper leg acting rather dead! He whispered softly, "I can't believe I fell asleep!" She countered with "I can, you were quite active when you got home last night...you certainly rocked my world!" Still looking at her back and stroking the length of her hair, he smiled and thought, *honey it was all your doing, you used my parts and did it good.* Now verbally he said, "glad I could help."

Their day started in the kitchen with Clive and Crystal's mom over coffee and hot cinnamon buns fresh out of the oven. Vincent had 60 minutes to make it to base but listened to the plans that were in the works for the other three of them to meet with designers, engineers and contractors. Clive had made great gains with the designer firm that worked on the New Yorker. Their reputation over the last twenty years had grown them from a 5 man team to a corporation much in demand. Clive was lucky that his reputation had also lasted these twenty years because Martin, the owner remembered his early days and was pleased to grant Clive and Crystal an on-site visit/ appointment on Shelby Street in New Jersey. Martin remembered working with old houses and working with one would be a great change of pace. Besides one never knows what could be found in an old house!

"So today's the day. Martin will be here as well as a local engineer and contractor. Hopefully whatever Martin comes up with is structurally sound for the bones of the house or the engineers can point him in another or better direction." Clive was excited, he hasn't seen Martin in quite some time. "Using a local contractor is good for business and should get us some brownie points going forward." Rita pointed out. "They were recommended by the lumber yard down on West Street, said the owner Samuel Wiggins knows his stuff, has a great crew and can be trusted."

"I'm off Vincent snuck in. Can't wait to see what comes of all of these changes". Crystal walked with him out to his car and wished him a good day. So far it was a great day, the sun was still shinning it wasn't too hot yet and Vincent was agreeable to change. So far so good!

The next month was a world-wind...a little demolition, a lot of deliveries of lumber, wires, windows, speakers, more wire. It was a good time to head to New York do a few shows and let the contractors do their thing. They had a town approved engineering plan and a building permit. Crystal felt she had the best of all people working on site and she needed to escape! Clive stayed behind to survey the goings-on and be with Rita! Vincent even stayed away from the house escaping to Massachusetts again while Crystal was in New York. What a difference a few weeks makes. When Crystal came back...wow.

What she loved about the house was the interior foyer...the staircase going up in two directions. It was still there and enhanced. The engineers liked it as well. The contractors liked it also. Back-up and come in the front door. The living room was still there untouched and comfortable. The office on the opposite side of the entry was now walled off to the entry and became the waiting room and office of the studio with complimentary curtains, rugs and furnishings to suit the rest of the house. The only difference... the filing cabinets and executive desk for Rita. There was a wide staircase on the back wall leading to the new rooms upstairs in this house. There was a sound room, recording studio with an interior wall of glass with mics and speakers and a sound-board bigger and more elaborate than the one in NY. Room for at least a six piece accompanying band, if not more. But the best part, for Crystal's needs, no appointment necessary. Rita was beyond thrilled. This was much more comfortable and more up-to-date than anything in New York and she'd already had four appointments this week with 7 more already booked for September.

The back of the house was under going a major change as well. Working with a landscape designer, Crystal ordered a built in pool with a pool house, fenced area for safety surrounded by large bushes for privacy. The two space parking was enlarged to six available spaces and a three bay garage. It's a good thing there were three aces of land to work with, but poor Miss Elise's gardens were now filled with a pool and evergreens. Miss Elise would approve of the changes because she loved Crystal and her house was filled with people and music.

Chapter 46

One year later the changes at 637 Shelby Street had brought about a complete change to the area. The hotel Crystal had seen on her first trip to Colts Neck was now a first class spot for writers, entertainers and military brass. It's dining rooms and function room hosted major events and concerts. The Captain and Suzie had returned to the house after retirement and Suzie worked some of the functions in the culinary line-up at the hotel. The Captain, Crystal's dad had taken an appointment as a military instructor of strategic armament right on the bass. There was no-way he could retire with his feet up and watch when the 'hippie' bands consisting of mostly young men with heads of hair just asking for haircuts came in to record their 'rock'n roll' music. He just couldn't watch the arrival of these guys in clothes that didn't match or hung off their bodies or looked like they fell off of the rag man's carriage. These guys and their bands had strange names to match their appearance and sound! He wondered what happened to Peter, Paul and Mary or the Everly Bros. The recording studio was a money maker but he preferred the military structure and uniforms. Rita stayed mostly at Shelby Street while Clive traveled back and forth to New York. Crystal's schedule wasn't as hectic as it was a few years ago, but that suit her just fine. She was now working on her 7th song after seeing her second, Black Water Blues to receive a review from both the R&B and Pop Radio stations. Vincent's schedule was just as hectic. His calendar in the kitchen of the house for all to see, posted military exercisers and weeks away for training exercisers and classroom requirements, while the private calendar that only he and Crystal shared showed trips to Maryland and Massachusetts. Crystal's association with the Bursar's Unit was a constant, although she needed to navigate through the changes of personnel every now and then to keep current with her 'personal files'. No fires to put out there, thank goodness, too many people were now dependent on her. They didn't know she was their uncle Sam. What she really loved was the fun she shared with the Operations Center personalities. Her house remained one of large barbecues, fire-pit sing-a-longs and pool parties. Her association with Brad and his wild gang of lyric writers was one of patience and a lot of success. Brad had always worked with three other guys. Not many of the other three remained the same. Either Brad was a hard guy to work with or the others didn't live up to his measure and didn't last. But for the first few years, it was always interesting to see who would show up with Brad. Crystal and Brad had a discussion at one time pinning down the changes in the song lyrics by the change of the men writing them. For a time there was Henry who was older...maybe 45 or so, divorced and 'needing' to make ends meet. His contribution to "Maybe Someday' was sad and really down, while the others had written about the bright light at the end of the tunnel. Henry didn't last too long in Brads little group. Who needs a downer? Certainly not that song! Crystal had a lot of say and contribution to Brads work. She sometimes made many changes to Brads written words. If the words didn't fit, but the 'picture' the words were painting fit her music, she'd re-write, sleep on it, change a tempo, change a word to fewer or more syllables to make it fit. When she was happy, she'd congratulate Brad on another successful collaboration.

Being military and around military personnel on a daily basis you pick-up on vibes or snip-its of conversations that are 'for their eyes only' or 'the need to know' and you'd rather know the truth of a situation rather than the rumors that are fact based but mostly blown out of proportion. Such as it were after Labor day. Crystal had just returned from a two week stint in Atlantic City and was in the Operations Area ease dropping on many conversations all at once. There was tension in the air, but she couldn't gauge the importance of the troupes that were now associating the 'Cold War' with Khrushchev's outbursts against the US. She'd been on a beach or in a club for two weeks and away from her dad's influence or Vincent's knowledge of what has changed or what is going on. Being on base in the Bursar's Area she could feel the unrest in everyone's activities. She'd go about her business, do some shopping at the PX and go home. This went on for a few weeks, but it seemed to her that the 'cold war' was heating up. The dinner conversations at home were now being shared with two major newspaper publications spread over the kitchen table. It was the second week of October 1962 and President Kennedy and the Russians and now the Cubans were involved in a conflict that was bringing us very close to war. The base was scrambling to be 'at the ready'. All personnel vacations and leave times were canceled with every ship in our harbor moved out to sea and moored in a combat ready position. All air ships were held back for base and harbor protection. Things and people were becoming very tense.

Downtown, it was commerce as usual. Banks were open, kids were in school the supermarkets were busy and most of the people walking down the street had little to no idea the military bases around the corner were in preparation for war.

By the third week of October one of the papers printed a simple statement trying to put a simple explanation of the world's turmoil into prospect. It stated "President John F. Kennedy said the missiles in Cuba would not be tolerated, and insisted on their removal. Khrushchev refused." This lead to the missal crisis on Oct 27th that had the US and Russians holding their breathe in hopes a resolution could be reached soon and without blood shed.

The Sunday morning newspaper headlines said it all. **Saturday, 27 October 1962, ", was the closest the world has ever come to a nuclear catastrophe!**, as US forces enforced a blockade of Cuba to stop deliveries of Soviet missiles ...etc...

Sitting at the breakfast table Sunday morning reading these newspaper headlines was the first time Captain Harold Grandcockski and Vincent Clear could take a deep breathe and feel relieved! Vincent excused himself from the table and returned to his bedroom and physically shook thinking about his families so far away. His fears had just now reduced him to tears. Crystal had never seen him like this before. He wrapped his arms around her and held her and admitted he had been really scared for the past few weeks. He'd been so busy on base and so wrapped up in following orders and keeping his nose clean and mind sharp he didn't have time to think about the possibilities of loosing everything and everybody. Crystal was seeing a side of him she'd never seen before. Even after all these years and considering all the tales he could have told about his kids and their growing pains (even if she didn't want to listen). It made him very real and it showed the softer side of him. It also made her very nervous to think about what almost and could have happened in the past few days. So many times there are military operations that are happening that the common man knows nothing about, but there was military under her roof and there were facts that were just laid out here that shook everyone to their core! Wow, it really makes one appreciate what and who you have! The remainder of Sunday moved along at a snails pace. This household needed it's quiet and reflexive mood.

Chapter 47

February 1963 the record label Clearly Entertaining had it's first nominated entertainer selling over 500,000 copies of their recording. That "Gold" record brought a lot of attention and notoriety to Clearly Entertaining. Being classified as an independent label and being in the mist of many independents, they certainly climbed it's ladder of success under Rita's leadership and dedication to listing and promoting the sounds that were selling. Between 1955 and 1959, the US's market share of the major recording companies had dropped from 78 percent to 44 percent, while the market share of independent companies rose from 22 percent to 56 percent (History Of Rock, 2009).

Clearly Entertaining, played a particularly important role in the development of both rock and roll and country music, releasing records by some really big names.

It was the right time to exploit the music market. Rita's two right hand men were constantly on the look-out for the sounds and personalities that would appeal to the buying power of today. Dick Clark was recording his music, teen dance show live in New York City and the brightest and best represented artists were performing live. Clearly Entertaining's 'men' with their ears to the street, presented deals to the fastest growing talents of the day to come to NJ to record. One contract and done with a few of who would become the biggest names on vinyl put Crystal's company on the map. It was exciting and expensive, but this New Jersey's label offered state of the art recording equipment, less expensive (than NY rates) studio time, licensing and all the perks associated with selling yourself. That's what it was, Crystal had learned that right away. She had a great studio, just off the beaten path and rat race of NY city, was in the same neighborhood as a 5 star hotel, close to the airport and was really starting to give some of the bigger, older guys in the business, a run for their money. That buying power that kept the money circulating was primarily the teens and the twenty-something population. They were attending concerts, buying posters, trading cards and recordings. This age group and their likes and interests were felt and promoted in every venue from the music they were listening to to the clothing styles, automobiles, and vacation spots. Cigarette smoking, pot smoking, beer drinking and sex was for sale. It was the beginning of the sexual revolution and music played a big part in it. TV commercials and movies were also making a killing using these popular pursuits.

So far so good, Vincent's children are really good kids. They were at or approaching these formative years of needing to belong or acting out. So far the music hadn't infiltrated their every-day life or had any effect. Sure they loved music, held their transistor radios to their ear under their pillow after lights out at night and learned the dance moves to the newest songs, but they didn't go out of their way to let it affect their judgment in anyway. The oldest boys were through school and gainfully employed or nearly finished college. Next was Andi a senior in high school in Massachusetts graduating in a few months and Rockwell from Maryland in college living away from home. Then you bunch the remaining 8 kids in the 6 to 14 year old category and they seem to maturing faster than their older siblings. Maybe it is the music and TV ads. They just seem a generation separated from the rest!

Crystal is enjoying the traffic in and around her home and recording studio and now sometimes fills in on recordings if they need some piano accompaniment. This is a little known fact, she does not ask for money nor does she lend her name to the recording. She just loves hearing her little bit of piano on the radio later and knowing it's her label. What she finds really thrilling is watching and listening to Karen and Ruth, the two Gadder nieces from next door who are making a splash as back-up singers as needed. Crystal called them and offered them a chance to sing back-up for Carolyn Jonas who was recording her "Hands Down". The girls always enjoyed the sing-a-longs at Miss Elise's and now at Crystal's barbecues, and they were good. So once they agreed and worked with Brad and Carolyn on arrangement, it was a done deal. Their photos adorn the walls of the studio along with everyone else that has performed and recorded there. This a first for them, but they worked it into a lucrative part-time job and sung back-up for many other bands who recorded here.

Vegas still calls for Crystal maybe three time a year and Atlantic City a little more often. Vegas will change overnight if it means more revenue. The smoke shops have changed their supplies for sale, the clothing stores are now boutiques with fashions out of this world with prices to match and the clubs are scrambling to hire the next 'big band'. These wanna-bees are asking and getting enormous purses for their performances. Crystal is still performing with elegance and style and with a lot of her own material. There is still a place for her in Vegas because it is a town that caters to all ages and preferences. Atlantic City is a growing community of pleasure seekers of all ages, sexual orientation, income and ethnic backgrounds. This melting pot of people still enjoy and look forward to Crystal's events. No matter where she plays, Crystal enjoys herself!

Chapter 48

It's early in the morning and Crystal's phone is ringing. The caller identified himself as an EMT at Aspen Chambers residence attending to him at his residence in Grafton. "The house is on fire, there are many emergency people on sight and I am with Aspen. I found your name and number in his wallet as a person to call in call of emergency, are you Crystal Clear?" "Oh my god...yes I am, is he alright?"

"Mrs. Clear, he needs immediate emergency care." Crystal's cuts him off with, "Please tell me where you are transporting him to and I will make immediate arrangements for a military transfer." "Very good Ma'am, He is going to Worcester City hospital, refer to Medic carrier #108, they will have his information."

Crystal immediately called the base and they arranged for an emergency air lift out of Worcester, Massachusetts to the burn unit at Portsmouth Navel Station in New Hampshire. Portsmouth had all of Aspen Chambers information and were waiting for his arrival. The communication and cooperation between the Worcester, Massachusetts emergency people and the base was immediate and excellent. His health and burn conditions were assessed and the burn center at Portsmouth was the best place for him.

Now was not the time to panic, but it was not Aspen in that hospital...is was Her Vincent! She had to get there and on the double! Her leaving her house early in the morning and leaving just a note by the kitchen sink was not an oddity, so off she went. She had money in her purse, a couple credit cards and a glove box full of maps. She also had a clean pair of underwear, a new bra and a clean blue sweater in the trunk of her car. She just headed for the highway north, she'd stop and consult the maps later. Ordinarily she loved to drive, alone and fast. She was going fast, but this was no ordinary drive, she was nervous, afraid for Vincent and felt very alone! It's a good thing there was good weather. She felt she was making good time so when she needed to stop for gas, she made it a coffee break and checked the map., After making a couple of notes of when and where to change highways, she determined she was about four hours away. She'd make it there by lunch time. The car radio was a waste on this kind of trip, that's why she had an 8-tract tape system installed. Today it only helped her to pass the time listening to her own music because she was so mad at herself. *I'm such a bitch, I never asked about the family or the house or the orchard. How did it start...how bad was it? My only concern was for Aspen and his care. Vincent is a healthy man, I hope he wasn't burned too badly. OMG...Aspen/Vincent...That settles it...Vincent is still an active duty service man. He's at the hospital as Aspen, I can't think...I need to see him, talk to him, feel him. This is such a mess. Somehow I need to 'hurt' Vincent so he won't be AOL on Monday. It took twenty years, but now it is blowing up in our faces! Stop IT...you don't know what IT is yet...stop IT! I need to stop, where am I? Rest area, good, check the map. Good, 47 miles to go, almost there.* She got off the highway and followed the street signs to the Portsmouth Navel Base. Once stopped at the main gate, she was allowed to proceed because of the parking stickers belonging to another base on her windshield and her military ID. Having gotten directions, she parked close to the front doors of the hospital burn unit and was immediately escorted to the room of A. Chambers.

When she first saw him she was relieved, but then concerned because she saw the tube wound around his left leg and heard, then saw the swirling water action happening. He was sound asleep. Sedated and resting comfortably. Sitting in his room listening to him breathe, she started to relax. After a while she walked to his left side and lifted the sheet to peek at his side and entire leg. His leg was all she could see. From mid thigh to his underarm area there was white gauze covering him. A silent tear slipped from her eye and then she noticed him looking at her. "Hey sailor, do you want to dance?"

She walked up closer to his head, bent a little and kissed his lips. "You are a sight for sore eyes Mrs. Clear, may I have a rain check? I seem to be incapacitated at the moment." He reached for her hands and held them tightly in his. "It was so scary Crystal, I guess Amy was aware of what was happening first and left our room to get Abby. When she left our bed, her movements woke me and I smelled smoke. Then everything happened so fast. There was an explosion, lots of flames then quiet. I only heard flickering flames no other noises no voices. Then I felt the heat. I couldn't see in front of me, I couldn't see anything, I felt turned around and lost, didn't know which way to go. I remember walking into a wall, I think is was a wall, it was so hot I jumped back, fell and burned my leg. I was looking for Amy, the smoke was too thick, I couldn't see anything and I couldn't breathe. Then I tripped on I don't know what and broke threw the stairway banister, front or back I don't know which. That hurt like hell and I fell again, I think, I don't know, then woke up outside being covered with a wet towel, sheet, something…what the hell, where am I, how did you get here. Are Amy and the kids here as well?"

A doctor entered the room right when Vincent stopped talking. All eyes were on him just waiting for him to speak and let us know how bad Vincent's inquiries were and maybe have the answers to some of the questions Vincent had just asked. "Good afternoon folks, I'm Dr. Bronson. Lt. We should have you out of here in no time. That gizmo that is wrapped around your leg is a cooling tube, running cold water around your burnt leg to sooth. We've also lathered your left side from your knee to your arm pit with a cooling burn aid to help in healing and to keep your burnt skin from sticking to the gauze we've laid over it. These burns on the top of your left leg and going up your side are second degree in nature and should heal nicely in a couple of weeks if kept dry and semi-covered. Your lower left leg however has suffered a little more damage in that the burns are all around your leg and nearly 3rd degree in nature. This means the burns have gone through the first, second and into the forth or more layers of skin. These burns will require more healing time and cause you a bit more pain. They need to be monitored closely for infection. Sir, you had no identification on you when you were brought in, I'll need your complete profile filled in at some point." Crystal offered to help with that. The doctor nodded and left the room.

"You know what that means...I need to think, maybe I can get you home to Colts Neck. You've been in an accident and landed here because of your burns. The name Chambers need not even be used. I'll fill in the profile as Vincent, have your treated and air lifted home." Crystal was still deep in thought and was pacing around the room when she heard the soft whimpering cry of an animal. She looked toward Vincent. It wasn't an animal at all, but big strong Vincent crying, saying the names of his children out loud one by one. He still did not know the fate of the other family members in the house. Now he desperately needed to know. Crystal kissed him gently and told him she'd make some calls and get all the information available and get right back to him. Thirty minutes later Crystal's heart was in her throat when she returned to Vincent and needed to tell him that everyone in the house had perished. When they had gotten everyone out of the house, and everyone sent to the hospital, there were the proper number of occupants and everyone was accounted for. They used the number 8 and as occupants of the house; husband, wife and six children. That was fortified using identification on most of the family members and relying on that number for the last victim that could not be identified, too badly burned. Amy and the kids died of smoke inhalation and that was the end of her explanation. She didn't need to go into the gruesome details of another death at the scene, but fires are like that. . gruesome. He'll get the details another time...this wasn't the time, he was heart broken enough, and needed time for Crystal's words to sink in; Amy and the kids all died. . .

A little bit of Crystal died finding out about Vincent's kids. No child deserves to die like that. The cause and more details of the fire will be found out at a later date, then they'll have to live through the nightmare all over again! It's the wrong order of things, no parent should ever have to bury their child. She couldn't sit still and was pacing Vincent's room again. She needed to get him out of here. Vincent had been sedated and was sleeping fitfully. The doctor now knew he was treating more than just burns on this man's body. The pivotal point of the fire had taken the lives of everyone that was there. This patient had escaped with relatively few burns and his life. The loss of everyone else in the house was now causing him a great deal of grief! The doctor needs to know they were his children. She also knows she has to get him out of here. *Think girl think…fill out the paper work with his correct information as Vincent. Get him back to Colts Neck. He'll be in the hospital and cared for as an accident victim. While he's laid up I'll arrange for a decent funeral for the Chambers family with a military presents…yes, I've got this..yea.. carrying back an urn of cremated ashes of Aspen Chambers to be buried with the rest of the family. We have to get home, I've got to get into the Bursa's Area and do the final paperwork, etc on Chambers. The sooner the better.*

I'm not thinking straight now, while I'm at it, I'd like to get rid of the other character as well. Now how can I make all of this happen??? Keep thinking keep thinking… it will come to me.

Using the tray table at Vincent's bed, Crystal filled out all the paperwork required for his care here and the request to get him moved back to NJ. Any rumors or snide remarks or questions at his being at the house in Massachusetts where this tragedy occurred were stilled when all concerned found out Crystal was his wife and had military connections back in Colts Neck. *This must have been his first wife with the house full of kids and Crystal his second, beautiful wife. All the staff was whispering.* They still made him out to be a bastard! Crystal heard some of the remarks and couldn't wait to get him out of here! Later that day, around dinner time, Crystal called home to let everyone know about Vincent's *accident,* where they were and that she was alright. About eight that night two light supper trays were brought in to them with an invitation for Crystal to spend the night in the empty room next to Vincent's, compliments of Commander Lewis here and retired Captain Grandcockski. With a wink, this orderly just said, "word gets around fast and you know some people in high places!". She smiled gratefully and accepted the food and the invitation.

Her nights sleep was nothing close to peaceful. Once she was awoken by the beeping sounds of an alarm down the hall. This disturbance was almost welcome because it got her dream cut short and out of the office where she was just creating the identity of Aspen chambers as per the request of her cheating, already bigamist, ling man of a husband. Waking up she still felt the extreme hurt and anger toward Vincent of that day. *Go back to sleep, what's done is done...*Finally asleep, this time the shift change and drug disbursing activity roused her from her dream of seeing Vincent standing under the welcome awning of the New Yorker, hugging and kissing a young woman with the most colorful head of hair, it was eye catching...but waking up, she was sure it was her Vincent and that was Rhonda!

It was finally morning and Crystal found out that her request for Vincent's being moved to NJ had been granted and it would happen in 48 hours. She made up her mind to spend the day with him here and drive back home tomorrow. That would give her enough time to check the news of the fire, investigate anything that she found hinky and still be able to check her files in the Bursar's Unit. That was her plan, but even she knew not all plans went in a straight line all the way to the finish line. As much as they could, they enjoyed spending the day together; her dreams aside and the circumstances of their confinement to these hospital walls! Vincent was brought out for two ice baths to treat his left side and kept calm with meds every four hours. The meds worked, he was quite mellow and talked about his kids lovingly while Crystal listened. She learned a lot about them and even more about him. They both learned that he would not be walking any time too soon. The burns to his left foot were quite severe and would need skin grafting. This decision would need to be revisited once he was settled and back at home base. The doctors were talking to him about time healing all types of wounds, physical as well as those of mental anguish! They realized he was suffering from both right now and would need time to heal and mourn and grow stronger.

Crystal hated hospitals, but these doctors were all right. She could actually feel compassion when they were talking to Vincent. He was just slightly left of center with one foot on another planet, but that held the pain away and the agony when his family started to cross his mind. Once again Crystal spent the night in the room next to his, and thank goodness all dreams were nullified by the sleeping pills that she requested. She shared breakfast with Vincent before heading for home. She wanted to get there in plenty of time to set the ground work for his *accident* story and be there when he arrived home. The only thing wrong with that plan was the straight line that brought her right into Grafton. Sitting at Howard Johnson's in Grafton Center having lunch, she was listening to many conversations about the fire and the Chamber girl and the way they found her in the orchard and what really happened to her. Who could have done such a thing, that poor girl. And if he didn't die in the fire, we'll have a rapist in our neighborhood. They need to find out how that fire started and find the man who harmed poor Andrea. And if she was not among the family members who else died, who was the 7th victim? Was it the rapist? Serves him right, but who was he? Anyway, with Mr. Chambers being in the hospital, and Andrea being found, the victim count was now down to seven.

These were the most confusing conversations she had ever easedropped on! Crystal's mind went into overdrive.... *The Chambers girl alive! What was she doing in the orchard? OMG, Raped...Vincent will have a.....! Where is she now? Does she know about the family?* Crystal was just about to tear into the newspapers she had picked-up on the way in and now she was afraid to. When her coffee arrived, she starting reading about the fire, the family and Mr. Chambers being taken to a military hospital by helicopter. The news that filtered out of NH was that Mr. Chambers didn't make it either. So far that was the only good thing that Crystal had heard since she got here. The papers were asking the same questions about the 7th victim, and about Andrea turning up alive, but offering no answers. Good, Aspen Chambers was dead. She'd make the funeral arrangements later when she gets home, this works nicely into her plans. Now the only thing that fretted her was that when Vincent finds out his daughter Andrea is alive but with unrelated injuries, he'll want to see his daughter, make sure she was all right and find out what happened to her. Rightly so, but this could never happen! Daddy Aspen is dead. Dead to everyone, even this daughter who could really use his love and support more than ever, but Dead is Dead! The papers were suggesting that she was brutally raped and left naked in the orchard. Kindly neighbors found her and had her taken care of. Currently she was in St. V's hospital learning the sad news of the rest of her family. *The poor kid, she doesn't even have a house to go home to. I remember Vincent saying she has a best friend, so much so, they seemed joined at the hip. I sure do hope that's true, she'll need that friend to lean on and for help. I don't even want to go to the top of the hill...I want to remember his house and his family the way I saw them a few years ago. Stupid, what am I doing in Grafton…learning and feeling…that's what! These feeling will help me to understand and cope with Vincent's feelings and moods...I hope!*

Chapter 49

Suzie and the rest of the household were on pins and needles waiting for Crystal to get home. Everyone had questions about Vincent's health, about the accident, about NH, and about him getting home. As calmly as she could over a couple of rum and cokes Crystal retold the story about the accident on highway I-95 in New Hampshire. "Vincent's jeep was clipped from behind by another vehicle who took off, then Vincent's jeep careened off the road, was taken out by a large rock. The back end of his car clipped the rock and caused him to loose the tire and rim as it broke off of the car. That action flipped him over. This immediately caused a fire and Vincent was burned severely on his left side. Once he was identified as military, Portsmouth Naval Hospital was the best location for him, they have an excellent burn unit and then I was called. I left immediately which you know and I've been with him ever since." "So, how are you and were the hospital personnel cordial and helpful toward you?" "Yes dad, thank-you for that, I'm fine. I slept in the empty room next to Vincent's and they brought us both meals. What a horrible way to spend a few days in beautiful NH. But he should be home tomorrow afternoon and then there will be talk about skin grafting on his left foot. He has second degree burns from his arm pit to the top of his knee and third degree down the rest of his leg with his foot being the worst. No other injuries from the accident, thank goodness! Thanks for the help dad, air lifting him home is the best way." "What was he doing in NH in the first place?" Suzie asked. "I guess Vincent and four other buddy's were invited and went to a bachelor party Friday night and Saturday they each got in their own vehicle and headed home, all in different directions. I guess next weekend the wedding will be out of the question for Vincent!" This little gab session ended when Crystal wanted to take a shower and change her clothes before dinner, then she wanted to head over to the Bursar's Area and see what she could accomplish.

Chapter 50

It had been a long time since Crystal had been on base after 6pm. It was dusk outside and very quiet. Everyone seemed to move in slow motion and without making a sound. She entered the Bursar's Area and didn't know a soul. Every eye was on her as she moved around the room like she belonged there and had business there. No one said a word when she went behind the second door, closed it gently and turned on the lights. *This is eerie she thought, I'm here, they didn't stop me, can I stay and do what I usually do?* All the while turning on the machine and entering her pin number while logging on. Getting comfortable and staring down at her fingers, she didn't know where to start. With the silent one...she typed in Keith Rogers....etc, more than she remembered, popped up. This was her personal trophy, he was a rich man, next. Aspen Chambers....etc and there he was, for the last time, almost! Now she knew what to do. Deceased, April 12, 1964, all military survival benefits to be paid to Andrea M. Chambers.(Item #3 Docket 43917 for M-SS ###-##-0569) Daughter of deceased and wife Amy Chambers also lost to the fire. Andrea being a minor and the only survivor of the *fire that destroyed the family home is entitled to and will receive full scholarship funding to the school of her choice along with the survival benefits. The fire also took the lives of his 5 other children. Funeral site Grafton, Massachusetts, Four man military entourage, 21 gun salute at Funeral --date TBD, details with Rooney Funeral Home, Worcester Street, North Grafton, 617-VE9-2022 not final.* After filling in all the lines on all of the forms the government thought they needed, Aspen Chambers was no longer. Just a few details to be gotten to in Massachusetts when the other bodies were released for burial. Sitting there rereading all that she had done, she felt numb. Except for the name Aspen Chambers, the text was factual, complete, precise and almost final. She sat there on auto-pilot...her fingers working and her mind set to be impersonal and professional, it's the only way she could get through this task! Crystal's thoughts now starting running a-muck! She sat for several more minutes to relax, regroup and really think about what she wanted to do next.

She'd wasn't done yet. Next, Crystal took wifely license to think about doing away with Reginald Sabers! This was an evil thing she wanted to do. But in the last few hours she had drummed up scenarios where Vincent would want to visit and dote on Rhonda and those kids more often. He'd want to talk about them more often, be a better husband and father to them...more often. Where would that leave her? For more than twenty years she has shared him. Rhonda would be looking for him to retire soon and move in with her full time. That would never happen. Had he thought about that? Better him gone from their lives for good, now... rather than later. She'd cause him a little more grieving now over the lost of his Maryland family due to his demise from a training exercise in VA. This family would be alive and well, he'd be the one missing! It all started with Rhonda, but it was going to end now! Well she had thought long enough.

Reginald T. Sabers...etc...and there he was for the last time, again... almost! Again she knew what to do...(Docket #16-449, M-SS 741-1289) Deceased April 12, 1964, Norfolk, Va all military survival benefits to be paid to Rhonda Sabers, his wife at 5 Lost Road, Towson, MD. All surviving children under the age of 22 are eligible for government educational grants and scholarships. Prepare documents for Rockwell Sabers, Rachel Sabers, Ruby Sabers, Rose Sabers, and Riley Sabers. Receive final body handling, casket or cremation from wife. Delivery of deceased to local mortuary as directed. Four man military entourage, 21 gun salute at funeral, date TBD, location TBD...done!

A few blanks to be filled in at a later date and these files could be closed for good. Feeling satisfaction with what she had accomplished tonight, she logged off and shut down her machines, shut off the lights and stood in the dark, empty room. *He's going to hate me, I could log back on and put everything back to the way it was, he's already hurting, whats a little more. I've been hurting for over twenty years...I don't want to fling it in his face...but..how does it feel?...! It's done, leave it...we'll learn to live with it!* She stepped out of the room and joined the personnel in the other room. Every single face she had seen earlier was gone. It was now 11:15 pm and there had been a shift change. Nine new faces were now starring at her, like where did you come from, hey I know you, "how the hell are you" said Neil, as he approached her with a big hug. Hug they did with surprised looks on each of their faces. Neil was a character she'd met back when Davies was giving her driving lessons. Thank goodness for Davies, he saved her from much ridicule and teasing and laughter back then and Neil was the heckler behind most of it. "Hey blondy are those your wheels out there? You can finally drive? I didn't notice any dents or scrapes!" Still encased in their hug, Crystal let him have it...she boxed his ears! "Hey everybody, this is our resident celebrity. In case you haven't met her, this Crystal Clear, now famous pianist and song writer. Be nice to her and she'll invite you to her next barbecue, she's also famous for them!" Hellos all around and the room and it was once again comfortable. With very little additional conversation, Crystal said her good nights and left the building.

Driving home her head was filled with what she needed to do next to prepare for two funerals. It's a good thing she made notes all evening and had a step by step itinerary to follow before needing to get back into her files. She also had to prepare herself for the conversation she needed to have with Vincent. *He's gonna kill me. He's not going to know what to do with himself. The man hasn't had a single hour all to himself without a wife or children in 21 years! Tomorrow will be the first day of the rest of his new life. I'm sure I'll get the silent treatment for awhile, but once his burns heal, I'm the only one that he has to take to bed now. Glory days, I haven't been able to say that for almost 21 years! Starting the day after tomorrow life around our house is certainly going to be different, particularly when he comes home from the hospital.*

Rhonda was notified by two Army Sargents at her house about Reginald's death. She was presented with a death certificate dated April 12, 1964. For the next 30 minutes she silently cried and listened to these two men talk about a training exercise on base in Arlington, VA at Fort Myers, going terrible wrong and five servicemen being killed. Reginald was among those that were killed that day. Then she was informed that the Army would be financially responsible for his funeral here in town. They got the funeral home information they needed as well as the cemetery name to contact. Then they asked her preference on a closed coffin or cremation stone. At this she was bewildered, a lot of information all at once and now she couldn't think. It was told to her that Reginald's body was too badly damaged for her to see , therefore they repeated the remains options. With a steady stream of tears she chose cremation.

Crystal was elated at this option, it was cheaper and she could handle the physical urn, choice of stone and let the Funeral Home help Rhonda with the words to put upon it. A four man team traveled from VA to Towson, MD on April 19th, and gathered in St. Mary's cemetery to say good-bye to an Honored Military man, faithful husband and loving father. These were the words Rhonda had chosen for his grave marker stone, depicting an angel with wings spread wide. Under this stone was the urn that was buried, carried to this location by the solemn military team. It was a somber gathering including the children listening to prayers and the 21gun Salute all in Reginald's honor.

At the end of the day on the 20th Crystal breathed a big sigh of relief when she was able to access the Reginald file one more time to put the final finishing dates and comments on it. She made sure her name and Vincent's and the name Clear with any of their personal banking information was erased and would never be seen again. Any other military expenses being used against this name would be on the Docket Number only. Reason for use: Rhonda's final expenses and the children's education. Applications (which could be copied) in each child's name for secondary educations and instructions with Docket number (which had all Reginald's pertinent information) were also hand carried to Maryland on the 19th. This was done...Closed...one down one to go.

The Massachusetts funeral was still many days away. The Navel investigation into this matter was held up by the number of autopsies that needed to be conducted due to the nature of the fire. It had been determined that the fire was set and it turned into an arson investigation. An interview with the surviving Chamber's daughter Miss Andrea Chambers, was halted because of her injuries, current condition and age. When the name Chambers hit the news, the firm of Baker and Comstock vigorously searched their files into the name of Amy (Samson) Chambers, daughter of Martin Samson, winner of a Nobel Prize and worth millions. Upon the death of Aspen and Amy the children's financial well being fell on the shoulders of their firm. Mr. George Comstock was to become Andrea's executor, and funds could be released under his name to suitable people of her choosing as well as to her.

These facts and other tidbits were printed in the local area Worcester, Mass newspapers. Crystal made a point of keeping up to date with these items in order to keep Vincent up to date when she felt he could handle more news, more heart-break, more her voice delivering this news. She kept the new papers well hidden in their room at home. They were for his eyes only. There was a high school picture of Andrea in the paper a few days ago, he'll want to see that. He was doing well once he was back at home base at Colts Neck and the skin grafting on his foot and ankle went very well. Crystal waited until after this surgical procedure to sit with him and share the news of Andrea's ordeal and of Reginald's demise.

To say the least his mood was black. The doctors were aware that he had suffered a personal loss of many friends in an accident and was dealing not only with his body injuries buy also with him grieving. Crystal's heart went out to him for his loss, naturally, but she was also concerned at how he was taking it. Three situations that snowballed into complete loss of two families. Him finding out that Andrea had been spared the fire at the house but was raped! He wanted to kill the bastard! Not being able to go to her and share the grief and loss of the family was bad enough, but she would need him to struggle through the next years of her life. She was alone and that broke his heart! He needed her, the only one he had left of what he had built with Amy in Massachusetts. And now with the current circumstances, he'd never be able to see her again! He was dead to her! And Rhonda, poor Rhonda! She's now alone to raise the kids alone. "In all aspects...I'm dead to all those who had loved me. Dead to all those that I loved! I'm Peter Rabbit, I've fallen down the bunny hole...I can see them, but they can't see me. Crystal, you killed me!" The tears running down his face, imploring her to undo all that she had done...it was killing her. She wanted to hold him, but all she could do was whisper... "I'm still here!"

He cried...she listened. She cried, he yelled. "You had no right to do that to me." The entire afternoon was full of accusations he threw at her with Crystal's defending herself the best she could. He had done wrong, she had done worse. He took another wife...then he took another wife!! Children shouldn't be treated this way. Children needed full time dads. He used his children as ponds, she didn't love him enough to have his children. (that one hurt!) He expected too much of her, she bent over backwards to give him everything he wanted. This went on for hours. There may be no way of mending these two human beings! Crystal went home.

Crystal threw herself across her bed and cried. It had been a hell of a two weeks! There was no one she could talk to. She wanted a drink. Sitting at the kitchen table with a rum/coke, playing solitaire, Suzie joined her. With the comforting words of a mother-in-law, Suzie thanked her for loving her son this much. *If she ever knew!*

Chapter 51

Nine days later Crystal moved Vincent home. It's a good thing their room was on the first floor of the house. Using crutches, it was an easy walk from the driveway; just inside the back door, down a short hallway to their bedroom. He admitted it felt good to get out of the hospital and come home. Everything here was familiar and easy for him to get to. Gathering at the kitchen table (everyone preferred it over the formal dinning room) for most of their meals, Vincent was a little more on the quiet side than usual. In their bedroom, behind closed doors, he didn't speak at all! The anger that radiated off of him toward Crystal was palatable. Their king size bed wasn't big enough to hold both of them and all the baggage they both brought to bed every night. Neither one of them could sleep. This had gone on long enough, maybe two weeks. Crystal had had enough! She talked with Rita and they booked her two long weekends at the New Yorker. She could sleep there! Vincent had people enough at the house and was close enough to base to look out for himself. For this episode, she was done!

Chapter 52

For Crystal it felt so good to be back in New York. It also felt like 'coming home'. Her show case was now a piano bar again sporting many pictures of yesteryear. The Marquee at the door merely said: The Show Case Featuring...The bar was long and black with tall bar stools with crystal like seats. The lights hanging from the ceiling were crystals that shown brightly or just evening light. The floor was sparkled with inlayed crystals and black grout lines. The piano in the back corner was a miniature sleek baby grand on a three-foot raised platform edged with shinny crystals. Crystal, standing just inside the door way was looking around with tears streaming down her cheeks. Never in her wildest dreams could she ever imagine a whole room whispering her name with such elegance. At just that moment in her thoughts, strong arms wound their way around her shoulders and said, "you can't sneak back to New York without me knowing about it." She rounded and finished the bear hug with Mr. Brentwhistle. "It's gorgeous" she gushed. "I know" he said, Shall we..." as he lead her to the piano. Once they were both sitting on the piano bench he said, "Now tell me what's going on with the lug-head of a husband of yours". "Being layed-up and inactive is really hard for him. Along with loosing friends and grieving and being stuck in the house, and knowing that I can get away anytime, like this, he's going nuts. It will, or he will get better. I'm better already, just being here!" she gloated. "Great, now please play something for me, please." She started in with a few cords and said, "how about my new one, Brad flew a title by me, I loved it, so now I need to write the rest of the song." She played on, a few bars and then a few bars more and then stopped, "It's a beginning she said." He dropped a kiss on the top of her head and said, "it's gonna be another great one" and exited the room. Three songs more and she had a slight audience. She thought, *this brings back memories.*

She played a 'free' shortened program for the lunch crowd that gathered in the show case. She announced and many posters that were being exhibited announced the same, that Crystal would be preforming in the Great Room tomorrow night as well as Sunday night and next weekend also. Having driven for the last three hours, and now having spent an hour in the new and reorganized show case, she needed to get to her room, freshen up and maybe take a little nap. Sleep, it would be a welcome thing! An item in short supply lately.

Crystal had her own room in the suite that was occupied by her mom and Mr. Brentwhistle. It had been a few months since she had been to New York and when she walked into her room she noticed it had also had an overhaul. It was lovely. Pale green with darker shades of green in a mosaic like pattern separated by silver lines wallpaper with a hint of celery green carpeting. Everything was dramatic but yet simple. The chase-lounge facing the TV was reupholstered in a velvety material of darker green with head and arm rests of material matching the wall paper. Now she noticed the bedspread and shams were a match to the chair. Very charming but in the way of her nap...the spread hit the floor and she made ready the bed for pillows and an occupant. A quick run threw the bathroom, stripping out of most of her clothes, she appreciated the bed, it felt wonderful to her. And sleep she did. When next she opened her eyes it was 9pm.

Nine pm. on a Friday night in New York City. She wasn't working and she was alone. A quick shower and a french braid in her hair and she was ready to go. When in New York, you dressed like New York so you could always be ready to go...but where...then it hit her, a bite to eat and a drink up on the 40th floor. The elevator button now announced the 40th floor as the Velvet Room. She stepped into the Room at 10:10 and went directly to a round table about three rows back from the band. They spotted her and she gave them a little salute of recognition.

The only thing wrong was that Johnathan was missing. At that they went into the song that had became Johnathan's recognition of her, Rum and a Coke. She smiled brightly, stood up and waved. In turn, they each waved back. She drank more than she ate that night, but it was all good, she was back in bed by 2:10 am after meeting the new band member, Hucksly, just plain Hucksly.

Crystal working the New Yorker again was the best medicine. The unadvertised shows were a sell-out. Her performances were spotlight perfection and it reminded her why she loved this business. The applause and adoration was her validation. Sure, the income from record sales made her a very rich woman, but the personal, up close connection to her fans was renewed appreciation each time she took the stage. This music never gets old. She was beginning to, but with make-up and distance under bright lines, it didn't show. Her body of over six feet tall was still as straight as an arrow and her hair was still long and the envy of every girl/woman who longed for long hair. Her years of experience just made her a better performer and able to connect with her audience better. Here in New York, life was good. Back in Colts Neck, not so much. So, Sunday night, go to bed and go home in the morning and come back for next weekend or just stay, make it a mini-vacation and relax.

It was just after midnight and her show was over but that didn't mean the night should be over. With the decision to stay the week, she headed for the elevator and the 40th floor. The music was wonderful and as she sat down, round table, third row from the stage, her drink, a rum/coke was delivered. It's nice to be known and remembered she mused. The only thing Vincent remembered about her was the ability to sexually move her. To sexuality bring her to heights to which she never wanted to come down. Now with this train of thought she scanned the band members, but there was no Johnathan.

With a quick wave of her hand a new drink was delivered and she wondered if Vincent even knew her birthday or remembered their anniversary. Did he know if her ears were pieced? Did he know her favorite color or her favorite song? Did they have a special song? Most couple do. These were strange thoughts, but to think of it...they never talked much. Except for the first year of their marriage they've had a 'house mum'. Really, what was his favorite color or for that matter favorite meal. It's been ages since she needed to cook for him. They really never needed to 'take care of' one another. She knew he was born in up state New York and his birthday was March 21, their anniversary July 7. Did he know the titles of the songs she'd written, did he even care? Did she know what really turns him on? Oh yes, he is a boobs man, but beyond that...? It's 1964 and we've been married nearly 19 years and we still know very little about one-another. *Stop it...this is bullshit, I'm just adding to my mood. We know more about each other than most couples. He knows what I'm capable of and I know he had 12 children. It would HAD being the operative word. Now there's only 7 and that's why we're in the mess we are in right now...grief is a hard period to life to live through. But in all actuality, there are No children in his life any more. I saw to that! It can't be undone and I wouldn't if I could. Those chapters are closed! He was selfish in opening them, and I was selfish in closing them. We hashed this out...the words were spoken. Our life goes on. I hope our marriage goes on. I could have blown it! Should I be home? No...I need to validate what I've done once and for all and bury it...move on. Vincent needs to heal and learn to live as only Vincent and appreciate what he does have and visit only in memories that which is gone. Right now I need to go to bed...I'm tired.* She had her own key to the suite and when she got there it was all quiet with a light on over the sink. She giggled and went along to her room.

After breakfast daily, Crystal filled her week with the piano upstairs in the Velvet Room until 3:30 daily working on her next single. Afternoon shopping and an evening meal with Mr. Brentwhistle about 8:30 and that rounded her day. It was a simple schedule and gave her plenty of time to rest and reflect and regroup with words and feelings to bring back home. She used some of those words and feelings in her new song Lonesome Lady. It fit! As much as Vincent had lost, she also lost Reginald and Aspen. They were no longer her worry or responsibility. When she looked at Vincent, that is who he was. When he left the house, that is who he was. No more traveling to other states to assume the identity of these made-up men with real wives and other responsibilities. His work load was so much less now. His worries all in front of him, here at home not hundreds of miles away. After years of carrying those worries and added responsibilities, he was free. He just couldn't see or feel it yet. With all of that off of her shoulders and him hating her because of it, she was indeed a Lonesome Lady. By Thursday afternoon Crystal had the song nearly done. She called Brad and they made plans to meet in the Velvet Room at 11am the next day. He was happy to see her and to hear the arrangement of Lonesome Lady with her input of mood, lost love, loss of life, old age, too many responsibilities, falling down, feeling low. "Okay Brad, is that enough to work with??? Now he was sorry it was Friday. So much to do and it was the weekend. It was just the way he was built, he had a hurdle in front of him and he needed to dismantle it immediately. He asked if she'd be around next week for a pow-ow, but she said she doubted it. She counted that if he really thought he had something, there's always room for him at her house. He kissed her on the forehead and said see you next week and he was gone. He was a delightful little man and he treated her like gold. She gave him his first big break and he has been under contract with Clearly Entertaining since it's start-up. All of those words she just filled Brad's head with, she felt! It was time to try something new, different. But What? Maybe there was something in Andrea's life or even in Rhonda's that they, she and Vincent, could be helpful with, on the side lines of course. It was an opportunity to do something with Vincent to better their lives. It sounded good. Would he be able to think of something? At lease she had something she could talk with him about.

Feeling a little bit better, at that, she was willing to put herself out-there, in their lives, she'd be interested in what Vincent would come up with. She just hoped it wouldn't be anything she'd want to reject immediately, that wouldn't make for a lasting conversation. Vincent/ Reginald met Rhonda in New York, was there something in New York that could rekindle a thought or memory for her, something they could help with, without her knowing? She'd bring that up to him. Andrea on the other hand was a different story. Since her family's death, she has found out she is a wealthy woman having something to do with her Grandfathers invention and its military use, still today.

Crystal found that she couldn't sit still. Her mind was running a hundred miles an hour. Her Songs, her husband, her life. So many things had changed. She was soul searching. So many things weren't the way she thought they would be. Some twenty years ago she and Vincent lived in this small house not too far off base where they both would go every day. But every night, god knows they lived for the nights and for the weekends. They knew each others bodies as well as the floor plan of their little house. They climbed around each others bodies and touched every part of the each other's body and explored each others body more than they explored any other thing that they came into contact with on a daily basis. She knew how to make him come, he knew how to make her squeal with delight and sexual satisfaction. He would touch, she would tease, they came together and before they knew it, it was 7am again and their attention and bodies needed to be sharp again, but on base, not in bed. Vincent had his job and told her in no uncertain terms, it was his life's ambition. Twenty or twenty-five years, make the grade and retire with a decent pension. That left her to find an equally time for-filling and satisfying position, job, career, or money making situation. She had done that. In twenty years, he never gave her an option. He just plotted along doing his thing, never giving her a second thought. His thoughts of her were only those of need. What she could do for him, as it turned out… in or out of bed!

Was she really ready to make the offer to do good by one of his, even with her eyes wide open? She had hurt him, maybe this could help. Not yet, she wasn't ready, she didn't want to rush home. The more she thought, the more she held back the tears. Stupid, why…she still had an hour or so to use this piano, and use she did. Abuse was more like it until Mr. Brentwhistle showed up to inquire about the 'noise' coming from this corner of the room. One look at him and she fell to pieces. The poor man didn't know what to do! Here's this hulk of a woman ready to cover him like a blanket, all arms and tears and sniveling like a baby! He just held her, pushed her hair away from her face, reached for his clean, white handkerchief and pressed it into her hands. It took quite a few seconds, but her sobbing ceased, she leaned back from him, blew her nose and said thank you. "I love the song you were playing, but not the way you were playing it." Brentwhistle said. She merely looked at him and gave in to the hick-ups. "Men can really be beasts at times, can't we" he offered. She still said nothing. He continued with, "I'm guessing that's why you don't want to go home.?" He made it sound like a question. "I know I was wrong, but he was way more wrong. We tried talking, but it turned out all wrong!" "I talked with your mom this morning...Vincent is is the same rut you are in. Go home and try talking with him again." "Not now" was all she could come up with. "OK, join me for an early dinner and a drink, you get a good nights sleep and start out fresh in the morning." She relented with "a drink sounds good." "Pull yourself together and meet me in the Starlight Room in 30 minutes." Her response was an affirmative shake of her head as she headed for the door. Just in time, it was later than she thought, the Midnight Men were just arriving.

By ten o'clock the next morning she was on the road heading home. Dinner with Clive was delightful and it helped her to shake her mood. It was also the final time he was going to ask her to please call him Clive and not Mr. Brentwhistle anymore. Enough was enough and this time he meant it! Her recorded music in the tape deck all the way home was good company for her. She made good time and was heading in the door at 1:30pm. Lunch was over but she was starved.

Left-over chicken and potato salad jumped out at her when she opened the refrigerator door. At just that moment Vincent appeared beside her and said. "I'd like a little of whatever you're having, I missed lunch." "Great, you pour us each a glass of ice-tea and I'll fix us each a plate." They ate in what could be described as a comfortable silence. She was glad to be home and he was happy to see her. A trip together to the pantry and they washed and dried the dishes and put them away. Totally skipping the dishwasher. While she was drying her hands, Vincent just leaned against the door way and looked at her... really looked at her. She hadn't seen that look in his eyes since the first time she saw him. In her high school football field graduation day. And then later that day, standing toe to toe with him with not much clothes on, he couldn't look away from her. He couldn't get enough. His eyes spoke volumes then as they were just now. Her panties were wet, but she needed to be more mature and not jump his bones! The aura surrounding them was super-charged but still silent. The blood running through her veins was hot. The sweat that was running down her neck caught up with the chill that was running down her spine and she wasn't sure she could break their eye contact. She wasn't sure of anything until the towel he was holding on to was wrapped around her back like a sling and it was being pulled, pulled by him, pulling her into his chest, with his eyes still boring into hers with such feeling. With her right were he wanted her, he dropped the towel and rubbed both of his hands down the length of her hair to her hips and waited. His eyes were imploring, begging for a sign of...and she caved! His lips came down on hers and her arms held him for dear life. They could both feel it. The I'm sorrys were next and then she talked to him of her thoughts about trying in some way to help Rhonda or Andrea or both if they could in some silent way.

By now the rest of the household knows that Crystal is home and the two love birds have kissed and made up. It makes it a lot nicer place to be when everyone is getting along. Rita came bounding into the kitchen all excited and told Crystal she was home just in time. She had a 3pm recording appointment with Loretta Lynn, they had broken into the Country artists and it was exciting! Roy Clark's was next on Monday afternoon, after the Country Music Festival being sponsored by the Colts Neck, Fairmont Embassy Hotel. Suzy's been really busy over there in the kitchen for two days. These were Rita's milestones in growing Clearly Entertaining and Crystal was very proud of her mother. These two had come a long way in their relationship and their respective careers. Vincent felt very much on the sidelines listening to these two strong, accomplished women. *What had he done or accomplished? A military career coming to an end and then what? He had nothing. A wife that traveled, no children, nothing to fall back on except his good looks, gift of gab and love of travel and seemingly the ability to do so with Crystal's schedule. Think man...think!*

By now everyone had gathered and dispersed from the kitchen and once again Crystal and Vincent were alone. Vincent's depression was back. Crystal's second sense instantly recognized his darkening mood and suggested they take a walk. With a little coaxing she had him out the door and walking and talking and throwing ideas around in regards to her thoughts of helping Rhonda or Andi. After walking two or three blocks, they were standing in front of the hotel building neither one of them had ever been in before. Vincent said "let's go in and have a drink". "I don't know what's wrong with me, but that always sound like a good idea", was Crystal's instant reply as she was holding Vincent's hand and heading toward the side door marked, Embassy Lounge.

Once inside siting with her favorite rum and coke, Vincent brought up Rhonda. Crystal swallowed hard and thought, *I guess I'm going to have to put up with this for a while.* "I only put eyes on Rhonda's father once, the morning he disowned her for being with me. The day I married her." "and her mother?" Crystal asked. "Never had the pleasure, but Rhonda spoke of her fondly as a strong, tiny French woman from the old country who was brow beaten and obeyed her husband without question." Crystal could see he was off in a different world as he was talking, relating his first dinner with Rhonda and her story of her parents sexual habits as told by her very open minded mother. Vincent's smile reached Crystal's face and he blushed! They laughed together and ordered another drink. "Ya know, Rhonda's folks were jewelers working on 5th Ave, maybe they are still there all these years later. To my knowledge, Rhonda had never seen her mother again.

Drinking their second drink Vincent became quiet again, deep in thought. Crystal's apprehension in asking him for his thoughts were founded in his last outburst about Rhonda, but she persevered anyway. "A penny for your thoughts, Mr. Clear". He reached for her hands, held them to his lips, laughed out loud and said "We're rich, aren't we?" He kissed each finger and laid her hands back on the table. "What are you…" Crystal couldn't even finish her sentence. Vincent leaned back and said, "my thoughts are all over the place…look at this place, are you comfortable? Crystal merely shook her head yes. He said, "think about the 300 plus miles between here and New York City, we build one every

100 miles in the smaller towns nearer to the advertised, local current events or attractions." Confused, Crystal said "hotels, bars, what are we building?" "It's a brain storm, we have so much to talk about. We could trademark them, like Howard Johnson's, and build them everywhere! It would keep me busy for years. More upscale than Howard Johnson's and you could play in the piano bars." Still confused, but happy to see Vincent excited about a project, she repeated, "what are we building?" He said "Motels." With that and a deep breathe he ordered another round of drinks.

Not too much later, Crystal was recognized and their private little afternoon delight was interrupted by piano requests and autographs. Thirty minutes later the entire hotel knew Crystal was in the house and Suzie and most of the kitchen crew were present to say their hellos. Naturally their drinks were on the house and they returned home hungry again with a lot to discuss. Their eight o'clock supper of scrambled eggs and toast was accompanied by a discussion of a road trip back to New York looking for ideal places to build a motel. Not just any motel, but maybe a 12 to 18 room or little cabana like cabins with a front desk that was also a dinning area seating upward to 100 people with a side lounge/bar area. That was just one idea. Now their talking a little up-scale, just a little, to make the traveler feel special. In this area, include a pool. Now Crystal's excited using these dinning rooms as wedding venues, where the wedding party can stay and not drive drunk. So many ideas, so much money, but unique ideas, build them all alike, build a uniform look, a uniform name that becomes household and rolls off the tongue like McDonald's! "Then when we get to NY look into the Jewelry stores for Rhonda's mother, just her mother." Vincent snuck in. Crystal was hoping that subject was closed!

Crystal was scheduled to play at the New Yorker next weekend, in eight days. The motel idea was still very much on Vincent's mind and he wanted to accompany Crystal when she drove up. He had 21 Personal Leave days left to his Military career. It was over in 10 months, it was the first time he didn't look at this time with trepidation. Retirement with nothing to do was nothing to look forward to, but now...he begged her to please not dismiss this an an idle idea, but one with merit until it proved to be otherwise or too much. He promised he'd work it through with professionals and keep her in the loop. The first step, he's was taking Wednesday, Thursday and Friday off, "so can we please leave for NY on Wed morning?" He was fun, like a little kid with a new toy! She agreed, it would be fun to get off the highway and drive through the little towns along the way and see the landscape, shopping areas and feasibility of starting a new business with no experience. No experience in buying land, building a building, getting food and liquor licenses, just doing what he wanted to do, silly-nilly because he wanted to! *Sure we'd play with his new toy until he breaks it and forgets about it! She'd be spending time with him in a happy and good mood.* Then he said when she was busy practicing, he'd go to the Jewelry district and look in the jewelry stores for Rhonda's mother. By now she should be retired, but if he could find her and she could spend some quality time with Rhonda, it would be a great present for both of them. His thoughtfulness softened Crystal's feelings toward his search. If he found her, they'd find a way to make that happen!

For the next few days Vincent had his nose in maps and on the telephone with Real-estate agents and looking into rents, the Sq. Ft. and rental prices of business zoned rental properties. He also drew his ideal motel footprint if it were to be built, keeping in mind Crystal's idea of a high class or wedding or reunion venue. This was something that really interested him and kept him out of his own head where he gets lost in his own memories, kids, wives, loves, schedules, and Crystal. He was learning these things were not paying enough rent to continue to live in his head anymore! None but Crystal remained as a constant and physically appealing thought and person in his life. He realized she was still bending over backwards to fill his wish list on this new venture. The one he was heading head first into. The family having just dealt with the lumber yard down on West Street for the expansion of this house, Vincent visited with Samuel Wiggins, the owner, with his questions and his sketch of his ideal motel. Samuel was really excited until he found out this building idea out of his area, but remained the professional and helped Vincent all that he could. They talked about the cost of lumber, electrical, plumbing, etc. Looking at the stretch,

Samuel was able to ball park the lumber and roofing materials by the sq. ft. measurements of the building Vincent had drawn. Samuel gave it to Vincent as 'food for thought'. They talked for a good long time about the cost of building vs. renting and the pros and cons, long term of both. Prices sure have gone up since the remodel of his house in Massachusetts, but he found a new respect for this gentleman. Vincent had learned a valuable lesson in talking with Mr. Samuel Wiggins, Listen and Learn! His twenty years in the service had taught him to stand at attention, ignore and tolerate, go threw the motions and go home. In two hours he learned he knew nothing and had a lot to learn. He needed to talk with Crystal a little more seriously about the money to take on this kind of venture. He hadn't lost his enthusiasm for the project, he just wasn't sure how deep his wife's pockets were.

That night after dinner and everyone had vacated the kitchen, it was once again, just Vincent and Crystal looking at the numbers Mr. Wiggins had given Vincent along with the advice of hiring a reputable engineer in the town in which you are working. Don't handle everything on your own, have a great lawyer and general manager. Crystal listened to Vincent's words and she also heard his enthusiasm and excitement and willingness to take part and learn. "Crystal, do we have the funds to take on a project like this?" he asked nervously. She smiled, took his free hand and answered sincerely. "It would be great to do a feasibility study in the area that you choose, but that also takes a lot of time and money. So you do your due diligence and investigate the area you choose in regards to it's proximity to the highways, recreational areas, auditoriums, beaches, or anyplace people would gather and need a place to stay. Look at other 'fine' dining areas with weddings or large parties in mind, and of course other hotels in the area. Once you come to the conclusion that this is a great area, now we look for a suitable building to remodel or a piece of land on which to build. Done right, yes, we have the money to start ourselves in the motel/restaurant business. We need the right look and the the right name. See what you've done...now I'm excited. Let's do this! What do we call them?"

"Call them?" Vincent asked quizzically, "how many are we building?" Crystal just lightly giggled and said, "we've already got the right attorney, the right manager would enable us to build many motels." "Okay," Vincent continued the idea, "one every 100 or 150 miles straight into and through NY into Ct then MA to Cape Cod, then up through NH and into Me. With the right name and the continuity of look, we can build a chain of motels. Run them right, we build a good reputation and the sky is the limit!" "Oh my gosh Vincent... you've been bitten by the ambitious bug...it'll make you a millionaire!"

"OK, just think. Just the front, the entrance, if you will, has to stay the same. We build a stone wall surrounding a fountain at our entrance. The building has a stone veneer front and double entrance doors. If we design something really eye catching...add a little bridge over water...and do the same at all of our motels, it could be our nitch along with our name. Come on Crystal, think of a really good name." "Well, we've already trademarked and incorporated 'Clearly'...now think of somehow to use it." was her immediate response.

"Like, Clearly Comfortable or Motel Clearly Comfortable or Clearly the Best Motels or Clearly Motels. Then we work on the slogan...Clearly your best nights sleep or Clearly, your first choice in motels or we keep thinking..." Vincent put his fingers threw his hair in exasperation. Crystal followed up with "I really like your idea of standardizing the entrance area and making it reflect a statement of tranquility, charm and welcome. Of my gosh, listen to me...you've rubbed off on me, I'm excited! Little touches of sameness throughout each motel will reinforce the standardizing effect we'll need to stick to. Like maybe each dinning room will be upholstered in the same print, the same color with the same carpeting running throughout. Buy in bulk and save money."

"Come walk with me outside, we both need some fresh air." Vincent held her chair and took her by the hand and walked her outside. "Remember what we did out here...a million years ago?" he said as he looked up into the star studded sky. "Let me tell you a secret" Crystal whispered for his ears only, "we may have been alone out here that night, but dear ole Miss Elise watched our every move from her deck balcony right up there" as Crystal's head and thumb pointed up toward the upstairs deck. "No way" Vincent whispered back. "I saw her that night and I was determined to give her a good show. I never said anything and she was none the wiser that I knew she was watching." "You do have secrets Mrs. Clear, don't you?" She turned to face him and draped her arms up over his shoulders and leaned in a little and said... "I only tell you the very best ones. But right now how about a dip in the pool before we head to bed.?" "As much as I'd love to" he said with a little tinge of remorse, "but I'm not ready to beat my leg up that much yet, you go ahead...I'll be happy to watch you swim naked for as long as you want.

Chapter 53

1964-5

The next morning Crystal headed over to the Bursar's Unit, knowing she'd be away for a bit of time, she wanted to check on the remaining of her personal files. *Oh yes, we'd have enough money to pursue the motel business. Keith's accounts are very healthy and growing, ours aren't too shabby either. You're right Mr. Clear, I do have secrets and for years I've kept them very well!*

When she got home she needed to still a niggling feeling she had about Aspen's/Vincent's daughter Andrea. Had they found the rapist? Had they identified the other body? Did she have everything she needed? Was she financially well enough off? Who did she have in her life to help her with the baby? Vincent hadn't said anything about her, neither had he shared any of his feelings or thoughts about all of the other family members in his life. As much as it pleased her it also concerned her that he might be bottling up feelings that one day may make him burst! She made a decision...she'd find answers to these questions!

So while Vincent was on base for the rest of the day and the rest of the household was busy with their own pursuits, Crystal closed herself away in her bedroom with the yellow pages and her address book. Her first call was to her lawyers office. She was looking for the name of a private detective that could be trusted, who did they use? She was excited in a strange way, because she also felt deceptive. Having gotten two names to contact she was on a roll. First, Mr. Allen P. Henshaw only took local cases. Didn't travel out of state on cases...what good was he?!! Next she was talking with Clarke, interesting young man, who answered his own phone was eager and ready to help, could start now! He asked, "Oh, I was referred...that's always a plus, may I ask by whom?" Crystal didn't feel this was a secret so she willing said "Hudson, Wyett and Comstock, my attorney's." She heard a sigh, a quick giggle and "are you really Crystal Clear or are you pulling my leg? Why would Crystal Clear need a detective? Dad is always setting me up!" Crystal counted with "once you're on retainer I'll be happy to tell you why I need a detective as long as we have it in writing that these are private matters to be held in strict confidence, even from your father. So which one is your father, Hudson, Wyett or Comstock? Because if we work together, I'm sure he'll want to know what I needed you to do." Now the poor kid was shaking in his shoes. "Oh Ms Clear, I'm so sorry I didn't mean for us to get off on the wrong foot, of course your matter would be held in the strictness of confidence, when would be a good time to meet?"

Crystal invited him to her suite at the New Yorker, Saturday afternoon at 1pm. Vincent will think I'm practicing and he'll be off to 5th Ave inquiring about Rhonda's mother. While I'm at it, maybe I'll ask young Mr. ---he never told me which one was his father! I'll ask about Rhonda's mother, too. Feeling like she had accomplished something, something really out of the ordinary, but once again 'for herself only' she was headed to the kitchen in a really good mood.

Cheerful moods all around the kitchen over coffee with Rita and Vincent. Rita was all excited about her after noon appointment with Loretta and she could tell Vincent's mind was far away and thinking a million different thoughts. His leg was giving him very little trouble these days and the pain had subsided greatly. Suzie was still over at the hotel working in the kitchen getting ready for the Country Fest that would be bringing in hundreds of people all weekend long and her dad was on base doing his thing in a classroom. It was a wonderful thing, everyone has a good thing going on and everyone seemed happy. Vincent broke the quiet when he said, "OK, are we ready to go and buy some land or scout out some properties for sale?" Rita's eyes fell on Crystal. First there was a hush that came over the kitchen then Rita couldn't hold her questions any longer. "What are you two up to and what are you buying? Vincent couldn't get the words out fast enough. "We're building motels and function venues and swimming pools and clearly broadening our reputation to include statewide recognition. You see how I used the word clearly?" Crystal got up and wrapped her arm around his middle saying, "down boy, we'll leave soon." To Rita she said, "we are toying with," but Vincent interrupted her and finished her statement saying, "we are investigating the possibility of building and running motels with upscale restaurants and lounges from here to Maine. We are in the talking stages with some numbers and many ideas so we are leaving very soon for NY, to get Crystal there before Friday noon. That will give us some time to look at what might be available to build on or remodel between here and there. With me being retired very soon, I'll need something to do for the next 20 years or so. The more we talked about it, the more excited we both got." Rita's eyes and head turned from Vincent to Crystal as she listened to Vincent rattle on. "It does sound exciting and very interesting. Good luck, have fun and please talk to Clive before you buy anything, please!." Rita got up, hugged them both and headed back to her office. Crystal's face was lit with sparkling eyes, rosy cheeks and a smile that radiated warmth, love and excitement. Vincent's head-first approach to this new idea had him in over-drive and he was chomping at the bit to get going. "I like you like this" Crystal said to Vincent as she cleared the table of their coffee snack. "You are percolating with ideas and excitement and it's catchy! If you have a bag packed, then we're ready to go." He swept past her and retrieved their packed bags from their room and held the door for her to join him in an exit.

So far it had been a seasonal summer, but not today. The day started off hot and it was forecast to get even hotter. Riding with the windows opened only moved the hot air around, but at least it caused a breeze, but it also made conversation nearly impossible with the road noise. About an hour into their ride Vincent convinced Crystal to veer off of the highway onto a more country road where they stopped for ice tea and a hot dog. It was nice to just stretch their legs and walk around a wooded lot next to a baseball field. No traffic, no noise, just a few older men walking dogs and kids on bikes. One hour away from base and life was already so different, but the temperature remained the same, hot. Back in the car, still heading north, they stayed on this secondary road just scouting out what was around and sure enough about 10 miles from the hot dog stand stood a motel. The Rainbow Motel looked more like a page out of an old fairy tale book with 8 individual one room tiny cottages each painted a different pastel color. No pool, no restaurant nothing to entice a traveler to want to stop there, and even on this day there were no cars parked there. Vincent said "one down, I'm sure many more to come, just to show us what not to do with ours. "I hope we don't see many more. Why would we want to build one if the ones we see aren't busy?" Crystal asked in earnest. "Because. Look around. There are no attractions, beaches, camping areas. No signs of coming attractions at a concert hall or auditoriums. That is what we are looking for, then a great piece of land to build on or a building for sale that we can turn into what we want." The enthusiasm was back in his voice. The we can do this attitude was in his voice and in his waving arms at the lack of entertainment in the neighborhood in front of them. Every time he started talking about the project in front of them, she felt more sure their money was going in the right direction. Traveling north still, both of them quiet thinking their own thoughts, Vincent was busy looking out the windows and taking in the landscape as Crystal drove on. They had just past the signs welcoming them to Passaic. Then the other signs started catching their attention. Home of the Passaic Panthers. Crew racing finals this Sat starting at Fells Point on the Hudson River. Willows Pond Camp Ground 3 miles ahead on the right. St. Mary's Bingo every Sunday night. Passaic Stone Chasms, Route 140, 12 miles . "Crystal lets head to the Stone Chasms. Check out the area and look around. There Route 140 just ahead." Again riding in silence, both of them checking out the area, it was beautiful. Large mature trees on each side of the road, with a house now and then and now a school and a ball field. Long stretches of road with nothing, not even a filling station. No motels either. Street lights up ahead, road signs indicate a four way intersection. The red light gave them a minute to check-out their surroundings. A strip-mall on their left (drug store, hair salon, convenience store and bank) in the middle of the parking lot, a drive-through Kodak, drop your film off stop. Across the street a busy filling station and smoke shop. Now they saw signs for the Civic Center Play House (no directions). "That's encouraging" remarked Crystal. "Now you're getting the hang of it" Vincent immediately responded to her and rubbed her shoulder. New sign, Passaic Stone Chasms, 2 miles. After traveling the two miles and taking the right at the Stone Chasms sign, they pulled into a parking lot that had an information booth dead center. Needing to stretch their legs, Crystal parked and they both walked to the booth and had a wonderful and very informative conversation with a park employee in her 70's. Henrietta was more than willing to tell them all about the area and the park. The park consisted of picnic areas and picnic tables. A child friendly play ground as well as tennis courts and a basketball court. Miles of hiking trails and rock climbing. Many trails with Chasms and they were labeled by difficulty. Rangers patrolled the park and they communicated by radio. This was a township park and didn't charge for it's use, other than the complimentary donations requested quarterly with the real estate billing. "Are you folks looking to settle in this area?" Henrietta asked. "No, actuality we're looking into areas that could support an up-scale motel, lounge, dinning venue type establishment. Where do young couples celebrate the party part of their weddings, or what is available to serve 100 guests with dancing for an anniversary party?" Crystal asked while Vincent had wondered away to the boys room. All excited Henrietta replied with out-stretched arms and fingers pointing, "those types of parties are all booked out-of-town at the Ole Mill Brook Tavern. A great place, but we have nothing in town. Just around the corner up the street (where she was pointing) near the Civic Center, a big-time developer just high-tailed-it out of town, they couldn't leave fast enough when they were caught lying and stealing about what they wanted to do on the piece of land being offered by the Sullivan family in town. Don't know much more than that except the Sullivan's are lovely people and the land has been in their dwindling family for generations. Vincent arrived back just in time to hear the part about the dwindling family. "What do you mean about or how is the family dwindling?" Vincent asked. "Boy, I guess you guys really aren't from around here." Henrietta whispered. "First, about two years ago Matte Sullivan, about 90 years old living here all of his life on the same piece of property his father, grand father and two great grand fathers before him died in a boating accident with his only son, never married and only grandson. That leaves his only daughter, Mary, age 68. Now, Mary , who buried her husband about 6 six years ago, perishes in a hotel fire in Cincinnati just 6 months ago. This highfalutin developer conned the family lawyers and town officials past the clause in the family do's and don't s in selling requiring no hotel or other establishment be built taller than two stories on the property containing 10 acres. The bill of sale was just about to be finalized when the town building manager asked for a scale drawing of the proposed building for the site and it was a 16 story hotel building. All negotiations were stopped, sanctions brought against this developer and that is where we are today. A beautiful 10 acre lot still for sale." "So if we are planning a one level , single story building it would fit within the parameters of the sale agreement?" Vincent said out-loud. "Yep.." Henrietta supplied. "I like you folks, so what are you looking to build and why?"

Vincent went into the front of the building idea with the stone wall and bridge and fountain leading to a registration area for the motel and the entrance to the lounge area to one side and the dinning room to the other. We are still in the planning stages and looking for towns where it would work and land to buy or buildings to buy and rework to our needs. He also explained he was about to retire from the Navy and needed something to keep him busy for the next twenty or so years. These motels will help to keep my entertaining wife close to me. She can entertain in the lounge. We'll make it a piano bar. This intrigued Henrietta. She asked if Crystal had recorded anything that she might have heard on the radio. That discussion lead to them changing the radio station Henrietta had tuned behind her. Within minutes Crystal's Black Water Blues was blaring out of the speakers. Smiling from ear to ear Henrietta indicated she'd visit the lounge to listen to Crystal play if the bar tender made a decent Bloody Mary. She wished them good luck in their land search and motel endeavor as they left the area with Black Water Blues still playing on the radio.

As Crystal and Vincent were leaving the parking lot they both started to talk at the same time. Both saying how much Henrietta reminded them of dear Elise. She was a fond memory that they would share forever. She'd be excited over their new idea.

On the road again in the direction of all of Henrietta's pointing they drove straight to the corner lot of 10 aces for sale. In unison, "PERFECT" came off of both of their lips! Crystal couldn't wait to pull over and park. The northern most edge of the properly was tree lined. Mature oaks standing mighty and tall and elegant. As they walked to the eastern most edge they encounted a sunken foundation of some sort that had a back yard of Willow trees surrounding a gazebo and overgrown gardens of years past. Turning and heading south on the property there was a long meadow filled with wild flowers, long forgotten bee hives and three rod-iron benches beneath a stand of maple trees. They walked back toward their car which was the western most side of the property that faced the road. All the while they were walking, they were talking. They needed a number to call a person to talk with the particulars in the sale of this property and when could they meet! In their minds they were sure they'd found their first site and couldn't wait to move on it. What made it even better was the Civic Convention Center was diagonally across the street and could handle the over-flow parking for any event held at the motel.

Back in the car heading to New York and the New Yorker they talked all the way as to how to get Mr. Brentwhistle on board with their ideas and this location. They had copied the listing agents name and phone number and needed a place to sit and have a good meal, stiff drink and a room for the night. Enjoying their first drink, Crystal used a house phone to call up to Clive and invite him down to the Terrace Room for a chat, a very important to her chat! Having heard the urgency and excitement in her voice it only took him 5 minutes to join them.

Clive actually sat and had a cocktail with Crystal and Vincent. After the second drink and all of the dreamy stone wall, fountain entrance details were discussed as well as the lounge, dinning room, venue possibilities and the at least 18 motel units, they went on to describe the 10 acres they had walked and fell in love with, not two hours from here. Once again he assured them that this was something he was sure he could assist them with. He was honestly excited for them in this endeavor. He said "let me make a couple of calls and on Monday we can take a ride and look at and walk this property together." Crystal whined, "why Monday, it's only a couple of hours from here, we can do it tomorrow morning, make some calls, talk to some people and be back here before dinner. Then there's still all day Friday before I need to work again." "Oh, you're still that impetuous little girl that can't wait. Wait for the calls to be made and the contacts to be scheduled. Maybe my contacts will need all day tomorrow and Friday to scout out the 'lay of the land' as you will, it's zoning, price and feasibility...then get back to me. That's a lot of work in two days on really short notice." "Sorry Clive, I know you're sticking your neck out again for me, for us and we really do appreciate it. We're staying the night, OK to use the suite? Then in the morning we'll be taking off early to scout out what we can find in Connecticut." "Oh course Crystal, that's your room, use it at will. Can I ride back with you two on Monday, maybe we'll have a lot to talk about. A 10 acre lot in New Jersey and whatever else you two find. Some fun days ahead, I can just tell!"

Clive kissed Crystal on the cheek, shook Vincent's hand and left them as their entree was delivered. Their evening meal was devoured with conversation all about the 10 aces and how and where to start building on that lot. It had never taken them that long to eat a meal before!

Vincent was spooning Crystal in her elegant room in the suite behind door 4001. She had been using this room for the last 2 years every time she stayed in New York, but she still felt as though she was intruding on Mr...Clive's personal space. That was nonsense of course, it was bigger than most 2 bedroom, 3 bath ranch houses you drove past on route 2. But still...the elegance! Vincent was feeling a stir he hadn't felt since the fire. He rubbed his left leg against the sheets to test it's tenderness and it felt fine. With that movement Crystal asked him how he felt after all the walking they'd done on their motel corner. "I love the way your phrased that, but really I was testing the friction factor of movement on my leg." As he was talking his penis was making it's way between her legs and his hands were busy on both of her breasts. "My leg has kept me from doing many things lately and one of those things is going to be rectified right now, as long as you are on top." His hands found their way to her breast and his fingers were ever busy on her nipples, squeezing her beasts together and rubbing his fingers between the caverns he made between them. His breath on her neck between nibbling kisses and words was driving her crazy. He whispered what he wanted to do to her right now and what he wanted her to do in return. As he talked and caressed, Crystal could feel herself being swept away on a feeling of sexual euphoria, the abstinence of sexual contact had given his touches, his words his attention new meaning. It was almost like the first time! Her body was reacting with such need it felt wonderful. He could feel Crystal's body starting to throb and her breathing taking on a different rhythm. "Slow down girl, we have all night... please turn around so you can touch me." In a heart beat Crystal had turned her body to face him and she cupped his penis in both of her hands. His hands were back cupping both of her breasts and their mouths were together in a kiss that only love can create. With their mouths still busy with the kiss and his hands still foundling her breasts, Crystal had him on his back with her vagina snugly nestling his penis deep inside. Before she broke the kiss, she traced her finger around their mouths, then let him suck on it before she sat up. She sat up straighter and leaned back which drove his penis even deeper inside her and it hit a spot that caused immediate cries of almost anguish and hip and body gyrations of euphoric proportion. Then the tears, uncontrollable tears of joy, contentment, and love. The unexplained emotion experienced when all good things and feelings erupt at the same time. Orgasm extraordinaire!

That was too fast they both agreed, so to cool things off for just a minute to let Crystal's nerve endings and clitoris relax to a near normal state they lounged face to face in the bed and talked about motels again. The conversation was fruitful in that they agreed on the exterior of the front entrance, size of each motel unit, how many depended on the size of the lot on which they were building or the size of the building they were remodeling. All of these someday motel dreams were hatching while Crystal's right hand was stroking Vincent's growing penis while her left hand was rubbing the inside of his left upper thigh. All the while Vincent's two middle fingers were inserted into Crystal's vagina as far up as he could get them in this half laying position, while his other hand was busy drawing circles around her nipples and pitching each one every now and then. So much for a cooling off moment. So much for treating an injured leg carefully. He ceased all hand movements, laid Crystal on her back and mounted her with the swift movements of a love stared, sexuality deprived grown human man. His hands found hers and brought them up above her head, while she lifted her hips and brought her long legs up and wound them around his hips. They moved together until neither one of them could breathe. Their coupling was long and hot and sexually exhausting, but also mutually satisfying.

"If I had know that sleeping with you in this bed in this room was this sexually explosive, I would have insisted it happen long before this." Vincent said while resting on one elbow looking down into Crystal's dreamy eyes. "You do say the nicest things, Mr. Clear... without thinking first. You were always too busy elsewhere, remember." Crystal let the words slip before she could stop them while struggling to get out of bed, out from under Vincent's legs. "Ouch, that hurt" Vincent let his words out.

Now standing he turned her to face him while he apologized for his retort because she was absolutely right. "I know sometimes it's hard for you to not throw in my face my past actions and decisions and I love you all the more for still being here for all that I've put you threw over the years. Thank you for still loving me and doing to me that which you just did...can we do it again...now...please!" "I do still love you, more..." he didn't let her finish her statement, but rather cut her off with a smothering kiss as he walked, shuffled her back toward the bed.

They left the hotel by 9am the next morning in their quest to find another great spot to build a motel. Again it was a great day, sun shinning, blue sky and very few clouds. Even the clouds that they had built last night were gone with more sexual exploits and the morning sun. On the road for only about 30 minutes and they agreed they were starved…time to stop for breakfast. So once again they got off the highway on to a road called Cross County Road and happened upon just what they needed, a sign that read "Home Cooking" 6 am to 7pm. Perfect! Looking over a map between where they were just now to the Northern most New England States, they decided Woodstock was their next destination. Great, one pot of coffee drained, a stack of pancakes, a plate of sausages and home-fries along with two fried eggs each, devoured and they were on the road again. Woodstock, NY here we come. We don't know why other that's the direction in which we are heading.

Feeling good so far about where they were headed, crossing into New York gave them a feeling of closeness, yep anywhere along here would be great! Vincent once again was being instructive in looking for signs of people gathering. Crystal took her next right and was now traveling on a more rural road. One lane in each direction with churches and schools and filling stations and a post office and convince store. She felt like she was in Mayberry RFD, but even better there was a sign. More like a pole with many signs on it pointing to and listing the names of many ponds and camp grounds. This time Crystal took a left and it brought her to a major route sign and a four way stop with street lights. Across the street on the left was a major supermarket, bank and Kodak Drive through. On her right a filling station and seasonal ice-cream shop. Very clean, very pleasant town. She drove straight ahead. More signs for local ponds, fishing areas, and picnic grounds. On her right a drive-in movie theater, now showing Bye Bye Birdie. She was now on a straight-a-way that seemed to go on for miles. There was a right coming up and she took it. Good choice, the center of Woodstock straight ahead with a Welcome Center. Needing to know more about the area, Crystal and Vincent wandered into the center with a million questions. Mrs Wilson, the woman behind the counter was an upper middle-aged long time resident of Woodstock and she seemed to know everything and everybody. They got their heads filled with local history as well as why Woodstock is a good place to settle and raise a family.

So their question of "would it be a good place or a good idea to build a motel, up-scale dinning room, venue offering location with a pool and lounge here in Woodstock?" She was so excited. " Yes, Yes, we need something like that. Visitors for Golf Tournaments, or Stadium activities and big weddings or graduation functions all need to use out of town locations, we have nothing in our town. You'd be the first, so build it fast, we need you!" Crystal's question was "whereabouts are the function halls in your neighboring towns" Vincent asked, where would be the best place to build our motel, where is there land for sale? These answers took another half hour to explore. A very pleasant lady, but she sure could talk! Next they took a ride straight through the center of town to Mill Street and came upon the most lovey spot they'd seen in town so far. An area of about 100 aces that was flat from the road for about 50 yards then began to get hilly the deeper you looked into the field. It wasn't much of a hill, but just enough to separate you from your neighbor on the other side. The frontage of this field was at lease 200 yards if not more. Across the street was the Ridgewood Country club and Golf Course (no dinning area, large lounge) The end of the field hosted a 'small' for sale sign: Call Todd at 458-221. Mrs. Wilson said Todd could be a tough customer to do business with. Next Mrs. Wilson told them to check out the big abandoned Agway building on Southwest Main Street across the street from the entrance to the Railroad Museum. At least they wouldn't have competition in their lounge in this area. A nice part of town, not too far from anything and it was on a very large lot. The building itself was at least three stories and had a foot print of about 200 by 200. A lot to work with. It also had a for sale sign with the agents name and number. Having made notes about the two places they looked at in town, they headed to Gainesville, the next town over to check out the function houses that were getting all of the business of large gatherings. They drove there, stopped in for a drink at two places and were glad they did. No competition in their minds! We'd be shinny and new and friendlier! They agreed! Time to head back to New York, her bedroom was waiting for them.

It had been a long day, but a fun packed learning experience and they had come away from it with two great leads with names and numbers. The drive back to the New Yorker seemed fast and effortless, they never stopped talking and dreaming about the locations they had looked at. The only problem, they each had their favorite and it wasn't the same one. After voicing their likes and dislikes on each property they agreed it would come down to the money...the purchase price!

Once they had settled themselves into the steak house for dinner, and ordered their drinks, they called for Clive to join them... again. He was genuinely happy to see them and share a drink with them. He listened to their adventures and their pros and cons on each of the possible sites, and was over-joyed at seeing Crystal so happy and animated about the prospect. He tucked the names and numbers they handed over in his shirt pocket and said he's run these be George tomorrow when he calls about the Passaic Property. Ya know...better still, it's still early, I'll go and call George right now and start the conversation about Woodstock and whatever else you two bring to my attention." Before leaving the table, Clive mentioned that he had talked with Rita earlier in the day and she was equally excited about the motel ideas. She said it would be a great way for you (looking at Crystal) to keep your name and career alive performing in your own lounges! If you two can 'play with' the word *Clearly* in naming the 'chain' of motels, most of the legal work would be more than half done. "Vincent, if you've got your mother-in-law on board for this venture, you'd better find properties and I mean fast! Crystal, she's ready to advertise their existence and openings!" Once again he kissed Crystal on the cheek and shook Vincent's hand before walking away.

Crystal watched Clive walk away and was thinking that she had no idea how she was so lucky to have Clive Brentwhistle as a friend. He had just happened in her life when she needed a "career protector" and "career builder" to get her started and on the right road of success. She had tried many times over the years to thank him and talk with him about the chances he had taken for her, but he waved her away. He said he felt like the winner in the relationship. He saw a diamond in the rough and helped to polish it, it grew into the crystal it was meant to be! He admitted to her a number of times that he thought Vincent wasn't good enough for her. Over the years he'd made that comment a few too many times because he could see her hurt feelings or foul mood was all of this doings. Clive had never meant to be the cause of additional hurt feelings for Crystal, but he had and he was sorry for it when she defended Vincent and tried to hide her feelings. Lately he has told her how happy she looks when she is with Vincent, that he can really bring out the 'happy' in her. And happy she was.

Back to the here and now she looked over at Vincent and said "all done?"

"If you mean eating…yes, but I'm really looking forward to a happy ending once I get you upstairs."

The next morning, Friday, at breakfast they were discussing the fact that they'd never had a camera. After ravishing Crystal half the night, Vincent approached the subject of driving to Vermont and taking his time to scout out possible motel sites. He'd buy one of those Instamatic Kodak cameras they see advertised every where and drop it off in a finishing store to be mailed back to them. He'd take a picture of every detail as well as the listing agent's name and number. Crystal thought it was a great idea until he said it being that much further away he said he'd head for New Hampshire first, today and find some sites, spend the night, then tomorrow drive up through Maine, find some properties and head south through Vermont, take more pictures of properties there, spend the night and drive back the rest of the way on Sunday and be back by her intermission time Sunday night, that would give him all three days to scout out New England. "I'll buy more than one camera he added! He smiled and added you need today to practice, I know you…and for a while on Saturday as well and Sunday you'll want to sleep in late have a lazy breakfast and hang around until show time…I know you! you're working… the most important part, we can share a night cap together Sunday night…and we'll be waking up together on Monday morning!" She smiled back at him knowing he was mostly right, but sleeping alone in that warm bed they just left held no excitement for her. "I'll miss you and miss out on the adventures of seeing our possible sites." "Yes, you will, but I'll be so busy and driving so much and eating crummy food along the way, you won't be missing much. You'll be here eating wonderful food, bathing and sleeping in luxury, and don't forget, you're working." With a pout she relented and blew him a kiss.

After breakfast, now 10 am, Vincent said, "great the plans in my head are set and the route I'm going to take are so up on the air, I'll just head north for New Hampshire and do the best that I can." He kissed Crystal good-bye at the elevator and descended to the parking garage. Once he was gone she worried why he hadn't mentioned Massachusetts as a possible motel site. Maybe the memories were too difficult for him, just better not to go there!

Crystal had just a few hours before her meeting with Mr. Clarke. ., the detective. Practice a little now and a little more later...that will work. At precisely 1pm the front desk called for Crystal and she admitted Clarke into her suite. *Gosh, he's a living doll, he's young!* While shaking his hand they both took notice of each other's height, Crystal was his equal and he was startled when he exclaimed, "not just beautiful by freaking tall too!" Crystal dropped his hand, closed the door, laughed until he looked embarrassed and then she said "freaking!...what's that?" Poor Clarke didn't know what to do, so he opened the door and left, waited 10 seconds and knocked on the door. In those 10 seconds Crystal's heart fell, and now she felt bad...! Hearing the knock, she carefully opened the door and Mr. Clarke Comstock introduced himself and said "I do believe you were expecting me".

Sitting at the dinette table enjoying coffee and the best coffee cake Crystal had ever tasted, they got down to business. Crystal touched lightly on a couple of items she needed help with, he stated his fee and told her he'd bring her compliments of the coffee cake to his mom! Now it was Crystal's turn to feel embarrassed. Past all of the little small talk, Clarke said he'd been through the police academy after college when he figured out he really didn't want to sit in an office all day and be a lawyer. His dad and the firm had hired him on occasion to help with their cases, and that kept him involved, and sharp but not as restrictive as a cop. So what he could do for her would be above board but without certain boundaries. He was licensed, promised 100% confidentiality and they were in business. It was then that she went into more detail of the things she needed him to look into. At this she disclosed the Sabers and Chambers names and the Massachusetts and Maryland addresses. She also included Andrea's dilemma that she wanted to know more about as well as the unidentified body left by that horrific fire. By looking into the fire maybe he could kill two birds with one stone. Identify the unknown body and find the rapist! "You do lead an interesting life Mrs. Clear". Crystal just shook her head and said "you don't know the half of it." Clarke perked up and said, but there lays the problem, I need to know the rest of it, because it sounds like one thing is related to another and all roads will lead back to the same place or person, so if you can fill in the blanks before I leave you today, that will save you money and me a lot of time." In what was going to be a meet and greet and come to an understanding of working parameters, turned into a three cocktail luncheon and Clarke filling a notebook of Crystal's words! Before he left, Crystal penned a personal note, on her personal stationary to his mom for the fantastic coffee cake. Signed the note and slipped it into a sliver lined envelope. She made Clarke promise to deliver it to his mom.

Monday, nearly noon time driving back to Shelby Street and home was a trip and a-half! Vincent driving, Clive in the front seat with him and everyone talking at the same time about the same thing with no one hearing a thing and no facts or stories being understood with Crystal's Pretty in Pink tape playing in the 8-track player and rain splashing down on them by the buckets. Crystal just gave up and laid down on the back seat which she occupied all alone. She'd never been in the back seat of her own car before, but today seemed like the perfect time because Clive and Vincent started talking before they left the Hotel. It was now well into the first hour of the trip and they were still like two old Navy buddies sharing stories and ideas until Vincent said, "Hey Crystal what do you think?" Her time alone with her own thoughts was now over, they asked her a question.

Had they actually agreed on something and wanted her input… 'that's a novel idea" she replied back, having no idea what they were talking about. "We thought so to, Clive returned, we'll have to run it by Rita when we get back" "Whoa.." Crystal said, sitting up and looking at the two of them. "I told you she wasn't listening to us. She has no idea what we've been saying" Vincent said with a laugh. "Sorry Crystal", Clive put in, "we agreed we like <u>Clearly Comfortable</u> as the name of your motels." "That's a good one" she agreed. Clive continued with "once Rita hears it, if nobody has come up with anything better, she'll have the advertising campaigning in full swing if you don't put a stop to her! "Once we're ready, I'll let her. We'll need all the help we can get" "Crystal", Vincent said "this is a sound idea and it will be a sound investment. Buying the property wisely is the key and then I don't believe in failure." "He's right Crystal. Buy right and you won't fail." *Clive was on board, Rita said she liked the idea, was there something wrong with this picture?* "Clive, have you heard back from any of your contacts on the properties and Vincent how many rolls of film did you go through on your trip through the New England states?" Vincent answered first. "Three rolls of film, one for each state, I didn't want to mix up the states or the properties so I kept them separate. Hopefully they'll be back on Friday." Next Clive merely said, "I haven't heard from either one of them yet...when we get to the house I'll call them both." The rest of the ride was civil and mostly quiet listening to Crystal's music.

Rita was in the recording studio with Loretta Lynn and her entire ensemble. Suzie was in bed sleeping, she had worked the entire weekend on the Country Music Festival, which was a great success and of course Harold was on base in his classroom, readying the next class of sailors for their missions. Our three travelers had just trudged through the pouring rain with their luggage and folded-up carry-ons and made it in the back door before the next set of thunder and lightening.

"Do I set up a round of stiff drinks or make coffee?" Crystal asked. Vincent offered to make the drinks if Crystal would be so kind as to start lunch because he was starved. Clive said he wanted both after he took care of his luggage and wet shirt. Ten minutes later they were eating grilled ham and cheese sandwiches and enjoying their cocktails and still throwing ideas around about the motels.

Clive was the first to excuse himself saying he had calls to make on the properties in Passaic and Woodstock, NY. He was also talking to developers working with the list Vincent got from Colts Neck local hardware lumber store. Once they had building plans, an engineered drawing would be able to fine tune that list to a bankable number. Crystal added that she was very happy with the engineering company and personnel that worked on this house, as she spread her arms wide. "I think they'd be easy to work with again, besides they liked Mom." Clive just shot her an unfriendly look and said, "You and Vincent are the ones that will be working most closely with them, so as long as their fees are in line, Wonderful. They're right down the street as I remember, right?" "Right, Crystal concurred. Then once we have the site, we need to hire a construction company. Do we hire locally for each property or one firm and offer them the 5 or 6 builds as they come along? "Boy, girl, you've really been thinking about this." "Of course, it's our money, spend a little to make a lot...right?" "OK, let me go make my calls." Clive said as he was leaving the kitchen. Vincent also left the house heading to the clinic on base to have his leg checked before he could return to active duty tomorrow.

Crystal had a thought up her sleeve, she'd see about those 4 months! With a lot on her mind and time before dinner, she wanted desperately to play the piano. Having been told that her living room was a totally separate entity from the recording side of the house, she slipped behind the piano and started with Pretty in Pink went on to Meadow Memories and was startled by a woman standing behind her with her hands wringing excitedly in front of her..."Your THAT Crystal Clear. Loretta Lynn whispered in awe...," Clive was on her heals, breathless. "Loretta, Rita's daughter Crystal, Crystal, Loretta Lynn." Both women just starred at each other while Clive caught his breathe. "Rita has told me so many wonderful things about you Crystal, and about your house. It's been my pleasure to record my "On the Land" album here. Please excuse my bursting in on you but I got away from Clive...again...and followed the music." See looked over at Clive when she added the...again. It was Crystal's turn to to be inquisitive..."What do you mean, got away from Clive...again?" "Oh you caught that, did you?...Well Clive and I have a bit of a past. Not a history...just a little... past!" Loretta let slip. "Well he has a story to tell and you are welcome here any time, please make yourself at home and remember us for your next recording". "Not just a cliche...but I will and I'll' be happy to pass the word about your great studio. It has more than Nashville so we'll be back."

Clive saw Loretta out and returned to the living room about an hour later to tell Crystal the good news about the land in Passaic. "We got an inside scoop that that property has been fought over, been sub-divided and for sale for so long, they can't wait to get rid of it!" "Who died and how many ghosts will haunt us?" was Crystal's first reaction to his news. "Does it matter, we have a starting price on which to bargain, stall somewhat, counter offer and then move quickly. We get deed in hand, break ground and Vincent won't know what hit him he'll be so busy! By the way, where is he I wanted to tell him too." "He's still active duty, remember...he's on base. Really a doctor visit this afternoon." "Oh yea…" Clive muttered, "then you are going to be the busy one for the next...how many months...four until his release? If you guys want to get this moving, you'll need to sign the purchase and sale agreement, sit with the engineers…" he let the words dwindle away and finished with, and you still have Atlantic City in two weeks for two weeks! Those words were sinking in as she remembered Loretta Lynn's words...a little past. She'd have to remember to bring that up when they sit with Vincent later.

Crystal's head was filled and started working overtime as how to get everything done in a timely manner, done properly and improve Vincent's odds at handling most of it himself. Her thought of earlier had returned with a vengeance as how to get Vincent released from the Navy earlier rather than in four months. First she'd make sure that it was what he wanted, she's do that tonight, then tomorrow when she was in the Bursar's Unit, she'd perform miracles! Just then she had a throw back to the days of Else...the aromas waffling from the kitchen were making her mouth water. Suzie was up and working on dinner, just then her dad came in the front door, dropped off by of all people Jim Davies. Jim was heading out back to park the jeep and then coming in for a quick hello. Crystal was always happy to see him.

Dinner that night was crazy. Noisy with everyone talking about their weekend. The people they saw, the property that they saw, the music they herd. By the time everyone had told their story and related their experiences it was well into bedtime. The left over thought was, can't wait to see the pictures of the properties in New York, New Hampshire and Vermont. Everyone would be waiting for the mail man to come.

The next day, Vincent and Crystal left for the base together. Crystal dropped Vincent off on the shipyard side of the base and she went along to the Bursar's Unit. Everyone was happy to see her and anxious to know more about her motel dreams when she started talking about them. They all agreed that she had more ambition than anyone else they knew. She just shrugged and said "I have a retiring husband that I need to keep busy doing something!" Vincent had indeed agreed that if she could get him released from the Navy 4 months sooner, he'd be all for it! So by the time Crystal left her work post in the Unit, she knew Keith Rogers was going to come in darn handy and Vincent would be getting an 'Early Release' notification in his pay next week. This type of early release had been happening on this base for the last three months. Vincent's release was coming three months shy of his original release date.

The rest of the week was low key and almost back to normal. Rita had appointments every day, Harold and Vincent left for the base together in the morning Suzie went shopping and planned meals and Crystal practiced and toyed with composing every afternoon. The difference was Clive was in the house, on the phone and making notes about different contractors and building inspectors in different towns in three New England States. The man was perfectly content keeping busy with the abstract. Until the phone rang and it was in reference to the offer they had proposed for the land in Passaic. Crystal answered the phone but was too chicken to continue with the call so she handed the phone to Clive who turned on his business voice and listened, shook his head yes then no then said there were too many bodies buried on that property to expect to sell it at that price after all this time. Be real, be responsible and know when a real offer is being made because tomorrow this offer goes down when we buy in New York to build the same motel with the same celebrity following.

Crystal's stomach was churning by the time Clive got off the phone., but he was all smiles. Just then the mail arrived and turned Crystal's entire being to Christmas morning with the anticipation of opening presents. She promised Vincent she'd wait for him to open the mail if it arrived when he wasn't home. That promise was killing her now. Then Clive said "that pompous ass wanted thousands more for the land than we offered. Watch This!" Clive picked up the phone, called the Passaic property people again, but needed to leave a message. Unrehearsed he went into a narrative that made Crystal cringe! His booming voice said "Crystal just signed on the Woodstock, NY property and currently we can only go as high as was offered, and it will be our last. ... because the deal is now in the hands of the bank. Notes are to be signed tomorrow at 2pm, our offer is valid only until then. Cash could be dispersed as early as 9am Saturday at your location pending a purchase and sale agreement. Call us us if you think we can come to a deal on this otherwise they'll continue to look elsewhere" Crystal just looked at Clive in awe..Rita had arrived in the room when Clive was leaving his message and she just ginned from ear to ear. She had heard him deliver messages like this before. Loud, without question and final. "They'll call back before dinner" Rita declared….. Clive just winked at her. "But that was a load of bull Crystal declared!" "Only we know that" Rita clarified.

When Harold and Vincent arrived home later that afternoon, everyone huddled around the kitchen table with a beer and looked at the pictures that had arrived in the mail earlier. Crystal was all excited and sorry she hadn't been there to scout out these locations with Vincent last weekend. There was one picture she couldn't put down. It had been taken in Vermont. The picture had been taken from across the street and showed a large area on which stood two deer with a back drop of Mountains, not too far off in the distance. There were trails, presumably ski trails lining them. When Vincent realized the picture Crystal had zoomed in on, he set up four more pictures showing the immediate surroundings of that field, That field had a sign boosting 8 aces. Now you could see it bordered a 4-way stop with signs for that skiing area, a funeral home diagonally across the street a convenience store and gas station and another clear lot on the on the 4ᵗʰ corner. "This was a beautiful area, but we'd need to know more about it. There was no one around for me to pick their brain about the town or what else was around there. Definitely food for thought thou." Vincent liked the way Crystal's eye lit up on that picture. He liked it too. "Okay, scoot off of the table, we need to set it to eat" Suzie instructed. Just at that moment the phone rang. Rita said "told ya" and answered "Mr. Brentwhistle's line, yes sir, I'll tell him your holding" all the while her smile was growing.

Dinner was a celebration that night. They had just bought their first piece of property for their first motel. "Clive you're a master at that sort of thing" Vincent congratulated him on their behalf. "Don't be too fast, you need to drive to Passaic Saturday morning and finalize the deal and deliver the 'cash'.

Crystal said "really, cash! They made you stick to that, not a bank check?" "Nope, I offered cash, that's what sealed the deal, girl." "Alright, I'll call the bank tomorrow and arrange for that and have it in a nice, little, case." She said this in a sing, songy, voice. Clive then said "as long as you're going that far, I'd like to see the property and then can you get me back to the New Yorker?" Rita piped in with "I want to go too, I'll stay in New York for a few days." Harold merely said he wanted to be the first to stay in the motel! It was a happy gang with congratulations all around.

The next day Harold and Vincent needed to head back to the base, but Rita and Crystal had the day to scrutinize the pictures. Crystal had definitely picked out the best Vermont site but she and Rita were not in agreement for the new Hampshire sites. Naturally they needed to know more about each one, but in that they were 130 miles apart, one a skiing community and one a water sport location. Build on both! Now they were in the middle of charting the mileage between Passaic and Woodstock, NY, Londonderry, VT , Waterville Valley, NH & Wolfboro NH, with Plymouth, MA and New London, Ct. also in the plans for building. All locations held interest for them to be represented in and they were far enough apart to attract business and be self sufficient and help to grow the name and build a strong reputation.

When Vincent got home that night, Crystal's head was spinning after looking at the pictures he had taken. Clive had made a couple of calls to the phone numbers he saw in the photos, but he was waiting for call backs. Yes, she had the money for one or two more properties as the lawyer had explained. They'd use one property in escrow to buy the next, so on and so on until they had what they wanted and all were operational and making money, then one by one, year after year they'd be released from escrow and all be held by the corporation as assets. Her attorneys were on board with this as were her accountants and it only took a 30 minute phone call to asses it's competence and ability to sustain itself. After-all, dirt was going nowhere, buy as much as you can afford! The bank called her at 1:30 to inform her that her withdrawal against her account was all set and in cash as requested and she could pick it up anytime. So far it was too easy. Everything had fallen into place so fast. It's amazing what money can do and it was her money. (at least most of it...Thank you Keith) Vincent had spent the day away from the house and didn't know what was going on all day, so once Crystal got him up to speed and all filled in, she was exhausted and ready for bed. From a piano player to a motel owner. From a career sailor to a motel owner...were they crazy? They looked at each other and laughed. Turned out the lights and had sex like it was going out of style. Crystal woke up and got up once during the night. She needed to check where she had stashed the cash! Yup, still there, feeling better, she got back in bed and snuggled up against Vincent. All was right in her world.

Chapter 54

It was an hours ride to Passaic and they had an 11:00 o'clock appointment at the First Chapter's Bank of Passaic to deliver their purchase price and get their purchase and sale document. Crystal and Vincent were in the front seat with Clive and Rita in the back. It was a nerve racking, exciting ride with conversation overload. Vincent had made Clive feel like the benefactor of the entire process by all of his help. This definitely helped to change Clive's feelings in regards to Vincent' s worthiness of Crystal. For the first time he saw a man totally supportive and genuinely in love with the woman and her abilities. It warmed his heart to feel Crystal had finally corralled her love of a man and music in the same place even if it was in a chain of motels. Now she needed to get back to work and let Vincent build them. The conversation also included the 'little bit' of a 'past' Clive had with Loretta Lynn. It was a mutual attraction of two people outside of a phone booth in the Stardom Hotel, downtown Nashville about 25 years ago. Two people, each waiting for a call that never came. So in the fifteen minutes that they gave each other to talk and flirt and gradually hold hands and wait for their calls, they made plans to have coffee later that afternoon. Before Clive walked away a happy young man, he stole a kiss and never looked back. As he was walking away, Loretta got her call which eliminated her free time that afternoon, so their coffee date never took place. It was about 10 years before they saw one-another again.

The meeting at the bank was quick and to the point. Crystal and Vincent had their piece of paper stating that they were now the owners of the beautiful lot at 246 Lower Point Road, Passaic, NJ and they were well on their way to the next step of being motel owners. They left the bank hand in a hand with smiles that could light up the world. Now Clive was behind the wheel of the car and they headed directly to the New Yorker for a celebratory lunch. During lunch they discussed hiring a lead contractor and letting him decide on local builders or building a crew to build all the motels. At least, with a Lead Contractor he can deal with the building mangers and inspectors of each town. He would be responsible for making sure all building codes were enforced. But first they needed to sit with an engineer and draw what they wanted. Vincent cleared his throat audibly to get everyone's attention while he produced a large, very large as he was still unfolding it, graph piece of paper. First he addressed his comments to Crystal, sorry Crystal that you've not seen this yet, but there have been no moments for us to sit and look at this. To the rest of the table he announced that this is what he envisioned the motels to look like.

The paper was turned so Clive could see it more clearly, then turned again so Rita could grasp it's enormity and then turned again so Vincent could show Crystal a couple of key items that he was sure she'd appreciate. It took a full ten minutes for the first comment to be spoken. In those ten minutes Vincent was getting very nervous. He had no idea what any one was thinking, least of all Crystal. He had been so proud and pleased with the effort it had taken for him to draw what was in his head. It was not to size according to the graph blocks, but he had noted approximate size of each room he had illustrated. Then it happened, Crystal cried, Clive slapped him on the back and Rita got up and kissed him on both cheeks. "What an undertaking you've imagined!" Rita exclaimed. Clive jumped in with "you're giving the engineering company a lot to work with, they'll be pleased. Then Vincent looked at Crystal's face. It was covered with tears and all blotchy and he couldn't read her thoughts or her mood. He reached for her hands and offered a penny for her thoughts. Everyone waited and she finally said, "how could you take all of my thoughts and the pictures I had in my head and draw them on this piece of paper? It's exactly what I'd love and exactly what I pictured. Thank You." She blew her nose and willed herself to stop crying. Now Vincent felt validated..all by Crystal's words. The rest of their luncheon was filled with conversation around the drawing.

A few hours later when they arrived back home to Shelby Street, Harold and Suzie were waiting for them with baited breathe. Rita had called ahead and told them all was all set at the bank and Vincent had a drawing of what he dreamed the motels could be. Once again the drawing was spread across the kitchen table and they were sharing their ideas and dreams with her dad and his mother. It wasn't that it was terribly late, but they had put on a lot of miles, expended a lot of nervous energy and accomplished a lot today, so they excused themselves from exhaustion and retired to their room.

Now behind closed door, the pair smiled at one-another, removed their clothing and fell into bed. Was it the bacon aroma finding it's way into their room or the sunlight streaming in their easterly window that finally woke up the sleepy couple a mere 10 hours later. That was a gift! It was Sunday morning and they didn't really need to get out of bed, but that bacon sure smelled good! It was their folks on the other side of that door, so with robes and slippers, just like little kids, they found their way to the table for breakfast.

They had the day to just veg by the pool and make a list of what needed to be done and the calls they needed to make. With Vincent's drawing burning their fingers every time they looked at it, they wanted to call an engineer so badly. "How about the one that worked on this house," Crystal inquired? "I don't know, I wasn't here, you and your mother dealt with him...did you like him and get along with him?" "I wasn't around much either, Rita ran that show. Clive met him, I guess he was okay." Well, we can call him tomorrow make an appointment with him and run our ideas by him. The scope of the job is a lot more than just this house, maybe he can point us in the direction of a contractor. One with experience in many states." Crystal reminded Vincent that she could made some calls tomorrow but she was also in the packing mode to be away for two weeks. He'd have a lot of work to do on his own. "It's going to be a tough 4 months with you gone a lot of the time and me on base Monday through Friday." Crystal got up, sauntered over to Vincent's chaise lounge, kissed the back of his neck, apologized she was so pasted out last night and told him she'd have a surprise for him in his paycheck on Friday. "Now you've done it, with you in that 'barely a bathing suit', kissing me and telling me I have to wait until Friday for a surprise, what do you think I am?" With the smile in his voice he made fast work with his hands getting her out of the top of her suit, sitting her on his lap facing him and nibbling heartily on each breast in turn. She could feel the lump she was sitting on and she didn't want to think of him wasting the effort. "Never waist a good thing" she said to him and relieved his penis from his trunks and untied her bottoms and shifted herself up and down fully upon his prize. It was too hot in the sun to be doing what they were doing, but it felt so good! It felt like it was going to be fast... c'est la vie! They had plenty of time and now plenty of energy...they'd just do it again, it wasn't too hot out, everything felt great 'out'.

"Ya know", she said "we never did know how to just take it easy and relax, look at how we just spent most of the day!" "Relaxation is over-rated as far as I'm concerned," Vincent counted with. "I enjoyed this a whole lot more than lying on my back with no one on top of me!" "Glad I could please, because tomorrow you are back to work. I'll drive in with you and check on my *things,* put some time in at the Bursar's Unit if they need or want me, do some shopping and be back here by 2 o'clock, make some calls, the engineer first and then be with you for supper. It's going to be a short week with me out of here Thursday afternoon. Travel to Vegas is so much faster and more comfortable being able to do it by air. Performing there is so much more fun now, it's not such a drag getting there, I guess I've aged!"

"That's the way you put it, I say just like some other things, you've gotten better with age! Besides age is just a number and the only number I'm concerned with now is the number of motels we are going to be able to build. Did you know we are up to 6 sites. Beautiful, ripe for the buying with price tags, if not affordable, in the ball park with people we can talk to. Go do your shows, make lots of money and bring it home so we can spend it." Vincent was really on a roll. His future looking a little brighter with plenty to focus on with keeping his mind off of his losses and more on what they could build.

In the two weeks Crystal was in Vegas, Vincent had purchased two of the six sites they had looked into and was in the process of making appointments in these towns with a Certified Building Contractor, Foster Bull and approved engineers building plans. The contractor, Foster would hire his own crew and work each site as it became available. On Tuesday of the second week Clive had met Vincent on the Woodstock site and congratulated him on his work to date and his retirement. That's when it really hit home that he was retired from the Navy. Crystal had actually managed to make magic happen—again-- and now he had the time to devote totally to this project. Clive made him realize again how special Crystal really was.

Tuesday night back at home on Shelby Street, Vincent needed the name and number that was associated with the Londonderry, Vt property. He searched his truck, the kitchen draw where nearly everything ends up and was now in their bedroom going nuts as to where he should look next. Crystal was a very organized person, everything had a place so where was her place for these property names and addresses? He'd already looked through the desk in the living room, kitchen telephone desk and now the bedroom desk. Next he ventured into the night stand next to Crystal's side of the bed and came across an address book. Perfect he thought, I bet I've got it, but what he saw floored him. This little black book had the names and birthdays of each of his children, by mother and state. The account numbers and dates the savings accounts were opened for each child. On other pages he saw the log-in and SKU information for the names of Reginald Sabers, Aspen Chambers and Keith Rogers. Who the hell is Keith Rogers. Just like the others he had a DOB and complete back story of parents, education and military service. Still active…. That bitch! No wonder why she never runs out of money. She made me and Rhonda live on military pay and she plays with this guys money!

Vincent didn't sleep very good that night. He was too busy trying to figure out how he could use his new found information, he'd also forgotten what he was looking for in VT. He knew he would use Mr. Rogers very soon, on second thought…*forget it…he's been around a long time, don't mess-up the good thing that's happening now!*

Late Sunday afternoon Vincent picked Crystal up from the airport. They both had so much to tell and ask. Vincent first. He was so proud of himself for the acquisition of the second and third properties. With Clive and Rita on board and the building permits in hand, they break ground in NJ tomorrow. The attorneys assured them that holding one property in escrow was enough to start the build on the next property, so New York's Woodstock site could start as soon as 3 weeks from tomorrow if they didn't run into any problems. Vincent wanted to start in Vermont next but needed Crystal's help with that site. Crystal was so happy with Vincent's progress and enthusiasm. "Of course I'll help in any way that I can, I want to be actively involved as well. What do you need next?" Crystal was sitting side saddle in the front seat while Vincent was driving just studying his strong masculine profile and trying to keep her hands to herself. Vincent, being the master of camaraderie asked about her two weeks, her performances and her success with her new song. Her home comings were always filled with lots of conversation and sex, the best part of coming home.

The next morning Crystal was anxious to do something, anything to help move the project along. Once again at the kitchen table she and Vincent sat and examined what had been done to date: Hired the Engineering firm, settled on size of motel footprint to include 18 rooms, lounge area, dinning room for 140 people, large kitchen, front desk and business office. Each motel will have a swimming pool and bath house. Those plans will come later. Purchased the land in Passaic, NJ, hard ass building inspector needed more on the engineers plans, Woodstock, NY, purchased land is close to here, all plans accepted break ground in three weeks, offer pending in Londonderry, VT. Apply for food and liquor licenses where land has been purchased. And what in everything that needed to be accomplished did Crystal want to tackle?

Crystal's head was spinning! Vincent had already done so much. Her heart was bursting with pride for him and at what he'd already accomplished, all she could do was smile and say, "I want to go shopping".

Vincent took those words to heart and was ecstatic! "Wonderful, I'll have plans for the entrance to the front desk and business office for you and you can start there. We need flooring, probably title, wall covering; paint, paneling, wall paper, you choose. A business desk, front counter at check-in...I'll have that built, a couple of chairs in the office. Remember you buy in lots of 6, all the same color, we want to build a theme and…." "Stop, Stop!...please", Crystal nearly shouted to get his attention. He stopped, looked at her with a gigantic smile and asked "what, not that kind of shopping?"

This was the speed at which Vincent's mind was racing. There wasn't enough time in the day to satisfy what he wanted to accomplish.

Two weeks sped by so fast and it was Monday of that pivotal third week. The week they had been waiting for to break ground in Woodstock. Foster Bull, the contractor had been in touch threw out the last two weeks with updates on crews and equipment and materials and had only good things to say about the town and every aspect of the project to date. The plan was to meet him at 8 am today on the site. "I'm so excited" Crystal said as she slipped her shirt over her head. When she popped her head through the neck hole, Vincent was there, so close, lifting her hair through the hole and nibbling on her earlobe. "We'll never make it there on time if you continue with this current activity" Crystal could only whisper her fears as it was already too late. Her hands found his prize already large and pulsating while he transferred his mouth from her ear to her mouth. He sat, she sat on him and their Monday was off and running with all things accomplished, in the right order and with plenty of time to spare.

The drive to Woodstock on this sunny and mild Monday morning was delightful. All nerves aside they knew they had plenty of time, hit very little traffic and enjoyed Crystal's music all the way there. On the approach to the property they saw Foster who directed them to where they should pull over and park. He was already in control and had equipment on site with more on the way. "This is so exciting" Vincent said on a sigh, as he watched and held Crystal's hand so tight! Ten minutes later Foster was standing with Vincent and Crystal explaining the plan for the day and the process going forward. He handed Vincent the schedule of work to be done with manpower and equipment and a time line and the money he would need by weeks end to keep the project going. He said the weather looked good through Thursday, Friday up in the air. The weather would always be a question in this type of construction. He said he'd give them daily reports and in those reports the look forward and what he'd need from them. As much as they wanted to stay and watch what was happening, this little speech sounded like, OK we're busy...please leave! They knew they didn't have to, but they also felt somehow in the way.

So by 9:30 they were on the road again and headed to the New Yorker. They were antsy and excited and wanted to share with Clive. But being in New York with virtually nothing on their plate that needed to be done, Crystal suggested to Vincent that they visit the jewelry section and look for Rhonda's mother. In his surprised shock he didn't hesitate to take her up on her suggestion. After walking down one side of the street and stopping in at least four jewelry stores, talking to every store owner and clerk and having no luck and then doing the same thing across the street, they finally came across an old man who remembered Marie Tuffin, that beautiful little French woman tied to that horrible, but ingenious cutter, Oliver Tuffin. After getting an ear full of her good qualities, they found out she passed on about two years ago. But wait, he indicated...opened the top draw to a desk, rummaged around a bit and came up with a Memory Card with Marie's picture and dates on one side and a prayer on the other, there was a little stack of them. He slipped one out of the desk and handed it to Crystal with a sincere feeling of loss. Walking away from the store, Vincent did have a moment of loss as well. Once again for Rhonda, never having seen her mom again and now knowing she never will. Crystal was beginning to see and feel the change coming over Vincent and she was afraid he'd slip back into the hole of depression and self woes-is-me! He had come such a long way in healing, she'd hate to see him slip back now with all the good things in front of him. This was their way of finding a way to help Rhonda, now they needed to help her bury her mom as well. They'd send the card to her, anonymously of course, from New York and be done with it.

Back at the New Yorker, as always, Clive was happy to see them. Vincent had learned to always have a few of those little instramatic cameras on hand and told Clive he got pictures of the equipment breaking ground! Clive had been very instrumental in hooking Crystal up with a designer to help with the carpeting and booth materials and colors for the lounge and the dining rooms.

Claire was also a gem with every other aspect Crystal asked her about. She asked the questions and got out of Crystal's head the exact look Crystal was trying to achieve. She made this shopping very easy. She also had Clive's flair for fixing prices and delivery dates. She and her firm may not have been the cheapest, but they were the best! Rita was no slouch either. She had the grand opening advertising for Clearly Comfortable nearly ready to go. It only needed Crystal's blessings and availability. But that was also Rita's job to book Crystal where she could make some money. If Vegas or the New Yorker had her working, the motel Lounges would need to wait their turn. Crystal would be doing record sales and autographs out of the motels as well. Claire said she wanted to be one of Clearly's first guests in the rooms she was helping to design and outfit.

As was planed, there is a bridal suite with a king size bed, whirlpool tub and wet bar. There will be six rooms with two queen beds and walk in showers, six rooms with two queen size beds and full bathrooms with tubs and showers, there will be three king size bed rooms with tub and shower bathroom and there will be two rooms with four twin beds, full bathrooms with tub and shower. The twin size bed rooms will be access available from the queen bed rooms. Crystal and Claire had a ball with colors and carpeting for these rooms. Crystal learned how to work with engineered drawings and how to purchase beds and nightstands and suitcase valets by size to fit in the rooms. Each room also had a small closet with ironing board, iron and four coat hangers. The bathroom would have two bath size towels, two face clothes and two hand towels. A hair dryer and an assortment of soaps, shampoo and conditioner. With one non-slip item for the bottom of the tub. They decided white for all of the towels.

Ten weeks later, they were now digging in Passaic, NJ, the first land purchase they made. This had better be a good investment because to date, this town had not been friendly. Foster Bull turned out to be a "Bull" to be reckoned with. He won each of the sticking points on the plans, the distance to water, and hours of operation. The building committee tried telling him the equipment needed to be stilled by 4:30 daily and couldn't be run on Saturday. "BULL" In three weeks, working 8am to 6pm, six days a week the structure was built, weather tight and paved. It was on a Monday, Crystal and Vincent were walking around the front of their building and low and behold a familiar face showed up. Henrietta from the Passaic Stone Chasm. "I've been keeping an eye on this place. I knew it was you two that bought this land. Good for you. Good for this town. You two are just what this old place needed. New business, new life, new attraction. And Crystal, I love your music. I'll be the first one in your lounge to hear you play live. I can't wait." With that, she was gone. Crystal and Vincent just watched as she turned, walked to her car got in and drove away! "That was a little bizarre" Crystal said in disbelief, "that she just turned and went away!" "Yea??..." Vincent second that feeling. "Maybe it's this town. Everything is just a little bizarre. We've awaken the sleeping ghosts on this property and they've come to haunt us!" "Let's hope not", Crystal said seriously!

Crystal was alone on the Vermont property the following week when they broke ground in Londonderry. Not really alone, Clive and Rita were with her but Vincent was in New Hampshire. This was a first for Clive and Rita, therefore they brought a different feeling of excitement to the prospect. Forest was now accustom to Crystals appearance on the first day, this was their 3rd first day together and it actually made him feel good that he was doing everything just right and she was there to show him and his crew off. Forest found working for Crystal and Vincent very easy. They had set up the parameters of his job description and were paying top dollar for exemplary workmanship and leadership.

He was the guy dealing with the different towns people and building departments. It made what Crystal and Vincent had to do very easy. They were merely filling out a bunch of forms applying for the liquor and meal/food licenses. Truth be known, the attorneys were actually doing that. Crystal's signature was required after they did the work. So now number three was in the works, Crystal had signed quite a few documents and signed many checks lately. She was still being assured that there was enough money and it's pay-back was just around the corner. She was standing on property she owned, but she'd never been there before. She chose this location from the pictures Vincent had taken. She turned around and could see the ski trails etched into the mountain side. It was a gorgeous view, one she would never tire looking at. At that moment Rita could see the dreamy look on her daughters face. She didn't say a word, just stood closer and shoulder hugged Crystal and broke out into a proud smile herself. "Clive, can you help me back at the car." Rita was saying as she was walking away from Crystal and Clive. "Oh yes, of course, I'll get the tools." Clive was on her heels as they walked back to the car. The ever vigilant Rita had a sign in the trunk of the car. Future Site of CLEARLY COMFORTABLE MOTEL...Featuring...Pianist... recording star, Crystal Clear in the Crystal Light Lounge opening night! Now she, Rita, had to remember and book Crystal in the lounges for each of their opening nights. Just part of her job! That sign was erected at the edge of the property, easily seen from the street.

Chapter 55

Crystal and Claire had copied the dropped crystal lighting look of the lounge in the New Yorker, to give the motel lounges a warm and comfortable feeling. A gray and white cloud looking carpeting covered most of the floor in the lounge. The exception was under the bar stools, the front of the fire place, and the dance floor. These areas had black tiles embedded with shinny crystals and the look was duplicated on the bar top. The booth material was black and soft to the touch. All the booths had dropped crystal lighting over shinny, thick epoxy, stone top tables. The same stone as the outside exterior front of the building. The inside back wall of the lounge featured a fireplace with the same stonework. Black, shinny tables with the same stone top and black upholstered chairs surrounded the dance floor and made a homey feeling near the fireplace. The black title floor at the fireplace reflected it's peaceful fire-light. The look and feeling of the lounge was one of comfort and elegance!

Claire and her team worked miracles in their designs and colors to create just the look that pleased and reached into Crystal's and Vincent's thoughts and wishes. On paper everything looked perfect, wonderful. From the exterior of the building, to the lobby to the lounge and dinning room and kitchen. The motel rooms were large enough, had the amenities to please, TV and telephone and 4 of the six locations had room access to the pool. The other two locations were going to feature indoor and winter ready pools. The banquet areas were to die for...picture a wall of glass on the western most side. The sunsets were magnificent! These colors of light pink and orange and blue and green played into the marble tops of all of the dinner tables and the copper which outlined the bar, swagged glass covered light fixtures and wall sconces enhanced the golden hue of the room. It was like walking into a mid-summers dream! There wasn't a function you could think of that couldn't work with this decor.

Vincent's trip into NH just secured his feeling that there would be two motels here. One in ski country and the other lakeside appealing to two mind sets and vacationers. Now to find the sites. He had approached the state pretty much on the north western side that put him square in ski country. Entering Waterville Valley. Sounds great...oh look... Crystal will love this. Out came his cameras. Church steeples, horse barns, split rail fences all pristine white stretching for miles right into an area marked next 6.8 miles, 3rd expansion. *What does that mean...?* He drove the next 6 beautiful miles of tree lined, single highway, nearly straight boring miles. Nothing here. Then is opened up! The billboards advertised the ski resort area of Valley Heights and Waterville Ravine The coffee shop on the next corner had a sandwich sign advertising lunch specials as did the trolley dinner next to the college book store. Bethlehem College. Proud supporter of Army recruits. The next few miles represented life in a small NH town complete with two schools, post office a supermarket and central town meeting house. Perfect place to stop and inquire about the 3rd expansion. What were the first two?

The wealth of information Vincent picked up here was invaluable. First he had the town clerks explanation of the expansion happening around here. He showed Vincent maps of the town and how it was separated into three and what changes, what advancements were being made mostly on the governments dollar. When the expanded sewerage lines and pumping station areas and electric grids took up most of the time at the town clerks window Vincent needed to extricate himself from this building. He went back to the corner coffee shop for lunch and to study the towns information on the three step expansion and the maps at how it would impact the area. Deep in study over the maps, information and turkey sandwich in front of him he barely heard the offer of help to try and figure-out and understand what all this could mean to this small town.

When he finally looked up he saw a knock-out of a women leaning over his table and reading over his shoulder. "Do you need help in figuring out what all this means?" she asked again. This time he was looking at her with great interest, she smiled walked around to the other side of the table and sat down. "This means the town is growing, the schools will have a better accreditation, we'll have more first responder agencies housed right here in town. You know, police, fire and ambulance. Better highway equipment and personnel. The Bethel Hospital built 10 years ago on highway 120 just 4 miles from here was in the first money the town got from the government. We've been growing every since. I don't feel like I live in the boonies anymore! Most people around here love all of the changes. It's the old folks who don't like it much." Vincent just sat and listened to her talk. Without knowing it, she answered a lot of his questions, but naturally he had more. But she had more to say… "so what do you want to build around here? A mall we need one or condo's or 100 house communities, or cul-de-saks?" Vincent shook his head and said "nothing like that". "Good she said, the new convention center in the second expansion has brought a lot more traffic to around here, but there is still more to do in that expansion. There is still land for sale and other building going up. Before you know it we will be a small metropolis. At least that is what the papers say. Good for us!"

Now she was drinking his coffee. She needed to wet her throat after all of the words that were just spoken. All the while she was talking he was thinking *Is she a nut job or just lonely? Do I dare ask what else is being built? Is she for real? She 'seems' to know what she's talking about. Where did she come from? Is she alone? Who is she?* He was about to ask what else was being built, but she had just picked from his plate the piece of turkey that had fallen from his sandwich, chewed and swallowed and said, "you'll not want to build a multi level office building or a bank because that's been done. Really nice too. So far everything is in good taste and adds favorably to our town." Vincent finished his sandwich and said he was ordering apple pie for desert, would she like a piece as well? She was excited by this and accepted with, "I hope you are going to build a bakery, we need a good one of those. We need things like Dunkin Donuts or Kentucky Fried Chicken or Block Buster, like I see advertised on TV, but you need to build the building because we don't have any rental property anywhere in this town." The subject was changed to how long she has lived in this town while they were eating their desert. He found out she was born here and never left.

When he stood up to leave and pay the check, she looked him up... and down... and whistled...then said, "you sure are a big one! Wait a minute." She climbed up on her chair, leaned toward him, wrapped her arms around his neck and landed her sweet tiny lips on his in thanks. This didn't cause too much of a scene as there weren't too many people left in the shop. He instinctively lifted her from him and set her gently on her feet in front of him. He then looked down at her with the biggest smile and said "my, you are a tiny one!" They walked out together and once on the sidewalk she asked him if he needed any help to find what he was looking for. Totally intrigued by this little one he said "sure, can you show me what's around the new convention center?"

Once she was sitting in his car she again thanked him for the apple pie and said that's why she was showing him around. He asked her where do couples have their wedding dinners or pictures taken around here. She replied simply "anywhere they want, we don't have anything special around here." She was delightful company and kept talking about the changes around town and what the towns people were hoping would be built around here to boost it's economy and popularity.

They were driving around a more populated area now and he could see the new buildings. He had just encounted the only street light the town has. So far in this town there were many signs for the different ski lodges and coming attractions for the convenience center. He also drove past two sites for sale that could work for his purposes. Now a little more excited about this small town because there were no hotels, commercially known dinning places places like McDonald's or Burger King or the large all you can eat Coral type establishments. There wasn't even a Dairy Queen. He turned around in a local market parking lot and drove back to the first Property for sale sign he had just pasted and parked. "What are you looking to build in our little town? Tell me and I can... maybe point you in the direction of the perfect spot." She looked at him with quizzical eyes that never stopped smiling. Finally he told her of the motels he and his 'partner' were building around New England. She was intrigued and asked him all sorts of questions and wanted to know more about 'them'. His excitement was peaked again and he told her specific things about their appearance, their size, hopefully their draw for large gatherings such as weddings or anniversary parties or even their high school graduation because she informed him their local high school was so small. He said "in this area we are also looking to include a four season swimming pool on the grounds of the motel." She was all excited about this revelation because their skiing traffic around town is a major economic boost and now with the convention center there will always be travelers around town. "OK," she said, "turn around and go back the way we came". "Why?" he followed up saying, I didn't see anything there to look at". She sighed... "that's because I didn't know what you needed and didn't take you on the right streets."

So back they drove past the convention center, the new banking and insurance buildings and took a left. Immediately they were once again on pristine farm land which hosted a huge barn that advertised hay rides, weekly square dancing, riding lessons and community gardens. At the end of the next field, which he was told was the community garden the road ended and they took a right. On his right was the most unique stand of three buildings he had ever seen. The large semi-circular driveway brought you up close to the mote and covered bridge to the front doors. The miniature castle looking structures also had gun torrents. The sign on the center buildings front door identified them as the Oldest Glass Factory of New England. "These are really unique little buildings, but not at all what we had in mind, even to remodel.' Vincent said seriously with regret. "You silly man, look across the street". She could see his smile building as he took in the site across the street. On the lower most southern corner of the property stood the most magnificent fountain Vincent had ever seen. He needed to see more, be closer, so he moved the car to the curb at the for sale sign. The sign forgotten for the moment, he wanted to look at the fountain. It stood at least 14 feet tall with six pillars of stone, the same stone at it's base and little sitting ledge about 14 inches wide running the entire circumference of its 14 foot width. There was a center spicket that shot to the top of the 14 foot pillars and cascaded back to the center at the same rate the water flowed down the pillars. Now out of the car, and walking around this magnificent structure, Vincent guessed the middle pool to be approximately 2 feet deep because he could see all the coins at the bottom. He just sat on the fountains ledge in awe while taking in the stonewalls that ran along the property as far as the eye could see. Still looking around he saw the same stone wall coming up the roadside from the north. Falling in love with everything he was seeing he went back to the property listing and took a couple of pictures. 9 Acre Lot for Sale...fine print (almost washed away by weather) Fountain and all stonewalls must be maintained. No sub-dividing. This time Vincent made sure to get the fine print in the picture.

Vincent walked back to car and saw an 'I told you so' grin staring back at him. "Is there a place fairly close that we could get a drink? Vincent inquired to her. "Sure, turn around and go to the end of the street, take a left." About 10 minutes later they past into a different town and then she pointed out a log cabin establishment with a sign, Limited Menu.. Well Stocked Bar. This will do nicely Vincent said while parking. They were attended to by a grandma looking older woman with full cheeks and pudgy hands. Once seated Vincent spread his information on the 3 Step Expansion Project flat out across their table. He started firing questions and found out that the fountain site was in project #2 and owned by an eccentric old timer by the name of Mrs. Mildred Congress Willoughby. Her father and husbands father were both pillars of this community and the two family thought they owned and could ran everything in sight. Now she is just about the only one left of the two families and she still holds her head higher than anyone else in our town. She holds it that high just to look down on everyone else and that is her only piece of property left. There was a high price set with the stipulations on the fountain and the stone walls and keeping it as one piece of property as the fine print stipulates, hoping to ward off anyone that would be interested. He also learned that no one was really looking at that property because #3 was just announced and that has residential lots for 60 houses in area BJ4..on the map and 60 more in EJ 2 with 6 more areas of house lots of 120 feet frontage minimum located, in P2-3-4 and T-4-5-6, that appears to be on the other side of town. This kind of growth was OK'd and subsidized by the government stimulus program in the water and sewer departments. It's also what is going to bring the work force into town and fill all of the openings that the new businesses will bring. The Expansion leaflets were very helpful and informative. Now that he'd driven around the town somewhat he could picture where the growth would be. Building their motel on Lower County Road on that beautiful fountain piece of land would put them in the back yard of the Convention Center and around the corner from 'down-town'. Yup, right where he wanted to be. Now that his mind was made up, he sat back to enjoy his beer.

Off in his own world and feeling good about the progress he'd made this day and wanting to contact Crystal and rave about Lower County Road and it's water fountain, he'd just about forgotten the tiny woman sitting across from him. He should know better than to get lost in his own thoughts and have Crystal on his mind because he was really enjoying the fact that his penis was being delightfully exercised and growing exponentially. Working on his second beer and having thoughts of Crystal's hand working to make his day even better, he closed his eyes to relish the sensation even more. He also missed the fairy, light-weight, settle her weightless little body straight down on his now exposed manhood. His gasp was silenced by her sweet little lips settling over his. "Don't worry our corner is dark enough, there is no one paying us any mind. Besides, I needed to remind you that I was still here." She pushed back a bit to look him in the eyes and repeated what she had said before. "You really are a 'big' one! Would you please buy me another rum and coke and then we can go somewhere so I can really enjoy you?" The rum and coke comment struck a cord and he deflated immediately. Cupping her face with his hands, he kissed her gently then lifted her up and off, smiled and said, "gladly".

The drive to her little cabin was fast and not too far, she drove. Once inside her small little place she was fast and she continued to 'drive'. She was driving him crazy because he couldn't believe he was attracted to this tiny little creature. She undid his belt buckle and unzipped his pants then proceeded to lift her top off. Bra-less, because there was next to nothing to hold in place, she watched him slipping his pants down his legs while he was gawking at the biggest, park pink nipples he'd ever had the pleasure of, oh screw it...nibble and suck at! Now, it was her turn to gawk... at his maleness! "I knew I was going to enjoy you, by the way, what is your name?"

Settled on her little twin sized bed with her naked and riding as much of him as she could handle, he finally said, "Keith Rogers. Gladly, being at your service. And may I ask, to whom I am servicing?" She giggled a sweet little laugh and said "Tina Willoughby." The name stilled him immediately and she laughed, "I'm not the one you need to be afraid of." "Oh yes you are, you're the one who has me by the balls, literally!" "A lot of good it's doing me. It's the second time today I've tried and you can't seem to keep it up! Really, I AM a woman!" "And you are the sweetest, tiniest woman I've ever had the pleasure of having!...now and again later and again after that. He protested... "I assure you, I do have staying power." And prove it to her he did.

"I love your body, tiny Tina, it moves in ways I've never experienced before. And your breasts change color with your excitement. You're intoxicating! You are every bit a woman and you make what you have work for you in ways that are unforgettable." "You talk like you're leaving Mr. Rogers." "I am, I need to, the sun is coming up..." But she advanced on him so fast with her hands wrapped around his penis and her tongue down his throat, she gloated and asked him "what else is coming up?" "OK, to have your tiny body wrapped around me one more time, I will endure that tiny bed of yours."

It was after 2pm before Vincent left Tina's little cabin. There had been two showers, supper and breakfast before he could pull himself away from her charms. Heading back to Colts Neck, he talked to himself all the way. What was it about that tiny woman? He loved the way she laughed, so easily. The way she wound her body around him, she'd go up, then down and when she settled, there was so little weight to her. She'd latch on to one of his nipples with her teeth and massage his balls. He was smitten, that what he was, smitten!

Yes, he had so much to tell Crystal. He was good at sticking to the facts at hand and not incriminating himself. There were years of practice on that subject, so back to the important facts. He was glad he had dropped the Lower County Road film at a Kodak Service Box, the prints seem to come back so much faster than using the US Mail. He couldn't wait to tell her about the huge fountain and beautiful stonewalls bordering the property. And best of all, the location was great. It would be easy to advertise and the need was great! The only draw back, the price. He had no idea how much, but it would be worth haggling over. Rita and the attorneys seem to stream-line this end of the business and get what Crystal wants. Their hand holding and arm twisting is worth paying for. With this one included, they had some pretty spectacular sights. Clearly Comfortable is off to a really great start and Vincent was looking forward to reviewing everything with Crystal later this week. They had scheduled this time together to do just that! Look at the sites, the files on each including licenses applied for, still pending or granted. Look at the orders, sent, pending or items received, from building materials to the bathroom shampoo. They wanted to look at everything including how much they've spent so far and what was to come. All of these things were being taken care of by others, but they wanted to stay abreast of everything. In the last few weeks talking with employment agencies in the towns where they were building, Suzie felt a little left out and felt she could contribute by overseeing the hiring on the culinary side of things. Naturally working with local agencies, but looking at the resumes and getting a feeling for the caliber and experience of the person. Vincent loved this idea because it was right her alley and she needed to feel wanted and needed. The Captain had his thing (on base) and this could be Suzie's. So far, making this a family affair with Rita at the helm, was working great. Vincent was so proud of his wife and couldn't wait to get home and get caught up.

Exhaustion hit him right after supper. All the driving he had done, and the tiny bed he had slept on the night before. These towns needed their motels. Crystal was of the same mind, very tired. A lot of driving, much conversation with Rita and Clive and a great deal of fresh air has just about knocked her out. The comfort and warmth of Vincent's body snuggled close to hers and her hand resting on his upper, inner thigh, made sleep come easily, she was a happy girl.

Chapter 56

God god...2:40am...Tina, what the hell did I do? I can't be doing things like that again...you stupid ass. Crystal is too good for me to walk all over her, again.! Tina was tiny with huge dark pink nipple clusters. Hair color? Face? Was she cute? How old? She was there... she offered it...she wanted it. I can't go back there...I

"Hey Vincent, you okay?" Crystal said in a hushed tone. "Your thrashing around, your breathing was different, talk to me" Crystal waited for Vincent to talk, or sit up...anything. Finally he spooned her, whispered sorry in her ear, cupped one breast and settled back.. This was enough for Crystal, she slept. But Vincent was actually suffering from a touch of guilt. His 'sorry' just now wasn't for waking her, his gut was actually nauseous and his thoughts were hateful toward himself. He had taken other woman before, but felt the need, the gnawing, aching need to make the pleasurable act binding and married those two woman. *Tina? What was That? Be still you fool. Make the contacts tomorrow, buy the land and proceed with hast and caution. Crystal will love it and I can go on to the next site. Get out of town and wear off my guilt and sick stomach in Wolfboro, NH. Every thing is sailing along so smoothly, I can't mess it up now! I love Crystal, I do...I used the name Rogers...holy shit!*

Vincent saw 3:10am then 3:50, then 4:25, he felt if he rolled over one more time he'd surly wake Crystal again. Sleep just wouldn't come. At 4:55 he laid there and willed himself to sleep and it must have worked because; Crystal leaving the bed for the bath room at 6:45, woke him and he groaned.

Not five minutes later Crystal was by his side inquiring if he felt okay. She'd never really seen him sick in all their years together, tired yes, but not sick. He begged her for an ant-acid tablet and one more hour of sleep. He said he felt sure that would work wonders and then he could get back to work. She didn't feel that that was too much to ask, so she woke the little tablet and let him sleep. At 9am when he rolled over and awoke to the hum of the washing machine, the dryer the dishwasher and rain hitting the window.

Vincent was sitting at the kitchen table with his first cup of coffee when his mother came waltzing in all excited with her news of culinary personal and agencies and meeting with people in all cities where they were building and getting that portion of their business up and running. He knew this was one of the things on their list to go over. Next Clive came in for another cup of coffee, Vincent didn't even know he was in the house. Rita joined them for a few minutes also excited about her full day in the studio with a popular singer working on her thirtieth album, looking for a new label. Aretha Franklin would be doing Who's Zooming Who here for the next several days. Today she's working on Freeway of Love. This end of the house could not escape all the excitement brought in by all that was going on. Crystal was no where around, she was on base checking her personal files. She'd be back by 10:30, the appointed time to start going over their 'lists'. Vincent had the next hour to himself to make the call to the broker of record for the properly in Wolfboro and make his appointment for the end of the week. This timing would work great, because Crystal was booked at the New Yorker for the weekend. Vincent excused himself from the kitchen to shower and dress for the day and make his call.

At precisely 10:10 Crystal was back with fresh danish and proceeded to make fresh coffee. Now spread out on the dinning room table were piles of folders, each representing a build site, they sat down to work. Crystal, with her mind satisfied that her personal files were secure and Vincent so busy and his mind so full of this project and the next site, the last location had not yet revisited his mind. With calendars, address books, employment agency numbers and personnel names, their attorney and Bull's number on speed dial, they were pretty much undisturbed and busy until after 3pm. The rain had stopped but the day remained cool and gray. They decided to walk to the hotel lounge for a cocktail and unwind a bit. They knew they'd continue to discuss 'everything', but that place wasn't home. It had a different aroma, a different feeling and different enveloping warmth.

Once seated, each with their drink, Crystal with her french braid tucked up under a stylish Italian silk as to help not be recognized, they started all over again, discussing everything they had just looked over. This time it was a conversation of self congratulations and happiness in the colors and styles and appearance and simple sophistication that they had so far seemed to achieve. Nothing was too over stated, but rather comfortable and attractive. They sat there just looking at one another, happy in their thoughts and with one another. This contentment brought about conversation about the people in their lives. How much Rita had contributed to the family and the corporation. The new recording studio and ability to juggle many things at the same time. Suzie pushing her weight around and becoming a major contributor in handling the dinning room, food and an event planner for each motel's event center. And then there was Clive. He had managed to hire a manager in each location handling every facet of every operation for each motel. Suzie may have started the ball rolling for each kitchen, but this manager finished the job with hiring the right people for food services, hiring staff, and bar tendering. There were cleaning services and staff for the motel rooms, laundry services needed everywhere there was a towel and landscaping and yard plowing for the winter. There was no service not tended to so far. At this they felt that they had hired all the right people. And they hadn't even had a grand opening...yet. The enormity of starting a business and then doing it again, all the same, in six different locations was...nuts. Once they reached this decision, they just giggled and ordered another drink. Crystal then invited Vincent to join her in New York for the weekend, but he informed her, he'd be in Wolfboro, NH while she was in New York.

Crystal's life had pretty much stayed on the same track, while it seemed that Vincent was recreating his life to fit his future. His future looked bright and busy and fulfilling and put him at the top of the heap for the motel business. He could recreate himself in each location as he wanted. As the money man, the maitre-D', the ass-hole to please, the answer man, the bosses husband, or have no role at all. He could build his name as the one to please, when the staff knew he was coming, everything needed to be spic-n-span! He knew he had a formidable and large physic and could play it any what he wanted. While Crystal remained the entertainer and the one with her name on the building! When she was in the house, the house was immaculate and running to capacity! That was the plan!

Chapter 57

Before Crystal even took the stage Saturday night, Vincent had the purchase and sale agreement for the most pristine 6.5 acres across the street from Lake Winnipesaukee faxed to the attorneys office. It was the beginning of the Wolfboro, NH project. Besides the beautiful lake. there were two draws to this location. Across the street there was a canoe club and snorkeling shop, right on the water and around the corner there was a Civic Center which hosted many events annually which always drew a crowd. Besides their weekly hot-rod gathering from May 1 through Labor day, August always has the Antique Road Show filmed there for a week. In September the Miss NH is held here at the Civic Center as is the Registered Dog Kennel show taped there. The Civic Center has a very professional team of promoters that keep the Center busy. That could pay off wonderfully for the motel. Having accomplished his goals for this location, Vincent hit the road again heading for Plymouth, MA.

Heading south to Massachusetts, Vincent's hands got sweaty and his heart had skipped a few beats. He just crossed the state line and entered Tyngsborough, a town he had never been to before or streets he had never traveled on before. Fine, just fine. Not all of Massachusetts looked like his Speer Street, he's sure he'll not bump into his daughter Andi over here. Just being in Massachusetts was messing with his head and his broken heart. In all the years he and Amy had lived here, they'd never traveled to Cape Cod. Plymouth, the town most on the channel and just before the bridges, that is what he was looking for. That's what

Crystal wanted… the feel of Cape Cod without the traffic and hassle of the bridges, so Vincent had his work cut out for him!

He had already spoken with Mrs. Lois Parameter of Parameter Realty right on Rt 6 in Plymouth, You can't miss us, we're in the shadow of the wooden windmill just behind us. And sure enough, 75 minutes later Vincent was making his approach to the wooden windmill and saw their office immediately. Lois was a pleasant woman and got the gist of what Vincent was looking for immediately. She explained that their area didn't have the attractions he was looking for, people just drove through town and continued to the Cape. They had the first Christmas Tree Shop and Basketville Stores that people drive from far to visit, so if you are offering an attractive lounge and dining room, that will do well in our area, we are surly lacking! Promoting your banquet room for large functions is also something that could do well around here. So after looking at some of the listings in her book, they took off for a drive to look more closely.

After an hour-and-a half riding around with Lois and learning the highlights of Plymouth and seeing the limited sites she had to show him, they returned to her office and Vincent said his farewell. Maybe there were other listings with other realtors, so far he was disappointed. It was a gorgeous area with beaches and historical sites of interest, and the ferry to Martha's Vineyard, just not what he needed. He continued to ride around and take the back roads, which lead to more back roads which all seam to get you back to route 6. So he went down Rt 6 another half a mile and took a right, he knew that lead to the beach, then he saw it! He was on top of a little bit of a crest, looking down to the ocean and half way down he saw it, a field of wild flowers, an old foundation sunken-in and the back of a sign. *Oh please be a for sale sign…what a site!* He slowly drove down to the field and tried to judge it's size, drove around to the front of the sign and sure enough, For Sale (by owner). He parked the car and walked to the sign, took a picture and prayed the vacant area in front of him was included. The sign stated 3.5 aces of field and 3 aces across the street, negotiable. That's what they had lawyers for…to negotiate! In his mind…SOLD! Now he was excited! *What a view!* From where he stood he saw only a few beach houses, many foot paths and countless patches of sea-grass all leading down to the white sandy beach before the beautiful blue ocean. He sat and couldn't get enough of the gorgeous view. *I was was in the Navy for 20 years, but still hadn't seen anything quite like this! I could live here! What it is about Massachusetts?* He drank it all in and got back in his car and drove out of Plymouth. He was thinking..*she's either gonna love it or think I'm crazy because there are no immediate 'attractions' to make people want to stay there. But there are...we'll just have to advertise more and sing the praises of the entire area!* While driving *he realized no motels to stop at, not even a good looking restaurant to entice him. That's all in our favor. It's still light out, I'm sleeping with my wife tonight, 3 hours and I should be there.* The thought of Crystal's warm body next to his while listening to her latest mixed music tape, kept him company all the way back to the New Yorker.

Chapter 58

1972

There weren't too many birthdays or anniversary's that Vincent remembered to shower Crystal with gifts or tender moments, so when he did the earth stood still for her. Today was one of those wonderful exceptions. He remembered Crystal's 45th birthday, arrived back in town to swing into the florist and pick-up the biggest bouquet of yellow roses and hand write her card, to say she was caught off guard is an understatement, this caught Crystal totally by surprise! The roses were exquisite but the personally written card was to die for! Vincent's handwriting expressed love and thankfulness for 'all'. Their years together, lots of adventures lots of luck and You always in my heart. The 6 motels carrying their name was keeping them busy, but they did it mostly together. At 45 years old on this 7th day of July 1972 he was so happy to have her!

Crystal loved life and everything it had brought to her. Her music, her home, the studio, their family, she felt loved. How many 45 year old's live with their mother? Now add dad and his new wife, who is Vincent's mom and for good measure add in mom's lover who just happens to be her boss. Yes, she is a happy woman surrounded by all of her favorite people. So to make this day even grander, Vincent planned a barbecue for dinner with half the base and Brad arriving with his gang. Just more people she considered family. A barbecue can make any day a great day, so to keep the reputation of having the best barbecue parties, even this Tuesday was going to shine and go in the record books as one to remember. You'd never know it's a Tuesday night if there is a barbecue on Shelby Street. It was rowdy, it was loud and it was fun, Karen heard about it, called Ruth and that added another layer of music to the affair well beyond midnight!

Finally Friday, Crystal's getting ready to head to New York and all of a sudden Vincent decides to join her for the ride. *Ah shit Crystal grumbles. I needed this ride to think, I'm a wreck…how can I play nice, nice with him? On the other hand maybe he'll be good company and he'll talk all the way.* With coffees to go they were heading for New York City. Crystal loved to drive, it was a mind relaxing exercise when she could talk to herself and always leave her dilemmas and problems behind, but this drive started off differently. Crystal started the ball rolling when she thanked Vincent again for the umpteenth time for the lovely flowers and the impromptu party for her birthday. She voiced how genuinely surprised she was by his generosity and the care he took with all of the preparations. He was reading her like a book and thought it would be easy to persuade her of his newest idea, she was in a thankful and good mood! Vincent had his own agenda and needed the 3 hour ride to discuss it with her, so with her kind words and positive attitude, he gushed his "Your welcome, it turned out really well. It was fun, and I loved the look on your face when the flowers arrived!" Then the drive became quiet, too quiet, too long so she pushed the buttons and her mixed tape began to play. Not ten seconds later, Vincent pushed the buttons again to stop the tape, but before he could speak Crystal asked "OK, what's on your mind?"

Then the flood gates opened! Vincent was all excited about dropping her in New York and heading to Connecticut to find a spot for another motel. He started listing towns and major routes and informed her that he had a couple of the little cameras with him so he could keep her informed every step of the way. The first six were built and making money and needed very little attention from either one of them and there were still two more states in New England that needed to be explored. I can start in Connecticut and be back by the end of your intermission Sunday night. Then we'll have a nightcap together, discuss what I saw, talk about your shows, sleep in the 'wonderful' bed of yours and be able to drive home together in the morning. Now he looked at her face and she was grinning from ear to ear. Without breaking her grim she asked, "Are you done? You can breathe now...how long have you been thinking about this?" He grinned right back at her and said "You know I love sleeping with you and that bed does wonderful things to me! That's what takes my breathe away." "You ass, I'm the one that takes your breathe away, so you'd better be back to be ravished and with acceptable pictures to boot!"

"Are you serious, we can do it again? Then I was thinking when you go to Vegas in September I could go to Maine and look around for suitable space there as well. Then when I call Bull, we'd be offering him two build sites." Long pause…. "Like I said before. How long have you been thinking about this?" Crystal was completely taken back by his logical train of thought and suggesting two builds right off the bat! "It will be easier for us this time around, we know what to do and I think we can count on the same people to make sure we hire correctly. At least we know where to start. And to answer your question, I've never stopped thinking about the last two states. It's just lately with everything running smoothly and not much to do, I need a new adventure. Only this time it will be an adventure of location, not scary are we doing the right thing, kinda thoughts! We did good six times, please can we do it at least these, two more times?"

Chapter 59

By the time Crystal pulled into the self parking garage at the New Yorker it was all set, Vincent Was heading to Connecticut. Once again he was like a kid in a candy store. He promised he'd be back by 11:59pm Sunday night, catch her final curtain and be ready for that night-cap. They were both excited about this prospect. Vincent had done it again, sold Crystal on his exciting venture and flew away on his magic carpet. At least that's the way Crystal saw it! On the other hand, she had to admit, he did good work, the motels were exceptionally well done and had a great reputation! Here we go again was her feeling when Vincent kissed her good-bye and left the garage.

Her head was working overtime and she talked to herself all the way to her room. *Had he done the mileage between sites, what towns was he headed for? He mentioned near the airport, colleges in both Ct and Ma as a draw for a motel. Be good Crystal, have faith!! He needs this to stay busy. His life has been in turmoil for 5 years now. I'd say he is doing remarkably well! He is still a virile man with many attributes, I should know. Unless he does it on the side, there has been no news nor has he mentioned his families in quite awhile. Cause for concern...I hope not...that was a lifetime ago...I hope he has been able to move on, these motels should be just the ticket to occupy his mind and his time; I can't deny he needs the diversion, at least these are healthy ones...expensive but healthy and lucrative! I am a little older now and not much has happened in my life to change or alter my course of career or ability to continue to build motels. Thank You Vincent, but I want to go with you when you head to Maine...September would be a grand time to travel north for great foliage, then when we get back I can head to Vegas for my one month's pre-holiday shows. After that I'll see about taking a couple of months off. Gee... am I building a mini Maine vacation in my head. In my head and in my panties, yup, Vincent you'd better be back here Sunday night. I can just picture the Maine sky line from our hotel room. I want a build with this view! Very colorful in front of a mountain with their peeks lost in the clouds. A sunset that radiates every color of the rainbow and then some! OK, I'm on board, more than I thought I would be. Maine in September. Fresh caught lobster and clam chowder. OK girl, get your head out of the clouds...lunch must be next.*

Her room felt a little stuffy...it shouldn't, the hotel was air quality controlled. One call down to the front desk had her head reeling with the news that the entire fourth floor was without proper ventilation or air conditioning. The mechanical works had zoned out and failed about 8 hours ago. Being a Friday in New York City in July heat every air conditioner in the city was working overtime. Many had failed! The maintenance department for the hotel was in a scramble to fix the problem with no success... yet. Eight hours without proper ventilation in this heat was cause for concern. *They'd get it fixed...go and eat....*

Walking outside was no walk in the part...it was too hot, so she ducked into the first 'sub-shop' advertising air-conditioning. It was small, it was cool and it smelled like everything they had ever grilled! She couldn't stay. She crossed the street and was greeted with the tallest, longest cockroach she had ever seen just walking out of the ten-foot double sliding door, open to the sidewalk to the 'Jack-in-the-Box'. Nope don't want to eat there! Now she found herself at a 'Juice Bar'. Inside was cool and smelled sweet, the menu listed many different blended drinks using many different... even exotic juices. Boy were they expensive, but nothing to eat. Moving on, feeling like a tourist in a city she had never visited before she could feel her hair sticking to her neck and her sandled feet start to melt into the sidewalk from the heat. This is not a city to get lost in or drop to the ground from heat exposure of exhaustion alone or without identification. If she went on too much longer without food, that's what she felt would happen to her. Now she was walking past an outside coffee shop that didn't offer more than egg sandwiches, she didn't want that. She wanted to be inside where it was cool eating something ... *who is that touching me and walking me briskly into, my hair is in my eyes and I can't reach...Clive!*

"I need lunch too and you looked like you were ready to drop right there on the street! It's cool in here, sit down and talk to me." "You sure are a sight for sore eyes, I thought I'd see you around four when you made your entrance upstairs." Crystal's cheeks were all flushed and her eyes looked glassy but she couldn't take them off of Clive. He said "we'd better eat quickly if we intend to make it there soon" Again, a blank stare from Crystal. "How long have you been walking around out there, lady?" "Don't know, but I'm hungry" Clive disappeared for only a few minutes and returned with ice water, ice tea and stuffed strombolis. Crystal ate like she had never eaten before. With the nourishment and cold drinks her color began to return to normal. Clive asked again, "how long had you been walking around out there?" Crystal tried to shrug it off like it was no big deal, but when he told her it was quarter before four right now, it stilled her. When she asked "where are we" it stilled him. They needed a taxi to get back to the New Yorker. There was no way he was going to let her walk the three miles back, not in this heat!

When they got back to the hotel, Crystal remembered the foul smell in her room and the heat! She went to the desk and inquired into another room and was told to wait a minute. Clive went straight up to the 4th floor. For the next five minutes of so she became a people watcher; waiting for, she didn't know what. People are really strange! She saw stripes over plaid, colors to laugh at; these girls thought they looked so fine! And guys wearing neon and carrying pocketbooks. She saw one gal with hair cut to her ear on one side and pony-tailed on the other. Strange...really strange. Finally Mr. Brentwhistle came out and sat next to her in the sunken, elaborately decorated waiting area in front of the reservation desk. "Sorry about your room Crystal, but you can imagine that with a whole floor not usable right now we're in a bit of a pickle. I do have a room for you however; have you ever slept on a water bed?" Crystal broke out in a half smile and said "that sounds like fun". Brentwhistle handed her a key card for room 3914 and told her housekeeping would be along to help her get whatever she needed out of the room on the fourth floor, don't know how long you will be displaced like this, but at least we got you a bed! "Not to worry and thanks, I'll be ready for my show by 8.

Crystal was accompanied to the fourth floor by a young man with a valet cage and they nearly emptied her rooms. Next up to room 3914 they went. The layout of the room was the same but the decor was entirely different. *OH fun she thought, it'll be like staying someplace different. Wait until Vincent gets a load of this. First* she sat, then layed on the bed and bounced her bum! Above her head was a net of purple with large green leaves and tiny white flowers sprinkled all over it. The wall paper all around the room was textured white with small green leaves and small purple flowers. The bed spread was white with green threads running through it. A person with a wild imagination did this room. Crystal loved it! No more time to recline like this. Time to get ready for the show. The room had rejuvenated her, the shower invigorated her and the lateness of the hour made her nervous as hell.

Hair done in a french braid with a black ribbon braided throughout, long black shirt with a slit half way up her leg, tiny silver slippers all topped with a sparkling silver tunic, light-weight jacket. Now she added dangling silver tear-drop earnings that caught the light every time she moved. She was the picture of pure perfection! Now to sound like angels tip-toeing across the piano keys and the night would be a success. She still got nervous until after the first applause. That was acceptance, and then she could really turn on the charm and continue the show at ease. She wasn't really new at this, but each audience made her stronger.

Twelve fifteen and all is well. Before the show was over there was standing room only and that's because the eleven o'clock shift leaving... didn't! They lined the walls of her theater and stayed until she was done. Crystal's personality and show and appearance captivated everyone at the New Yorker. There was nothing about her that people didn't like or admire.

In the meantime Vincent had a leisurely ride up to and through Connecticut scouting out the interesting and available land to build on. He knew what he wanted and felt he'd know it when he saw it. He also knew the area in which he really wanted to look so with his eyes wide open across Connecticut he still headed north to the Bradley Airport area. But taking the side roads and traveling right, then north and west again, he had no idea where he was but there it was...for sale...6.5 aces. Flat, beautiful with a broken down barn sitting in the middle collecting every piece of rubbish that blows across that field. He needed to get closer, read the sign and take several pictures. Tariffville, don't blink, you'll miss us! Is what the sign said. Call Todd at 5889 for more information. Not much to go on, but at least he had a name and a number. He drove on for another half a mile straight to the Farmingdale Race Track.

Huge area with loads of parking and signs and pictures of horses everywhere you looked. *Now that's more like it...an airport, rail station close by, surrounded by colleges, major race track. Keep driving what else is there?* Past the track he entered an industrial area with a fire department and police department. He turned right and drove straight into a shanty down-town area. Not much of a draw or even to look at but it had a bar, and that was enough for him. Not too bad and it had a limited lunch menu. Wonderful, a beer and a burger, a map and a chatty bar tender, just what he needed.

Waiting for the burger, Vincent chatted up the bar keeper and found out almost everything he needed to know about the area. Including this November, the state had a gambling question on the ballet. Allow it or not...yes or no..simple. "It'll pass hands down, then watch this area grow," the bar keeper predicted. *That's all I needed to know, thank you sir!*

It was only 2pm and Vincent felt like he had the tiger by the tail. This area was just 15 minutes to anywhere you needed to be, a rail station, airport, major city and hospitals. Colleges in every direction to bring in the overnighters, parents, grandparents. Crystal's major question .. where do couples go for a wedding venue, or major celebration of any kind. He still needed to ask that question, so next he ventured to the next intersection and took another right. This time the area was an out-skirt of a college. He drove around a little more and found the

Tariffville Central Library. *Why not…look at a few maps, get the lay of the land, ask about Todd and the land for sale, ask the venue question if there is anyone around that 'wants' to talk. This could be a valuable few minutes or a big waste of time…*

Men don't have the same kind of "women are looking at me" antennas that most women have. When Crystal walks into a room, or down the street, she knows she is being watched. Not so with Vincent. His tall, dark, and handsome physique causes even some men to do a double take, he's that tall and that good looking, but he rarely thinks about it. So this Friday afternoon when he walked into this library looking like he had a million questions to ask, Ms. Shirley was right there to lend him an ear or a hand or whatever else he was needing! Now that feeling on the back of his neck told him that Ms. Shirley had her tentacles out and she was sniffing! Not a great way to size up a woman, but she was downright possessive, like stay back he's mine! Taking advantage of her 'friendless' she confirmed with the help of maps that he was right where he wanted to be. The town had everything and more with gambling almost here. She also conveyed the fact that most brides hire a hotel hall in Hartford for their nuptials and dinner after. She didn't know of too many other types of large gatherings. Most people around here are not the party type of people. Not until you get into the college crowd. The horse track has a couple of bars, but she could not go so far as to call them lounges. No restaurants, just fast food. She had no information on Todd. Not his family or connection with the land. Once he got back to his car, he could not call it a complete waste of time, he did find out a few things. Still driving around, heading in the direction of the train station, he'd find a phone and call the Todd number.

The 30 minute drive back to the train station did not net him any further lots or buildings for sale. The call to Todd was fruitful, Todd actually answered on the third ring, he said he'd meet Vincent on the lot in fifteen minutes. Fine, why not, he'd drive back. After kicking up dirt and road trash for an hour, walking the land with Todd and taking more pictures, they landed back at the bar where Vincent had his lunch. Todd was an old farmer, no family left. He was the only son of an old farmer and lost his only son in Viet Nam five years ago. The stress of that killed his wife of 47 years. No reason to hold on to the land anymore. "You want it, give me enough money to live the rest of my life comfortably" was all he said! "I'm not a gambling man so I can give a dang about the race track or any other kind of game of chance!" Knowing what he and Crystal had paid for similar acreage he threw the old man a low ball number and after almost physically chocking, Todd put out his hand to shake on it before Vincent could change his mind! Now Vincent 'almost' felt guilty for his low offer, but proceeded to write up a simple purchase agreement for Todd to sign and had the bartender sign it as a witness. Took a picture of the document and the bartender, the bartender took a picture of Vincent handing Todd the prerequisite twenty dollar down payment (2 $10 bills) to seal the deal, just because. After another beer he thought, *how easy was that! The cost of a couple of beers, this was a walk in the park. Wait until I tell Crystal about THIS transaction.*

Now that it was pretty much a done deal, Todd and Vincent shared another beer together and started talking like old friends. Vincent told him the plans for the land and the building that they intended to build. Told him the name of the chain already in existence, but he didn't know one motel from another. It came around to the fact that Todd and his wife loved to listen to music together. They loved to dance or just sit on their front porch and listen to the radio. Vincent shared that he was recently a retired Navy man and his wife was a pianist with a few records of her music playing on the radio. Todd added he still loved to listen to the radio, "who is your wife and what are the titles of her songs. Vincent complied with Meadow Memories...and Todd but cut him off with "Oh, I love that song, I love it both ways, with and without words! Son, I think you're paying me way too much for the land, I'd have given it to you for a meet and greet with your wife!" Vincent slapped the old man on the back shook his hand and told him he had a reserved table in the lounge for a beer anytime he wanted to come and listen to Crystal play.

It's not even 6pm, it's still Friday and Crystal's working. Now what?

Vincent got in his car and headed south. Not even 60 minutes later he was in the middle of a traffic jam. Cars all over the place, street lights every 200 feet, do not turn, left turn only, one way-do not enter, Hartford Medical Center, turn here with a large arrow. *Oh, so I'm in Hartford. This is rush hour. Get off the road you fool. Find a place for dinner and get off the road!* Easier said than done, but Kens Steak House sure did sound good so he followed the directions from the bill board, thanked the road gods that he still had daylight and was parking his car safely twenty minutes later.

He'd had enough of a bar for one day so he opted to sit in the dinning room. When being shown to his booth, he felt a pair of eyes follow his every step. He ordered a drink from his waitress but in doing so made eye contact with the stunning woman sitting at the bar who had watched his every move. When his single cocktail was delivered, she surmised he was alone. Within minutes she slid into the bench at this table opposite him and said "I'm drinking vodka tonics, would you be so kind! He merely lifted his left hand a tiny bit and his waitress gave him an affirmative wave. *Wow, he thought, not even 8pm, no...closer to 7:30...is she working or really hard up, I'm twice her age!?*

Her drink arrived and she said "thanks, I'm Donna". They drank in virtual silence until she said "and your name is?" "Keith" he answered immediately.

"I'm sure you've heard this many times, so I will repeat, you are a very striking woman, with that head of red hair. So are you flaunting a natural look or a certain bottle brand?" She just starred at him, juggling in her mind her next comment and response (*I'm not going to waste a perfectly good drink on him, but if I had a glass of water, he'd be wearing it!...so here goes...*) while rubbing her bare foot (she kicked off her heels) up and then slowly down his leg, she leaned in a little closer on the table, showing no bosom, "there is only one layer you'd need to peal away to check out the real thing." "That's a very bold and forward statement to be making to a man you've just met." He met and held her eyes. She shared right back and didn't miss a beat with "I know what I like when I see it, so if you want to see it will it be your room or mine?" She downed her drink, slipped her feet back into her heels and stood by his side of the booth, "which will it be?" Taking the challenge, he downed his drink, stood, took her hand and said "Yours."

Twenty minutes later, after holding her hand the entire time they crossed the street and went to room 412 of the Embassy of Hartford Hotel, where he didn't have to wait long to see the real thing. "Peal away and feast your eyes" she said this while lifting the hem of her long dress up to her knees..."you can help ya know, I don't bite." With the invitation made, he proceeded to lift the dress over her slim body and over her head. Her arms went straight up to enable him to lift the dress away from her body. In doing so he removed the one layer and witnessed the most perfect, mannequin molded, feminine body he had ever seen! Firm and tight, nipples dimpling on top of beautifully rounded breasts no bigger than a 13-year-old's. Pulling his eyes away from the entire form, he let them fall on the strawberry patch that looked like it was ready to picked! He asked, "what is the drinking age in Connecticut?" She giggled (started advancing and unbuttoning his trousers and loosening his belt) and replied, "I am plenty old enough to enjoy a cocktail in a public place and experienced enough to want to play with a prick longer than I've ever had before! "I want you to rock my world, while I give you a wild ride!" "Lady... you're on." Again she giggled... "Not yet, but very soon, soon indeed!" as she led him to the bed.

Vincent left room 412 of the Embassy of Hartford Hotel at four-fifteen in the morning with Donna sound asleep on her side of the bed. *Damn Crystal's still working and it's only just Saturday.* He walked to his car in the Steak House parking lot and drove away. Drove to places unknown, but at lease at this hour there was no traffic. Then it hit him...*I'm starved, I haven't eaten since lunch, many hours ago.* Then he saw it...a billboard advertising Denny's open 24 hours, serving breakfast anytime. *Perfect!*

Sitting at a table 30 minutes later savoring his hot, black coffee, he needed to think of something to do to fill the rest of his day, two days actually. Somehow he needed to inform Crystal that he had found and put a down payment on the perfect Connecticut piece of land, they'd be ready to start building again. He felt proud and happy of this accomplishment and also sexually spent and used by that little red head. *I managed to fill her all right, she'll not want another long, wide, stiff penis in a while. She'd better 'stick' with the little boys! Good glory be!! What have I become? I've kinda had three wives in the past twenty-five years and never cheated on them. What am I doing to poor Crystal. She'd never forgive me for this! Back-up you fool...who are you kidding...I've been cheating on Crystal her whole married life. I think the University of Connecticut is here in Hartford someplace, I'll find the library and fax Crystal the bill of sale and copy of the Purchase agreement that I have from Todd. He was a sweet old man. He'll love Crystal.*

After his hearty breakfast, Vincent was now finishing up with more coffee and a sweet cinnamon roll. Reading the paper he was just trying to kill time before getting back on the road and finding UConn. In the paper he found the actual street address of the school so he felt one step closer to communicating with Crystal. *Damn it, I'll be faxing these items to Rita, I'll have to call Crystal and tell her about it and the old man Todd. It'll be nice to hear her voice. I just can't call her too early, she was up until after midnight finishing her show.*

When Vincent was back on the road again, there was a little bit of pink in the brightening morning sky. No more self recrimination, he felt good. Driving around in the city in the morning with no traffic was easy. Finding the school was also easy and didn't take any time at all. Vincent found that when driving around the campus it brought back memories of being on the grounds of Rensselaer Polytechnic Institute when Rockwell and Kevin were in school. *Not good Vincent, knock it off,* now he realized he was talking to himself... *thinking about his son wouldn't do him any good. He'd been doing so good lately and Crystal was a champ in giving him 'chart-blanch' to keep him occupied! You have a job to do, so get on it and phone home.* Still driving around he found the cafeteria that he'd need later, but right now he was still looking for the library. *All of these old brick buildings covered with ivy and topped with flags a flying, carbon copy of Rensselaer in New York. Oh Rockwell whatever happened to you? You've left a hole in my heart and a question in your mother's that we still can't fill. Someday...maybe...please!!* There, the library. *Good, time to change my thinking.*

The young library aid, that helped Vincent to first copy his documents and then using those copies fax them to Rita, was immediately smitten with Vincent. She couldn't keep her mind on his business requests, but rather totally on him! She asked "are you a teacher here?", all breathless and flirty! Before he knew what was coming out of his mouth, he was Mr. Keith Rogers, the new Professor of Business Practices. "It's an elective course as a freshman, but a must pass the next three years in Law, Business Law and Civic Responsibility. I'm afraid I'm going to be a very busy man. What's your major?" With a frown and downward glance she answered, "English Lit, none of your classes fit." *He was immediately relieved.* "Well, thanks for your help, I know it's only July but I've got a million things to do. First a phone call... then..."she interrupted with, "the cafeteria has a lot of phones."

He couldn't get out of there fast enough. Too young, too eager and too much! But when he stepped out into the sunshine and ivy covered walls again his thoughts turned back a few years and....*Some pictures and certain feelings or some thoughts are triggers, he was missing his kids, his kids were now in the heavens and in the hands of God. Andrea's child would be about 8 years old now...I can't even claim my own grandchild... thanks Crystal...knock it off, it's not her fault...I screwed up and caused a lot of people a great deal of pain. Crystal's motives were always good. She managed to do exactly what I asked her to do. Enough...someday I will be a fly on the wall and know what my kids have been up to. But now step it up and find those phones. So next* he headed over to the cafeteria. The first thing he saw when he walked in was a wall of pay phones. *Wonderful, a quick coffee then I can call Crystal. No, still too early.* He grabbed a coffee and a local newspaper. Killing time he read most of the ads and a couple of feature stories that peaked his interest. Still too early to call, but look at what just walked in that totally peaked his interest! After paying for her coffee and English muffin, she made a bee-line for his table with a shit-eating grin and said, "Civic Responsibility how nice, I'll finally have someone with some intelligence to talk to. Mr. Rogers, I presume, Maggie Henderson, nice to meet you" she said as she sat down opposite him at his table. "How..." was all he could get out. "My daughter over in the library. She didn't lie, you are the prettiest and biggest thing around here. Can I help you find your way around"? "Thanks, but no, not just yet. I needed to let some people back home know that I made it here okay, hence the library, but that being done, now I'm waiting and wasting time until my next appointment." "Ya my daughter showed me your notes for your fax, are you buying land and building a house? Across from the race track is not the best location for that...all the traffic and noise...it gets pretty busy over there." *Oh how he loved hearing that!* Just looking for now. *Holy shit, too early for this, I've got to get out of here and never come back. I'd love to sweep her off her feet. She looked and almost sounded like she'd be a good candidate for some action tonight, or now as a matter of fact or at least later today. Down boy, get out of town...now!*

"Nice to meet you Maggie Henderson, looking forward to some interesting conversations" was all he said as he walked to a phone booth and called Crystal's room number. It went unanswered, he was concerned and called the desk. Now he finds out she in a different room and this gal can connect the call. Crystal sounded wide awake and very happy to hear his voice. All excited she couldn't wait to tell him about sleeping on a water bed last night. "We'll need to christian it when you get here," she said. He told her about the land and the area and about old Todd. He also told her he sent, he hopes binding information to Rita, because he believes he bought the land. Now she was over the top excited and said she'd call Rita as soon as they hang up. "When are you going to get here?" she asked. He hemmed and hawd, but finally said, "just like I said before, before your curtain call Sunday night. I promised I'd be there and I will." "Why, still late Sunday? You did your job, Now what are you going to do?" "I thought I'd take a ride up to Hopewell Junction and look over Grandma's old place. I can't see me sitting around the city waiting for you to finish. We'll have a great night-cap and head home Monday morning just as planned." As always she caved, said "miss you loads, but Sunday night it is, drive carefully" and hung up! Relief washed through Vincent because he knew he had just bought himself all day today, tonight and until nearly mid-night tomorrow night.

When he hung up and pushed himself away from the wall with the hand he had holding his body in a leaning position with, there stood Maggie. Wanting and ready to continue their conversation. "I heard enough to know that you have until midnight Sunday, so what do you want to do? I could show you around the school, show you around Hartford or take you home and show you all of me and what you'd be missing if you choose either of the first two options." She merely ran her index finger under the collar of his shirt to the back of his neck, then slowly back again, never loosing eye contact with him until she moved that finger to outline his lips. She watched her finger for a heart beat, until the lips started to smile then moved her eyes back up to find his eyes also smiling back at her. My car is in the lot parked right next to the one with New Jersey plates, so if you follow me, you can save me the chore of having to make my bed.

Vincent walked with Maggie out of the door, down the steps to the parking lot where they each got in their own cars. Out of the lot and three turns later Vincent was being shown into a mid-century mansion with pillars at the front porch which hosted front doors that stood at least fourteen feet tall. Once inside, there was no time to look around and take in his surroundings. Maggie was a fast woman and didn't waste any time getting him up the stairs, through her dressing room and into an elegant bedroom, where in-deed, the bed hadn't been made! While slipping off his shoes, Maggie had her hands busy at his clothing and had him comfortably in bed before she even had the pins out of her hair, but when she did, they released almost as much hair as Crystals! She knew she had his total attention at the drop of her hair. So working her long dress up and over her head, left her naked and ready to play.

Every woman marveled at Vincent's manhood and stamina. Maggie was no different. But without knowing it, Vincent was learning to play games. He kissed and fondled and fingered and teased, snuggled and spooned, sucked and rocked. He came and made her come, not once by several times, the groans and whimpers and breathing that filled the room gave credence to the sexual behavior happening over and over again. Since Vincent hung up the phone with Crystal, at least five hours ago...he hadn't said one word! Even now, with Maggie leaning up on one elbow watching every move Vincent made, he dressed, stood in front of her mirror, combed his hair, went back and bent over her, fondled her left breast, kissed her lips and left. A few minutes later, from her upstairs window, she watched him leave her house.

Damn, I starved. I like Hartford, there are plenty of places to eat. Twenty minutes later he was pulling into First and Last Tavern of Hartford, a little place serving Italian. He shouldn't have looked so hungry and comfortable and sure of himself all at the same time because that look had the three waitress all wanting to be his server. They were working, so flaunting his maleness and flirting with the three of them got him great service, a huge helping for desert and three phone numbers. The third was written on the back of his American Express charge slip in the lips of a smile, under a note...off at 3. He guessed she was the one closest to his age, the tallest and by far the prettier of the three. He liked women with very little make-up and understated jewelry, she fit that bill as well.

"Appreciate it" he said, as he signed his slip, and let is fingers linger on her hand as he returned her pen, then added "only passing through on my way to New York." He winked and walked out.

Early afternoon on this beautiful, sunny, Saturday, Vincent was now on his way to Hopewell Junction, just as he told Crystal. His grandmother was long gone, but he loved that area and he enjoyed driving so it was just the right time to take this ride. His work was done, he believed he bought the right piece of land in this area for their last motel and spending his leisure time doing the things he enjoyed was his right. He knew he'd be bored in New York with Crystal working so here he was. *A race track, are they running this weekend? There are signs posted all over the place...I'll go and find out.*

Thirty-five minutes later Vincent was back in front of the track reading the headlines for the weekend races. Sunday, tomorrow Post Parade promptly at 1pm, 11 races including two trifectas, a quinella and a daily double. Pulling his mind away from the tract, he now focused on the land across the street. *Yep, this is going to be a good place. It's going to set a different tempo, but I bet it will be one of our best! Okay my time schedule is now set...drive to Hopewell, spend the night and get back here by post time. This is gong to be a great weekend!*

Vincent drove straight to where grandma's house used to be. Now he drove around town some more, a little slower with his eyes wide open. The 80's hadn't been good to his childhood memories. The church was still there but the addition to the library was huge and it backed up to the playground which encompassed four tennis courts and two baseball diamonds, all new. The growth in the town was tremendous. The new school...no, two new schools. One elementary and the high school just off the center of town, wow! *I'm heading back toward grandma's. This is unreal...her house gone, her fields, the entire area, now all built up. There has to be 50 or more new houses around here! I should never have come back! This is not where I built all of those special memories. I've heard it said "you can never go home". Of course not, they ripped it all out and changed everything!*

With his heart a little crushed, he took the other road to get back into town and noticed HIS elementary school house of one story, consisting of four classrooms, one in each corner, with a wonderful center activity space, was now a two story center building with one story additions on all four sides. The sign out front still read "Hopewell Center for Learning, grades 1-6". The town now had two elementary schools and a new and larger high school. *I'm glad I'm not raising kids in this town. But the growth everywhere must be about the same. It's just my town isn't the same any more!* Knowing he wanted to head southwest in the direction of Hartford., he drove into the late setting sun. *Baloney, I don't need to do this, I don't need to arrive back there until tomorrow noon time or so. I'll just get out of Hopewell and hope for the best.* When he was driving along side of the river and saw the signs for Fahnestock State Park he remembered a quaint little town and headed in that direction.

Nothing is quaint anymore. Henderson's Hardware was still on the corner as he remembered but it was adjacent to a bridal and tuxedo shop. There were gas stations on every corner with drug stores, doughnut shops, McDonald's and supermarkets everywhere he looked. He just pasted a billboard advertising the new "Out-Door Mall" at North High-Land Hills...*Boy things have changed! There, the hotel...a good meal and a good nights sleep and I'll head back to the race track in the morning.*

Vincent pulled around front of the Pelton Arms Hotel and idled at the Valet sign. A short middle-aged man in a blue uniform with white shirt and tie arrived to relieve Vincent of his car and wished him a good night. Tucking his ticket in his back pocket, he proceeded to the reservation desk to get a room for the night and inquire about their dinning room. *It was a good time to check-in, 5pm on the dot...all rooms should now be cleaned and available...he was thinking like an Inn owner!.* Anytime he stopped at a place like this he always took their advertising brochures and made mental notes on everything. What do they do that we could do or do better? Stops like this are always a learning experience. He was assigned room 535, non-smoking as requested. Entering the elevator he made note of the music, nice touch. His room had a king size bed, was nicely furnished with dark wood end tables, a tall dresser and a long narrow table of the same dark wood. The table had matching holstered arm chairs in a masculine green plaid on each end, which accented the lighter green carpet and pull drapes. On top of the dresser stood a TV with remote, and alarm clock on one end table and matching lamps on each. The bathroom had a mounted or hand-held shower nozzle with an adjustable head. *Very nice, that's our next upgrade.*

Still taking everything in, Vincent went back to the elevator and selected the restaurants button. The door opened to your choice of Chinese cuisine at Nancy Chang's or burgers at Johnny Rockets or Italian at Vinny's or good old steak at Beef & Chops and last but not least an All American Buffet...4 choices $6.95, 6 choices $8.95...all you can eat, one trip through $12.95. *This is unique, he thought.* Having taken only about six or seven steps away from the elevator, he still stood there quite perplexed as to what to choose for dinner. He stood on a tiled floor, about 12 feet around showcasing each restaurant with lovely plants at each door opening and a hostess ready to seat you on your approach. He was quite confused until Michele linked her arm with his and announced she had been craving Chinese food all day. "When you are really hungry nothing satisfies with all of the different selections, especially when ordering with somebody else, then you have double the selections." As she was pulling Vincent toward Nancy Chang's she went on and on about how much she loved the MaiTai's at Chinese restaurants. Before actually being shown to their table, Michele turned to Vincent and said "I know this is terribly presumptuous of me, but I hate to eat alone." Vincent simply said "me too", and they were shown to a table. Immediately their drink orders were taken and they both ordered a MaiTai. Now, Michele reached across the table to shake Vincent's hand and introduce herself.

Their dinner was wonderful, despite the way it started, they learned a lot about one another, enjoyed another drink and ate to their hearts content. Vincent was looking forward to an early shower, he missed his this morning, a little TV and a good nights sleep. He had a room waiting for him and he honestly wanted to get back to it. Michele was a lovely woman and a great conversationalist and she greatly appreciated Vincent picking up the entire dinner tab. Vincent thought with his peck on her cheek, he had said goodnight to her at the elevator, but she followed him right in and road to the 5th floor with him. She also got out on his floor. "This is quite a coincidence", Vincent said to her. She replied with "No it isn't, I'm coming with you". "Ms. McIntyre I am a married man" Vincent said as he unlocked his room door and started to walk in. "I wish I were a married woman Mr. Rogers, but I'm not. If I were, I wouldn't need to stalk good looking hunks like you, get what I want and in return pleasure the hell out of you." He was in the room, she followed and closed the door. As she proceeded to unbutton her blouse, she said, "come on Keith, your wife isn't here and I am." The blouse landed on the bed and she removed two condoms from her skirt pocket and put them on the bed table. Now the skirt joined her blouse on the bed. She slipped off her sandals, walked over to Vincent and helped him take off his shirt. She sat him on the bed and untied his shoes and relieved him of them. Next she helped him take off his pants. He played dumb and said "It's been a long time since a woman has undressed me. What else are you going to do for me?" "You said shower, right?" She went into the bathroom and turned on the water in the shower. By the time Vincent got there, the room was nice and steamy and she was stark naked. He was quick to loose the rest of his clothes and they both stepped into the walk-in shower stall. It was almost sensual with the way they approached each others body, slowly and gently. Now came the soap, slowly and in a cleansing manner, for each of them. Michele stepped very close to Vincent, took his hands, got up on her tip toes and asked him "are you afraid of me?" He lied and answered "no, I'm just not accustomed to stepping out on my wife." She asked, "do you like my body?" She was still very close to him and only touching his arms or chest. At the question Vincent reached up and cupped her breasts, leaned down to her ear and softly said, "Yes, very much," At that she reached down and wrapped her hands around his penis and said "I'm glad I picked you, you are magnificent! I knew the minute I saw you I wanted you inside me. You were so easy to talk to, I know you will be very easy to ride, that's my favorite sexual position because it gives you favorable finger access to my clitoris. Touch me there and the organism will be immediate! I want to enjoy you for a long time so don't be to fast to make me come, it makes me tied." He asked "are we done in the shower...can we go to bed now or do I need more lessons?" She giggled and said "Oh let me count the lessons I could teach you Mr. Rogers., but only after you shut off the water and follow me." Like the good little student, Mr. Rogers turned off the water and followed Michele to the bed.

Michele was a very appreciative woman when she had Vincent on his back and she was applying the condom to his engorged penis. "Oh yes, I definitely want to ride this for a long time. Just make believe I'm you wife and get bored, I know how to please myself." "Believe me girl, you won't need to do that, and believe me, my wife is not boring, but please take it easy and be careful, that might be too much for you, as she was still 'handling" his penis. You're young and small and may not be deep enough to take the whole thing all at once." The concern in his voice really touched her. Now it was his turn to giggle a little. "Ya know Michele, it has been a hell of a long time since I've worn a condom, it rather feels good, nice and tight, like I expect you to be."

She bent down over him and kissed him soundly then straddled him and slowly lowered her body down over his penis that was reaching up into her, but not enough. She lifted her body and tried again, but entry was not happening! He rolled her over saying, "sweaty, I've fathered 12 children and never left a woman in my bed without tears of joy, quivering joints and exhausted beyond orgasmic pleasure. Prepare to be exhausted."...and in doing so kissed her with a vengeance. Tongue working her mouth while his fingers worked her clitoris and he bent her leg to fold his penis behind her knee. She moved and he moved his penis between her breasts, while tweaking her nipples then moving his mouth to hers again for a kiss that would moisten every part of her and allow him to gently push his penis into her waiting and wanting hot center. He'd push and stop, repeat, push and stop, she'd lift her hips for more, he'd push again and stop she whimpered a little, he asked "do you want more", Oh yes...big sigh...please" he pushed once more and felt a barrier, he reached her end. He filled her, now it was time to move her to fulfillment! He pulled out a bit, pushed back in...relaxed...pulled out a little more, let his body weight down on her a bit more. Pulled nearly all the way out and slowly filled her again. His kiss had her hips plunging him even deeper, had him pumping her until he felt at the point of no return and he stopped! She groaned and held his ass down until she could breathe again then her tongue found his and his penis took on a mind of it own and pulsed inward and made him retreat to just repeat the entire process. He couldn't believe her stamina, but he matched it and when the organism started again he laid her over and he stayed on his side, held her arms above her head with one of his hands while the other helped to push her ass into him for deeper penetration. He continued to kiss her with tongue matching the penis trusts until she broke. Body gyrations, tears and hiccups until she laid flat from exhaustion, then he cupped one breast and sucked gently on the other while gentle cupping and squeezing her throbbing pussy. "That's more like it he said… Are you happy yet? He then added, that was really good, much better than this morning."

"Okay Michele, up and at-um… as he sat up in bed...I need a good nights sleep, I have an appointment at 1pm tomorrow back in Connecticut and then another at mid-night with my wife in New York, busy day coming up. And I am looking forward to another sexual, very robust trip... or two around the world... on a water bed... to boot!"

"Twelve kids? Did I hear you right, and she still wants to mess around? You did her this morning and still had the energy I just felt?" Vincent got out of bed, bent over Michele and gently kissed her lips and responded. "Hell no, this morning was a professor at UConn and the twelve kids were with my x-wives. Now, get up girl, I want a good look at you as you dress and watch you ready yourself to leave, then I can sleep alone and peacefully." "You're kicking me out! After what I just let you do to me?" "You've been fed, thoroughly cleansed and fucked by the best and one of the biggest, you said so yourself, but you'll never see me again, so please get up and leave."

Vincent watched Michele as she got out of bed, snatched up her clothes and went into the bathroom. At precisely mid-night she walked out of his room, all put back together looking like she did when he met her earlier. He then made a quick trip into the bathroom, set his alarm clock for 8am, turned out the lights and proceeded to think about his twelve kids. Instantly his mind was back on 5 lost Road and Rhonda was packing Rockwell off for college. All the kids were around the car when we left the driveway to drive him away. *I can picture their long faces because Rockwell was going away. The little ones really loved him, he was good with them. The little ones...Andie's wasn't little anymore... Damn these college buildings have my mind all mess up.*

Eight am, the alarm clock is waking Vincent. *As much as I hate waking up alone, if it's not with Crystal, I'd prefer it!* He sniffed his pillow, it still had the sent of Michele. He sniffed her pillow and it defiantly had the sent of sex. At one point she had her pillow down on his stomach and when she turned, her cheek hit his penis, so for a slit second he thought she would put her mouth down on him, go deep and really pleasure him. *Oh Rhonda, I really do miss you at times. Someone wrote a book about someone like you....Deep Throat! I've never had the nerve to ask Crystal to try and do that to me...I wouldn't want her to try and picture you in that position down on me. She's a pleasure just the way she is...tonight...!! Damn, I'm as hard as a rock. Where did the condom go?* Once his hand was wound around his penis he forgot about the condom, thought about Crystal's hair hanging down over her breasts and relieved himself

Chapter 60

1975-80's

Noon time back in Connecticut heading to the race track, Vincent decided to pull over and call Crystal. He needed to hear her voice. Not Donna's or Maggie's or Michele's...*what's gotten into me...three woman in less than 36 hours. I've never been like this before. I didn't even compare them to Crystal, I just used them. They came on to me, I was weak and I let myself be lead. Dam-it they used me! I need Crystal...I want Crystal and that is such a great feeling...to know without a doubt that I love my wife. At least in that relationship I know where I stand. We use each other in the ways of the flesh, sex, and trust. I'm bad...she trusts me. I have broken every rule ever written about a monogamist marriage. She claims she has never, not even once broken her marriage vows. I trust her. She trusts me and I'm the biggest fraud and worst husband that ever walked this earth. I don't deserve her or her love, but without it, I'd die.*

Once he heard her voice and they talked about her show last night and the fact she loved being on the water bed and she couldn't wait for him to get there, and yes the twenty dollar down payment on the land was legal and binding, he felt like Crystal's husband again and not this over-sexed teen aged kid out for his jollies. Just hearing her voice this noon time had him weak in the knees and wanting her more than he had in a long time. "Crystal" he said...she waited. "Vincent is there sometime wrong, are you alright?" He was quick to answer her this time. "Oh, I'm just fine. Short pause... Crystal, I miss you. I missed you in my bed last night. I thought about you this morning sitting on the side of the bed with your hair falling down over your breasts and I grew a boner that almost hurt, I needed you! I hate cold showers." (he lied) Immediately Crystal responded with, "you'll have me tonight as many times as you can handle, believe me I'm looking forward to it. I'll need to start saving these bedtime experiences for the month I'll be gone. I always miss you so much. I wish you'd come with me." Just the thought of her away made his heart plunge! Why did she have to bring that up now? "I love you Crystal, I know I don't say that enough, but believe me I do. I'll remind you again...tonight." Crystal was quiet a minute and through a tear chocked throat ended the call with "I love you, too...till later, bye" and hung up. All these years later they both could still cause heart throbs.

Vincent drove back to the track and parked his car on 'his' property, crossed the street and bought a program. Not knowing 'anything' about the races or the horses or the owners, it was a shot in the dark to bet on anything! But being the type of man he was...he talked to a few people found out the basics, and put $10 down on each race. Everything to win, naturally...the max on each race the max on each horse. That done, now he wanted to get home to Crystal.

Building across from a race track could be run. Just with the adrenaline he felt by placing his bets, and walking among the people gathering and parting with their money, he felt this could be something he would want to learn more about. These thoughts could wait, his other thoughts of Crystal wrapping her arms around him and holding him close and the sent of her made his drive back to New York well worth while. She'll be over the top happy to see him early and waiting for her.

Vincent made it back to the New Yorker ten minutes after Crystal's show started. He decided to use this first hour to find her room, have dinner and find a seat at her show. She needn't know he is there, he could watch her and maybe distract her during her second set. That would drive her crazy to see him out of the corner of her eye and not really be sure of what she is seeing. He's done this before and has a good time doing it! Sometimes she makes remarks during her show about wanting and missing someone so badly, she starts seeing things. Other times she starts to pay Boggie-Woggie just to see if he jumps out of the audience to stop her. Her audiences never know why she doesn't finish that particular selection. Just a few minutes before Crystal is about to start her second set, Vincent is escorted to a table four rows back from the stage. The lights are still set to intermission so Vincent has an opportunity to look around at the people, their ages, their attention, the way they are dressed, the way they are looking around at everyone else. Amazing, she still draws crowds of all ages, seemingly of all interests and all income levels. Tonight's program could be considered high-brow because of the instrumental accompaniments and yet these 21-29 year-old's can't wait for the second half of the show to begin. *I couldn't be more proud of this woman. And to think I wanted to stunt her musical growth and career. I am a low life of every sort! I really do love her!*

The lights started to blink and the orchestra started it's warm-up chords, the black, heavy drape parted and Crystal walked to center stage. She was a vision from head of silver hair to toes of sparkling silver. The orbs of glass in her ears and hanging around her neck caught the spot-light and sparkled as bright as her smile. The long red, body fitting dress Crystal wore was split up to her knee on one side and allowed her to slide on to the piano bench with elegance. Vincent couldn't take his eyes off of her. The minute the lights hit her walking out on to the stage he was like a smitten kid, needing to get close to the prettiest girl in the room and scared of rejection!

Once she started to play, he knew every song, he knew all the words, he could picture her years ago struggling with the right tempo or timing to make it just right. Then, Meadow Memories! Having just left grandma's area, he could picture it the way it was when he brought Crystal there. The meadow where they frolicked and swam and made love. The first time the words were spoken and she cried over joyed. When he realized he needed to wipe away the tear that just fell from his eye, he knew, in his heart he knew. After all of their years of marriage how could he absolutely show her how much he loved her!

Waking up in the arms of the person you love has to be a gift. One that she has experienced many times in her life, but his morning there was something different. Gentle, giving, considerate, loving, let me count the ways. Last night was magical. He arrived earlier than expected and caught most of my show. Then the delivery of my favorite flowers during the last number. He marched right up on stage, placed the beautiful bouquet of yellow roses right on the corner of the piano and sat next to me while I was trying to keep my composure playing that last piece. At its conclusion he announced, sorry folks no occur tonight. You've had her for more than two hours. It's our 35th anniversary and I haven't seen her for two whole days. Thanks very much and God-speed! And the curtain was pulled! He made arrangements for that as well. And today look at him sleeping like a baby. He said he had one more surprise for me but I'd have to wait...what in the world is he up to? She was awake, so why couldn't he be?

Rolling over and running her hands down his chest to his sleeping penis, it was time everything woke up. She wanted everything up so she started working at it. Satisfied with her results she said, "I'll take care of that if you tell me my next surprise now." The poor guy hadn't even opened his eyes yet, but he was letting his brain fog clear up before he corralled her and helped her mount him. With her on top and being properly filled, he didn't need to open his eyes to picture her and feel her warm, naked breasts being swayed across his chest as she teased his penis with her movements. He prompted her to lift her arms so he could get the full roundness of the breasts in each of his hands. He switched that up a bit to lay her on her side so he had more hip control at bringing her to a better place to fondle and suck those voluminous breasts "Good morning Mrs. Clear, when did you say we were going to Vegas? I decided I'd let you take this with you." Those words stopped her completely...he said, "please be fair, don't stop what you're doing, why do you think I want to go along?" She completely froze now but in doing so put a clamp on him so tight, he came in an instant! Tears of joy and her arms around him in a vice grip, so tight he couldn't move 'anywhere'! He let her relax a bit and said "if you still want me to!"

Chapter 61

1980's

Over the past few years, Crystal had spoken to Clarke Comstock on numerous occasions covering a number of topics. During their very first meeting it was understood that he would work the locations and the names Crystal had given him and report about their work, hobbies, circle of friends, family entanglements, financial status and major changes in those arenas. To date there has been virtually no surprises about the people or their everyday lives. He'd work the names or locations when it fit in his schedule as there was no rush on Crystal's part, she just wanted quarterly reports, even if there was nothing much to say. She was informed, but knew that Andrea Chambers was a very wealthy young woman since the fire due to her mom's family inheritance. He also told Crystal that Andrea's daughter was also another beautiful young woman, and they were both doing fine. The fact that Andrea had a girl was news to her, but hearing she was a cutie pulled at her heart strings! If that news affected her like that, just imagine what it would do to Vincent! The one new fact that had surfaced was that Rhonda's mother was killed in a hold-up in the jewelry store where she worked. That had happened February 10th 1967, just a few days before Valentine's Day. He had no word on her father. After this last brief conversation, Crystal terminated Clarke's involvement with her affairs. He had found very little and the family members were seemly adjusting very well. Clarke offered his services if she ever needed him again in the future.

Vincent had been Crystal's champion twice in accompanying her to Vegas in the early 70's. The first time Crystal got to show him around and played tour guide and was proud of all the new things she could show him. She was performing the casino circuit all week so Vincent only stayed Friday, Sat and Sun. He flew home on Monday, besides the motels were so new and so on his mind, Vegas was too far away. A couple of years later Crystal convinced him to return to Vegas with her for a week before her shows were to begin just to be vacationers and see the sights. They had a ball making a car trip to the Hoover Dam. So much history and marvel to lean how it was built. They were like little kids all alone and doing what they wanted to. That night back at their hotel they booked a three day bus trip to the Grand Cannon. All excited they boarded their bus with 58 other people from all over the United States and a few from Canada to learn about and explored one of our nations greatest national parks. They were not disappointed. More than once they asked each other, why hadn't we done more of this, taken more vacations, seen more of our country and its broad history and vast beauty. Their three days went by too fast as do most vacations. That left them two days to spend with Peter and see the Vegas he had learned to enjoy through pictures and on horse back. Peter having spent many weekends or more at the motels opening, had learned an appreciation of Vincent and his coping mannerisms in regards to the motels and his love for Crystal. Peter reckoned in his own heart that he had been too hard on Vincent and judged him unfairly in his feeling for Crystal. They seemed to have a good life and Crystal made a point to keep him (Peter) in it!

Beyond this the 80's were actually a blur...Everyone was so busy! The motels took all of Vincent's interest, time and energy While Crystal's career still carried her to Vegas to perform, down to Atlantic City and naturally New York. Plus she was playing in the lounges of her motels, each, once a month. This was the time when she and Vincent got to spend the most time together and they loved it. These three cities were becoming a home away from home for her and they treated the motels like home so all was well in Crystal's world. Then Los Angeles was introduced into the mix in the late 80's and it was beyond a big deal.

She was invited to perform her first hit song Meadow Memories on national TV during the Grammy Awards. The program was also going to high-light the songs rendition with words and invited Brad and his team to the awards.

Vincent was so proud of her, he was bursting with enthusiasm when Rita and Clive said that they wanted to go to California with them. The invitations came with contracts of acceptance with penalties if there was a breach of contract. Both Rita and Clive looked at these contracts as the normal type of contact for this type of exposure. Crystal was over the moon excited and nervous to be performing live in front of TV cameras, but of course she signed the contracts with pleasure. In the next following days Rita had their hotel reservations made and all flights booked and confirmed.

The trip to California was 6 weeks away and life needed to go on normally until their departure, but it was so tough to go about the every day as normal. There was nothing normal about going to California to perform on live TV. Crystal had done well on her other first performances but this one was scary. One week after returning the signed contracts she received a telegram notifying her that she had been nominated for a Grammy with Meadow Memories for her first recording. The same day Bradley Cooper receives a telegram nomination for the Word writer of Meadow Memories. Crystal was at home when her telegram arrived and Brad was upstairs in the studio when his telegram arrived. You'd think there was an earth quake when the telegrams were re-read to everyone in the house. The house expounded with voices and music and people. The excitement was palatable and shared by everyone. It was later in the afternoon that same day the postman returned with another telegram. Rita signed for this because Crystal's hand was shaking too much. The telegram was address to Crystal Clear in care of: Clearly Entertaining. It Was a Grammy nomination for the Record Label. There wasn't a dry eye in the house. Then the champagne was opened and the rest of the day was lost in praise and congratulations. That night Crystal finally drifted off in a peaceful nights sleep in Vincent's arms.

They arrived in Los Angles four days before the Grammy's. The hotel was marvelous, Clive's reputation preceded them, therefore their red-carpet treatment started there. Then the nerves started getting jittery in Crystal. What to wear, what color to wear how to wear her hair---up, down, braided? When and where could she practice? How many audience seats did they have? Brad and his whole team was here. Their first night in town they were invited to dinner anonymously. The note addressed to Crystal read: This invite is for Crystal, Vincent, Rita and Clive. You cannot refuse this, meet me in the hotel lobby at 6:30...you'll know me when you see me. So many wonderful things happening. So many surprises. Why not, they were new to town, didn't know a soul, didn't know where to go.

February in California was like September in New Jersey...what to wear, short sleeves, a jacket, sweat shirt? All of the above were packed, you'd think Crystal was going away for a month, she wanted to be prepared for anything! It was a great evening...she opted for a long sleeve, Kelly green, mock turtle-neck shirt and black jeans. Her earrings were stud pearl and she wore a drop pearl necklace. She felt pretty and understated. Dressed like this she felt relaxed and at home. Ready to go, the four of them exited their elevator and scanned the lobby for a familiar face. Crystal's little screech of delight and her vault into Peter's arms solved their mystery question. "Of course I'm here for the Grammy's, (he answered Crystal's searching eyes) but right now I know this neighborhood delight called La Scala Boutique, off the beaten track and we can talk and eat there." Peter had Crystal's hand and was leading them to a mini van he had parked on the curb.

"I try not to miss any gala event" Peter was saying as he drove the few miles to their destination. "I get some of my best candids at these events. It's my bread and butter with the celebrity magazines, you know, who's who and what are they doing and then who are they with?"

Dinner was a delightful Italian smorgasbord with every noddle imaginable available with white sauces, red sauces, flat breads, crusty breads, hot, spicy or regular meats. It was an all-you-eat fare with a huge sunken salad bowl in the middle of the table. The house wine was lite, white, semi-sweet and delicious, even to a non-wine drinker. Peter was saying he subscribes to 'Inside the Lime-Light' an international spy-glass to what's happening and when. "I get the scoop on such things as this weeks Grammy's and who is being invited and looked at before the media at large or the public. I knew you got your invite, I knew it 3 days before you did. (with a sarcastic tone of voice and a slant to his eyes he continued with) thanks for giving me the heads-up, what if I didn't know? You know I'm going to give you the best pictures of your life!" With that he stood, saluted Crystal and toasted "To our very own almost Grammy winner...Crystal Clear"...Here, here was heard round the table!!

For Crystal the next 3 days were a blur. She got to practice in the quiet auditorium at the hotel and shopped for a new gown to wear for her performance. She found a shimmery blue number that hugged her body in all the right places, fell to the floor at her toes, had a slit up to her knee for easy access to the piano bench and a neck line that afforded her the use of her own jewelry to finish the look of simple elegance. Her hair had been pulled back over her ears and held with a ribbon of the same material as her dress. One thick soft curl of hair was draped from back to her front and fell over her left breast to nearly her waist. She was a vision of loveliness!

At 4pm the day of the Grammy's, a black stretch limousine arrived at the hotel to whisk Crystal and Brad (he was staying at the same hotel) to the Shrine Auditorium and Expo Hall in downtown Los Angles. They sat opposite each other in the very back seat of the auto and just smiled at each other. When he said "good luck" that broke the sound barrier and they talked and giggled and gushed all the way down town like two little kids. They walked hand in hand into the building and Peter never missed a beat or a smile or a look! Crystal never even saw him.

Three hours before show time, in her dressing room with Rita and Clive and Vincent they were seated by a sumptuous buffet certainly for more than just four, so when Peter knocked on her door he was swept into the room to eat! He said thanks, just a quick bite, I don't want to miss too much out there. He downed a huge sandwich, a bottle of water, kissed her on the cheek and said "knock them dead out there" and left. Crystal was reminded of Miss Elise just then, it's was the first time she had ever heard that phrase.

Rita and Clive ate heartily, were thankful they didn't need to venture out for their supper while Vincent picked, then picked a little more but not enough to consider it a full meal. His inners were too wound up just looking at Crystal and thinking about what she must be thinking! He'd seen her nervous before a show before, but this was different. Everyone was lost in their own thoughts, the room was nearly silent and there was a knock on the door. Everyone but Crystal nearly jumped out of their skin. She calmly opened the door and came face to face with the director of the program. She had just made his acquaintance three days ago when she was practicing in the theater of the hotel, but was surprised to see him here. Crystal invited him into the room, invited him to have a bite with them and offered him a beer. He shook Vincent and Clive's hands, nodded toward Rita and took Crystal up on her offer. He sat down with a 'hump' "this is the first time I had a moment to sit all day, thanks so much for your hospitality, I'll take that beer and help myself to a sandwich and get to the point of my visit." In between bites he finally got to the explanation and the total point of the visit. Brad was being recognized and nominated for his words to primarily, "Black Water Blues". With everyone out there today it came down to Rita, right here, this Rita to remind us that you wrote the musical score and recorded that song, so rather than a recording playing in the background as we honor Brad and your label...would you kindly play "Black Water Blues" on stage behind Brad when he takes the stage? Crystal's eyebrows were arched so high in astonishment and total surprise, she gushed with pure delight in accepting his invitation for her to play a second number. With all eyes on Crystal he broke the silence with, "this could be the Crystal Clear or the Clearly Entertaining show tonight by all the times you, your songs and your label are going to be mentioned. After finishing his beer he walked to the door, turned around and looking straight at Rita said, "you have a very beautiful and talented daughter Ms. Dunski and I'm glad you found me for that little talk earlier. Thanks for supper and all of you, enjoy the show." with that he left.

"Mom, what was he talking about, little talk?" Crystal immediately asked. Rita looked around the room and let her tone of voice speak for her when she answered Crystal's question. "I was talking with Brad and he told me they were using piped in music for Black Water Blues and I hit the roof. My little fury was witnessed by a few people and when I explained my outburst, it was immediately decided to ask you to play that number when the announcements were being made. All those people out there wouldn't be wrong to think Clearly Entertaining plus Crystal Clear and Brad writing for Crystal Clear and working for the Clearly label equaled they have the best of the best here...they know it!" Crystal got up and hugged her mom, "thanks mom, you're the best and the best manager too. Are we being paid for any of this?" Vincent just shook his head and muttered "show business!" Clive added his two cents by saying, "that was certainly an interesting supper and added drama by our dear Rita, it definitely helped the time to pass by. Crystal you'll need to dress pretty soon so your mom and I will be in our seats hobnobbing with all the other anxious people out there. Have fun and good luck." Rita kissed her daughter on the cheek and was led from the room by Clive.

Vincent went to Crystal and wrapped his arms around her saying, "you've worked so long for this, you deserve every accolade they want to give you out there, I'm so proud of you." That praise from her husband made Crystal go weak in the knees. "I can usually please so many with my music, but on so many other occasions you've had your feelings hurt because I choose my music over you or your needs. It's been a tough go sometimes, but I just got the best award I could get having you here with me and being proud of me." "You are really good and very talented and I am so sorry for being such a cad sometimes. I'm not proud of myself but I need you to know how much I love you and want the best for you." He ended that tender moment with a kiss! Just then an announcement made them jump a mile ...20 minutes to make-up. Vincent offered to help her dress but she wisely declined.

Once the make-up was on and she was dressed, the back-stage area was crazy exciting! She met so many people she'd only seen on TV or in magazines. She found it amazing how many people knew who she was. She assured herself it was her hair...celebrities don't know piano players, but Oh...she was so wrong. She was more than that, she was a celebrity pianist and song writer with a past and a following and tonight a Grammy winner, but she didn't know that yet! Once being told where to stand and then where to advance to once you heard your name seemed simple enough; until the music started and the noise became all you could hear and the people started scrambling in all directions behind the stage curtains and the lights changed and the nerves set in and she felt turned around then she heard the opening bars of "Meadow Memories" and her name and a kindly soul led her by the elbow to the stage in time to hear the magical results of the winner of the Grammy for Best a-Capella artist. She was stunned...When she was handed her trophy and asked to say a few words, she saw Peter not 10 feet away, behind the stage curtain just beaming at her and flashing away, she turned back to the audience and started with "I won, I really won...Thank you a million times whoever made this a reality, I thought I was invited here to play my song." The MC then asked her to follow him and they went to a sleek baby grand where she took her seat and played her best rendition of Meadow Memories. Upon completion the curtain was pulled and she could join her family in the audience seats. Two more awards were given and then she was listening to the names for song of the year and the Grammy goes to Crystal Clear for Meadow Memories. With rubbery knees she stood in place and needed a push to move. Once on stage, again she was handed the trophy and spoke into the microphone. Short and sweet with many thanks. This time she was walked to the side stage which lead to back stage where she let the tears fall, but Vincent was there to hold her up. She was so happy to have his strong arms around her for support. Because from there she was lead to the piano which was now back stage to be reintroduced to play Back Water Blues for the introduction of the Brad as a nominee for Composing and arranging...little did she know that this was a shared nomination. Five minutes later, after playing her heart out, she was back on stage with Brad accepting the Grammy for composting and Brad word writing and arranging Black Water Blues. But it wasn't over yet, before the end of the night Crystal added one more Grammy for

Recording Artist of the year. At this time they acknowledged Crystal's recording company: Clearly Entertaining and listed her and Brads accomplishments as being recognized by, the Recording Academy of the United States for "outstanding" achievements in the music industry.

There were many invites to parties everywhere in LA after the awards, but Crystal and her little posse opted to return to the hotel for a night-cap and relaxation. For Crystal sleep wouldn't come easy tonight but she definitely needed to get out of the lime light and relax.

"Mom, Clive did you know any of this. Did you know I was to receive these awards? Who nominated me or us or the label?" It was a question on Crystal's mind for the next umpteen years.

Chapter 62

1994

Years later while driving back to Shelby Street from Maine. Crystal's nerve endings on the back of her head told her something is up...Vincent has been too quiet. He had been great company on this trip and they really enjoyed themselves, but now in the car...she asked..."Hey Vincent, what's up, you're too quiet, where did you go?"

"You really are a mind reader Mrs. Clear...Okay, there is something I need to discuses with you because it has been on my mind and why shouldn't I ask you about it"? "For heavens sake Vincent, spit it out, what's on you mind?" Crystal was a little short with him. "Well a number of years ago when we were starting the build in Vermont I went into you bed night stand looking for a name in Vermont but found a couple of other things instead. That which really bothered me was the name of Clarke, a detective. What did you need him for?" This was so out in left field, Crystal mind went blank and her hands got sweaty. Thinking quick she tried to dismiss the entire thing "it was nothing", but Vincent wouldn't let it be. So she fest-ed up with "I needed him to check on Reginald's and Aspen's demise in the real world. What was going on in Grafton and on Lost Road." Vincent was extremely quiet now and she was afraid she had crossed him in some way.

Several miles later he asked, "so what did you find out. Anything about Andrea or Rhonda or the kids?" Crystal swallowed hard and repeated that Andrea had a little girl and they were doing just fine because Andrea had a substantial inheritance from her mom's father's estate and Rhonda and the kids were also doing just fine because they found out Rhonda's mom, Marie Tuffin was killed in a jewelry heist and they sued the city of NY and the store and were awarded a sum of money with which they've done quiet well with. "Remember we were told Marie died, we even have her prayer card. We just weren't told how she died." He was quiet again. Then... "Anything else?" "No, not since then, but I could call Clarke and ask him to dig around again...make sure everyone is doing alright." "Since I can't go myself or even be a fly on the wall, yes please, call him again and ask him to check on my kids. A few years back when I was driving around the college towns looking for land, using the college library's for info or for their phones, I would get such a heart ache thinking about Rockwell at college or going home and seeing the kids. I didn't even know Andrea had a girl. She must be about 30 years old now and I don't even know her name.

All Crystal could say was "I'm so sorry Vincent." He responded immediately with "I don't blame you for what you did. Well, maybe a little, but you let me have them for more than twenty years, for that I thank you. You are a much bigger person than I would have been. Can you do me a favor?" "Name it, if I can, I will." Crystal's hands were still sweaty and she was afraid of what she just agreed to! Vincent said, "When Clarke is looking around ask him if he can take pictures of my kids, I'd love to see them grown. I don't know what you tell Clarke, I don't know how you explain these people to him, I don't care, but that is my wish." He now engaged the CD and Chrystal's music filled the car.

When they got home, Crystal needed a drink and to relax, she'd been keyed up since Vincent's questions and request. Having been so busy with the motels and the studio and piano engagements for the past several years, she hadn't visited her 'files' lately. Since the death of Aspen and Reginald, the only disbursements from those accounts should be the death benefits and college funds if applied for. She needed to wire the names and account numbers of the saving accounts she had started for the kids to her attorneys so they could disburse the funds at their 21st birthdays. Oh that would be tricky...it's the only thing she would be asking her attorneys to do in that regard. *NO, she'd need different lawyers to do that, not use hers...do not involve them in something that was 'unlawful'. She didn't want to use Clarke again either. She didn't want to use anyone that was that close to her or Vincent to dig into their personal matters. Now she was nervous all over again. Was relaxing a good idea? If he saw the name Clarke, he must have seen Keith Rogers. He didn't say anything about that! Was that a shoe to be dropped at a different time? Now she was paranoid! Relax, think...I'll use Clarke, really, why not?! I'll call him tomorrow.*

They had gotten home rather late that evening so while Crystal showered, Vincent had buried himself with the newspapers he'd missed and had collected at the house. After driving for hours, Crystal had had it and went to bed early. She had a fitful nights sleep with dream after dream about days gone bye. The fire in Grafton, layering lie upon lie to get Vincent back here to NJ to heal. Manipulating the system to bury Aspen and his family with grace and military grandeur and trying to picture Aspen's oldest daughter pregnant, scared and alone! And then to do it all over again in Maryland for Rhonda and Reginald's family.

Too much! 3am and she was up and pacing the floor. She knew Rita and Clive were in NY..she had checked and the studio was dark and all locked up as it should be, but she hadn't heard a peep out her cad or Suzie. That's a chore for tomorrow. Vincent rolled over with a loud snore, then settled on his side peacefully. After using the bathroom, Crystal tried to settle back in bed. Sleep came but this time her dreams were scattered and didn't make any sense, full of loud noises, loud voices, thunder and crashes. She was glad to wake up at 7 and leave the chaos behind!

Wrapped in a wonderfully warm robe and slippers she made it out to the kitchen and made coffee. Two cups down and working on her third while reading some of the papers Vincent left behind, she heard noises coming from up stairs, good dad and Suzie were home. The aroma of coffee always works, the sleepy heads were drawn to it! By nine-thirty breakfast was finished, all cleaned and everyone engaged in their own activity. Crystal had already called Clarke to find out he was now a lawyer at his dad's firm, but left a message for him and expected him to return her call. The studio didn't have anyone booked until Thursday so the house was really quiet. Crystal liked these times, it was when she'd go to the piano in the living room and play to her hearts content. She'd close her eyes and picture Miss Elise just standing there listening to her or as a youngster catch her dad looking up over his paper with a look of extreme pride. If she tried really hard, she could hear her mom humming as she played. Wonderful memories, wonderful thoughts, then the phone rang.

It was good to hear Clarke's voice. How could he help her. She was tongue tied, she needed Clarke the PI, so that's what she said. He laughed said he worked with a really good one, one he knew she could trust, did she want him to set up a meet? It was all settled, Friday at 1pm in her suite at the New Yorker. This worked out really well, she was playing the New Yorker this weekend so getting there a day early was no big thing. Vincent was even going to drive up with her because he had business at the Woodstock motel.

Friday afternoon 1pm Crystal got a call there was lawyer on his way up to see her. When she opened the door she was startled. An older, better looking Clarke was standing there with a package in his hands. "Come in, come in, nice to see you. What are doing here and what are you hauling around?" Clarke walked in, kissed her on the cheek and said, "good I smell coffee." Still surprised to see him but delighted she said "what are 'you' doing here?" He replied all smiles, "I'm the one you trust and mom just baked her coffee cake, so I'm glad you have coffee on." Sitting with their snack, Crystal filled him in on what she needed this time, including candid pictures, as many as he could safely get. Same people, same locations, what has changed in their lives? Clarke was wonderful and asked no questions. He didn't know Crystal's relationship to these people, nor did he ask. He had his assignment (and was tired of the rate race at the office) and he was happy to do it. He had earned her trust last time, so she was happy to be working with him again, on this but held back the name and bank account numbers on the other matter.

With Clarke on his way, Crystal promptly called the bank and made an appointment for later the same day. Working with a clerk at the counter who had no idea who she was, these transactions went off without a hitch. *One more trip to my private files in the back room at the Bursar's unit and my last favorite man Lt. Rogers will be discharged from the service with no additional duties or payments due him. These bank accounts to be transferred. Retired name Chambers, A. has been archived as deceased along with Sabers, R. paying out survivors benefits and any educational benefits duly applied for any time in the future. No more attention to these files required! Monday...it will be done! Just having made up my mind to stop all future access to these files is such a relief. When it is done I know I'll sleep a lot better! It's only Friday...I can't wait until Monday night when it is done.*

Sitting with Clarke, and finishing her business at the bank made the afternoon just fly by. There was no time to sit in on the Midnight Men's practice. It was coming up to dinner time and Vincent promised he be back in time. So she figured a quick shower and she'd dress for dinner and be ready and waiting.

Chapter 63

Crystal is 73 YEARS OLD

"New Years Eve 1999, a toast to our hostess and benefactor and still the most beautiful woman in the world, my wife Crystal Clear." Crystal had chosen the Clearly Comfortable motel in Waterville Valley, NH for this celebration because it had been snowing and had fabulous views, plus the fountain was always a draw for her. They had the motel and dinning room all to themselves and were celebrating and remembering and were happy they had the entire weekend to do so. They were using tonight, Friday, December 31, 1999 to say goodbye to everyone they'd lost in this century and be happy to move into a new century with everyone they still had. Crystal's toast started with remembering Miss Elise fondly because without her she wouldn't have the house she does or the recording studio or the memories. She went on to say, "it all comes down to the memories. Tonight only, Johnathan can live large because he created many memories for me. Dad, most of the time, larger than life, living the life he loved and to the end with the woman he loved. Suzie, able to share to her end, her life with the 2 men that meant the most to her, her son and my dad, again, under the same roof. My Mom. I could write a book on my mom's virtues, abilities, strength, creativity and honor. She went from a married mother of one...Me.. to the First Lady's, 1st lady, to running a recording studio and handling all of the legal matters and advertising and scheduling and...so on and so on...She did it all! And Clive. We could each write a book on his virtues and contributions to our life! He'll always have a piece of my heart that no one else can touch because he meant that much to me. His encouragement and leadership and patience and praise...I could go on, but I don't need to because I know you all feel him too. All of these people I loved and will miss forever, but am happy I had them in my life. Now lets eat and drink and enjoy the people we still have in our lives...Happy New Year!"

At a minute before midnight, Crystal started playing Auld Lang Syne, but at midnight she let the TV take over so she could enjoy Vincent's kiss. The 1900's had been good to Crystal. She married the man of her dreams, had a career she loved, traveled a little, had her mom back in her life...in a big way, had four gold albums, 2 Grammy Awards, had written 11 songs and with the help of others, had two, Multi- million dollar corporations. As was in evidence by the people around her, she was rich in many ways!

So far the evening had been stupendous. Crystal enjoyed the people that were with her, the food was marvelous, naturally their room was comfortable the Midnight Men performed beyond her exceptions, so on and so on..she couldn't say enough good things about her environment or the way she felt. So when there was a knock, an out & out slamming on the locked door, the door that announced...Closed Private Party---everyone was startled and froze in place. Vincent and Peter went to investigate, but when the door opened just a bit, this little bit of a woman burst in, took one look at Vincent and jumped his bones...literally..locked her legs around his middle, arms around his neck and yelled Happy New Year, missed you Mr. Rogers and planted a lip lock on him!

Once the little lady was shone out, and the excitement was over, it was getting to be late for all of these old folks so the party was over. Crystal and Vincent made it back to their room, but all the while Crystal thought it quite the coincidence that she called Vincent Mr. Rogers. She could have chosen Peter, but she didn't, she aimed straight for Vincent. Crystal's high of the evening was crashing down on her in a big way. In all the years she had been duping the government out of money, using false names and made-up identifies, she never thought the game would end outside the military gates. It had gone on so long, she didn't know how it would end, prayed things would just play out and end. Glad her dad was never made aware of her thievery, that would have killed her! The few times she thought she was caught and her dad knew what was going on, she thought she would die! But tonight, it was straight in her face, coincidence or not it needed to end. She never wanted to feel this way again!

Her favorite motel, a new year, need to start it right. Vincent had a thing for red. So tonight when Crystal emerged from the bathroom she didn't need to catch Vincent's attention, the very red, very long (remember, she is very tall) very showy, thin flowing red robe over the most delicate 3 red meticulously placed roses, took his breath away. He got out of bed to help her with her robe, stepped back and asked her how she kept the flowers in place. Crystal, also knowing that he has a thing for warm caramel, used the candy as glue. She was so ready for him to devour her. For years they had been playing with each others body, tonight Crystal had this planned and was looking forward to it, so no Mr. Rogers was going to ruin this playtime for her. Crystal told Vincent that it was a tasty magic that held the roses in place, but he needed to be gentle, enjoy the experience and tantalize her at the same time. And gentle he was...his tongue, the taste of bourbon when he kissed her, no complaints...hers tasted of rum... A warm tongue on her breast did feel better than a cold one and a hungry and warm mouth felt marvelous when he discovered the roses were of frosting and had the flavor of caramel. The heat Vincent produced transferred to her and the gentleness and calm and tantalizing feeling he was managing to control in himself was about to let loose in Crystal. He could feel her heightening emotions, so with more control he had ever felt, he stopped all motion except to gently rub his hand down her left leg very slowly, and recite some of the words in Meadow Memories " a moon lit sky above snow covered mountain peaks, a peaceful and serene place where lovers need not speak". She froze, held his hand still and said,"those are your words... of many years ago". He merely said, "and you capitalized on them, made your first million and shared them with the world." "Yep, your words, helped me to paint a picture, just like tonight, out the window what do you see? A moon lit sky above snow covered mountain peaks, why do you think, besides that meadow, that this is my favorite place? That sky, those mountain peaks, the snow, the serene place and here we are... lovers, long after those words were spoken or the song written. You recited those words, you found this place and you are defiantly my lover." "I'm glad about that, happy new year Mrs. Clear." This time his kiss tasted sweet and of caramel.

The next morning, 11am New Years Day brunch, served in the lounge was first, plentiful, tasty and heartfelt! Peter showed his appreciation for this invite by presenting Crystal with a handsome photo collage of all of the opening nights at each motel. Throughout the years, Peter was the first quest at each motel. He would take oodles of pictures, send them off to the local newspapers and the gossip magazines, out-do the local press each time and promise to be back for the next one. They both claimed it was the best way to stay in touch, so for the years that it took Crystal and Vincent to build eight motels, (yes, eight...they added Maine and Connecticut) they saw Peter on the average of once a year. These were great visits, and it had all started 45 years ago. Some times he didn't come alone. He'd have an exhausted entertainer in need of some R&R, or a complete models company for her shoot in the mountains, or on the beach. Bull couldn't make it to the party last night, but he showed up for the food this morning! He remained a good friend and worked on other projects for them. Brad had grown from this goofy kid with grand ideas of being a great song writer into a very responsible man of many talents, had written the words to each one of her songs and been a valued employee for more than 30 years. When Crystal found talent or made a friend it was a treasured relationship and she saw to it that the camaraderie lasted.

Just looking around the room and thinking, her feelings went from awe to thankful, then a little melancholy but fell like a bang on regret. Outside of Peter she never had a best friend. She never had that girl friend to talk to or confide in or gossip with or miss when she went away to school or away for a job. The girlfriend to hang with and talk about boys when they were growing up or about clothes and styles when they could afford to buy their own clothes. She'd never been anyone's maid-of-honor or asked to be the Godmother to anyone's infant. That type of close relationship with another woman had never been in her life. She had never shared, therefore, wouldn't know how to share that kind of a special moment. *What's wrong with me, I'm 73 years old, have made a fortune many times over, am married to the love of my life, shared most of my shinning moments with my family and closest friends and are looking at and sharing with most of them right now. I've not missed a thing! I've lived my life on my own terms , experienced more life and love, personal growth and adventure than most in even a longer life. And I'm not done yet. These motels are my home away from home and the pianos are always waiting for me. When we get home to Shelby Street next week, I need to make an appointment with I don't know who or how, to look at my long ago personal files, to fix… or stop…or terminate these illegal activities. Who was still drawing from these accounts, she needed to know. How many kids were using the academic funding provisions? Not fair to pull that, but!!! My heart isn't strong enough anymore to think about getting caught! But that's enough for now…look around and enjoy what you've got!* At that moment her eyes fell on Peter. She knew he'd be packing and getting ready to leave tomorrow. It was getting harder and harder to say good-bye to him. They were the same age and could complement each other on their still youthful appearance. To date they both still had good health and their own hair! But how many more times would they cross country to be with each other? *Enjoy him now, fool…discuss that later!* With the party still in full swing, people were starting to talk about packing it up and moving on. They had the rest of today, Saturday and then Sunday to get ready for the new work week on Monday, that's always hard after a holiday. But it must be done because the motel is open for normal business on Monday.

Over the years Crystal had seen to it that each motel had a complete face lift every 8 years. The look of the motels were always kept the same and under great management latest longer than other corporate sites such as Howard Johnson's or Kelsey's Kettle. Over the years the motel's competitors were the Country Inn's, but they were smaller and more expensive. Super corporate management kept the motels active with each of the towns activities and celebrations. After all this time, their future still looked bright. Crystal wasn't ready to completely retire yet, so between her lively fingers and good local bands, the lounge was still a great night spot. Their dinning room, banquet rooms were as attractive for any venue, including a formal wedding or 50th wedding anniversary party. Good taste and great service never go out of style. Crystal's motels were a testimonial to that.

Mid Saturday afternoon Vincent wandered back into their room to watch a football game and promptly fell asleep. None of their guests were in the lounge and it was too early for dinner so Crystal sat at the desk in the office. Being alone wasn't a good thing, the Mr. Rogers episode crept back into her mind. Sitting still wasn't happening either so she went to the kitchen with a question on her mind. Did anyone recognize the tiny woman who caused the scene last night? Oh yes, many in the kitchen knew exactly who she was. The last of the Willoughby's. At one time that was a powerful name in this town. It sounded familiar to Crystal, but she couldn't place it or know why it rang a bell. Finally to help clear the look of confusion off of Crystal's face, Virginia, the oldest waitress reminded Crystal that the Willoughby's used to own this property. The dawn...now Crystal remembered the name! Now she asked if the woman lived around here. Of course she did, and very well!

Twenty minutes later, Crystal found herself face to face with Ms. Willoughby, wondering why, why did she really come here! Ms. Willoughby stepped aside and invited Crystal into her home. "Boy, you're another really tall one, sorry I caused a stir at your party last night, but I saw him through the window, no mistaking that man, although I admit, it's been a hundred years since I last saw him. He hasn't changed too terribly much, just a little older with some gray hairs. I think age and gray hair on men looks really great sometimes, he's no exception. *Does this woman ever shut up...she does seem to know Vincent, did he introduce himself as Rogers? Did she show him around the first time? He knew I'd love the fountain, but didn't want to come back here..why?.. her??* He was like a little boy the other time we met. He wanted to show his partner a picture of the fountain..I said partner..are you married.. and we went from there straight to my place. You're a tall woman, you must know...but I'd never seen one quite as big a him. I think he was a little taken back by me and my size, so I played that up some, it was fun to see his face when he saw my flat chest all nipple-puckered, but he sucked them anyway...he's good! Can I make you coffee or tea, will you sit awhile? I'm sorry, I'm Tina and you are?" "Good strong coffee would be wonderful while you tell me the rest of this interesting story. What did he say his name was?" Crystal needed to sit, she also needed something stronger than coffee, but the story was riveting and she wanted to hear more. She was already sick to her stomach so what the hell. "Great, coffee it is, do you do cream or sugar or brandy? At this time of day, anytime really I prefer the brandy, but that's why I need to watch out I don't drink too much coffee. I offer coffee to all of my guests, because, you see I don't like to drink alone. You're really good for my memory, after we ate apple pie, I made coffee for Keith as well. Yes Keith Rogers, that was his name. A real gentleman he was, every time I was needing to climb on a chair to reach him, he'd lift me up like I weighted no more than a feather. I must be a light-weight, because I had his meaty stiff out of his pants and I sat on him so gently he didn't even know what I have done until I was in face for a kiss. That was at the restaurant where I was picking turkey off of his plate, that's why he offered me apple pie. I must say, that was a disappointing feat because not much of him reached up inside of me. Not until later, back on my little twin bed where I lathered him up good and I slid right on down. Coffee's ready, don't move a muscle, this is fun, you are good for my memories and this is a good one." *This bitch is a scream, if we weren't talking about Vincent, I'd really be enjoying this...now what do I do? Tell her who I am, play stupid, keep her talking, this was 35 years ago...do I care? OH, I care!* "Can I do something to help you, get the brandy?" "Hello no, I got that first" Tina said as she placed the coffee, brandy and mugs on the table at Crystal's reach. Crystal helped herself and offered, "sounds like quite the afternoon you two had." Tina laugh and corrected "afternoon, evening, all night. No matter how old or how big, boys will be boys, the next morning after the shower he thought we were all done. I let him think that until I knew he could go again, so with all of my womanly charm I dropped my big fluffy robe, stood on a chair, kissed him silly while undoing his pants and inserting that warm, swollen member right back where I wanted it. Before too long we were back on the bed and the pants that were in the way now, at his ankles. Next time you see him, ask him about his exploits on a twin bed! Can you picture that…him on a twin bed?" Crystal kept the mood light, after all this was a good piece of gossiping, so she asked, "Do you see Mr. Rogers often?" Tina immediately replied. "That was a one and only…hadn't seen him again until last night, that's why I was so excited. I often wondered what happened to him and then the land with the fountain was sold. Wow, that was a long time ago."

"Well, thank you for the wonderful coffee and your interesting memories, you should write a book, but I've got to be on my way now." Crystal felt like she was escaping. She knew she had to get out of there before Tina starting talking again. That little woman was too much! Her ride back to the motel was full of soul searching. How many other motels or towns did Vincent have an evasion about going back to? For all of her married days, Crystal still believed she had the love of her life. It's just too bad Vincent didn't feel the same. Some dogs never change, hers hadn't. She felt like she had nothing more she could give to that man. Her love, their first 20 years, he spent married to two other women, plus her, now she finds out that for the past 35 years, he's been playing on the side. During those 35 years he helped her build, maintain and improve a chain of 8 motor-lodges with fine dinning and banquet facilities. He committed the most fundamental error by 'playing where you work'. She gave him those 35 years of hard work and respectability built by that hard work. But now it just locks like what you see when you look threw a kaleidoscope; broken pieces of something beautiful all falling in on themselves! When you look at Vincent's life, that's all it is. Pieces of everything he's been given, that's the problem; not earned, broken into tiny pieces reflecting back at the viewer from the depths of a far away funnel unable to regroup and make whole and beautiful again.! It took that tiny woman and a brandied coffee to open Crystal's eyes. With those eyes now wide open, she needs to get her dignity and respect back in a place where she can flaunt them over him with a rightful authority once the unlawful military records scam is rectified and resolved. She realizes, that's all on her. Built from the ground up by her because of him! All of her unlawful acts motivated by his actions and his ability to twist her love for him into actions she'd regret if she didn't follow his heart felt requests turned immediate demands. He knew how and when to push her buttons, but no more! She couldn't wait to get home.

Chapter 64

1-2-2000

It was a very quiet ride heading south when Crystal and Vincent left Vt and headed home. Crystal's head was full of ideas of how to try and halt or stop all payouts of government money that she had misappropriated. She knew she needed to do this immediately. *Who did she know and when were they there for her to get in and do her thing It wasn't so easy these days. Everyone was always happy to see her, BUT getting behind the back door and closing that door felt...wrong. She honestly felt like she was being watched! It's about time all of those miss-handlings stop.* She was feeling heart sick, more than that, she was feeling nauseous and sick to the stomach. *Get home fast and do your thing. Make these feelings stop!* Vincent sat in the front seat next to Crystal all the way home and hadn't picked up on the fact that Crystal was having difficulty holding back tears or was uncomfortable to the point of feeling sick over a situation that maybe she hadn't shared with him. He never once asked her why she was so quiet or why hadn't she put her newest tape in to play. He sat with his own thoughts and future plans and hadn't given Crystal even a second, never mind first thought.

Home sweet home, the house looked so good to Crystal. Get in there, take a shower and go to bed. She was now exhausted physically and emotionally. The driving had done her in and her thoughts were killing her. *If that bastard even comes near me tonight I'm afraid I'll blurt out everything I've found out about him and Mr. Rogers. He can't even begin to explain himself. What is there to explain...except how does he know the name and situation of Keith Rogers? How long and how many women has there been? Do I really want to know. I couldn't let my mind work like that while I was driving. I couldn't let this burning desire to physically beat the loving shit out of him get the best of me while on the road...but now...my belly is on fire with anger and self pity! How could I have not known? Because he is that good of a liar and cheat and really practiced at manipulating me. I'm that easy and he's has walked all over me. Well, not any more, now I'm wise to his lies. Two can play at getting what they want.*

What I want is going to take a lot of patience and trial and error on my part. As for Vincent he had better grow accustomed to hearing no or we'll see or I doubt it or ya maybe and I can't and, not now a lot more often, I'm just not going to be that easy to get along with anymore! I need something else in my life to fill a void, because that is what he is going to be...absent...a void! There isn't one part of his life that I am not going to look at. I cannot hurt Andrea or her daughter, but if Amy were alive I sure would do a job on his relationships! Rhonda, you don't know how lucky you are to no longer have Reginald in your life. Maybe somehow you'll find out. I've only begun to deceive! Oh, Johnathan, I was such a fool!

It was just twilight, it was too early to go to bed. Besides in this mood she would never sleep. A little rum and coke while sitting at the piano sounded really good to her. Forty minutes later having played all of her original songs and being rational and kind to the piano keys she realized Vincent hadn't even peeked in at her at all while she played. Was he hiding and avoiding her wrath figuring she wanted to 'discuss' the little lady that had a neck hold on him. He was mighty quiet on the way home as well. *I wonder what he thinking about. More lies to pad the answers he needs to feed me in response to my questions. He knows they are coming. She sure did open my eyes.*

Nice and relaxed, the piano and the rum had done it's job. She could go to bed now. Alone, which was fine, feeling a little mellow. which was also fine and ready to sleep which was great! The morning sun, shinning straight into her eyes had done it's job. Nearly thirty years of waking up the same way had never grown old...she loved her home.! Stretching her arm across to Vincent's pillow and feeling cool sheets alarmed her. She sat up and looked across, not even a head print in the pillow, no wonder she slept so well. He wasn't here, he never came to bed last night. *We'll' have to try that more often, a little piano, some rum and no Vincent...I slept great!*

If he's here, he'll arrive for coffee. If he doesn't, I'll check the garage for his car, then wonder if he's even in the same state. I'm beginning to think I don't know him half as well as I thought I did. It's a hell of a way to start a new year, We're too old for this shit! One cup of coffee down and still no Vincent. *It's sad I need to check the garage...but...no car!*

She felt sick to her stomach again. Monday morning and the studio staff was arriving, it was a bright and brisk January day with the promise of many great things about to happen. It was her belief of every morning, she always thought of her cup as half full and had faith that only good things would happen. So why did she feel sick to the stomach with additional feelings of dread? Needing to really start her day, she dressed, made the bed, tidied her room, poured another coffee and headed for the studio office. There were three messages on the phone. In a hurry she engaged the answering system hoping at least one message was from Vincent. One hang-up, the second from Clarke, she skipped it for now, finally the third was Vincent. He said he dozed on the coach until 6am and has been driving around since then, can he please come home now to talk? And at that moment he pulled into the driveway. Crystal went back to the kitchen and waited for him to come in but busied herself with making another pot of coffee. When Vincent walked through the door he looked tired and 20 years older!

How can that happen, she thought, he looked like himself last night, his soul searching really did a job on him. I've never really been a hard woman to live with so what was he expecting me to say or threaten since I found out about little Ms. Willoughby? This is different, interesting, he's scared!

Vincent dropped a string tied box from Sargents Bakery on the table while Crystal just watched him take off his jacket and look around the room trying to find her. He sat in his chair and cut the string and announced he brought 'melt-a-ways' straight from the store... still warm. These were Crystal's favorites! Fifty years ago was a very long time ago, she offered coffee from the pantry. Sitting across from one-another, silent, just observing was torture. Crystal started with "how many others?" then reached for the pastry box. All of her concentration was on her fingers and the way she nibbled on her melt-a-way...down one side first, then up the middle, three bites and it was gone. These were a specialty of Sargents and she loved them. It was kind of Vincent to remember and bring some home.

"You could have lead with any number of questions, why did you ask that one first?" Vincent looked more than tired, he looked beaten and ready to throw in the towel! "Are you going to be ten times more angry if I say ten? Are you going to ask me where and with whom and when? It really doesn't matter now anyway...once was too many and you seem to have found that one out! Let's just say, your career was not good for me. Your being away and leaving me to entertain myself lead to mischief. I had three women in my life for more than twenty years and a forty or more hour job that more than filled my dance card and kept me satisfied. Then you took that away from me. In my bed you were more than enough for me, but my bed got mighty cold. So no matter where you were, I needed to keep my bed warm. So I guess that answers one of you unasked questions...I would take a woman 'anywhere!' My bed, her bed but never in our motel. You gave me plenty of opportunities to meet, get friendly get laid and come home. The first twenty years of our marriage laid the ground work for my being able to get it up and keep it up from Massachusetts to Maryland and back to New Jersey. I was younger, playing with three younger women then and you guys used and almost abused me! I loved it, and then I missed it! So I improvised!"

"You're making this out to be all my fault! You're not a man, you are a bastard and a user. You never knew the meaning of a committed relationship or the meaning of staying celibate in your marriage. First you cheated on me with Rhonda then on Rhonda with Amy all the while still coming home to me. I've been such a fool...so you see.. that tiny Tina and her little twin bed was only the first outside of your marriages that I've found out about, I don't need to know more...GET OUT...NOW"

She didn't know where the courage came from to actually say all those words and kick him out, but now she waited. Waited for him to lift his body out of the chair and actually leave. He was looking at her with disbelief in his eyes. "You heard me, get out. There is nothing here for you any more, there is nothing more I can do for you...get out---NOW"

At those words, Vincent left the kitchen, went into the bedroom got a warmer coat out of his closet, never looked back at Crystal and left by the back door. It took forever for Crystal to hear the car start, but once it did, he drove away toward the base. Poor Vincent, there is nothing left for him there either.

Just now she didn't care where he was headed, but somewhere down deep she was concerned for his well being. She walked into her bedroom and looked in the mirror. She didn't feel as old as Vincent looked just now. She didn't think she looked as old as her age. What do seventy-three year old woman look like? Crystal was thinking... Vincent's grandmother always looked old...she died at 79 and looked ancient. My mom, Rita, really started showing her age when she started to stoop, her hair thinned and the lines on her face got deeper and deeper. Is that my future? I hope I take after dad. He still had most of his hair and was straight and tall until the day he died. This is depressing, she thought, go do something good. The piano was beckoning.

Having played through her repertoire left her feeling like she could tackle the world, but what she really needed to do was to get on base and shut down her files for good. That was the next thing on her list but her feet felt heavy, full of lead, any excuse not to leave the house in case Vincent came back. To what end? So she could throw him out again...she grabbed her jacket and keys and headed to the base. Driving down to the Bursar's Unit she realized and hoped that this would be her last visit, all done, kaput, no more. The skeleton crew on duty was happy to see her as usual and didn't question her use of the back room, for which she was thankful, she didn't need any flack now on her final visit. With the door closed and her fingers busy, the files popped up immediately. Dated today January 3, 2000 all files were made inactive and archived, sealed in encryption and password protected and buried. Lights off and she left that room for the final time. Driving home she remembered she needed to listen to Clarke's message and most likely return his call. What he had to tell her were also things she'd just like to bury and forget, those were Vincent's people. But she didn't know how true a statement that was...yet!

The call was answered by a sweet, young woman who made the appointment for Clarke to visit her here in New Jersey. They set the date and time for this Friday afternoon at one. She now had the rest of the week to be nosy upstairs in the studio, play her piano or bake. She was becoming rather good with creating breads that required yeast, she also liked baking things with layers. Pineapple upside-down cake, cherry or blueberry cream-cheese strudel or this wonderful concoction called 'better-than-sex'. It had a thin chocolate cake bottom--- shredded coconut, chocolate chips, nuts, heath bar candy all smashed up and other tasty things all mixed up, topped with more cake and served with Baileys liquor poured over the top. For an old lady, this was definitely better than sex! It was so tasty and lip smacking she decided it would be the Friday afternoon snack delight to serve Clarke, so she set herself up to be busy. At least that was her plan until she heard and witnessed the ruckus outside in her parking area...What the hell, police, an ambulance, barking dogs and people all over the place. Brad from up stairs came running down caring a microphone and recorder over his shoulder and ran out the back door, yelling..."these are great sounds, keep them coming! Crystal was right behind him to find out what all the commotion was about. The noise was deafening, more people walking up the street to see what was going on...most of them with barking dogs on leases. From the other direction the police had the street blocked. Brad and Crystal walked behind her garage and pool fence to try and see more. There it was, one car hanging over the stone wall and heading down hill toward Mr. Gadder's house and another car smashed into Mr. Gadder's house at the right hand corner. "What a mess" Vincent said from right beside Crystal. "Where were you hiding?" Crystal asked. "Not hiding, just resting, sitting by the pool until I heard the crash." Brad heard the sirens of the tow truck in route and was delighted when the dogs all started barking again and the cops directing people to move away from the obstructed driveway and hill side, for Brad, the more noise the better. Crystal was satisfied, she knew what all the noise was about and started walking home. Vincent caught up with her, took her hand and walked along side of her. There were too many people around for Crystal to make a fuss or a scene, so she just continued to walk home. Vincent opened the back door for her and she walked in, washed her hands and resumed greasing her baking pans for her cake, neither one of them spoke a word.

Supper that night was much the same, Crystal cooked, they both ate. Vincent cleared his place and returned to the den to resume watching TV. Crystal finished in the kitchen and retired to the piano and played to her hearts content. Many times she could feel Miss Elise or her dad watching from a few feet behind her. It was a comforting feeling, but after a couple of hours her back starting complaining so she quit and went to bed. She slept like a rock, again...no Vincent. So be it...up and out of bed she went to the kitchen and started the coffee. After a quick shower, she sat with the morning paper and her coffee contemplating what she would do today. There were so many closets and trunks that needed going threw, that would be a good thing to start with as soon as...that thought was cut short as she heard the water running in the shower. Vincent! There was enough coffee left, he'd make do as she went upstairs to tackle a closet or two.

The first closet was her mom's. Vintage clothes in really good condition, all styles come back around again, it's too bad they weren't closer to the same size. Crystal was way to tall and about four sizes bigger than her mom. She bagged all of this clothing and started on the shoes at the bottom of the closet. *Mom you had really little feet...look at these things, how did you walk in these heels? And these clogs! They're gross! That's it, everything is going.* Everything was bagged and put in the corner for the Salvation Army. In the same room, the next closet was Clive's when he was here. There were three black suits complete with vest and cummerbund and pocket handkerchiefs. To complete these outfits there were two white shirts and one off pink shirt. His black shoes were spit polished every week and it showed. His jeans, t-shirts and bathing suit were folded and on the top shelf. The only other thing was his bathrobe on a side hook. It was the only thing that smelled like him and she hugged it. She had done really good so far, but the closeness of Clive tugged at her heart strings and she was momentarily lost in memories. *Straighten up and fly right Crystal or you'll never finish this project.* All things bagged and she was on to the next room.

Feeling like she still had some energy, going down stairs to talk to Vincent just wasn't in the cards yet. So next was dad and Suzie's room. The next closet was her dad's. This one she found a little harder to handle. It smelled like him and she could picture him in nearly every shirt she handled. Before putting anything in a bag she made sure to check every pocket, he was notorious about pocket change. You were never broke if you had a quarter on you. One of dad's favorite sayings. The memories helped her to finish his closet. Once again, everything bagged and ready for the Salvation Army. This closet was empty and swept out, on to the next. Their weren't as many memories in Suzie's belongings, they were easier to bag and forget, but the closet wasn't empty. There was a travel bag on the floor and it was heavy. Once Crystal had it dragged out and opened she found it full of Vincent's belongings. *Odd she thought, up here, why? Forgotten? Maybe Suzie offered to empty and launder everything? Must be, these things are old.* Once again she went threw every pocket to make sure she wasn't giving away any money or old mail or secrets. There were racing brochures and betting forms and betting receipts. *This is the race track across the street in Connecticut. I wonder if they are any winners here and if they are still good? Wouldn't that be a kick in the pants. Oh ya, credit card receipts he never gave me, I can see why, one person cannot eat or drink this much at one time. She must have been really good to him! Knock it off Crystal, next pocket...more receipts and a copy of the silly bill of sale that bought the land in Connecticut. Holly shit! Look at the dates on these things, look at the locations, look at the money amounts! I don't need to ask him where or how many any more...I think I know. Boy was I stupid!* She stuffed every piece of paper she could put her hands on in an envelope, closed the travel bag and put it in the corner with the other items waiting to go to the Salvation Army. Down stairs she threw the envelope in Vincent's lap, he was sitting in the den, and she hurried from the room.

The kitchen still smelled heavenly because of the cake she baked yesterday, but now it was getting to be supper time. She didn't have much of an appetite after finding Vincent's little bag of lies, so toast and soup was all she prepared...for one. After a brisk 40 minute walk outside, she returned to the house, washed up, brushed her teeth and went to bed. Surprisingly she slept liked a rock.

Morning came and she stretched across to feel for Vincent, but he wasn't there. There wasn't even a head print on his pillow. *No wonder why I slept so good...two nights in a row...maybe I could get used to this! That's a nasty thought.*

When Crystal got up she found a note next to the coffee maker. "Gone to cash in a winning ticket, be home for dinner, please." *That's an odd request now ... the race track ticket... he's gone to Connecticut?*

It was going to be another long day for Crystal. She continued cleaning out odds and ends up stairs left by Clive, Suzie, mom and dad. Their personal dresser draws filled with their underwear, nightgowns, jewelry boxes, address books and in mom's case her diary. Once the draws were emptied, the books were put back into the house library, some jewelry and wall hangings put aside to be donated to a good cause, and the rest readied for the trash. That left two rooms up stairs totally empty and ready for a good cleaning. It was a good feeling to have accomplished so much in just two days. And besides that Crystal had prepared a pot roast for their evenings meal when...and...if.. Vincent got home.

Now what, as Crystal sauntered threw the dinning room and with no particular direction in mind and laid her arm full of materials on the table and just stared at the lot. She remembered when her mom died picking out her funeral outfit and using a few pieces of her 'inexpensive jewelry'. That's when she carried the red-velvet box of her expensive, exquisite jewelry pieces to her own room. What she had here was her moms costume jewelry box, her daily calendar, her favorite hair comb, that was probably worth a kings ransom and a little photo album that she'd never seen before. Still standing there she decided to get a drink and dig into some of these unknown treasures. Once in the kitchen, she checked on the pot roast, it was doing just fine; needed about another hour. With her drink in hand she headed back to the dinning room to first check out that photo album.

Sweet! The first few pictures were of her as a baby, she'd never seen these pictures before. Next, one of her mom and dad together...they looked happy, the back was dated 1929. Next, dad and a dog. That made her stop completely. *They'd never had a dog, why not? She'd never even thought about having a pet. It's not too late, why not...I don't travel nearly as much as I used to, Vincent would probably love it...besides when we do travel, she could come with us. It could be fun! That's a tomorrow thing.* The next picture was of her mom. Her mom at about age 40 in a handsome yet feminine business suit standing in front of the desk in the Oval Office! (the back: sure enough! ... 1946 at the White House) Crystal knew her mom had a very prestigious position in Washington DC, but to see the picture...WoW! Lastly, two pictures of Clive and Clive and her. Next, Crystal held her mom's diary, *to look inside or not look inside, that is the question. Nope..I've got my memories, I've got my own set of problems, this could open up a whole new set of circumstances... not gonna do it!* She set the little book aside to be destroyed. *I never had the time...but now I'm glad I never wrote in a diary. If it were found, we'd be in jail!*

Her thought process had upset her, it didn't take much these days, so off to the piano she escaped! An hour and a half later, she was sitting at the kitchen table eating her pot roast supper all alone. Really she was just pushing the potatoes and carrots around on the plate. He had asked for supper, the cad didn't even know enough to come home and eat it! If she had a dog she could at least feed her the meat! Its no fun eating alone, Vincent didn't come home again.

Dang-Blast-It...that window and the sunshine, I swear I just fell asleep, maybe I'll move upstairs on the other side of the house. I need to shake up MY world, do something different for ME...get out of here and have fun, but only after coffee. Even the coffee didn't do much for her, the thought of breakfast held no appeal either. She woke up alone again this morning. After a quick clean-up around the house and one load of laundry she headed off for the PX. Still having access to the base and a military ID, the PX was still a draw for her. She could loose herself wandering in the isles.

Even after all these years, everyone was always happy to see her. She pushed her shopping basket up and down the isles, shopping mindlessly but taking note of the other women in the store. She never peopled watched as much as she did today. Women of all ages of many different cultures and colors most of them with short hair. At least those were the ones standing out to her. Did she dare...Why not!

Giving herself enough time to think about it while finishing her shopping, driving home and putting everything away, she still had that URGE! Feeling giddy inside, like she was embarking on a new experience, she went to the yellow pages to look for a salon. She called and made an appointment for later today and now felt nervous. What to do until then...? Piano...no blues, peppy tunes, smile songs. She started with Lady in Pink and went on to Bow Ties and Brownies. She was in the grove and played for the next two hours. When she felt finished she looked at her hands, her nails particularly and wondered if the salon did manicures, she was in desperate need. *Yep, today is a me day.* After wandering up stairs, just to be nosy and see what they were working on she figured it was time to go and find that salon. Grabbing her pocket-book and making sure she had her car keys, she was off.

She felt like a little kid, sneaking off to do something...what? Naughty, bad, mischievous, it felt good! Her mood had definitely taken a turn for the better and she was enjoying herself. Then she noticed her hands were sweaty on the steering wheel...she was nervous and she was there! Doing this was totally outside of the norm for her. Paying total strangers to take control of ... "Hello, Crystal Clear, it's the real you...I told the girls you called and made an appointment. Never in a million years did we think you'd ever really do this...come in I'm Patty and she's Chris, that's Carol in the back hall folding towels. So where do you want to begin." Crystal sat in chair and asked if they did manicures, she' be interest in that as well. Also, did they have an association with Locks of Love because if she was going to go through with this she wanted to donate her hair. Carol joined the other two women and assured Crystal that every inch of hair they cut off would be donated. "So let's get started before I change my mind" Crystal whispered. "If you're donating, we wash first" Patty said and helped Crystal out of the chair over to the washing section. While washing Crystal's hair she remarked that this chore was going to be so much easier from now on. "What style cut are you looking for, does your hair wave or curl easily?" Crystal was at a loss. "Since I'm a teenager long hair is all I've known. It's never seen a curler or a perm. All I know is that it is thick and takes forever to dry." "OK, first we'll trim up the ends and donate nice clean, trim locks, probably about 18 to 20 inches long, that'll leave about 10 inches for us to work with." Crystal gasped, "that's a lot to cut off"---changed your mind---we can do your nails and call it a day! After taking a very deep breath Crystal said "let's do it!" The three women applauded her!

A few hours or so later Crystal left the salon with clean, polished fingernails and a hairdo so simple and easy to care for, she was immediately sorry she hadn't done it years before. Now that all the weight was off of the shorter, much shorter ends, they wanted to spring back and bounce a bit. The body her hair exhibited was something she'd never seen before, she loved it. The drudgery of showering and washing all of that long hair was now gone, how nice! There was a form Crystal needed to fill out to donate her hair, but there was also a very sweet card for her to sign personally to the recipient. Feeling wonderful about the time she spent on herself and the good feelings she had about donating her hair, she drove to Wyette's General Store for an ice cream sundae at their lunch counter to celebrate. Her smile didn't dissipate until she got home and Vincent's car still wasn't there.

Supper really wasn't needed tonight, she had just finished a wonderful ice cream sundae, so a little later she'd pick at something, now she just wanted to settle in and read a book. What a novel idea, she hasn't wanted to do that in forever, but right now she was looking forward to it. A number of years ago she had joined 'a book a month club'. Vincent laughed at her as did her mother. Her mom remembered how it was like pulling teeth to get Crystal to read anything in grade school! But collect books she did for a few years, they looked good in her book case. They were all still there collecting dust. It seems her interest ran from mysteries to romance to the girl next door type of books. She picked a mystery and wandered into the living room and got comfortable in one of the over-stuffed chairs. Judging by the 82 pages she had read and the fact that she needed to turn on a light about an hour ago, she guessed she'd been in the living room nearly two hours. Maybe some cheese and crackers and a glass of milk was in order, she made her way back to the kitchen to find Vincent sitting with a beer at the kitchen table. She was startled to see him there, but when he looked at her, the new her, he was very startled as well. Neither one of them said a word. He finished his beer, got up and went to take a shower. Crystal went about collecting her cheese and crackers and settled at the table. Once again, just like the other day, she thought; *this isn't what my life should be like when I'm 73 years old, I'm too old for this shit! And her thoughts were back on her cheating husband...not her book any more.*

For the rest of the week she didn't see much of Vincent, he wasn't home, he must have found something to do. Crystal was just waiting for one o'clock today to meet with Clarke because it was the only appointment she had and couldn't wait to get it over with. He seemed anxious to meet with her, especially coming here to Shelby Street. She didn't get out to New York much these days, so meeting here fit his scheduled just fine. Since Rita and Clive have been gone she was pretty much retired. Her schedule is flexible as she plays primarily only in their own lounges, at the motels on the weekends. With eight motels in seven different states, if she chooses to work every weekend, it can still keep her mighty busy! Every now and then the New Yorker will call and book her in one of their lounges. It's fun, they take out one of her old posters and advertise and usually fill the space for the weekend. New York is still a fast pace and interesting city, she never gets tired of it! Vegas and Atlantic City are now catering to the younger set and the more pop music. The Big Band days and Crystal's type of music just doesn't fill the stadiums any more. It's OK, she's busy enough. She doesn't need to compete any more for record sales or radio play. She's happy in her little nitch. For the last few years Vincent had been going to the motels with her for the weekends. They'd drive up together, they have breakfast and dinner together, Crystal plays on Saturday night and they drive home together on Sunday.. It had been working out really well. Truth be known she hadn't noticed Vincent being particularly careful not to be seen at the motels or in the towns, maybe Connecticut more than the others, but that's only because that's where he just got caught! This meeting with Clarke is really his, I wish he was here...too late, Clarke just arrived.

Chapter 65

2000's

Clarke was a really interesting guy. He just got back from a holiday visit to Switzerland. Skiing was his thing, so when he met a gal that loved the sport as much as he did, they married and have been traveling together ever since. He explained that she is also a lawyer in a different New York firm and they have it worked out that they both take the month of December off each year. He has a little more flexibility because of his relationship in his firm so he can take on clients or investigations as it strikes his fancy. His wife gets extremely jealous of his time out of the courtroom. He admits, she works harder than he does. Like this weekend, he is starting here, but heading to Atlantic City as soon as their visit is concluded. Crystal's almost a little jealous, she hasn't gambled in a long time. With this chit-chat over, it's now time to get down to business. Crystal invites him to sit at the kitchen table and promises a delectable surprise as soon as he says what he has to say.

He gives her a quizzical look and then starts spreading pictures across the table. He said he started in Massachusetts and found Andrea Chambers on Robins Nest Dr. in Grafton. The picture is of a lovely colonial house with a slender woman of about 35 standing there with her three children. The house belongs to her mother Andrea Chambers now 54 years old, the next picture. Crystal looks and admits they are all good looking people. *So that's Vincent's daughter and his grand children, if he only knew.* Clarke then continues with the story behind the people.

Ms. Andrea Chambers is a very educated woman, she works at the largest hospital in Worcester, it's about 7 miles from her house. Working in the criminal behavior/physiological department of that hospital helped her in her biggest and most important case of her career, more than that, her life! You see the younger woman, it's her daughter Maddie. When Maddie was thirteen years old a childhood type of cancer was discovered in her body. Andrea went on a wild search for a blood type donner to help her daughter. The search was wild because Andrea was the only surviving member of the Chamber family burned out of their house in April of 1964.

Her mom was an only child with no living relatives so that side of the family was no help and it was the same on her dad's side of the family...no living relatives. *Crystal's mind was blinded with sorrow... Vincent might have been able to help!* A local blood drive to help Maddie turned up a possible match as did the country wide search of Maddie's blood type. This possibility was in Maryland. To investigate the possible match from the local blood drive, it meant traveling to Arizona. *She wasn't a match to Vincent, small saving grace. He couldn't have helped in that regard after all.* The participant in the blood drive had married and moved. Andrea questioned the validity of the sample and the persons name, location, of everything. The match was coming from her mothers side of the family, which made her look at every piece of paper left from her mothers personal file. Andrea had looked at these papers before but nothing jumped out at her. Now dates and locations are ringing bells as is one familiar name. Her mother's maiden name was Sampson, this potential donor's maiden name was also Sampson.

Clarke indicated that Andrea did travel to Arizona where she did in fact confirm through many documents and the unmistakable likeness of her (Andrea's) own eyes to this newly found relatives eyes that they were undeniably related. "Don't ask me how I found out, but I guess Andrea and her Aunt Dora both have the same color green eyes with a speck of white in the pupil that comes off like neon! I guess at first, Andrea was pretty freaked-out over this, but it also proved to be the final and best link into family." Clarke took a breathe and asked if Crystal was following him so far. Crystal asked... "So when everything was said and done, the Arizona woman came back to Massachusetts to be a donner for Maddie?" "Yup" was all he had a chance to say because Crystal immediately followup with, "did Andrea find out how her name was Sampson, if her mom didn't have any relatives?"

"Quick story---Dora grew up in foster care, kinda always looking for a family to belong to and it happened on a military base in the library. She found some 'records of fact' and it read like her life story, so, many inquiries later and a blood test to confirm, that she was in fact the illegitimate daughter of the Pulitzer Prize winner of 1927, Martin Sampson." Crystal was all ears and mighty interested in these stories, forgetting that they all revolved around her husband. "Wow, you sure were busy, I'm glad it all had a happy ending. Now how about coffee and a piece of this wonderful cake I make called Better than Sex!" "I'm all for a piece of cake, but better than sex, dear Crystal you've been married too long if you think cake….." He just shrugged his shoulders and almost felt bad for her.

While enjoying and savoring every bite of his newest best desert, Clarke informed Crystal that he wasn't done with his report on the people she had asked him to look into. But then he informed her that he'd get back to that when the organism that hit his brain subsided and expired after he had another piece of this indescribable cake! Crystal counted with "that's why its called 'Better than Sex', silly!

After a long break of just eating and getting caught up on people and vacations and trips and New York, they talked about the passing of Crystal's mom and Clive in that horrific bridge accident. With the support of everyone involved and with each day that passes with eye witness accounts, police reports, skid marks and generally good detective and police work the bus driver did all he could to avoid the accident. The bus company is cooperating with everything they have been asked to do and to surrender; such as maintenance records and reports, tire inspections, everything down to replacement windshield wipers. It was a gorgeous day on October seventh, the accident should have never happened. The bus passed all of it's tests so it is completely on the two ass-hole motorcycle guys trying to ride the top rail. How they got up there is anybody's guess. No one so far has come forward with that information! All fifty-seven souls on board that bus should have made it home safely that day. It will take years to culminate all aspects of the case and get it settled, but at the end of the day it will pay out millions!

Crystal your cake was delicious, but speaking about court cases, that's what next in the things I found out. I didn't even have to leave Massachusetts to learn that in 1982, once Maddie had survived her ordeal, a doctor colleague of Andrea's talked her into pursing the search for the Maryland donner match.

It turns out that Rockwell Sabers and his best friend Kevin... remember the kid with the broken leg back in the 50's were the one's raising hell in Massachusetts in 1964. They drove up to take revenge on Mrs. Chambers because Rockwell found pictures of his dad with her (supposedly her, a beautiful blond woman)taken on the vacation he had taken with his boys in 1955. Somehow Rockwell had it in his head that Mrs. Chambers had met his dad in NH while they were there and he had pictures as proof. In the meantime it was Kevin who took Andrea from her bedroom the night Rockwell set the house on fire. Kevin brought Andrea into the orchard that night and raped her. He had been drinking waiting for Rockwell to avenge his revenge so when he took Andrea, he was stinking drunk and the rape was brutal and mean. It was also how Andrea ended up pregnant. That's the reason why Andrea survived the horrible fire at her house. She wasn't in it!

It was the same Kevin who received blood transfusions from Rockwell during his bought with his cancer in his broken leg back in the 50's. Andrea being a doctor, a very smart doctor figured out that the blood transfusion from Rockwell to Kevin, changed Kevin's blood type to that of Rockwell's. Once Dr. Andrea and her friend Dr. Gayle had the proof of the blood angle they needed to identify Kevin as the rapist because it was Rockwell dead behind the garage at the Chamber's house. But that's how the two boys ended up with the same blood type and ended up being a match for Maddie. But wait, this still needed to be thought through...it was the Sabers blood that was the match... more searching. It took some time and more travel for Andrea and her friend but they got the job done. It turns out that Andrea's dad and

Rockwell's dad were the same man. In finding all of this out, it's a good thing that he was dead, because if he weren't, he be spending jail time as a bigamist!

Andrea was incensed to think it was her mother that was cheating with Rockwell's father and she wanted to see the pictures. Kevin said Rockwell had proof and he kept them in a leather bag. That bag had been in the trunk of Kevin's car all these years and was looked at in the police station in Maryland with Andrea as witness. It was indeed a picture of a beautiful woman, but not her mom! So the revenge was all for naught. The death and destruction was useless. So many people were hurt. And two families were torn apart. As it turned out, Rockwell took the lives of his half bothers and sisters, all but one. The court case I spoke of was Kevin extradited back to Massachusetts to stand trial for the statuary rape of a minor...Andrea was still 17 years old... three months away from her eighteenth birthday in April of 1964, and accessory to arson and murder.

Now Clarke slid a new pile of pictures for Crystal to see. First was the picture of the bungalow on 5 Lost Road. It had quite an upgrade since the death of Reginald. Next a picture of Rockwell taken when he graduated from college, that's as old as he got, next of Russell and his wife and three kids, Rachel, who incidentally looks just like Andrea, then the twins Ruby and Rose now in their forties and the youngest, Riley just closing in on forty-three. "Traveling over to Maryland to get these pictures was a little eerie after getting all the facts before my arrival." Clarke just shook his head and repeated "eerie".

"Just to ease my own curiosity I looked into the identity and service record of both Reginald Sabers and Aspen Chambers because the kids seamed to lack for nothing, had great educations paid for by the government and their dad's GI benefit, plus savings accounts for each child at their birth. He did a good job for a man who never existed and he did it twice! Crystal, this is the second time you've asked me to look in on these families, if you ever need a lawyer, a know a few that are really good. I know these things are none of my business, I was just curious." She looked at him and thought for a minute. "Have you ever had a best friend, neighbor, colleague, teacher or acquaintance that hinted at a situation, but never asked for help or suggested that somethings weren't quite right? Years ago this is how it all started...I was more curious than you, I am down right nosy, even all these years later! I'm sorry to hear that there was tragedy, death and criminal behavior associated with these families, but when looking at all these people over nearly forty years they fit the national average on each count. To look at the lot of them, they look well adjusted and happy. That will be my take-away and now I can leave it at that! As far as the money goes on my mom's case, you know I don't need the money, I just want those two young men that caused the accident hung by their balls and really, really hurt! What they did was negligent and criminal."

Clarke was satisfied with Crystal's response to his query. "You made me wonder for a while, while I was driving back from Maryland. I did question what you had to do with these people and their lives. OK, so we are done with them, I did my job?"

Crystal smiled at him, covered her hand over his and shook her head in the affirmative, just like old ladies do! Clarke held her hand for a minute, said that is was always nice working for her and took his leave.

It was still early and Crystal was once again wondering where Vincent took off to. Clarke had no sooner left the driveway and a beautiful, spanking new, gold colored Lincoln Towncar pulled into its place. Crystal was standing at the door to see Clarke off and saw this car arrive and park. Vincent got out of the car all smiles, did a half bow and did the arm extension of 'offer.' It did warm Crystal's heart! She loved that car. Vincent came nearly 'skipping' up the walk way, approached Crystal, encircled his arm around her waist and walked her back into the warmth of the house. "So what do you think?" He didn't give her an opportunity to say a word. "It's registered in your name because the insurance was cheaper that way...you're younger than I am". "In that case..." she grabbed her jacket off the hook and put her hand out to Vincent, palm up.

Ten minutes later, cursing down the road, she said "it handles like a dream and the ride is so smooth. How and when did you do this"? "I'll fill in all the blanks if you buy me supper". She thought real quick about the conversations they need to have at home around the pictures Clarke left and said, "sure enough." He slipped in one of her tapes and the sound was divine! Driving this wonderful machine and listening to her music, she took her time, even took two back roads to get to Davinci's, one of their favorite places to catch a quick meal.

Once seated with her drink of choice, Rum & Coke, and Vincent with his beer, he started spreading out and flattening papers and receipts in front of her. "What's all this?" she asked with a wrinkled look on her face? First she saw the paid in full receipt for the car that he bought in Connecticut. She saw first the state and then the amount, took a deep breathe and asked, "how?" His smile was wide and proud! He then turned a few pieces of paper for her to look at. They were the betting receipts she had thrown at him yesterday, but they were stamped 'processed'. "What does processed mean?" she asked. Again he smiled and turned a yellow sheet of paper toward her so she could see it clearly. A 1099 needed to be processed because he ran into taxable dollars! She looked back at the bill of sale and the price of the car and then he pushed an envelope toward her and she saw it contained cash. "You did good...you did really good." Her words made him blush and start gushing "I've never won anything before in my life, it was a shot in the dark the day I placed these bets, didn't know one horse from another. My ten dollar bills did a lot of good that day, it's the same day I bought the land for two $10 bills and wrote up the bill of sale for the guy to sign. I haven't been to the races since. You keep me too busy!" She looked at the bill of sale for the car again. "You did good with this too, it's only got 67 miles on it...it's band new?" "Well, I've driven it a little...more like 267miles now. I knew you were mad, so I stayed away about 200 miles longer." She reached across the table and touched his hand, he turned it over and grasped hers. "Lets just call a truce and enjoy our meal, shall we" she suggested.

With the morning light, Crystal found Vincent sitting at the kitchen table looking at the pictures Clarke had left. There was a peacefulness that touched Vincent's facile features. A look that only another parent could really appreciate, but it was apparent that Vincent needed these reminders of what he had helped to create. He hadn't seen his children in a long time, he was lost in love at this moment, she hated to disturb him. Having poured her own coffee, she joined him at the table. "You made beautiful children, Mr. Clear." *and immediately caught her own mistake, they were Sabers!* "I'm not sorry I wasn't here with you yesterday, the kids look too much like me. Your detective was able to be more open with you alone. He would have just looked at me and his flood gate of questions would have opened." "Clarke's not like that, what you're suggesting would have been very unprofessional of him. As it was, when he had finished telling me the tales of everyone's life, he did ask me if I needed a lawyer." Vincent just studied her face now..."and do you, need a lawyer"? "No, I do not, and he was satisfied with that." "So what are the tales of everyone's life?" Crystal took a deep breathe and said, "let's start with a the good story"

Crystal leafed threw the pictures until she came to those of Andrea. "Andrea grew into a beautiful, smart and accomplished physician. We knew she was pregnant and this is her daughter Maddie, with her three beautiful children. Two girls and a boy. They are standing in front of Maddie's house. She stayed in Grafton and works in the Medical Center in Worcester, only 7 miles away. Her husband was not with them the day these pictures were taken, he was at work." When Crystal looked over at Vincent his eyes were glassy, he didn't dare blink. He got up from the table and got more coffee.

When Vincent came back with his coffee, she reached for his hand and explained the rest of the information will be hard to hear. "Clarke laid everything right out there thinking that I was a friend of a friend and not emotionally attached to any of these people." "So tell me, don't hide anything!" Crystal started as gently as she could handling the pictures of the kids as she spoke and relayed the people and the places and the time line just as Clarke had. Several times Vincent shifted in his chair and a couple of times he struck the table to release some anger-frustration-hurt. Crystal asked if they should take a break, make fresh coffee, take a walk, change the subject. The facts are not going to change, even if we talk about this later. "It's not going to hurt any less later, please finish." Once Vincent stopped her to release the words building from his memories..."that was you the boys took a picture of, not Amy. In the jail room, Andrea was looking at a picture of you not her mother! That poor girl!"

They'd already been sitting there a couple of hours looking at the pictures talking about the fire. Talking about Andrea's ordeal and then the medial problems with her teen daughter. Vincent was just getting to the realization of Kevin not being in Grafton alone, not without Rockwell and Rockwell hadn't been seen since the night of the fire and his DNA surfaced from the scene, therefore the unidentified body behind the garage and the person who set that horrible fire was his son. And the way all the facts starting falling together, was by the forensic work done by his daughter and her equally gifted doctor friend from Massachusetts.

All this time Vincent was holding and looking at the picture of Rockwell, the one Saber boy who never aged past 25 years old. "All of this happened 36 years ago. When were all of the little side stories solved?" "Clarke said Andrea and her friend Gayle started their investigations around 1982. It took them a while to zero in on the two boys from Towson, MD, but once they got that far, Kevin was the weak link and once he cracked, all the truth came out as well as the pictures Rockwell had hidden for years. Kevin was arraigned in Towson District Court in 1983 and transferred to the Massachusetts court system in 1984. Kevin stood trial in Massachusetts in 1987 was found guilty on all counts. In 1988 he committed suicide in prison." Now Vincent blew his nose and wiped his eyes and asked is there anything else?"

"A little, Rhonda Sabers was contacted by Andrea with the support of her friend Gayle and after a few uncomfortable visits found pleasant ground on which they could be friendly. After all, everybody loved the Dad! To this day Andrea and your Rachel are good friends. That's good because they are the same age and half-sisters; (and after shuffling the pictures around) look at how much they look alike!" Finally, Vincent found something in this mess he could smile about. Then he asked, "Where is Rockwell buried?" "Rockwell was buried in an unmarked grave in Grafton, Massachusetts in 1964, as of this date, it never has been marked. That's what Clarke said."

Chapter 66

2003

Several weeks turned into several months where Crystal's working the motel lounges was becoming an interruption to her retirement. It just turned out that way...she hadn't really retired but New York wasn't calling her any more, neither was Vegas or Atlantic City. Her hands were telling her that enough was enough, go out on top and let the recordings be her legacy. Vincent was six years her senior and was not aging well after hearing the entire story of 1964 and the fate of a few of his children. His mood and temperament suffered terribly and his sleeping habits or rather lack of sleep affected his health in a very downhill manner.

Vincent, on paper, was still a man to be reconciled with. As when he needed to meet with the maintenance men and the oil company to come to terms on the discrepancy in gallons of oil delivered and the usage of the oil. Crystal stayed out of it...Vincent always made his point of fact and turned the situation into a win! He was, after-all a good business man! Just an aging, unhealthy, old goat who in public stood tall. In private, was moody, suffered terrible head aches had poor eating and sleeping habits.

Every now and then they would take a ride to one of their motels, Crystal would play in the lounge an unadvertised set to the pleasure of every person in the house! Once she started playing, more and more people would arrive and that always made her hands feel better! (in her head!) Once alone in her own room she would take more Advil and soak her hands in hot water to make her knuckles feel better. She knew cold, ice water would help more for the inflammation, but the hot felt so good!

Vincent would take the ride with her to the motels, mostly because he didn't want to stay home alone. He didn't drive any more and even Crystal made sure that she only drove in the daytime. Night-time driving was bothering her eyes. Too much glare! Getting old really sucks, but she wasn't giving in to it yet! She was slowing down, but still enjoying everything she set out to do! She learned that the silver in her short hair hadn't changed the Crystal, to much!

Aside from the motels, which was now a stand alone money-making operation run by a management company hand picked by her attorneys, Crystal still had the recording studio located in her home in New Jersey. Her home...the house was too big for her and Vincent. After talking with Vincent about it, it was decided to turn it into a hotel for visiting recording artists and they would move to a smaller house or condo or take a cruise around the world! Just not live there anymore...maybe.

The recording studio was another money-marker. But since the loss of Rita and Mr. Brentwhistle, Crystal had lost a great deal of interest in it's every day operation. Sure, she'd go upstairs and listen in when an artist peaked her interest. Or she'd use the equipment and technicians when she wanted to record something herself, but on the whole, it ran without her input. So now she was thinking , she was going to totally hire out it's management to a separate firm.

Crystal had put a lot of thought into what she planned to do with her house. Miss Elise would be proud of her as was Peter when she called him and talked with him at length about her plans and the help she would need from him. Vincent listened to her plans, but it was 'just' Crystal 'talking'. Vincent had little interest in much Crystal did or said these days. His days were filled with looking at his kids pictures and doodling. His writing didn't make any sense. He would fill notebooks full of nonsense. Most of his writings weren't even words! Crystal would leave him to his own despair and move on with her own plans. Vincent's despair was of his own making. Living in a mayhem world for so long, now he didn't know how to make do.

A little more than two years ago, Vincent convinced Crystal to drive him to Massachusetts to visit Rockwell's grave. They were heading home from their Wolfboro Motel, so a little detour into Massachusetts wasn't a big deal. A request to visit his son's final resting place was not an outlandish request! Standing on a flat piece of ground in a Grafton cemetery on a sunny Sunday afternoon in April stirred up emotions that hurt! The flat stone depicting angel wings and roses merely said, Rockwell-All is Forgiven. Crystal was shocked at the heart-felt decision Vincent had to make for those feelings! And he ordered the stone all on his own. Maybe now he could sleep better. After spending just a few minutes at Rockwell's site, walking back to the car, Vincent asked Crystal if she would drive him past Andi's house. Not really surprised because they were so close, she just shook her head, yes. In her own heart she really hoped 'someone' would be outside. Just getting out of the car, getting the mail, washing windows, someone...outside!

Crystal had just started the car and Vincent said, "Wait...Please go up Speer Street first, it's not out of the way, I just want to look." Crystal said nothing and slowly drove out of the cemetery and drove taking his directions to the top of Speer Street. Driving up, the apple trees in the orchard were just beginning to uncurl their green leaves and look alive, it was a quiet and peaceful place. Then, there it was a long low ranch style house with an attached two car garage with a basketball hoop over the doors. It looked like a well lived-in home not at all the same style house that burned down so many years ago. They say you can never go home again and this certainly wasn't Vincent's home!

"Thanks for coming up here, now let's try and find Andi". Crystal turned around in front of the fence at the farm, just like so many others before her had.

"I can see why you liked living here, Grafton is a really nice town." Crystal said this while driving away from Speer Street, still taking directions from Vincent to get to the other end of town. "It was even nicer forty years ago, but it still only has one set of lights at the lake. Here we are and wouldn't you know it...it's red" Vincent said at the stop. Left here and we'll travel Grafton's million dollar mile of Dunkin Donuts, pizza, Chinese food, banks, a liquor store, dry cleaners, beauty parlors, it's only supermarket, gas stations, CVS and a dentist. That's new". They traveled the next mile in silence just taking in their surroundings until their approach to another street light. Vincent said "bear left at this light, it's new too". Not too much further down the street they came to Wyman Gordon's, a large factory operated by the Navy. In it's hay day, the parking lots had three or four hundred cars in it's parking lots rather than only the fifty or sixty cars he saw today. "Slow down, take the next left and then in a half mile Andi's street is on the right.

"OMG...the girl at the mail box...slow down...stop." Vincent opened his window and spoke to the girl. "Can you help us, we're looking for Point Rock Estates on Creeper Hill Road." She was really cute, maybe ten years old and defiantly had a family resemblance. She giggled and said, "you are really lost, I know where it is, but couldn't tell you how to get there...wait a minute...Mom, she yelled." Now Crystal guessed it was Maddie approaching the car at the 10 year old's beckoning. The older woman, maybe forty, had the look of her mother, Vincent's Andrea! With a brilliant smile she said, "I'm heading there in a few minutes if you'd like to follow me, I'll be just a minute. Wait here." and she walked away. Crystal said "it's that Welsh blood line, it makes all of you look alike, it hasn't diluted yet! They all look like you!" Vincent took that as a compliment and beamed at Crystal. Within minutes they were traveling again on familiar roads, but encounted more traffic lights Vincent knew nothing about. The town is growing, it's too bad, it's not quaint anymore!

Vincent explained that he knew where they were going. Years ago Point Rock was a fresh water beach that was on Lake Quinsiamond and nearly every school kid went to swimming lessons there. Now it was a gated community built on the water for the over fifty population... Thinking out loud he said "had Andi moved here and now Maddie and her family have her house? How things change! Let's go home."

Chapter 67

2005

For the last couple of hours Vincent had filled his senses with family. He now relaxed silently in the car next to Crystal, who had her own thoughts on the last couple of hours. She couldn't wait to get home. At her age, she was beginning to feel the pinch of not having anyone else in her life to leave things to. Neither did Vincent, really. He was already dead to his families, this was the closest he dare to venture. They were all each other had. As she discussed with Peter briefly last week, she needed to get home and catalog and photograph her belongings for sale or auction if she intended to vacate her house and do a major remodel. She had mentioned this desire to Vincent as well, but his interest in her whims were nil! She'd proceeded anyway!

Moving into a suite at the Fairmont Embassy Hotel right down the street wouldn't be such an inconvenience. It would be nice to be taken care of and eating from the hotel lounge or dinning room and not thinking about cooking for a while. She needed to get home and arrange these thoughts into a workable timetable and talk to Peter again and work it out with him. Still driving in silence, she couldn't let her thoughts run away from her. This time she spoke to Vincent and let him in on her thought process to see if he had any problem leaving the house and staying at the Fairmont for awhile. He said he rather liked the place...after all it gave him the idea of their motels and that worked out rather well. So when they get home, the first thing to do was call Peter and see when he could get out to the East Coast for an extended visit!

Crystal is excited again! Vincent recognizes this and says...OH Boy!, here we go again!" Crystal counters with "your life would have been so boring if I didn't get excited like this." "When we were younger, I would be whisking you off to bed and taking advantage of your excitement, now I just let you call Peter." She smiles the all knowing smile, hugs him sincerely and disappears to the piano for the next hour or so. This is still how she thinks things through.

The next day Crystal was on the phone with the design crew that she had worked with before, made an appointment for them to come to her, had the town building permit department's email handy, called Bull to find out his availability and went upstairs in search of Matt, the head honcho up there, who would need to know what she was up to... this time! She was in such a great mood. Peter said he could be there the first Monday of the following month and stay as long as she needed him. She and Vincent had been living out of different rooms for so long now, not sleeping here and being at the Fairmont and still going to the different motels on a monthly basis would almost seem normal. For as long as she is able she is determined to continue at this pace. Vincent recognizes the bounce in Crystal's step and likes what he sees. She is a happy girl!

Chapter 68

Once Peter arrives it only takes about 6 weeks to photograph everything Crystal wants to sell. Peter is that organized! Some pieces needed to be moved and or staged. All needed to be cleaned and polished and seen in their best light. Some of the carpets were shampooed and photographed as well. Better to sell them than to rip them up and dispose of them. The pictures on the walls, the murals and landscapes had their frames touched-up and were well cleaned. All the drapes in the living rooms and all of the white curtains that were in the windows since Crystal got there, if they could be saved...were saved. Peter made the determinations that when ready, the washer and dryer and refrigerator would be donated to a homeless shelter down-town. All of the usable pots and pans would also be donated.

Peter's on-line catalog and portfolio of his photographs of all things 'Clearly' netted Crystal a pretty penny in the sale of everything! Everything except the piano!

For six weeks it wasn't all work and moving furniture and cleaning, a few of the days were spent with the design team, with Matt (from the recording studio) Peter and naturally Vincent. Trying to figure out exactly what she wanted to do with the building was the hard part. Foremost, keep and maybe enlarge the recording studio, would need more parking outback. Hi-end hotel the rest of the building? How many rooms. Make it a bed and breakfast..how many rooms...dinning room for how many. Breakfast a must! Offer a dinner menu to the public? Need more parking regardless...enhance the back yard and swimming area? Name?? Time line? Keep a personal suite on premises? More questions than answers.

Matt said he didn't need more space for the recording studio, even the large office downstairs could be reworked space-wise and the job could be a shared responsibly for appointments and reservations. If that's all he was needed for, he needed to get back upstairs, he felt sure Crystal would do good by him and his studio. "Just let me know when we're on vacation because of all the work that needs to be done" he smiles brightly and walks away. Matt was Crystal's major player upstairs and he made everything run like a well oiled machine. Rita trained him well and he has been making contacts and building contracts and making money for the label ever since Rita's demise.

Next, figuring space for the chefs kitchen and major laundry room taken out of the equation, keeping an on-suite on the main floor for Crystal and Vincent and using the remaining space on the first floor as dinning space and office that leaves using the size of the bedroom and bathroom combo, divided into the building space now available and that means 18 rooms on the second and third floors. Adding sq footage to the building could mean larger rooms or more rooms. Everything was food for thought. Peter came up with the name for the door as CLEARLY IRRESISTIBLE (B&B).

Things were coming together...Yes, Bed and Breakfast ... keep the foot-print as is, that's still 18 guest rooms. Yes, a lighted fountain out front with a foot bridge to the front door, No stone work, keep the integrity of a mission style home. Rework downstairs office, keep piano in living room/main dinning room. This was Crystal's last go round and she wanted to be included in every major design and decision. She'd use Claire again and that design team, then step back once everything was underway. The back yard pool area and garden needed to be tweaked just a little to bring it closer to the house for the guests.

Yes a B&B with breakfast every morning. A nice buffet style. Even dinner severed every night. A fixed menu, with a fixed price severed family style and offered to the public, one seating and done, just like any families house.

She'd talk with the management company handling the motels for all the staffing requirements and see to it that, that runs smoothly as well. With all of this going on, she and Vincent should still be able to make their monthly trips to the motels. That will be their R&R...after-all it's too busy here!

Crystal was excited. They had so much. In a way, they found a way to enjoy every bit of what they had. The house was just too big and not enjoyable any more. Not with the family gone and Miss Elise just a memory. Maintaining their room on the back of the house near the back door will be just right. The people filling the house and the aroma of food and noise from all around and upstairs, knowing the studio is working to capacity and they have celebrities and wannabees in and out all the time, it is exciting! *Yes, everything is falling into place very nicely. We'll have more than enough for everyone. I had managed in the past to make sure everyone, had...the future should be no different. This nest egg should be big enough.*

Chapter 69

2010

With everything running at it's peak of perfection with Crystal and Vincent enjoying their self made retirement schedule, the months traveling to their motels, melted away into years and living among the happy, excited young musicians coming and going and staying at their B&B and the towns people and other weary travelers stopping in for dinner, their B&B's reputation mandated a bus stop on Shelby Street!

When home and reading a book, out by the pool, Crystal never knew who would be joining her. A neighbor, a celebrity or Peter coming for an unannounced visit. The pool or the Tiki Bar at the pools edge on hot summer afternoons was always a favorite place to met up with friends. So in preparation for another busy season, the grounds are under going a Spring clean-up and the pool is being cleaned. Vincent is outside just enjoying the sites and sounds of Spring and everything waking up when he falls to the ground and never gets up. He is pronounced dead at the hospital a short time later. It's April 11, 2010 and Crystal's world has now changed forever. The hospital is kind and treats her with the respect due any grieving widow. The funeral director and everyone on base couldn't be kinder and more helpful even if it were their own family. Crystal hasn't needed to do this for thirteen years since she planned her own mothers funeral, but she was younger then and she forgot how much it took out of her emotionally. This was hard, very hard.

She withdrew into her own thoughts and her own rooms. For hours she'd just stare off into the distance and separate herself from everything...

She's talking to herself...remembering

Almost from the beginning, she knew Vincent was a cheating man. She also knew he loved her dearly..

There were many things that Crystal would do or try to do to include Vincent in her every day or her long term planning process. Her dressing was only provocative for him. She would flaunt and tease and do anything she could think of to keep him interested. She remembered their first home on a back road a mile off base. She'd walk to meet him and the closer he got, the more open her shirt would become. By the time they were face to face the only covering her breasts had was her long hair, very long hair tucked into the waist band of the front of her pants.. He'd smile, lift the hair out of his way and fondle her all the way home. By the time they reached their front porch she'd inform him that her panties were wet. That stroked his masculine appetite! He'd look for the same greeting the next day, and the day after that...it kept him coming home.

By the time they were in their second apartment, while home, she never wore panties, she was always available. Even that couldn't keep him home. This is when he took his first second wife! Not so much with her blessings, but with her help. Again, to please him in this regard, he'd come home to her to reap all the benefits of a husband. Their sex life was exciting, exhausting but not rewarding! He wanted children. In her mind he was never home long enough to make a good dad, he had a career, that is what she pursued, a career!

She tried many times over to include him in her overnight jaunts. First to New York, he did one out of every ten visits. Then to Vegas... he only went twice. He was never over-joyed with her career as a pianist, a concert pianist, it kept her away from home too often. By now he had a second, second wife. Guess who was never home now! But when he was...wow, the bedroom was steamy and Crystal was a happy girl. Somehow she could block his other women out of her mind. When he was home he was hers! When she wrote her first song, he needed to sit-up and take notice. She was good, really good. He got caught up in the melody and mouthed some words that stuck. To this day she can see his face listening to the music and almost singing the beautiful words. They came from his heart and painted a picture more beautiful than she could even imagine.

Military transfers are never easy. His last one put her in charge of finding housing that was close to the base and private enough for her to play the piano whenever she wanted or needed to. She also needed to be able to travel to New York easily. What she learned really fast was that this was a great transfer. The train into New York was a shorter ride and it's location put her near to Atlantic City where she could work as well. The house she found was a steal in all ways. It was huge, had all the amenities, a low monthly rent, had a great piano was owner occupied in the person of an almost elderly woman who kept to herself and loved to cook. She loved to remember Miss Elise, their house mom, who loved to listen to her play the piano.

These memories were mostly sweet. This big house easily became home. She loved being here. It was a good thing because she spent a great deal of time there alone. Her Vincent was quite the virile man, having a total of twelve kids in two different states. *I must have been a very lonely and desperate woman to still want this guy, either that or I was completely off my rocker! But I remember when I traveled or when I was in need, I had Mr. Purple!...OH, the memories!!*

I remember finding my moms diary back in the day...I never did read it, had no interest in a diary what-so-ever. But now, remembering my memories as they pop into my head... is fun. I have mostly great memories and they are worth thinking about.

Vincent, he would go off and be a dad with his kids, but Crystal would never let him bring that home. Remembering the vacation she planned for him and his kids...she became that proverbial fly on the wall and went along on the side lines. So that when he was relating the bits and pieces of Rockwell's friend Kevin and his broken leg and medical problems, at least Crystal could picture Rockwell. It was years later when she got the rest of that story! Vincent's kids were so much a part of him and not Crystal, one day she took a ride just to eyeball his kids playing in their respective back yards. Crystal went from Massachusetts to Maryland just to look at his kids!

Crystal's life began to change a little when she recorded her first original song. She was introduced to the likes of a recording studio, song writers, the meaning of record sales in the material world and how much that could be worth to her. Her piano playing was an art and it was worth selling and exploiting and it expanded her professional horizons exponentially! She also learned the worth of her best friend in New York and found the love of her mother after years of being physically and emotionally estranged.

Crystal had learned that she needed to live her own life...Vincent was certainly off living his. If the military wasn't sending him off to NH or down to Va for weeks at a time, he'd be off every other weekend to spend it with one of his other families. She had his love when it was convenient for him other than that she had Miss Elise always wanting to listen to Crystal's piano playing or cook for who ever was there. It was heart-breaking to Crystal when Miss Elise passed away, but it also a major stroke of income for her, as she inherited the property because according to Miss Elise, Crystal brought so much joy to her and life and love to the house.

This was now Crystal's home. She brought everyone and everything she loved under her newly renovated and enlarged roof. She now had private living accommodations for her mom and her NY best friend Clive(they were quite the item!) as well as her dad and Vincent's mom (who had been an item and caused the wedge in her mom's marriage, years ago) as well as her own recording studio and business office. Clearly Entertaining the record label and corporation was established and made Crystal a very rich woman. Vincent was in awe of Crystal's business sense and proud of her accomplishments and went along with everything she proposed to do. After-all, he was still a service man, but his retirement was looming in the not too distance future, then what was he going to do?

Tragedy happened in Vincent's life when his Massachusetts family perished in a fire. All but one of his children loss their life that day. He was there and escaped certain death by the care of one particular person on site. He was whisked away by ambulance, to a burn center, saving his real identity and letting that of the house owner perish as well. Getting him home to Crystal with his lower extremities burned and him still having trouble walking was again, quite the feat on her part. By now, for Vincent she is quite the liar and she does it so well! These injuries helped to expedite his retirement and left the question, now what!

There was no-way Vincent could retire from military life and go home and live with wife number two 24/7 as she would expect, so Crystal did the unthinkable and on paper the same way she created two service-men with complete pay and benefits, she saw to their demise. The Massachusetts man was already declared dead, so Crystal only needed to finish off the Maryland man. That done, now Vincent had no other families to travel back to. His physique took a beating all in one wack and he wallowed in self pity for awhile, but for what he had lost, he bounced back pretty quickly. He never verbalized to Crystal his feelings on the subject or threw in her face that which she took from him. At least he knew his Maryland family was well, just doing without him. Life goes on!

One gray afternoon Vincent took Crystal by the hand and invited her to go for a walk with him. They'd never done that before in their own neighborhood, but what the heck...having stopped for a cocktail at a local lounge, Vincent shares with Crystal his idea for future work, income, and staying busy. The idea of Clearly Comfortable is born all this time talking to herself.

Chapter 70

All the plans were made, service dates for May 10th after the cremation. Vincent and Crystal never spoke of their own final wishes so Crystal did what she would want for herself. There was a small prayer service held in the little church on Harding Street. She made sure to inform the funeral director of these, her final wishes as well when she ordered her own tiny burial urn, a match to Vincent's. With travel back to Massachusetts and a plot next to Rockwell's in Fairview Cemetery, South Grafton, she was ready for the burial on May 10th. Crystal had ordered a small flat marker; Vincent Octavio Clear, Loving husband and father, February 9, 1921-May 1, 2010...all words surrounded by roses and wings, also a match to Rockwell's that Vincent had lovingly ordered years before.

Crystal stood there alone, not really alone, Vincent was in the urn she carried by her side. She was alone in her prayers and with her thoughts. She didn't want anyone else there with her just yet, she was an hour early. She had done so much alone in her life, what's one more? She was sure Vincent was looking down at her, thankful she had followed through with his last wishes and brought him here. She was burying him with his son. She'd be buried alone, at home, with his name. Such were her thoughts when a black limousine pulled up to her side and the driver introduced himself as Chuck Holsteader, the baluster. She reluctantly let Mr. Holsteader take the urn from her and rest it on a black drape on the ground. He then proceeded to dig a small hole in the ground adjacent to Rockwell's stone. He asked was she was expecting any clergy or family to join her but when she answered in the negative, with his hand over his heart he started to recite the Lords Prayer. Crystal joined him in prayer, thanked him for his kindness and then slowly walked away. She couldn't bear to watch Vincent be lowered into that hole!.

Crystal left the cemetery and drove around the area for the next few hours just thinking, but also looking for a place to have lunch. She didn't know where she was, but she happened across a quiet little place with great food and a strong Rum & Coke. Now what? Back in the car, the one she loved, the one Vincent bought ten years ago, the one she couldn't part with, the one that drove her straight back to the cemetery. Standing in front of the newly laid stone on top of where Vincent will spend the rest of eternity, Crystal just stood and let the silent tears roll down her cheeks. There was no measure of time, but all of a sudden the hairs on the back of Crystal's neck told her she was not alone.

Slowly a lone shadow crossed over Crystal's shoulder down across Vincent's ground. "So, he's finally here to rest" the sweet feminine voice said. Without looking around, Crystal knew it was Andrea's voice, somehow she knew she'd see Andrea here before she headed home. "I read the obituary and knew you'd be up here some time today, I'm glad I caught up with you; so you are Crystal." Now Crystal turned to face Andrea straight on. Andrea saw Crystal's tear streaked face and softly said "may I"? She stepped forward and embraced Crystal in a consolatory hug that brought on more tears, from the both of them! 'I won't take no for an answer, you are coming home with me", Andrea held Crystal's arm and walked her to her own car.

Ten minutes later they were sitting together in Andrea's sunny kitchen just starring at one-another, reading each other's thoughts, like are we really here together...now what? Crystal started with "you have a lovey home, I love your kitchen". "Dad would have liked it too, you two should have visited for a while when you did your drive-by a couple of years ago. I knew in my heart that it was Dad, I just knew." Now it was Crystal's turn to hug Andrea's tears away.

"Can you stay awhile, tell me things. Share any or all of the life you had with Dad. I know what kind of a man he was, but he was still my Dad. I'd just really love to know what happened forty-five years ago and how and where he's been living." Andrea just slumped back into a chair and looked longingly, imploringly at Crystal, to-please-say-something!

Crystal took a deep breathe and started with, "he was the kind of man that loved with all of his heart and wore it on his sleeve. The only problem was he'd take off his coat, forget here he left that sleeve and move on to the next. I could reel him back in...and I did for years. I don't know what you know of his or our lives but I'll tell you whatever you want to know.

Three days later, yup, Crystal was still at Andrea's and still telling the stories of their life. Now she was sitting down to supper with Andrea and Maddie and Maddie's husband Ethan and their three children. Most of the stories of Dad traveling on the weekends to visit with his kids were the weekends Crystal traveled to New York or other places to perform. Until Maddie looked at Google and Facebook, they didn't know or had never heard of Crystal's career as a pianist. Andrea had a piano in her living room that no one played, but that changed when they heard Crystal play and when they You-Tubed Crystal's performing days. Now Maddie's three kids wanted to learn to play the piano.

When Maddie was in the house, they only talked about Dad's visits to Massachusetts and the family that was lost in the fire or Dad's and Crystal's life together. They talked a lot about Maddie's illness and cure and Andrea's travels and discoveries in that time period. Andrea did mention meeting Rhonda all those years ago and keeping up a friendship with Rachel, even today. Maddie knew the whole story of those happenings, but it was ancient history and not a reoccurring topic of conversation.

Andrea asked so many questions and wanted to keep the time line straight, but there was so much time to cover, they had just finished talking about the house on Shelby Street and turning it's upstairs into a recording studio and the name Clearly. This was also a new and strange name Andrea needed to be more familiar with as it grew in importance as the years went by. The studio and the recording label and the fact that Crystal had used that name since the day she married Vincent was honest and lawful. Andrea didn't know her Dad's name was Vincent, so that in itself was not easy for her to wrap her tongue around. Her Dad was Aspen, Aspen Chambers. The names her Dad used and built families around, where did they come from and how did the military support these fictitious people? Crystal, remembering Andrea was not only a doctor, but had an affiliation with the police department, answered a lot of these questions very coyly, not all together honestly or with much detail. This was still something that Crystal could get in a lot of trouble over. So, Reginald was a made-up name as well, not only Reginald but also Sabers! Andrea was still being blown away by the fictitious history her Dad had built.

"Did Dad have any family that we could have been enriched by?" Andrea asked very softly the next morning over breakfast. "Oh my goodness...his grandmother, who was in up state New York was a hoot!" The rest of the morning Crystal's stories were of the house and the food and the church and the meadow. A lot about the meadow, even the title of her first song and the words her Dad had said aloud. They became the first words written for that song, said with such feeling and insight it brought tears to both of their eyes. Andrea made the effort to request the Grammy winning song from the Google speaker on the counter in the kitchen. They both sat and listened to that sound, Andrea in awe that Crystal had written it and Crystal in memory so deep she could have stayed there all day! It's time for me to go home Crystal announced when the song had ended. Andrea objected, she still had so many questions and many things to learn.

"Tell you what...pack an overnight bag, I've something to show you. I promise before we get there, the rest of the story will be filled in." At first Andrea was very hesitant, but then also very intrigued. Within thirty minutes, the kitchen was cleared of breakfast and they were on their way. Maddie and Ethan had rescued Crystal's car from the cemetery days ago, so it way ready to go as well. Before leaving, Andrea called Maddie to let her know they were leaving town for a few days.

When they were in the car for an hour or so, Andrea insisted on driving the rest of the way. Crystal could give her directions without giving their destination away. When Andrea was behind the wheel,

Crystal called ahead to find out if 'her room was available'. "Wonderful, we're about an hour away". The conversation never stopped. Crystal had already told of Rita, her mom, and her story. Now of Vincent meeting her dad, the Captain when he was just a kid, visiting and 'being with' Vincent's mom Suzie. It sound like a twisted tale," but after Vincent and I were married, he took me to meet and visit with his family and that's where the meadow comes in and it was great! "Such memories, so the title of the song Meadow Memories was born then and there...but I digress! So for the next twenty years your Dad and mom enjoyed married life with your dad being an enlisted Navy man, home only every few weeks for a short time. At the same time, he was an enlisted Army man living in Maryland as Reginald Sabers, again with six kids and only home every few weeks for a short time. In between, he was home with me. I made a point to build a career and keep busy in his absence.

But back at the house on Shelby Street, the studio is going strong and needs a manager, my mom fills that position. I introduce her to my boss at the hotel where I work in New York and they have so much in common, they become an item and live in my/our house. My dad retires and he is finally with the woman he loves and had been pining for all these years, Vincent's mom Suzie and they also move into our house...remember I told you it was huge! Now comes retirement right after the horrible accident at your house. Sometimes I'm not proud of the things I did or the strings I managed to pull but I couldn't let Reginald be with Rhonda 24/7 x's 12 months a year at his retirement. Number one...he'd have gone nuts...number two your mom was gone, you had her money and your best friend and I got selfish and wanted Vincent with me for a change.

So as you know, Both Aspen and Reginald died in 1964. Your Dad at the fire and Reginald in Virginia, a base accident. Your Dad, Vincent, did sustain burns on his left leg and stwas hospitalized for a time that prohibited him from going to you. In his heart he wanted to, he wanted to commit murder when he found out about your circumstances, but factually he knew he needed to keep his distance, he was dead to all of his family. So now after months of healing and convalescence, he's bored. Still being a fairly young man he came up with an idea that would keep him busy through retirement and the rest of his life, but he needed money. "I had money, a lot of money and at some point I'd need more than playing the piano to keep me busy...so why not." But she stopped talking, took a breathe and then told Andrea to pull in here... we're here...this was your father's idea, look around...we built motels! Andrea saw the name on the sign...Clearly Comfortable...she repeated and said out loud..."Clearly"...she was in awe..

After parking, Crystal went to the desk and was surrounded by well wishers and convalescence at Vincent's passing. He was quite the gentleman at these locations and everyone loved him. Once she had her key, she walked Andrea to her suite, where they put down their bags and just looked at each other. They were in Waterville Valley, NH and now Andrea had a whole new set of questions. But first she wanted a tour of the grounds and the entire motel. She was blown away, it was wonderful and her Dad had built it!

As they walked around, around every corner Crystal was greeted with a hug or hand shake and conversation about Vincent. Andrea's heart was filling with pride for her Dad and enjoying seeing everything he had built. The swimming pool and cabanas, the lounge naturally with a piano and picture of Crystal, the dinning room, the colors and fabrics. Andrea just stopped and looked at Crystal and said "and we knew nothing of any of this". Crystal recognized a tone of voice and said, "let's go have some lunch."

Once seated in the lounge, Andrea let her tears of frustration, anger, pride, loss, carry her away. She didn't know how to put into words what she was feeling. She didn't know her Dad at all. What she had made him out to be since she's a little girl was all wrong. Crystal was working on her second Rum & Coke when she made Andrea talk about her father. What he was like when she was a little girl and what she would tell her friends about him. Andrea said so many nice and loving things about her Dad, and Crystal helped her to still believe all those wonderful attributes and more. Crystal made sure Andrea knew she was loved and missed and worried about and missed some more all the days of Vincent's life. Crystal tried to paint a picture of Vincent after being a Dad, as a man building something for his children after he was gone. "Your Dad and I didn't have any children together, but he had you guys and in his later years he did build a fortune.

"Is there any way you can communicate with Rhonda and have her and her entire family, I mean kids and spouses and grandchildren travel to Shelby Street, New Jersey and stay at the...Irresistible B&B, naturally at my expense, I want you and Maddie and Ethan and kids... all, if I'm right...all 20 of you to come to New Jersey. I need four weeks to get my things in order so anytime after that, please try to arrange it...please!"

"Have you lost your mind, I don't have that kind of relationship with Rhonda and asking Rachel and saying your name, she'd probably never talk to me again. I'd be siding with the unknown or the enemy! You are that in some circles, you know that, don't you?" "Do you still believe that after the week we've just spent together?" Crystal held her breathe waiting for an answer to that question.

"Never mind. I can make things happen a different way, do you like what you see? Did your Dad do good?" Just the look on Andrea's face answered that question. Crystal wiggled her fingers, she did this many times then got up and went to the piano. After playing 'Lucky', 'Cloudless Skies' and 'Lonesome Lady', three more of her singles, she was back at the table with Andrea with her mind made up and many ideas still being worked out in her head. Andrea, having just found out that Crystal wrote these songs as well, was in awe! After a good nights sleep they headed back to Massachusetts where Crystal said ado to Andrea and started for home in New Jersey. Her head was full of the conversations that she had with Andrea, the memories that popped out of her head that she hadn't thought of for years. She hoped she didn't bore Andrea or Maddie with her stories of Vincent and yesteryear. But now to work on the next thing. *Vincent, please forgive me, but I'm planning on giving it all away.*

Clarke will help but I'm going to have to tell him some truths that he probably has already worked out, but now he'll know for sure. The truths can't hurt you any more and I'll never divulge mine. My indiscretions made you out to be a superman of sorts, adding to their savings accounts each year on their birthdays. But also forgive me for taking your name off of the house or should I say B&B. For now I need to keep that as mine and I don't want an unforgiving son or son-in-law to try and take it from me. I need to find a way to invite them all to the B&B for a reading of your will. That's where Clarke comes in.

It was a long drive home, but with her mind working overtime and the planning process she had working in her head, the miles and the time flew by. The very next morning she was on the phone with Clarke's office to arrange a meeting. Once again he consented to travel to her and meet here on Shelby Street. The meeting was a mere four days away, but she had time to bake a cake!

Need less to say he was impressed when he arrived at a B&B no less! "Your office knew I was doing this, no one told you?" "Well, since the last time I saw you, I got married, honeymooned in Europe and I now work out of the new Connecticut office. Big changes for me, but I left word if you ever called and needed anything, they'd call me and I'd be on your doorstep! Did you happen to bake a cake?"

After coffee and yes, her 'better-than-sex' cake and an hours conversation about Vincent's passing and this new B&B, and his new wife, he said his wife was a great cook and could he please have the recipe for this cake. He said "I told my wife I was going to New Jersey for this little thing called better than sex and I'd see her in a couple of days. She was incensed! So I better bring her the recipe. So now you tell me what's going on and what you need." "Long story short, I want to leave the motels to all of Vincent's children! Please concoct your lawyer letter contacting everyone of them as recipients in his will." "But it's my understanding he didn't leave a will. What children?"

It took another hour and another piece of cake to fill Clarke in on the times and lives of Mr. Chambers and Mr. Sabers. "So in other words, he was a bigamist! I knew something was rotten in Denmark the last time we visited with those names! And you knew, where were you in his line-up?" Clarke's face had the look of surprise, but when Crystal answered "First." the look changed to shock! "No wonder you eat this cake, you had to give up on this guy." Crystal merely shook her head and said, "I never did. I loved the guy with the big heart." "So tell me again what you want me to do." Clarke said with still trying to wrap his mind around Crystal and the life she lived!

Crystal explained she wanted all of Vincent's children to come here to the B&B for the reading of his will. She wanted each one of them to inherit a motel. "You could step up at this time and offer your assistance in keeping the 'corporation' in tack where they were all owners of the corporation and all eight of the motels, or they could each inherit just one, keeping only two units in the corporation." "So you want me to lie and make-up a false will and then ambulance chance the family's inheritance." "Yes, exactly...see you're a natural." "You're a piece of work Crystal...I can't do that." "Of course you can...rework the words I spoke to a lawful give-away...offer to work with their attorneys if they have one, but speak up that your firm already handles the 'corporation'. Without getting to the dollars and cents worth of each motel, explain the corporation is wealthier handling all eight rather than splitting them up. Or the more I think on it...offer the corporation of motels to the Sabers and the B&B to Andrea. Go back to the office and wrap them all together...because I'm not going to live forever...I leave you the recipe to my cake!"

With the enormity of work that needed to be done, Clarke had already decided to spend the night and talk this through with Crystal. With recording half of her statements and coming to an understanding of what she wanted, Clarke was very proud of her. She was a very wealthy woman, mostly self made and she was willingly giving it all away to Vincent's children. He finally understood why she wanted to meet them all... first. That's why she was bringing them to the B&B. If they turned out to be snotty little SoB's, and couldn't change their tunes toward her...so be it...but at least she tried. If they turned out to be thankful, understanding human beings with broad shoulders and understanding and forgiving hearts, she'd be a happy woman. At the end of three days, Clarke knew exactly what Crystal wanted. She was a shrewd and thankful woman. Every piece of her property that touched Gods green earth was tied up with Clearly. The recording studio paid rent to the B&B and was it's own entity, therefore, Clearly Recording Company's earnings would be kept separate and half of every dollar, would be donated, split between the Shriner's and St. Jude's. At the end of the day, Matt or any future manager could become very wealthy, because to date the Studio was a gold mine and the other half of the earnings were employee profit sharing. Crystal could easily live off of the royalties from her recordings and original titles and needed nothing beyond her own lodgings at the B&B. After all, this had been her home for more than fifty years.

Chapter 71

2010

Two months later, the week of July 14, it was understood that the B&B would take no reservations for the entire week. All rooms were reserved for the Sabers and the Chambers. Crystal was ecstatic! Clarke had worked his magic and all family members would be in attendance. Naturally in the two months it took to get the correspondence going, the families had a chance to talk among themselves and try to figure out exactly what was going on. Andrea had confessed to Rachel that she saw and spent some time with Crystal and liked her. She didn't go into a lot of detail, she didn't want to open the door to discussion.

The invitation to the B&B was for each family member to be awarded their inheritance from the estates of Vincent and Crystal C. Clear, owners of the Clearly Corporations. For clarification, Vincent O. Clear was also known as Reginald Sabers and Aspen Chambers. Insomuch as Crystal Clear is still among the living, her interests in these corporations were liquidated to be included in these bequeaths. The meeting with all family members, and their attorneys if they wanted them present, included Attorney Clarke Comstock and was scheduled for one pm on July14th. These were the facts included in the certified letter sent to each recipient of the reading of the will.

The family's started arriving on July 13th and Crystal had a chance to meet and talk with each one of them. By six pm on the 13th, everyone had arrived and they were all enjoying the meal the chefs had selected for their first night. She had been a nervous wreck since yesterday waiting for everyone to arrive and afraid she'd be outcast as the enemy or the wicked witch of the B&B or the spiteful one who kept their Dad from them for the last 20 years. She had no idea which way the pendulum would swing. But it was with a happy heart Andrea was first to arrive and introduced each one as they arrived and walked in the door. To say the least, they were a handsome bunch. They all had the look of a Welshman and, Vincent! Even Rhonda was a pleasant woman, knowing in her heart what kind of a man Reginald was. She couldn't help it… "I loved him anyway!...you understand" She made a point to tell Crystal that Reginald was a good father, an attentive man to the kids needs when he was home. Many times he'd send them them trinkets from his travels or always birthday cards to arrive on their special day. Rhonda told Crystal that she believed that 'he' had a good heart over flowing with love. "After all, you stayed with him all these years."

With everything pretty much said and done, Crystal felt like she had very little left and nothing to do. She needed to leave the house before 1pm today, she couldn't be home while Clarke was in the dinning room singing the monetary praises of Vincent and Crystal and giving everything away. This is what she wanted...this is what she had asked Clarke to do. Turning to the piano and taking her mood out on the poor unsuspecting keys was her old way to relax and sooth her troubled mind. But with the fingers sore and the knuckles swollen and stiff, the quality and sometimes accuracy was suffering. So even this activity left her a little saddened at times. So she'd turn to the other thing that she still really enjoyed and that was going for a ride in the car with her tapes playing. It got her out of the house.

Downtown really hadn't changed much except for the mammoth Athletic and Sports fields that were built near the new ramp to the highway. This area had changed the most with new parking lots taking up many acres of land where little stores were put out of business.

Oh Crystal, stop thinking...Her thoughts were becoming very nostalgic... it could be fun...and all mine! Drive around the area again, there has to be a spot. Damn, drive around again...there at the edge of the parking lot, the perfect place, maybe...keep driving. Still driving around town and the outskirts of the city, her mind just kept going back to the spot she had seen earlier. Her entrepreneurial mind and the money she had in the bank wouldn't let her mind rest! *I can still do this...it would be small... it would be sweet and this would be the perfect spot* as she pulled into the parking lot and stopped and starred and continued dreaming. *Boy this had the same affect on her that the fields in Passaic or Woodstock or even Wolfboro had. She needed more information, were all of the empty store fronts being demolished or were they available for sale, could they be restored? After making may notes and jotting down the address she was anxious to get back to the house and have a conversation with Clarke. Her mind was racing a mile a minute, she hadn't been this excited in a very long time.*

When she arrived home, she went directly to the lounge and sat at the piano. The dinning room was still occupied with the family members but she could tell this was more of an informal conversation now as a few of them had cocktails and were milling around before dinner. Crystal stayed where she was and started playing the piano, just because. She also signaled over to the bar for a cocktail, why not? She'd corner Clarke when he would eventually find her. It's why she stayed at the piano and continued to play. A number of the family members found Crystal and congregated around the piano. For some people hearing an old song brings back memories or triggers a person in their past. A few people standing there right now were saying how much they loved this song, couldn't believe she wrote and recorded this song, right here, upstairs, years ago. They never knew who wrote it or recorded it, just remembered dancing to it at their school dances and not wanting it to end. A few even admitted buying it when it first came out! They had no idea she was 'that' Crystal Clear.

Andrea, Russel, Rachel and Rhonda made a point to talk to Crystal when she finished the song she was currently playing. They formed a united front in apologizing to her for having to liquidate her interest in the motels to make today a reality. They were beginning to realize how much the motels meant to her in her past. They said they understood today was totally her doing in granting what Vincent had built over to his children, but at what cost to her? Crystal just looked at Rhonda and said "Rhonda, are you going to run a motel and worry that the old man cheated you or pray the insurance will cover the costs to repair the front door a car just hit?" Rhonda giggled and said "hell no, I'm too old for those headaches." Crystal giggled back and said "exactly!" Rhonda stepped forward and hugged Crystal, saying "thank you, thanks for everything."

Crystal saw smiles on most of the faces and almost relief in a few others. She was learning the meeting with Clarke had gone well even though he sang her praises as being the driving force along side of Vincent and it was her money that was the down payment on everything the Clearly corporations owned. There was no way he was going to allow any one of the family members to label her the wicked witch of anything! And she was also the one that prompted this meeting today to settle the affairs with each one of you being Vincent's legal heirs.

Sitting with Clarke at dinner she learned that all the family members wanted Clarke to stay on as legal counsel for the motels and had elected Russel spokesperson for the Corporation for all eight motels, breaking that up didn't make any sense, it was better to stay the way it was. Andrea was the only one who wanted her own attorney sent copies of her personal papers and the Clearly Corporation papers on the motel. Since her dad died, they had taken care of everything for her. Clarke said "no problem, she was playing it safe. The entire afternoon went off with out a hitch. I think everyone was very surprised and then very excited at the value of properties. When I get their decision back to my office I'll be able to tell them a closer estimate at the taxation costs in reporting it six ways. They agreed paying a little on a lot of something they never had before was a no-brainer!" Crystal just had to laugh!

"Now," she said with a twinkle in her eye…" "Oh-oh" was all he could get out before she said, "you weren't thinking of leaving tomorrow, were you?" with anxiety in her voice, that made him pause before yes. And the puppy dog eyes and a set to her mouth when she said "Please stay on tomorrow, I need just a little more of your time and expertise before you go", he relented to hearing her out in the morning, doing what he could and heading out before the dinner hour tomorrow. She'd take what she could, because she knew once he got his teeth in it, he could follow-up from his office no matter where it was. Now relaxed she felt she could enjoy the rest of the evening. She was glad the family was enjoying her music, and she fore-filled a lot of their requests.

Knowing a big chunk of worry, manpower, expense and travel was now off of her plate, she was looking forward to pursuing just a little place, close to home and not overwhelmingly expensive. This had to work out. In her mind she was 'going home to a place she loved'. Before going to bed, Crystal made a list of the things she wanted to discuss with Clarke. If he could get the ball rolling on her purchasing a little shop already standing or a vacant lot, zoned for what she had in mind, that would be the first and biggest battle. Forty years ago they couldn't deal with the local vendors, but this time she could, she was building local. Her first call would be to Samuel Wiggins at the lumber store on West Street. No, she'd visit him or his son or his grandson, whoever runs the store now, she could taste the success of this venture. Success is sweet!

Chapter 72

July-2011

This was Peter's busy season, when wasn't he busy...in Vegas if you weren't busy, you were out of business, so with many hands working under his corporate title, he could afford to take a few days off. For Crystal, it didn't matter what time of year it was...he'd do it! She was so excited he'd be there next week. It had been 12 months since Crystal's first inquiry on 2 Line-Drive. Her little dream became a little bigger than first planned because there were many new shops opening along the newly developed area. Of course every shop owner wanted to be near the baseball diamonds, succor fields, hockey fields, basketball and tennis courts. She needed to be big enough to compete with wherever popped up next to her. The results were beyond her wildest dreams. Her first walk through her shop was exhilarating. It was just what she had pictured, it came out just the way she hoped it would.

Peter's first impression was one of complete surprise, but with Crystal it was just like her to turn back the clock more than a half century and invite him to sit behind 'her' Ice-cream Pallor!